James Wilde is a Man of Mercia. Raised in a world of books, he went on to study economic history at university before travelling the world in search of adventure.

Unable to forget a childhood encounter – in the pages of a comic – with the great English warrior, Hereward, he became convinced that this great fighter should be the subject of his first novel. *Hereward* was a bestseller and four further successful novels, chronicling the life and times of this near-forgotten hero, followed. *Hereward: The Bloody Crown* brings his action-packed story to a thrilling close.

James Wilde divides his time between London and the home his family have owned for several generations in the heart of a Mercian forest. To find out more, visit www.manofmercia.co.uk

HEREWARD

The Bloody Crown

James Wilde

BANTAM BOOKS

LONDON • TORONTO • SYDNEY • AUCKLAND • JOHANNESBURG

TRANSWORLD PUBLISHERS
61–63 Uxbridge Road, London W5 5SA
www.penguin.co.uk

Transworld is part of the Penguin Random House group of companies
whose addresses can be found at global.penguinrandomhouse.com

Penguin
Random House
UK

First published in Great Britain in 2016 by Bantam Press
an imprint of Transworld Publishers
Bantam edition published 2017

A CIP catalogue record for this book
is available from the British Library.

ISBN
9780857501868

Typeset in 11.5/14pt Sabon by Falcon Oast Graphic Art Ltd.
Printed and bound by Clays Ltd, Bungay, Suffolk.

Penguin Random House is committed to a sustainable
future for our business, our readers and our planet. This book is made
from Forest Stewardship Council® certified paper.

MIX
Paper from
responsible sources
FSC® C018179

1 3 5 7 9 10 8 6 4 2

For Elizabeth, Betsy, Joe and Eve

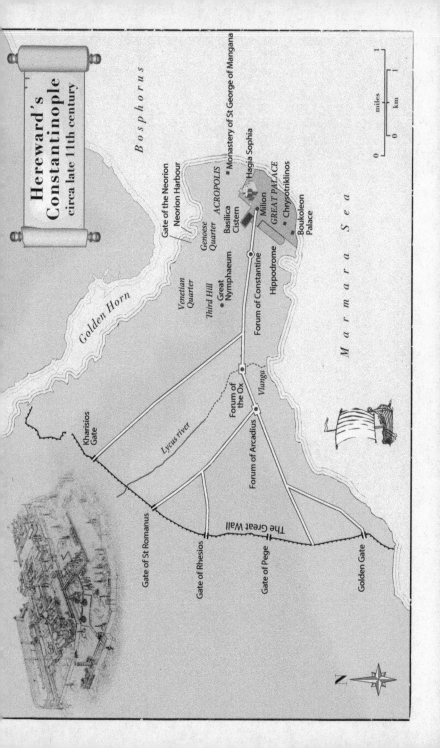

Hereward's Constantinople
circa late 11th century

Bosphorus

Golden Horn

Kharisios Gate

Lycus river

Gate of St Romanus

The Great Wall

Gate of Rhesios

Gate of Pege

Golden Gate

Forum of Arcadius

Vlanga

Forum of the Ox

Forum of Constantine

Venetian Quarter

Third Hill

Great Nymphaeum

Genoese Quarter

ACROPOLIS

Gate of the Neorion

Neorion Harbour

Basilica Cistern

Monastery of St George of Mangana

Milion

Hagia Sophia

Hippodrome

GREAT PALACE

Chrysotriklinos

Boukoleon Palace

Marmara Sea

miles

km

PROLOGUE

4 May 1079

Rain lashed down. In the suffocating darkness, the Roman warriors surged into the camp. Full-throated battle-cries drowned out the roar of the wind and the rumble of God's drums deep in the heavens.

From billowing tents, bleary-eyed fighting men scrambled out to look death in the face. In that moment, they knew that they had been too confident by far.

Axes swept down, blades limned with the ruddy glow from pitch-soaked torches sizzling in the downpour. Swords stabbed, spears jabbed.

One storm had masked another.

On the edge of the camp, Wulfrun of the Varangian Guard slid his axe out of the lookout's gut. He grunted with contempt at his enemy's failings. Too slow, too dulled by sleep. The man had seen nothing until the blade had torn into him.

Wulfrun wiped the rain from his eyes with his leather gauntlet and peered through the drifting clouds from the steaming campfires. The night heaved with battle. The thunder of running feet, the screams of the dying. Horses rearing, hooves ripping tents. And everywhere the constant thrumming of the rain on the too-dry ground, and on the trees that had masked the approach of the emperor's forces.

All was going as planned.

Shaking the droplets of blood from his blade, Wulfrun ploughed into the turmoil. Ahead of him, the men he commanded drove like a spear into the heart of the camp. In their crimson capes, with their circular shields marked with their sigils and their long-hafted Dane-axes in hand, the Varangian Guard showed no mercy. They were terrifying, to friend and foe alike. Wulfrun nodded. Here was why every man and woman in the whole of the empire knew the fearsome reputation of the emperor's elite force.

As he plunged into the churning mass on the edge of the tents, he drank in the chaos framed by the eye-holes of his helm.

In the wavering glow of a torch, one of the enemy's mercenaries broke free from the fight and pounded towards him. A Sclavenian by the look of him, from one of the Slav tribes on the edge of the empire, with his long braided hair and the spirals tattooed on the left side of his face. Baring his teeth, he swung his spear up. But Wulfrun could see the glint of fear in the man's eyes. The shock of the attack had dulled his battle-wits.

Without slowing his step, Wulfrun spun round the spear's tip. Whisking his axe up, he continued to turn full circle and hacked the blade into the Sclavenian's neck. He had wrenched his weapon free and was loping on before the other man knew he was dead.

And then the maelstrom swallowed him.

As the roiling sea of warriors swirled, he pushed on towards the centre of the camp where the tent of the traitor Basilakios waited. In his mind's eye, he fixed the location. The purple canvas, the dragon flag flying above framed against the ruddy sunset glinting off the Vardar river as he lay on his belly spying on the oblivious enemy army just before the storm broke.

Streams of black blood flooded into the swelling puddles. Wulfrun hacked down another warrior. The enemy showed little resistance, but he had expected no less. Not from the Frankish, Sclavenian and Arvanite mercenaries, nor from the faithless Romans who had flocked to the treacherous general's standard when he had risen up against the emperor.

Steaming in the deluge, one of the tents burned fiercely. In that glare, the night swooped away to reveal the clash of warriors seething through the camp. Axes flashed, hacking and slashing. Helms and hauberks glowed in the flickering light.

When he darted round the conflagration, Wulfrun felt a cold pang of shock at the sight that met his eyes. Painted red in the firelight, a figure from the very depths of hell loomed before him. A beast, it was, eyes white and wide in a face drenched in blood. The commander of the guard jerked back. He had felt no fear since he had taken the oath, yet still his axe froze in his hand.

But then the apparition bared its teeth in a grin. No monster this, but a man, though one yet born of hell. Hereward of Mercia swung up his dripping axe from the bodies littered around his feet and with a nod of recognition bounded away towards the general's tent.

Wulfrun grimaced. It clawed at his gut that the man he hated most in the world now fought alongside him as a member of this elite force. But as he watched his rival slash a path through the enemy soldiers as if they were boys on their first day with a weapon in hand, he could not deny that he was a skilled and powerful warrior.

Hereward's English allies followed in their leader's wake. They had joined the Guard at the same time, the ones he called his spear-brothers. Kraki the Viking. Guthrinc, the giant of a man. Sighard the red-headed youth. Wulfrun narrowed his eyes in suspicion. They were good, all of them. But though each man had sworn the Varangian oath to protect the emperor, they acted like a force within a force, their own tight-knit group serving their own ends.

Shaking off his thoughts, Wulfrun ran on. He would not have that English bastard claim credit for the capture of the treacherous general, or, more likely, the kill.

A moment before he closed on Hereward's men, they threw themselves aside across the swimming mud. Driving through them came four men on horse-back. They leaned across the necks of their mounts, digging their heels in to force the steeds to their limits. Wulfrun threw himself back too, just in time to avoid

12

being crushed under the hooves – these men would stop for naught.

As he reeled back, he locked eyes with the lead rider, taking in the leathery, scarred features of a seasoned warrior. It was Basilakios. No doubt the traitor and his closest aides were saving their own necks. Their destination could only be Thessalonica, a day away, where the rest of Basilakios' army waited and he could hope to defend the city against the emperor's forces.

Cursing, Wulfrun watched the four horsemen until they were swallowed by the night. Basilakios had only bought himself a brief respite. After this battle his days were numbered, he must know that.

As news of the disappearance of their leader spread, Wulfrun watched the resistance slow, then still. Heads bowed, shoulders sagged; weapons splashed into the swelling puddles. Triumphant, the soldiers of the empire began to round up the dejected survivors, ready for whatever justice would be meted out upon the emperor's orders.

Wulfrun stalked back towards the edge of the camp. The rest of the Varangian Guard tramped in his wake. Their work was done here. Let the foot soldiers clean up Basilakios' mess. He wanted nothing more than to be out of this endless driving rain before it soaked into his bones.

'Wulfrun. Hold.'

The commander turned to see his aide, Ricbert, weaving among the tents like a riverbank rat. 'The news is not good,' the smaller man said when he splashed to a halt. 'Brynstan is dead, cornered and cut down by five men so that bastard Basilakios could make good his escape.'

Wulfrun grimaced. Brynstan had been a good man, one of the Guard's best, and Wulfrun had made him second in command the moment he had become commander. 'Tonight we will mourn. Then I will think on the best man to take his place. The Guard cannot be left leaderless were I to die.'

'The emperor agrees. He has sent word that he would speak to you. Now.'

'Nikephoros is here?'

Ricbert pulled off his helm, the more easily to wipe the rainwater sluicing into his eyes. 'It seems our young general, Alexios Comnenos, arranged for him to oversee our great victory. Or not,' he said in a sardonic tone.

Wulfrun gritted his teeth. 'More games. What does Alexios intend in bringing the emperor here?'

'Who can tell? There are more plots and rumours circling the court than in the lowest pox-ridden brothel.'

'I cannot read Alexios' mind, but he circles always like a hawk waiting to fall upon its prey.'

'Blame his mother. She holds his reins.' Ricbert walked away, beckoning. 'I will take you to him.'

Wulfrun strode up to the emperor's tent on the ridge overlooking the camp. Two torches spat at the entrance. From inside came the glow of a brazier set up to dispel the rain-chill. With a smile etched with irony, Ricbert swept out one hand to usher his commander across the threshold. He waited outside, silently cursing the gusting downpour.

The warmth from the brazier was welcome. Wulfrun eased off his helm and shook the water from his face. He sensed other presences hovering in the gloom at the back of the tent: counsellors and lackeys, he guessed. The emperor would not be here without the ones who wiped his arse.

Nikephoros hunched over the brazier, warming his hands. Once he had been a potent general, with more than one great victory to his name, but many failures and humiliations too. Yet now he looked much older than his seventy-seven years, and frail also. The burden of ruling an empire brought to its knees by a litany of threats, and a daily assault of plots and curses and attempts upon his life, had taken their toll. His hair, what little remained, had turned the colour of hoar-frost, his face sagging and wrinkled, his back hunched. He no longer looked as if he had the strength to lift a loaf of bread, never mind an axe.

'The bastard has escaped.' Nikephoros looked up, his eyes glittering with the red glow of the fire.

In that moment, Wulfrun could see how the old man had clawed himself an empire. Weak-willed he might be, spineless, dull-witted, and a temple to poor judgement, but he was as vicious as a wounded wolf. And in his heart the furnace of ambition burned white-hot.

Under the last leader, the pale-faced boy-emperor Michael, Nikephoros had governed Anatolia as the *strategos*, and had commanded the army in the far east. His rise had been slow, but sure. But the first time he had been truly tested he had failed, and that failure had cost the empire much of its eastern lands. When the Norman adventurer Roussel de Bailleul had risen up, Nikephoros had fled like the coward he was, leaving the Caesar, John Doukas, to be captured and the army humiliated. The Caesar was only saved, and peace restored, with the aid of the Seljuk Turks, who demanded land – and lots of it – as their price.

Yet as was the way with the power-hungry, Nikephoros suffered no shame in his cowardice. One year gone, he had amassed his warriors and marched on the throne. Michael gave up with barely a whimper. How could he not? He had never had the heart to rule, and the empire's power had been ebbing away by the day under his weak command. If he had not gone, the people would have risen up and hanged him from the Milion mile-post.

'Basilakios' days are numbered,' Wulfrun replied. 'If it takes a week, a month, or a year, we will batter down the walls of Thessalonica and drag him back to Constantinople for his punishment.'

Nikephoros' mouth was a cruel slash in his wrinkled face. 'I have already given thought to that. Basilakios will have his eyes put out. Let my face be the last sight he sees.'

Wulfrun nodded. First a boy-emperor, then a savage old fool. The empire was destroying itself by degrees. His thoughts flew back to the day when Nikephoros was crowned by the Patriarch, Kosmas. Even then, everyone knew nothing would change. The people battled with starvation. Grain was too costly, coins contained so little gold they had the weight of an autumn leaf. The coffers were emptying, power was ebbing, and, unchallenged, the Turks drew ever closer. When he peered into days yet to come, he saw only darkness. But what could a man do?

'Draw closer,' Nikephoros said, beckoning with a wavering hand. 'Warm yourself. Will this fucking rain never end?'

Wulfrun stepped forward, but gave no sign of enjoying the heat. 'You wished to see me?'

'Aye. I am heartily sick of these rebellions against my rule. First Bryennios, now Basilakios. I am here by the will of God. Can no one see that?' He clenched fists that barely looked to have the strength to crush a sparrow. 'The battles . . . the constant battles, they weary me. But while we tear chunks out of each other, the enemies beyond the walls creep nearer. The empire must not fall, Wulfrun. That is why I seized the throne from that weak cur Michael: to save it.' Beatific, he pressed his palms together as if he were praying. 'Not for my own glory, whatever folk say. I will be the empire's saviour.'

Though he showed a cold face, Wulfrun made a silent plea to be saved from would-be saviours. Did Nikephoros truly believe the easy lies that fell from his lips?

'There must be changes if I am to carry on with God's plan,' the emperor continued. 'This opposition to my rule must end. We must show strength against our enemies, both within and without the walls. To

17

that end, Karas Verinus will now advise me on our strategies to fight the Turks and the Normans. He is a seasoned general with a mind as keen as a knife's edge. Some would say cruel . . . ' Nikephoros shrugged. 'But he is a man I would want at my side.'

Wulfrun winced. Karas was despised by all who knew him. A snake that could be trusted by none, like all his kin. This decision would come back to bite Nikephoros on the arse.

'A good choice,' he said.

'I have plans, too, for Falkon Cephalas . . .'

This time Wulfrun could not hide the tremor in his face.

'You do not value him?'

'I would not question your wisdom.' Wulfrun paused, steadying his voice. 'It is hard to find a space in my heart for a man who would have had me executed for treason.'

Nikephoros fluttered a dismissive hand. 'Days gone by, Wulfrun. Days gone by. Falkon is a bastard, but bastards are what is needed. And to lead our armies into battle . . .' The emperor raised his arm and snapped his hand forward.

From the shadows at the rear of the tent where the counsellors waited, a figure emerged. The face was spattered with blood, and the hauberk too, the long black hair rain-sodden. But the eyes burned with a sharp intelligence. Even covered with the filth of battle, Wulfrun thought how young Alexios Comnenos looked. And yet for all his youth there was no doubt that he was the finest war-leader in the empire, a worthy man to hold the title of commander-in-chief of the western armies. He had been born with a sword in his hand, Ricbert said.

'From this day on, Alexios will command all our warriors, and he will answer only to Karas,' the emperor said. 'This is how we will bring honour back to Constantinople, Wulfrun, through men like this.'

Alexios gave the faintest bow, seemingly at ease with his elevation to the highest military role. 'I serve at the pleasure of the emperor.'

Wulfrun felt a wash of relief. He could not fault Alexios Comnenos. His military leadership would take some of the sting out of the influence of Karas Verinus and Falkon Cephalas. Another appointment in that vein could have meant disaster.

'And through men like you, Wulfrun,' Nikephoros continued, wagging his finger. 'The Varangian Guard is my right hand, as always. No emperor could wish for better protection.'

'Our lives are yours.' Wulfrun bowed his head.

'I have heard the sad news that Brynstan died this day.'

'Worry not. I will find a good man to take his place in no time.'

'No need. I have already made that decision . . . with Alexios' guidance.' Nikephoros swept out a hand to the young warrior.

Wulfrun saw that Alexios was smiling. So soon? The young Roman must have raced from the battle-field to offer the emperor his advice.

Alexios stepped aside so that another figure lurking

at the rear of the tent could step forward. Wulfrun stiffened when he saw Hereward. This was the worst blow of all. 'No,' he said. 'This cannot—'

'The emperor agreed there is no better man for the job,' Alexios interjected.

Wulfrun tasted acid. Hereward and Alexios had been in deep for many a moon, and he could see that this had been planned for some time. Even had Brynstan not been killed no doubt Hereward would have been rushed here to take the credit for Basilakios' fall.

'Hereward the Bloody,' Nikephoros said with an approving nod. 'That is what they are calling you these days, is it not?'

'It is better than some of the names that have followed me.'

Nikephoros chuckled, clearly in awe of this warrior. He turned back to Wulfrun. 'You are old friends, are you not? From your days in England?'

Wulfrun fought to steady himself. Friends. He held the Mercian responsible for the death of his father. Though he had done his best to make peace with that, he would never forget it. 'We ran together as boys,' he replied in a wintry voice.

If the emperor heard the chill in those words, he did not show it. 'Good, good. Then the Varangian Guard will only be stronger with two such great warriors at its head.'

Soaked in gore, Hereward still looked like some apparition from the depths of the night. *Aye, Hereward the Bloody*, Wulfrun thought. Since that bastard

English exile had joined the Varangian Guard, it was as if he had set free the devil that lurked inside him. No other warrior could match him for slaughter in battle, nor, Wulfrun had to accept, for courage. Hereward, the man he had hated since they were both boys in Barholme, had become a hero, even among the ferocious ranks of the Guard.

Wulfrun sensed plots forming around him, though he could not see the weave of them. But there was no doubt that they were bad business.

Hereward strode over and held out his hand. Under the watchful gaze of the emperor, Wulfrun could do naught but take it.

'You cannot forgive me for the poison that was spread in days long gone,' the Mercian said in a low voice, so that the emperor could not hear. 'But I will be a loyal ally, you have my word on that. And you will need me, be in no doubt.' His voice became little more than a whisper as he added, 'There are worse days yet to come.'

CHAPTER ONE

East of Constantinople, Christmas 1080

The air reeked of death.

Droplets of blood spattered the face of the running man. Squinting through the sea of dark swelling among the trees, he tried without luck to see where the wind had caught that black rain. But he could not afford to pause to wipe the stains away.

At his back, the howls of the hunting band rang to even greater heights. They smelled blood too: his blood. Glancing into the gulf behind him, Hereward could see a constellation of tiny flames dancing nearer, always nearer.

Death was coming, and coming fast.

Branches tore at his face and snagged in his hair. Snarling roots clutched for his feet. Beneath the forest canopy, the night was so deep he knew it was only a matter of time until he fell. Then the pack would be upon him.

Skidding down a bank, he winced as thorns ripped the bare flesh of his arm. He was travelling light. The crimson cloak of the Varangian Guard had been left behind in the city when he had set off into the east five days gone. He wore but an oiled leather breastplate, grey woollen leggings and leather shoes. His Dane-axe was still under his bed in Constantinople. He carried only his gold-hilted sword, Brainbiter, his constant companion since he had been a boy, and a long-bladed knife. And on his left forearm, his round wooden shield painted red with his raven sigil in black.

The slope ended at a patch of marshy ground. He squelched through it and splashed into the chill water of a babbling stream. Keeping low, he darted along the course, hoping that he might buy himself some time.

Fifty Turks lay at his back, he guessed, all of them dressed in their felt *boerk* bowl hats and thick woollen *yalmas* fastened tightly across their chests. Some carried single-edged swords. Others were armed with bows, and those archers were so skilled they could take the life of a bird in flight. He could not afford to give them a clear shot. And there would be reinforcements nearby. Blood-crazed and hungry for vengeance, they roamed the lands even here, close to Constantinople.

As the banks on either side flattened out, he glimpsed more torches flickering on either side. Gritting his teeth, he lunged to his left, across the boggy ground and back on to the dry leaf-mould of the forest floor. Within moments, he had closed on the nearest torch. His enemies had formed a crescent around him, and this Seljuk warrior was ahead of the left flank.

Slowing his step, Hereward padded from tree to tree, never taking his eyes off that wavering light.

When the Turk wandered near to his hiding place, Hereward drew his long-bladed knife and ghosted out behind him. His arm flexed as fast as a striking viper, hooking the crook of his elbow under the warrior's chin and yanking his head back. With one fluid movement, he ripped the blade across the bared throat. So quick was the attack, the man could only let out a dying sigh.

As his victim slumped to the ground, Hereward sheathed the knife and snatched the falling torch. His enemies would be peering deep into the dark for their prey, not following the path of another light.

Before he could take another step, footsteps pounded near. Whirling, he glimpsed a contorted face in the torchlight. A glint of steel whirled towards him. Somehow he thrust himself aside. The sword whisked by a finger's breadth away from slicing open his skull.

Brainbiter leapt into his hand. As the Turk swung round for another strike, Hereward felt his chest tighten. If he allowed this foe to cry out even once, the entire hunting band would be upon him.

The Mercian thrust the brand towards the other man's face. Shocked, his assailant reeled away from the trail of flames. That was all Hereward needed. Lunging forward, he rammed his sword deep into the warrior's gut.

As he raced away, Hereward felt the weariness in his legs start to burn. He had been running from this hunting band since dawn, when they had spotted him on the edge of one of their burned-out villages. Their teeth had gleamed white among the black bristles of their beards as they wailed and beat their chests at the loss of their women and children, friends and neighbours. They would never have cared that he could not be blamed for this slaughter. To them, he was just another bloodthirsty Roman bastard.

Kraki had been right, he thought grimly. The Viking had mocked him for being so foolish as to venture alone into land the Turks had occupied. But the need had been great.

His nostrils wrinkled at the reek of smoke on the wind and he tasted bitter ashes on his tongue. As he crested a ridge, he looked down upon several fires flickering in the blackness below him. The dying remains of another Turkish settlement, perhaps the newest, and the one closest to Constantinople. How could they have advanced so far, so quickly? Why had the Romans not fought back sooner?

Hereward beat the torch upon the dry ground until it was extinguished. There would be light enough here. And perhaps, too, he would finally find the object of his quest.

Skidding down the bank, he prowled into the village. Clouds of smoke drifted before him, obscuring then revealing the massacre. Bodies sprawled everywhere, farmers mostly, but women too, and children. The attack had moved from hut to hut, he guessed, with stealth at first, until it had been impossible to muffle the screams. Hereward felt his stomach knot at the slaughter of so many innocents. This was murder, not war.

For a moment, his thoughts flashed back to another burning village in the frozen forest of Northumbria when he had been little more than a murderous youth. That was the moment when his life had changed, for the better, he hoped, and he had been led away from the road to hell.

But then his eyes watered and he jolted back into the present. Pressing on through the billowing smoke, he focused on the carnage around him. The embers of the houses still glowed red. This destruction had not been long in the making. Cocking his head, he listened for any sign that he was not alone, but the crackle of the lingering fires and the snap of the wood were too loud.

With his skin blooming from the heat, he reached the other side of the small settlement. The smoke folded back, and for a moment he was in a place of silence and stillness. Ahead of him, a pale shape glowed in the gloom, hovering just above the height of his head. He stiffened as he tried to understand what he was seeing. His sword slowly fell to his side.

As he stepped forward, the pale shape took on the form of a man, but something more than a man. Wings reached out on either side.

An angel.

CHAPTER TWO

'**D**o you like my handiwork?'

The wintry voice rolled out. Hereward whirled, but whoever had spoken was lost to the swirling smoke. Yet for all his wariness that vision hovering in the dark burned too brightly in his mind, and he could not stop himself from looking back. His neck prickling, he took a step towards the angel. As it gained definition in the gloom, the true nature of the thing revealed itself to him.

It was not one of God's messengers.

Here was what had driven the Turks to such fury. Here was the horror that had fomented a tide of blood, one that could drown all Constantinople if left unchecked.

On a great blackthorn, a dead man had been suspended. Stripped naked, his arms stretched out, his legs crossed at the ankle, his head lolling to one side. Hereward narrowed his eyes. This body had been arranged by careful hands, a warning, aye, and mockery too, that spoke to both Turk and Roman in its echo of the Saviour upon the cross.

Hereward found his gaze drawn inexorably to those *wings*. While his victim was still alive, the killer had plunged his sword into the back and severed the ribs down to the loin. Then those narrow bones had been cracked back and the lungs jerked out and exposed in fans of pink flesh.

The Blood Eagle.

Hereward had always thought it naught but a story told by Christians to damn the heathen Vikings who were supposed to inflict this torture upon the defeated. He had never witnessed it on the field of battle, never heard of its being enacted, until rumours had surfaced of one who had indeed committed this torture, and had been named after it.

A shuffling echoed at his back and Hereward turned. Surrounded by the orange glow of the fires, a towering figure began to emerge from the cloud of smoke.

'You have hunted me for days. Now you have found me,' the Blood Eagle growled.

His true name was Varin. Hereward had heard the older members of the Varangian Guard talk of him in whispers. One of their own, who had been consumed by such a blood-lust he had been driven mad, and disappeared from their ranks into the wilder reaches of the empire.

The Mercian drank in the disturbing sight. A head taller than Hereward, Varin still wore his crimson cloak, its colour dulled by the filth of the road and the cloth ripped into tatters so that when he walked it fluttered behind him like feathers. A mail-shirt, tarnished by age and beaten from battle, covered a leather breastplate. In his right hand he gripped his Dane-axe, the blade nicked and smeared with blood, and on his left arm he wore a blistered, faded shield marked with his sigil, the black silhouette of an eagle. Both his hands were stained red.

Hereward looked up into the orbs glowing within the shadowed eye-holes of his helm. 'Your reign of terror is over. You will return with me to Constantinople and face justice for your crimes.'

Varin's stare did not waver as he took the measure of the man standing in front of him. 'I have run with the wolves in the frozen wastes of the north. I have fought the Rus on lakes of ice and slaughtered Normans under a sun so hot their spilled blood boiled. I have walked with death all my life. And you would command me?'

'I too have walked with death.' Hereward held the Viking's unblinking gaze.

'Who sent you to claim me?'

'No one. I am here of my own will. The Romans had problem enough with the Turks before you began to whip them into a frenzy with your slaughter. The emperor and his greybeards could not let you kill and kill until the Seljuks laid siege to the city itself in their anger. But their plan to stop you was not good.' The Mercian remembered his frustration when the strategy had been described to him. 'Fifty men or more to ride into this newly lost land to bring you home, axes-for-hire captained by a handful of the Varangian Guard. The Turks would never have let such a force drive into

30

their heart, not after you had cut a swathe through them. Many lives would have been lost. I could not allow that to happen.'

Varin laughed, so low it was barely more than an exhalation. 'So, you disobeyed the orders of your betters.'

'One man working alone stood the best chance of capturing you. One man who could track you through these forests without drawing too many eyes. And I was the best man for that work.' He stiffened, hearing the cries of the hunting band as the warriors crested the ridge. Time was short.

Showing his jagged teeth, the Blood Eagle said, 'One man.'

'And if you will not come with me, I will kill you here.' Hereward drew his sword.

Unmoved by the threat, Varin cocked his head, listening to the horde sweeping down towards them. 'If my days are to end, so be it. I have done good work. But should we fight each other while all hell breaks loose around us? You may take my life, but the Turks will have yours.'

Hereward peered through the drifting smoke. 'I am sick of running.'

Varin shook his axe over his head. Droplets of blood flew from the blade. 'Then let us make a stand here. Odin will decide if we still walk this earth at dawn, or if we travel to Valhalla.'

'You and I against an army?'

'I like those odds,' the Blood Eagle roared. 'How many are coming for us? Thirty?'

'Aye, about that.'

The Viking's eyes glinted in the firelight. 'I have met these Turks. One on one and one on ten. Most are not seasoned warriors. They are farmers . . . wandering tribesmen who have scraped together enough gold to buy a sword or an axe. Many have never been on the field of battle and seen their brothers cut down around them. They do not fight to the last. They fight until they are afrit and then they run like frightened rabbits. And if there is one thing I know, it is how to make men afrit.'

'I am no novice at that myself.'

Varin narrowed his eyes. 'Good. Then we are in agreement. We leave our fight until our business here is done.'

Hereward nodded, pleased to accept the terms. With a man like Varin at his side, there was some hope. He raised his head to face the smouldering village. The howls of the Turks broke through the sounds of destruction. The hunting band was about to move among what remained of the houses. He glanced over to signal to Varin that it was time to begin their attack, but the Blood Eagle was already gone.

Sucking in a deep breath, Hereward let peace settle upon him. He was ready. Deep inside, he felt his devil stir, the part of him that lived for blood, for battle, for death. For a long time, he had thought it his curse: the thing that had made him hated by all he met, that had allowed anger to consume his wits and driven him to slaughter when a good man would have walked away.

But now he had made an accommodation with it. In battle, he fed that devil well and it kept him alive. In peace, it left him alone.

When he raised Brainbiter, the blade shimmered orange with the reflected light of the fires. His stomach prickling with anticipation, he bounded into the deep bank of smoke.

In that dense grey wall, muffled sounds came and went. A call and response rang out. The Turks sensed some threat. They were entering the village with caution.

When the sound of pounding hooves rumbled near, Hereward stepped close to a burning barn. He felt his skin scorch in the heat. Crouching down, he waited for the horseman. Instead it was a riderless steed that careered out of the smoke, its eyes wide and white with terror as it raced through its former home. As it thundered by, he glimpsed two Turks moving slowly in his direction. They looked right and left, their swords levelled.

Hereward stooped to pick up a stone and hurled it against the remnants of a timber wall afire across the street. The crack rang out even above the crackling of the flames, and the two men jerked towards the source.

The Mercian was moving the moment they turned away.

Darting across the baked earth, he rammed his blade into the back of the nearest man. Convulsing, his enemy pitched forward as the sword came free. The other warrior whirled at the death-cry, just in time for Brainbiter to rip across his bared throat. He fell back in a shower of blood, clutching for his neck.

Hereward was already moving past him, alongside a burning cottage.

Two more Turks fell in rapid measure.

In the glowing embers of another house sprawled the blackened remains of the innocents Varin had slaughtered when he had put this village to the torch. Hereward felt a jolt of disgust. For all that they were both warriors and members of the Varangian Guard, he must never forget that they were not alike.

As he rounded the corner, he glimpsed a band of ten men stalking towards him through the smoke. They cried out when they saw him and launched into a run. They thought him alone, a running dog waiting to be cornered.

Choking on the smoke, Hereward darted back the way he had come. More cries echoed when the hunting band came across his victims. That would only whip them into more of a frenzy. They would throw caution to the wind now, and that was what he wanted.

A house collapsed with a sound like thunder. An eruption of sparks whirled on the breeze towards the stars. Weaving around it, Hereward caught sight of three headless warriors – more of Varin's handiwork – but he did not slow his step.

Finally, the smoke cleared enough for him to see the angel suspended in the blackthorn. He had come full circle. Dashing behind the tree, he dropped low and pressed his back against the trunk, waiting out of sight.

The baying of the hunters grew louder and then ebbed away. The beat of footsteps slowed, then stopped.

Glancing around the tree, Hereward saw the group of Turks, rooted as they stared up at the Blood Eagle. He watched their faces lit by the fire, their eyes widening, the features growing taut. A familiar sight – fear. He didn't understand the Turkish tongue, but he knew they must be asking themselves what devil could do such a thing. And they were right: it was the work of a devil.

As a superstitious dread descended on them, they began to shift uneasily. And that was when Varin burst out of the swirling smoke. For all his size, he was as silent as a ghost. His axe swung. Blood sprayed. A head flew, bouncing across the dirt.

The Turks spun round, but they were caught by the speed of the attack. A collarbone cracked open, a chest peeled back. Varin was more skilled with his weapon than any man Hereward had seen. The Viking hooked the blade around the legs of another and ripped out the hamstrings. The Blood Eagle left his victims alive, to scream in agony and terror of the end that was coming. So throat-rending were those cries, they would roll out across the village, through the muffling smoke to the ears of the remaining warriors of the hunting band.

Varin knew how to create fear well enough.

As the surviving Turks milled, they finally found

their courage and their swords. Dancing out of the reach of that swinging axe, the men circled, waiting for an opening.

Hereward darted out from his hiding place. Where Varin was like a great oak, the Mercian was light on his feet. When his blade punched through the back of the nearest Turk, the other warriors jerked round, shocked. Hereward watched the calculations play out on their faces. Though they outnumbered their foes two to one, the Seljuks saw that they would not survive this encounter. As one, they spun on their heels and fled away into the smoke.

Varin watched them go with contempt. 'I told you. Frit.'

'There are near twenty more. If they attack as one, we are done for.'

The Blood Eagle wrinkled his nose. 'I would wager we will not see another Turk this night.'

Hereward cocked his head, listening. No war-cries, no call and response of hunting warriors. Only the crackle of the dying fires.

On the edge of his vision he glimpsed sudden movement. He turned, too late. Varin had rounded on him, flames flickering in the dark eyelets of his helm. The haft of his axe rammed up. Hereward's ears rang as he caught a glancing blow on the side of his head, and he spun back. Pain lanced through his skull. For a moment his wits flew away.

When his vision returned, he was lying on his back, staring up at Varin. The orange glow of the fires limned the Blood Eagle.

'I will mount you on a tree so all can see the beauty of your flight to Valhalla.'

The Mercian stared at the axe hanging over his head.

With a grunt, the Blood Eagle swung his blade down.

Hereward rolled aside with barely an instant to spare. He felt the rush of air from the blade, and the jolt when it slammed into the ground where his head had been. A cloud of dust swirled up as Varin wrenched the axe free.

Rolling on to his belly, the Mercian closed his fingers around the hilt of his sword and thrust himself to his feet. Though his instinct had been lightning-fast, he was still too slow. The Blood Eagle was bounding away into the trees with long, powerful strides.

Hereward cursed himself. He had let his guard down like a boy on his first day on the field of battle. His muscles burned from exhaustion and his head still rang, but he would not see his struggles amount to naught. With a snarl, he raced in pursuit.

CHAPTER THREE

Spectral hazel trees were beginning to loom out of the previously utter gloom. A glow of silvery dawn light seeped through the forest canopy as Hereward loped among the thick tangle of brush. His chest was burning and his legs were numb, but he did not slow even for a moment.

Ahead of him, Varin pounded on, seemingly tireless.

The night had passed in a blur of clutching branches, steep-sided valleys and sudden drops where the land had slid away. But Varin had spent long months in that trackless waste and he knew well the paths the forest creatures made, tracks that Hereward would never have seen. At times, the Viking appeared more beast than man. He wove through undergrowth without hindrance, as if he could sense obstacles before he saw them.

Yet still Hereward had kept pace with him, just close enough to hear the beat of his quarry's feet but far enough away to be lost in the dark. If Varin realized he had an enemy upon his trail, he showed no sign of it.

Finally the beat of footsteps slowed. The Mercian slowed too, dropping low to creep forward until he could see his prey. Varin was hunched over a babbling stream, cupping a handful of the cool water to his lips. As he slaked his thirst, his eyes darted around, like an animal's.

Crouching beside a blackthorn, Hereward waited and watched. Ahead, the trees thinned and the light of daybreak was brighter. A still lake stretched out beyond, the waters dark. There was only the birdsong for company.

For a moment, Hereward scanned the landscape. After the fall of Ely, the remaining English rebels had hunted deer in the vast, dark forest that stretched from the fenlands deep into Mercia. The bucks were fast and powerful, and he soon learned that he always needed an advantage to bring one down.

Keeping low, he crept among the trees. The Blood Eagle was stalking along the edge of the stream. Even there, Varin did not let his guard down. His axe swayed in his grip, ready to strike out at any moment. His head was half-cocked, listening for even the faintest crack of a twig.

The Mercian kept his breath tight in his chest, waiting for his moment.

When Varin stepped out from under the shade of the trees and looked out across the lake, Hereward knew he had him where he wanted him. Gathering speed as he padded forward, he rose up and then threw himself off the higher ground. Varin must have heard something, for he half turned, but it was too late. The Mercian slammed into the bigger man's back, pitching him forward. Crashing on to the ground, the two warriors rolled in a tangle to the water's edge.

Finding his balance, Varin pushed himself upright with a roar. But Hereward was ready. He thrust both hands into the Viking's chest, hurling him even further back. An instant later, Varin's eyes widened as he realized his opponent's plan, but by then it was too late. Deep into the sucking mud at the lakeside he sank, until it came high above his knees. The weight of his armour and his own large frame dragged him down.

Snarling with frustration, Varin strained to pull himself free, but the mud held him fast. Given time, he would drag himself out, Hereward could see, but that opportunity would be denied him.

The Mercian snatched the Dane-axe from where it had fallen.

'Fight me like a man,' Varin growled, seeing he was now at a disadvantage. His eyes darted to the swinging blade. Hereward could see from the Viking's eyes that he thought his time had come, but he showed not a flicker of fear.

In the instant that the Blood Eagle raised his shield and braced himself for the hacking blow that he expected to take his life, Hereward spun the axe round and thundered the haft into Varin's forehead. Stunned, the warrior crumpled into the black mud.

For long moments, Hereward grunted and cursed as he dragged the unconscious man back on to solid ground. Varin weighed as much as a mule, it seemed. Once his foe was free of the mud, the Mercian pulled his arms back and slid the long-handled Dane-axe beneath them to pin them before binding Varin's cloak tightly round the wrists and to the haft. The Viking was held fast. He could walk, but he could not fight. Only then did Hereward slump back on to the grass and breathe deeply of the cool dawn air.

CHAPTER FOUR

Barbs of sunlight glinted off the chopping waves. The shrieking gulls wheeled overhead and the wind moaned as the small boat strained against the furious currents.

'You owe me your life,' Varin said, the heat from his stare at odds with the chill of his whispery voice. 'Without me, the Turks would have long since hanged you from a tree, lopped off your legs and dragged out your guts for the ravens to feast on. Is this how you repay me?'

Blinking the sweat from his eyes, Hereward heaved at the oars. 'I take you away from your hard labours for a goblet of wine in Constantinople. Is that not payment enough?'

'You have worked hard to bring me to judgement,' the Blood Eagle continued with a wry smile. He was sitting in the prow, leaning back as if he did not have a care in the world. 'I hope you are well rewarded for your efforts.'

'Duty drives me, not lust for gold.' Squinting, the Mercian tried to see Constantinople on the horizon, but a shimmering heat haze hid the way ahead.

Varin snorted with derision. 'Duty? Then you now have masters who command respect, who command your sacrifice?'

'I took an oath.'

The Blood Eagle nodded thoughtfully. 'You are an honourable man. A rare find in Constantinople.'

Hereward's back was burning from the midday sun, but he could not afford to relax for even a moment. The currents in the turbulent Bosphorus were treacherous and claimed even seasoned sailors. He would be glad when he had come to the end of his journey. Some wine, some meat in his aching belly and a good night's sleep still seemed as elusive as a dream.

After he had captured Varin, they had trudged for a day and a half through the woods until they had reached the salt marshes. With what little gold he had in the pouch at his waist he had bought the use of a creaking boat that looked as though it might sink at the first wave. And then the hardest part of the journey had begun. He had been rowing so long now that even his strong arms had grown numb, and there was still the better part of a day to go.

'The empire has been cursed with weak emperors for too long now.' Varin settled back against the prow. 'Too much gold, too much wine, too many women, too little care. Too few wits. This empire reached from horizon to horizon and they have sold it cheaply like a poor merchant at the market.'

'What care you? You were well paid.'

Varin nodded. 'Aye. True.' His heavy-lidded eyes

seemed to stare at distant things beyond Hereward's ken. The Mercian had seen that look before, on men who had spent too long at battle. 'But gold is not enough to feed a man's soul. The gods have plans for all of us.'

'And what did the gods plan for you?'

'I was born to kill. That is the only skill that great Odin granted me. What use my sitting in the dark beneath the Boukoleon palace while Emperor Michael, that callow youth, gives away his empire to the Turks, piece by piece? The old man who followed him, Nikephoros, is little better. He fights to keep his grip upon the throne, but he shies away from taking a stand against the enemies outside the walls. No, Odin called to me. I answered.'

Pausing in his rowing, Hereward leaned down to scoop out the seawater that was starting to sluice around his feet. It seemed to be coming in faster now. What hope this vessel would keep them afloat until they reached dry land? 'And Odin filled you with enough hate for the Turks to make you slaughter them like a butcher's stock.'

Varin frowned. 'Hate? Not I. They were enemies. I felt no more or less for them than for any man who looks down a length of steel at me.'

'I saw the women and children lying dead in that village.'

'You would know my heart? You think what I do is easily explained? Is murder, nothing more?'

'It has been said that you hunt the Turks because of a blood-feud.'

'Aye. It has been said.'

Hereward could see he would get no more out of Varin on this front. Instead, he went on, 'You torture them. You sever their ribs and rip out their lungs while they are still alive. They die in agonies, choking. That is not how a good warrior treats his enemies. All deserve an honourable death.'

'You think the blood eagle is torture? It is an honour, reserved for the greatest of foes.' The Viking's voice rang with sincerity.

Hereward studied the face before him, trying to get the measure of his prisoner. Enough madness lay there to cast doubt on any words he uttered. But then all warriors were mad, to a degree. Yet there were no shifting eyes, no tics around the mouth, nothing to indicate cunning or deceit. He seemed a plain man, who said what he believed.

Varin leaned forward, grunting as he rested the Dane-axe that pinned his arms back upon the sides of the boat. 'The blood eagle gives wings to the soul and carries it on to the world beyond. In days long gone, we gifted it to our greatest enemies. The mark of the northmen for those who fought with valour, whose names would for ever be told around the fires. We know this from our old songs, from the verse.' He closed his eyes and murmured, '*Ok Ellu bak, At let hinn's sat, Ivar, ara, Iorvi, skorit.*'

'Then it is not a story told by Christian priests to make the English afrit of all northmen?'

Varin spat over the side. 'I heard this at my father's knee when I was a boy, and he heard it from his father afore him. Christians! Their churches may have spread across the northlands like a plague, and my brothers and sisters bow their heads to the cross, but in the villages, away from eyes of judgement, they hold tight to the hammer-tokens hanging round their necks. Some of us still keep the old ways alive. It is who we are, fire and ice and blood, the path of the All-father. We will never let those ways die.'

'I have heard that from other northmen,' Hereward said with a nod. 'Warriors, most of them.'

'They say we are a Christian land now, as they say England is too. But you know well the beliefs of kings and earls and thegns are not always echoed in the halls of ceorls. Good men do not easily forget the ways of their forefathers.'

Hereward baled out the seawater as he weighed these words. When he looked up, he caught a glint in Varin's eye and knew, a moment too late. Thrusting forward on the balls of his feet, the warrior half lifted himself from his bench. At the same time, he swung his torso to the left. The axe-head followed, slashing towards Hereward's face.

The Mercian jerked back. He felt the boat rock wildly beneath him. The blade whisked by a hair's breadth from his cheek. Throwing his weight forward, Varin rose completely from the bench and crashed his full weight down upon Hereward. Pinned in the bottom of the boat, the Mercian felt cold water flood into his ears, stealing away all sound but the throb of blood in his head.

Varin's face loomed so close their noses almost

touched. His features were calm, as if this were far from a matter of life and death. With a snarl, he wrenched his mouth wide and lunged for Hereward's throat. The Mercian smashed his head forward before those jagged teeth could clamp on his flesh and rip him open.

Varin jerked back, blood trailing from his nose. But Hereward rammed his head forward again and again. Pain lanced through his skull.

As the Blood Eagle reeled, the Mercian rolled him to one side and wriggled out from under his bulk. Shaking the throbbing dullness from his head, he clasped his hand across the back of Varin's head and thrust the Viking's face down into the seawater in the bottom of the boat. Spluttering and thrashing, the Viking tried to force himself up. Hereward held him fast.

When Varin was on the brink of drowning, the Mercian yanked his head up so he could suck in a juddering breath and then forced his face down into the water again. Three more times he submerged his opponent, and only when he was sure the fight had been washed from him did he snarl, 'Enough?'

'For now.' Varin spat blood and brine.

Hereward dragged the warrior up and hurled him back on to his bench in the prow. 'Are you mad? Without me, this boat will sink. Your hands are bound. You cannot bale. You cannot row. You cannot swim. You would only drown.'

'Aye. But I would be free.' Varin licked his lips. 'Free to choose my own way of passing. Free to walk into Valhalla with my head high.'

Hereward slumped back on to his own bench. When he resumed the baling, he kept one eye on his prisoner.

'I will try to kill you every chance I get,' the Blood Eagle said.

'Aye. That I am starting to see.'

'But you are hard to kill, harder than any other man I have fought. I will give you that.'

Grunting, Hereward pulled back on the oars. During their struggle, the boat had been caught in one of the strong currents, and he had to strain to steer them back on course.

For a long moment, Varin watched his captor, no doubt trying to understand this man who had risked his own life rather than ride with an army. 'Why do you bring me back to Constantinople?' he said eventually. 'Why not end my days in that village I set afire and be done with it? You would have saved yourself the risk of marching a captive through the enemy's land. No more bloodshed to fan the flames of the Turks' wrath, no more fear of sparking a war.'

'Is that what you wanted? To force a war?'

'Better now than when the Turks had grown confident enough to attack on their own terms.' He levelled his unsettling, unblinking stare at his captor. 'Speak.'

'I am no executioner.'

'As good as. The moment I set foot in Constantinople I will find myself without a head.'

'You will not be executed.'

Varin looked out to sea. 'I took you for a man of honour. Not a liar.'

'You have my word.'

The Blood Eagle shook his head, disbelieving. 'Now you speak like a madman. I am worth nothing.'

Hereward squinted towards the horizon. Now the day was drawing on, the heat haze was starting to fade and he thought he could just make out the gleaming dome of Hagia Sophia in the distance. 'In the Vlanga, where the Varangians are at ease among their own and speak their mind, your name is still on many a lip. A great warrior, they say, perhaps the greatest the Guard has known. A lost soul, driven to the edge of madness by battle.'

Varin snorted. 'What know you of lost souls?'

As he rowed, Hereward bowed his head so the other man would not be able to read his expression. All his men, his spear-brothers, were lost souls. They had fought hard to save England from the grip of that Norman bastard William, but in the end they had been defeated. And it had cost them their land, their families, their friends. They had been set adrift on the seas of fate with only what they could carry, and they had been struggling for long years now to carve out a new life in Constantinople. Once they had been admitted into the ranks of the Varangian Guard, fortune had come their way. But not enough to make up for what they had lost.

'I hear tell you are a man to be trusted. Loyal,' the Mercian continued. 'Yet now you have no master, no allegiance.'

'I walk alone.'

'All men need friends.'

'Not I.' Varin leaned forward, his eyes piercing. 'I have chosen my path. There is no going back.'

'Every man can change his destiny.'

Varin thought for a moment and then said, 'When I was a boy, I followed my father on a steep climb, to the upper reaches of the mountain Galdhopiggen. At the top, the wind cuts like a knife, and the ground and sky become as one. Giants live there, gnawing on the bones of men who get turned around in that white world.' He sucked on his teeth, remembering. 'As we sheltered in a cave, with a small fire to keep us warm, listening to the roars of the giants away in the night, my father told me a truth. In every man's life, he comes to the place where the roads cross. A man's days yet to come are decided at that place. A good life. A bad life. Fortune. Glory. Misery. We should all be wise enough to see that crossing when we stumble up to it, but we do not. Most carry on along the road they are on without even noticing.'

Hereward studied the man opposite him. Varin's head was bowed in reflection. Blood trickled from his nose and he licked away the droplets with a flick of his tongue. The Mercian felt acutely aware of the two of them, alone there on the heaving ocean, caught between sea and sky.

'Many do not see the crossing at all. But have no doubt, my father told me, all of what could be and what will be is decided by that choice, and once on the new road there is no turning back.' A note of yearning edged his voice, and perhaps of regret too, for those long-ago days. 'It has been many years since the gods brought me to my crossing. I thought my choice was a good one, that I would make my father proud. But the road I have walked has not been worthy. Still, I can blame no one but myself. This is my road now, and I must walk it till the day I die. You cannot change my fate, English. I pray to Odin only that you see your own crossing when it appears before you.' He nodded slowly. 'This is a truth.'

Hereward watched Varin hunched on his bench, his head bowed in reflection. He had expected to find some untameable wild beast when he had first set off upon the trail of the Blood Eagle. Yet there was more to this man than the ability to deal death. Honour, certainly, and perhaps even more. He was hard to judge.

But then Varin looked up as if he had been reading his captor's thoughts, and his eyes were mere pools of shadow within his helm. 'You are an honourable warrior,' he said with a nod. 'It is good to have faced you in battle. But you would have been better to end my days out in the forest. I cannot alter the road that runs away from me. And if the time comes, I will still kill you.'

CHAPTER FIVE

Fingers like Damascan steel crushed the tanned throat. The knuckles whitened. In the quiet of the chamber, the flailing victim's choked wheezes echoed no more than the rustle of autumn leaves.

Karas Verinus held the soul in his huge paws. Though he was a big man with shoulders broad enough to heave a mule, he was calm. He exerted no more effort than was necessary to complete the task. Once a general in the field, now the emperor's closest military adviser, age had carved deep lines in his face. The greying hair that tumbled past the nape of his neck had long since lost its lustre. But though he was no longer a young man, his strength had not diminished.

'You are a spy,' he murmured. 'A spy for the Nepotes.'

His stare unblinking, Karas held his victim's gaze. The other man's eyes were wide and bulging and filled with terror. He was half Karas' age, small and slim like a fawn. Only moments before, he had been offering a goblet of wine to his master. The deep-red liquid now flooded into the grooves of the flagstones. His clutching hands clawed at the air, their frantic scrabbling beginning to slow. There was nothing he could do to break that grip.

'No words are needed,' the general continued. 'No admission. I know the truth. I have known since you first became my servant. No plea for mercy, either. Save what little breath you have. It will soon be gone.'

He leaned in so that their noses were almost touching. Since he had killed his first man, more than forty summers gone now, he had always loved to watch the light dying in the eyes. What an honour it was to witness the moment the soul passed into the arms of God, to be there to guide it across the threshold.

The eyes widened a touch more. The flame deep within them flickered and then winked out. As the flailing arms fell and the body went limp, the general unclenched his fingers and let his victim fall to the stone.

For a moment, he surveyed his handiwork. Then he dragged the corpse against the wall and slid it behind a tapestry. Someone would find it once the flies droned and the reek rose. He would be long gone by then and no accusation would be levelled at him.

Barely had the tapestry flapped back into place when laughter rolled towards the door. Karas drew himself up, cracking his knuckles as the clacking of leather soles approached along the corridor without.

The candles guttered when the door swung open.

Shadows swooped around the opulent chamber. A blast of chill air carried the scent of spice from the Christmas feast. Distant voices rumbled dimly. The feast would be dying down soon, the guests ebbing away until the palace was filled only with the remembrance of the Saviour's birth.

Amid a peal of cackling laughter, the emperor lurched in. He was in his cups, the wine making his eyes sparkle and dart. No doubt he had spent the night trying to drown his terror of the threat posed by the Turks. He would need more wine by far. His ruby-red tunic was of the finest Syrian silk, glittering with gold filigree. Nikephoros had quickly learned to love a life of finery since he had won the crown, a far cry from the blood-spattered general Karas had fought beside on the eastern frontier.

The emperor was ushered in by his newest adviser, Falkon Cephalas, a man whose fortunes ebbed and flowed in that city where only success was valued. But Karas knew his type. A man like Falkon would never be down for long. He was short, with curly black hair shading to grey at the ears. His blue eyes seemed to see everything, but his features were oddly unmemorable. A man could hold a conversation with him and then forget he had ever been there. Karas watched the adviser smile as the emperor made some light remark, his short, flat burst of laughter perfectly timed and fading in an instant. He bowed, he swept an arm. He said exactly what his associates wanted to hear and no more. Karas' eyes narrowed as he scrutinized this skilful display; he would never be taken in. Falkon was like a poison that took a season to end a life, and those around him would be none the wiser when death came calling.

'Ah, Karas,' Nikephoros slurred. 'You were missed at our feast. There was a woman who ate fire and a man who became a bear.'

'There was much laughter,' Falkon agreed.

'I would not willingly have stayed apart from the celebration, but the news brought from our scouts in the west could not wait.'

The emperor's good humour drained away and he scowled. 'It is true, then?'

Karas nodded. 'That Norman warrior the Fox is readying an army. One greater than any we can bring to bear.'

Baring his teeth, the emperor jabbed one finger to emphasize his simmering anger. 'He is a bastard, that Norman. A bastard.'

Pushing aside his contempt for this husk of a man, Karas nodded in agreement. 'Aye. But one that will not rest until Roman heads are staked along the walls and this city is in flames.' Nikephoros did not deserve to wear the purple. He was too vulgar, with mud coursing through his veins and none of the bearing of a true leader. He had not even been a good general. But soon his rule would be over. Then fate would decree a righteous emperor would sit upon the throne, one with the blood of the Verini.

'Robert Guiscard is an adventurer, but would he risk all he has won in an attack upon this empire?' Falkon asked.

'He thinks he can defeat us.' *And he probably can,* Karas thought.

The emperor prowled around the chamber, plucking at his tunic. Karas felt only disgust. The stink of fear was all over the man who wore the crown.

'The Turks on one side, the Normans on the other,' Nikephoros mewled. 'Oh, why has God abandoned us? Why are we cursed to live in these times?' Whirling, he stabbed a finger at Karas. Clutching at straws. 'Our army is better by far than it was under Michael. We have spent good coin to turn our open hand into a fist. The Immortals are bathed in glory. The finest warriors in all the world now flock to our standard. Surely that bastard knows this?'

'Is the Fox not satisfied with Salerno and all the other lands he has taken from us?' Falkon's face showed no emotion, but his eyes had a faraway look, the gaze of a man turning over possibilities, calculating, weighing. Karas knew that look. It said: *What path will benefit me the most, here at the end of things?*

'Like all Normans, he hungers for the horizon and seeks to make all land up to it his own.' Karas fought to keep the edge out of his voice. These children would try to wriggle out of any fight if they could. 'Robert Guiscard is not afraid. He now has the blessing of Pope Gregory, who had wit enough to make the Norman his ally when he feared his own power was threatened. And the Fox is as cunning as his namesake, have no doubt of that. He has found a reason to attack the empire, one that seems honourable on the surface.'

'What reason could he have beyond greed?' Nikephoros blurted.

'He has taken up the cause of Michael Doukas, of course,' Karas replied, his voice filled with acid. 'You know full well that when Michael was emperor before you, he promised his son to the Fox's daughter. Guiscard's honour has been impugned, his daughter left with nothing when she could have had an empire to her name. Pope Gregory would not argue with that, nor would any other power in Europe. If Robert Guiscard wishes to attack, there will be none to stand in his way.'

The general strode across the chamber and plucked up the goblet where the servant had dropped it. Grasping an amphora, he slopped more wine into the cup and swilled it back. 'My scouts tell me he has sixteen thousand men at his back.' He wiped his mouth with the back of his hand. 'At their heart, near two thousand of the most seasoned Norman knights, men who crushed England underfoot, who have fought and won on every front. And he has a fleet of ships to bring them to our gates.'

The emperor blanched. 'And I have the Varangian Guard,' he murmured.

'Aye, they are a good few. But only a few.' Karas narrowed his eyes, watching Nikephoros shrink by the moment. Everything was coming to a head. Soon it would be time to make his move. He would be the saviour of the empire, not this weak man, and he alone would be well rewarded. He tossed the goblet aside.

Coming closer, the emperor reached out his hands like a boy begging his father for aid. 'Tell me, Karas. Never was there a greater general in all of the empire. What hope have we?'

Karas allowed himself a flicker of a smile. 'When there is a strong fist, a stronger heart, there is always hope. One thing we do not do is wait for the Fox to attack. We meet him head on.'

Nikephoros' eyes flickered with a pathetic plea. 'You have a plan, Karas. Good, good. I knew I could count on you.'

'Robert Guiscard will send out a war-band ahead of his army, to prepare the way. We will smite them. And then he will know he cannot threaten us. That defeat will make him delay his attack, and we can buy more warriors to strengthen our own army.' He paused, and added, 'With what little gold we have left in our coffers.'

'And beggar us?' Falkon asked.

'Beggar or corpse. Which would you rather be?' Karas held the other man's blank stare.

'But if we send our fucking army to crush this war-band, we are defenceless against the Turks,' Nikephoros said, frowning.

'Not the army. Only our best. The Immortals, and the Varangian Guard.'

The emperor gaped like a codfish. 'But . . . but who will protect me?' he stuttered. 'If the Varangian Guard are gone . . . And the people . . . those ungrateful cunts . . . they speak openly of rebellion now. The markets seethe. Wulfrun's spy, that little rat Ricbert, he says the traitorous families at court are preparing to move against me. I cannot be left unguarded, Karas. I must be protected.'

Karas' smile was broader this time, one that could have been construed as reassuring. 'You will have me at your back. And Falkon Cephalas, and all your loyal advisers. No harm will come to you. We will make sure of that.' He strode to the door. As the torchlight from the corridor flooded into the chamber, he turned back and drank in the emperor's frightened face. He would etch this moment upon his mind. 'All will be well,' he said.

The dim sounds of the feast rumbled through the stone walls as Karas made his way along the corridors and out into the chill night. The torches along the high white wall of the hippodrome were ablaze. Walking underneath them, he watched his shadow dance. Ahead, the dome of Hagia Sophia was silhouetted against the starry sky. Once he reached the Milion mile-post monument, he turned past the Basilica Cistern and made his way into the streets containing the fine houses of the wealthy. They were clean and whitewashed, with torches burning beside the doors.

Yet his neck prickled with an odd sensation. Nikephoros had been right. Rebellion was in the air, even here. Anger, hunger, fear. The cauldron of Constantinople was beginning to bubble, and he could not afford to wait much longer to make his move. Since he had returned to his city, he had laboured hard to place his men in the positions that would matter. Once his call rang out, they would rise up as one and there would be a slaughter the like of which Constantinople had never seen. The emperor, the Varangian Guard, Falkon Cephalas, all of them would be put to the sword.

And then, when terror was at its height and hope thin on the ground, he would march into the palace and Justin Verinus would take the purple. His brother Victor would be avenged and the Verini would rule, aye, for a thousand years, as was their destiny.

His warm smile faded after only an instant. Justin was not the best choice to be emperor, not by a long way, but what option had he? After Nikephoros, Karas himself would be deemed too old. But Justin was broken deep inside; he killed as other men lusted after wine or women. His hungers could be hidden for a while, but once the people discovered his true nature he would be dragged through the streets and hanged upon the walls.

Karas' doubts did not leave him until he reached the door of his house. Inside it was quiet, the slaves long gone to their chambers. A single candle guttered in the sparse hall – he had no need of finery, of comfort – but his nostrils wrinkled at a sweet, unfamiliar scent floating in the air. Honey, and the perfume of mullein flowers.

Frowning, he let his hand fall to the hilt of his sword as he walked through the echoing rooms. At the door to his sleeping chamber, he paused for a moment and then swung it open.

Golden in the glow of a score of flickering candles,

Juliana Nepa lay naked upon his bed, lustrous blonde hair falling across her shoulders. On her side, propped up on one elbow, she had positioned her body perfectly so that his gaze would be drawn to her breasts, and her hips, and the curls of gold that nestled there. Slowly, she ran one slender finger from her neck to the tip of a nipple, and hesitated there for one moment before continuing the line over her belly to her inner thigh, ensuring that his gaze would follow its progress and miss nothing that was on offer.

Karas met her sparkling eyes. Her smile was wide, inviting.

'Karas Verinus,' she breathed, 'I am yours to do with as you will.'

He felt no desire, only a deep cold in his chest. Since he had returned to Constantinople from his estate in the east, he had seen her at court and in the market, and every now and then their eyes had met. Yet they had never spoken, as befitted the representatives of two families bound by a sworn blood-feud that crossed generations.

His own kin, the Verini, and Juliana's family, the Nepotes, seemed destined to be always at each other's throats. They had jostled for power at the court for long years, and that history had been bloody. An eye for an eye, a tooth for a tooth. In recent times, Karas' brother Victor had taken from the Nepotes their power and their wealth, and in doing so had left Juliana's father Kalamdios so badly wounded that he was now trapped in his frozen body, drooling like a madman.

In turn, the Nepotes had clawed back their fortune and their position at court and had murdered Victor. Karas grunted. There was no love lost between him and his brother, but that killing had impugned the name of the Verini and that could never be forgiven.

It was true to say the families hated each other more than they loathed any other soul on earth. And yet here she was, presenting herself like an offering upon the altar.

'Take me,' she said, her eyes narrowing seductively.

Karas looked her over. At court, she seemed enveloped in a mist of innocence with her wide eyes, her open, unguarded mouth, her quick laughter, her excited gestures. Now he could see that persona was more than studied; it was a work of art that was well constructed and had to be constantly maintained.

'You give yourself to me despite all that has passed between our kin?'

'I do. It is wrong that two such great families should be at war. We gain no ground. We whittle each other down by degrees. Come – the time for fighting is past.'

Karas walked to the end of the bed. Juliana opened her lips, and opened her legs.

'Take me,' she pressed. 'You will never forget this night, I promise.'

'Your spy is dead.'

Taken aback by his comment, Juliana gave a puzzled laugh. 'Spy? I know of no spy.'

'He watched me so you could be sure of my movements. So you could be ready and waiting here for me.'

'I only want you.'

'You are a whore. I know it. I have heard the whispers in the taverns. You think you can bend any man to your will by spreading your legs.'

Juliana was stung, her cheeks reddening.

Karas showed a cold face. 'I am not my brother. I do not have his inhuman tastes. Power is all that concerns me.'

Juliana's smile faded. A small knit formed in her perfect brow. Karas could see she had not anticipated this response. He guessed she had never known rejection before, certainly not when she had offered herself so brazenly.

Karas twitched, a snarl leaping to his lips. 'You think I can be bought so cheaply? By a cunt that has been used to subdue any man you wish to quash? At Manzikert, I slaughtered so many their blood washed around my knees. I have choked the life from children, and thrown women into torrents to achieve my heart's desire. I do not waver when some woman spreads her thighs. I am not weak. Nothing – not my cock, not love, not fear, not greed – nothing moves me from the road I travel to seize what I want. And certainly not some child who gives herself value when she has none. I have had a hundred whores better than you. You are nothing to me.' Raising one arm, he clenched his fingers as if he were crushing her windpipe. 'Your life means nothing to me.'

Juliana's face darkened. She drew her legs up, but she was still naked in her humiliation.

Plucking up her dress from the stool beside the bed, Karas flung it at her. 'Cover yourself. You bring shame upon your head. And it sickens me to look at you.'

With a murderous scowl, Juliana wriggled into her dress. 'You will regret this, Karas Verinus,' she hissed.

'You are so used to seeing men fall to your charms, you forget who you deal with.' His voice became a growl. She saw something in his face at that moment. He watched her eyes widen and her mouth pop into an O. 'You have walked into the wolf's lair. You are alone, naked, defenceless.' Reaching out both arms, he said, 'I could gut you with my bare hands. Drench myself in your blood and rip off that pretty head. Then I would throw what remained into the street for the dogs to feast on.'

Blanching, Juliana began to edge towards the door. Karas crossed the room and kicked it shut, blocking her path to the only way out.

'Do not hurt me,' she said. 'I will do . . . I will pay anything.' She backed away from him and fell across the bed.

'You were too confident. Too confident by far.'

'Please,' she begged. Her hands were trembling. He could see that she knew what a fool she had been.

'But here, at this point, where all my plans are falling into place, I can afford to take no risks. You have had a lucky escape.' Lowering his arms, he cracked his knuckles and sneered, 'You Nepotes, you can never be trusted. You have no strength, no power, so you skulk in the shadows, watching. You send out your spies, and you bide your time waiting for the fates to conspire to give you an advantage. And I do not doubt that you all thought yourselves so clever for sending you to bed me here. You laughed, I am sure. But that means someone knows you are here, little girl, and I will not be tarnished by accusations of murder. For though the emperor would surely find some way to pardon me for it, the taint of the crime would follow me and that would hinder all that I have put in place.'

Juliana let out the breath trapped inside her in a juddering sigh. As Karas loomed over her, she cowered back across the bed. 'But know this, for all the good it will do you. Soon the Verini will rule this empire. Very soon. But you and your kin will not live to see it. I will take great pleasure from breaking the neck of each one of you with my bare hands. Judgement Day is coming for you all, finally, and it is coming soon. Your days are done. Your tale is over. Make your peace with God.'

Her face became ashen. As she mouthed a desperate prayer, Karas crushed her wrist with a hand that had choked the life from a man only an hour earlier. Dragging her squealing off the bed, he hurled her across the floor towards the door. Her humiliation was complete. Scrambling to her feet, she bolted from the chamber.

Karas grunted and said, 'Whore.' It was only a whisper, but it chased her out of the house.

CHAPTER SIX

Hereward marvelled at the transformation that had come over the Vlanga, there on the south of the city, not far from the Boukoleon palace. Though Constantinople was blanketed with a reverential stillness during the twelve days of that holiest of celebrations, here the streets throbbed with life.

Flickering torchlight turned night into day. Men staggered, carousing, their full-throated singing ringing out across the rooftops. Friendly hands swept up those too drunk to walk. Along the streets, groups of women huddled with bright eyes darting, giggling, feigning shyness but holding out the ribbons that were their tokens. And deep in the shadows of the alleys, pale shapes were entwined. The grunts of lovemaking rolled out.

The air reeked of wine and urine and vomit. The warriors of the Varangian Guard were at play.

With Alric and Varin beside him, Hereward nodded to the warriors he had fought alongside. Even in their drunkenness, they bowed their heads in respect. He was pleased to see them enjoying these moments.

Their lives were brutal, and death was always close. But they were well rewarded, no one could deny that.

This quarter belonged to the Varangian Guard, had been earned by them through blood and steel. For one hundred years now, successive emperors had understood how much they owed to the Guard's ferocity in battle, and their sacrifice. These warriors had been showered with gold. When the crops failed and grain was short, they always had bread. The best wine flowed for them. And they were so lauded for their battle-skills, there was not a man or woman in the city who did not think them heroes.

And yet for all their riches, there was a time of reckoning coming. Would they survive the seasons to come, when so many enemies were readying to bring the empire to its knees? How many of them would die for yet another emperor who barely deserved their loyalty?

'You are well liked,' the Blood Eagle grunted, reading the signs.

Hereward could see that selfsame respect in the men's faces as they glanced at Varin. They knew him, respected him, perhaps feared him too, though he had once been one of them.

'These men know a great warrior when they see one. You should take heed. This is Hereward of the English. He led the rebellion against the cruel rule of the Norman invader, William the Bastard.' Alric eyed their captive. Hereward grinned. The monk had been around warriors so long now that not even a man with Varin's fearsome reputation daunted him. He was tanned and well fed, and he carried himself with confidence. Life at the monastery was good for him, it seemed.

Varin nodded. 'You lost, then.'

'Aye. We lost,' the Mercian agreed.

'One battle,' Alric emphasized. 'But in life he has never been defeated. My friend led his men here from England, crushing hardship after hardship beneath the soles of his shoes. And though all the powers seemed arrayed against him, he brought his men into the Varangian Guard so they could be rewarded in the manner that they deserved. And now Hereward is second only to the commander, Wulfrun.'

Varin looked round. He seemed surprised by this information. 'Second only to the commander Wulfrun,' he repeated, adding sardonically, 'Then it is an honour to have my freedom stolen by such a great fighting man, and my days ended by his works.'

'Keep walking,' Hereward growled. 'You will not be killed.'

'And a warrior who can perform miracles too,' the Viking murmured.

Once he had moored the boat on the quayside as night fell, Hereward had led Varin to the monastery of St George where Alric had been awaiting his return. The monk was not only the Mercian's eyes and ears in Constantinople, but his oldest friend and the man he trusted above all others. From the day they had met in the frozen wastes of Northumbria when they were little more than callow youths, they had fought their way through battles large and small at each other's side. They had both paid high prices, Varin thought, eyeing the stump where Alric's left hand should have been. But they had survived. They were ready to face what was to come next, together.

Ahead, a ruddy light danced across the white-washed houses from the Yule fire. The bonfire blazed on the common land at the heart of the Vlanga, and the warriors milled around it with their mead cups. The Romans knew nothing of these traditions; like so many things, the men of the Varangian Guard had brought this with them from their northern homelands.

Varin smiled when he saw the fire. He muttered something, a prayer to Odin, no doubt. When they saw the Blood Eagle, the warriors' songs drained away and they clustered in groups, bending their heads together to discuss this turn of events.

As the men parted, Hereward peered into faces until he found Wulfrun. In the midst of the celebrations, the commander stood rigid and upright as if readying himself for battle. Ricbert stood beside him, his rat-like face lit by the flames as he swigged back his drink.

Hereward pushed his charge forward. Varin raised his head, dignified, though his wrists were bound with ropes behind his back beneath the tatters of his crimson cloak. As they approached, Wulfrun's face remained like stone, but his eyes burned.

'I have brought you a gift,' Hereward said.

'We thought you dead,' Wulfrun said in a wintry voice. 'Some wished it so.'

And the commander was among that number, the Mercian knew. Wulfrun still blamed Hereward for the death of his father, and however much he tried to come to terms with that, for the sake of peace within the Guard, probably always would.

Wulfrun turned to Ricbert. Waving a dismissive hand at the Blood Eagle, he said, 'Take this dog away and prepare for his execution.'

'Wait,' Hereward interjected. 'I have promised that he will not lose his life.'

'What right have you to do that?'

Hereward paused, choosing his words carefully to avoid a confrontation. 'I would not challenge you, you know that. But hear me out. Varin has lived among the Turks for long seasons now. He has crept along the edges of their camps, and watched their settlements, aye, and tortured their warriors to learn all that he can, I would wager. He has great value to us. You know the Seljuks will attack Constantinople soon enough—'

'Aye, because of the ocean of blood that this bastard has spilled,' Wulfrun spat.

'Be that as it may. We know a war is coming, and we need all that is in his head.'

'And for this you risked your neck . . . and disobeyed my word?' His voice hardened.

'For this, and to save the lives of good men who would have ridden into the heart of our enemies, outnumbered, when one would suffice.'

Wulfrun gripped Hereward's arm and steered him to one side where they would not be overheard. The

Mercian could hear the simmering anger in the commander's voice. 'You are fortunate to have friends in high places or you would long since be dead. But go against my orders one more time and I will gut you where you stand.'

'I am a loyal member of the Guard.'

'You think yourself above all rules. The great Hereward, the Englishman who fought a king and almost defeated him. You . . . and your spear-brothers. We are all brothers here, but you and your men, you wear the crimson cloak, but you stand apart. You follow your own path, and even when you seem to be doing my work, it is to your own ends. I rue the day we let you all take the Guard's oath.'

Hereward held out his hands, trying to placate him. He could not afford to make any more of an enemy of Wulfrun than he already was. 'This time, aye, you are right. I followed my own judgement. But, as you see, I have brought Varin back. His days of blood among the Turks are over, and, if God is with us, we will know peace for a while longer. And no life has been lost in the doing.'

Wulfrun was unmoved. 'Give me your word that you will not disobey my orders again.'

'I cannot do that.'

For a moment, there was only the roar of the fire and the drone of men at celebration. The commander scanned Hereward's face. 'Then you cannot be trusted, and I must treat you as an enemy,' he said eventually through gritted teeth. 'Watch your back.'

Wulfrun marched back to where Varin waited,

Ricbert's blade hovering over his chest. 'You are an honourable man, I know that. If you wish to keep your head upon your shoulders, swear an oath now that you will not return to torment the Turks, and if we have need of your axe . . . as we may in days to come . . . then you will answer our call.'

The Blood Eagle raised his head so that the firelight played across his features. 'I so swear.'

'Go, then,' Wulfrun spat. 'Claw out some living here in Constantinople, if you can. And I will pray that we have not brought those days of blood within our walls.'

Varin showed no relief that he had been set free from the fate he had imagined. Instead, he turned, levelling his cold gaze at the man who had captured him. The sheen of battle-madness hid whatever lay within those eyes. Hereward could not tell if the Viking looked at him with threat, or thanks, or puzzlement that someone had thought his neck worth saving.

'You will see me again,' the Mercian said. 'Have no doubt of that.'

Without another word, the Blood Eagle turned and walked away. Hereward watched him go, limned by the fire, until he disappeared among the milling warriors.

'You should pray that you do not see him again,' Wulfrun said with no pity whatsoever. 'A man like that holds a grudge for a long time.'

Hereward left the commander of the Varangian Guard to his contempt. With Alric at his side, he made his way back through the Vlanga's festivities to the great hall he had been given when the emperor had made him Wulfrun's second. Though it was no larger than his father's hall in Barholme, the whitewashed stone made it seem grander by far. Columns lined the door, supporting a small portico. His raven sigil had been branded into a wooden plaque that stood beside the entrance.

'You have earned this,' Alric said as if he could read his friend's thoughts.

'Small reward for losing England,' Hereward grunted.

Inside, the raucous voices of his men echoed from the feasting hall. Hereward smiled. Now he *could* imagine he was in his homeland once more. No one would think a Roman lived here. There was no gold, no marble, no light, airy chambers. Heavy tapestries darkened the walls. The floor was covered with straw and rushes. Wood was everywhere, good, solid wood – benches and stools – and he could smell the smoke of the open hearth-fire.

Yet for all the comfort it brought him, Hereward felt a pang of regret. Easing open the door to the feasting hall, he watched his men before they glimpsed him. There was Kraki, his face a mass of battle-scars, still wearing the furs and leather armour that had seemed a part of him since they had first met in cold Eoferwic. Kraki, who had only loathing for him in those days, but was now one of his most trusted allies. And Guthrinc, an English oak of a man, towering and strong, yet more gentle than any Hereward knew,

73

until he faced his enemies on the battlefield. Sighard, the red-headed youth, his cheeks flushed as he dawdled with some girl. She had dark hair and dark skin, and her dress was the blue of the summer sky. As she twirled a lock of his hair around one finger and laughed, Hereward noticed her bright eyes. They suggested she knew more of the world than Sighard, he thought.

And there was Hengist, driven mad by the Normans who slaughtered his kin, dancing around the table to a song only he heard. And Herrig the Rat, Hiroc the Three-fingered, and Derman the Ghost, like the others stripped to their tunics in the heat of the hall. They tore at their meat, their chins slick with grease, and threw back their mead as if there would be no tomorrow. The women who sought their favours filled their cups and held their eyes with lingering looks. They had all donned their finest silk dresses, splashes of ruby-red and emerald and ochre in the firelight. Their laughter rang up to the rafters.

Hereward set his jaw. How at ease they seemed. 'This a poor reward for all they have sacrificed.'

'You have given them all you promised – gold and glory,' Alric countered.

'It is a poor trade for a home.' He seemed about to speak further, but then caught himself.

The monk, though, knew him too well. 'You fear for their lives with what is to come.'

'Gold and glory are passing. Have I given them only a place to rest on the road to death?'

'They are warriors.' Alric frowned at him. 'They know death is always close.'

These men had given up all to follow him wherever he led. He felt the burden of what he owed them pressing heavy on his shoulders.

'No one here could ask for a better leader.' Alric clapped a comforting hand on his friend's shoulder. 'Put these thoughts aside.'

But Hereward knew he could not.

Stepping into the room, he boomed, 'The spear-brothers I knew feasted the way they fought – as if it were their last day upon this earth. Have you lost the fire in your bellies?'

A cheer rang out from the warriors. They pushed aside their meat and their drink and swept around him. The Mercian set aside his darker thoughts when he saw the fierce welcome in those faces.

Guthrinc wagged a finger, pretending to count. 'Two arms, two legs, a head. Is this a miracle I see before me?'

'Did you ever doubt I would return in one piece?'

Kraki snorted, waving a dismissive hand. 'Do not swell his head more. I would wager there was more running than fighting.'

Guthrinc eyed the Viking, one brow cocked. 'And you would have stood your ground against an army of Turks.'

'Aye.' Kraki shook his fist in the air with defiance. 'One man . . . an army . . . I am not afraid.'

'Ah, a brave warrior,' Guthrinc said with a slow nod. 'Or a jolt-head. I have yet to decide.'

As the Viking bared his teeth, the spear-brothers cheered, playfully urging a fight. But when he looked

75

around, Hereward could see that jocularity was only a mask to hide the worry they had shared that their leader would never return.

Sighard stepped forward, always the most honest with his feelings, as the young often were. 'Victory?' he asked.

'The Blood Eagle is here, alive, and all is well.'

'Did Wulfrun snap like a wounded dog when he found you had done a whole war-band's work on your own? And ignored his orders?' Kraki wiped lamb grease from his mouth with the back of his hand. 'Ah, fuck him. He has a face like a stone, and a heart like one too.'

Derman thrust a cup of wine into Hereward's hand. 'Speak. We would all hear what you have learned in the east. Is war coming? Will we soon be called on to fight the Seljuk hordes?'

The Mercian swilled back his drink and licked his lips. 'Aye, the Turks are gathering. It was always to be, but the Blood Eagle's slaughter has made it sooner rather than later.' He looked around at the serious faces. They were not afraid. That was good. It would take steel to carve a path through the carnage that was to come. Eyeing Alric, he added, 'Whispers pass through the court that we face another enemy too.'

'A Norman adventurer,' the monk said, picking up the telling. 'A great warlord, greater than Roussel de Bailleul. He was only interested in gold and power. This one wants to bring the empire to its knees.'

'This you know for sure?' Sighard asked.

'Fear has driven the Romans into the churches to

pray for their souls. The truth of these threats rings up to the rafters with every plea to God.'

'And what does the emperor do? Nothing, I would wager,' Hiroc grumbled. 'He was good enough when his own rule was threatened. He pursued the traitor Basilakios to the end, and blinded him in judgement. But does he have the stomach for a fight on two fronts, a fight against two great armies that turn us into dwarfs?'

'And we are caught in the middle,' Sighard said, rubbing a hand through his thick red curls. 'A few good men.'

Kraki swilled back the last of his mead. 'We have been here before. Hope was thin on the ground when William the Bastard besieged us at Ely, but still we fought him to a standstill. And we would have won if not for the treachery of churchmen.' His gaze flickered towards Alric.

The monk held up his chin. 'We are not all the same.'

'Be that as it may, what do we do now?' Guthrinc asked. 'Wait for orders to ride into the jaws of death?'

'That is our job,' Derman said. 'That is why we are weighed down by sacks of gold. It would not be honourable to flee from this fight.'

'No one is talking about fleeing,' Kraki snapped, glaring.

Slowly, all eyes turned towards Hereward. A silence fell across the feasting hall. In the glow of the fire, the women bowed their heads, pretending they were no part of this, but gripped by what they were hearing. Kraki was wrong. They had not been here before. Never had they faced so many enemies without a good general to lead them to the higher ground.

'Our fate has not yet been written,' Hereward said in a quiet voice that carried clear across the hall. 'Now, return to your feasting and keep your spirits high. I have more work to do.'

It was enough. The spear-brothers turned away, their voices growing louder as they searched for their cups, their meat and their women. They had long since decided to put all their faith in their leader, and they had not been disappointed yet.

'You shoulder your burden well,' Alric whispered, leaning in. 'You are a good man, and they know it.'

Hereward turned to his friend, shaking his head slowly. 'Make no mistake, when it comes to war, I am a devil. This fight will not be over soon. You know that to be true.'

A shadow crossed the monk's face at what he saw in his friend. But he nodded in agreement and said with a note of caution, 'You make things plain as day and night when you look upon yourself. Angels and devils. But men are men, and what do you call a devil who does God's work?'

Hereward looked back to the spear-brothers who had followed him loyally for so long. He had no time for the monk's clever words.

'I am a devil,' he repeated quietly.

CHAPTER SEVEN

Hereward pressed back into the deep shadows of the alley. In a swirling pool of torchlight, Wulfrun strode down the street ahead, his helm dipping down, his crimson cloak flapping behind him. Ricbert hurried at his side, holding the flaming brand aloft. The festivities were ending. The Yule fire would be burning low, the Varangian Guard drunk.

Cloaked in the dark at the Mercian's back, Alric waited until the commander and his aide had passed and then he breathed, 'Can we trust no one?'

'This has become a city of plots. The threat of an early grave drives men wild. Some seek advantage in the confusion, a new road to power. Others seek only to survive until a new dawn. But they will do anything to win their heart's desire. We can trust none of them.'

'This is a lonely road we walk,' the monk replied with a note of regret.

'Was it not ever so?' Hereward turned to his friend, trying to soften. 'And keep one eye on Neophytos. That bastard monk is as treacherous as any man I know. He has spun his lies well for his poisonous kin, the Nepotes. In their war against Karas Verinus, that family will do anything – murder anyone, cheat, betray, and in Juliana Nepa's case bed any man – to achieve their ends. But it is through Neophytos the eunuch that we will know when the Nepotes prepare to make their move.'

'He keeps his own counsel,' Alric said doubtfully.

'True. But his lips are loose when need be and he can be easily bought if you are sly.'

'Aye. Now he has been shaved, he can no longer lust after women. But his hunger for other pleasures never ends. A table groaning under the kitchen's finest meats and cakes will make his eyes sparkle.'

'Then return to the monastery. You have much work to do.'

With some reluctance, Alric nodded and walked away. Hereward felt a pang of regret for the demands he had made. By calling upon their friendship he was leading his ally further and further away from the path of righteousness. But the monk would never deny him. They had shared too much.

Glancing around, Hereward wrapped his crimson cloak about him and slipped across the narrow street. The houses there were whitewashed, with cool, fragrant gardens at the back. They were mainly the homes of wealthy merchants, and others who had made good coin in that city which loved its gold.

At a large house with a bronze plate stamped with a wolf's head by the door, two guards waited under a hissing torch. Hereward nodded to them and stepped inside. The indoor slaves asked him to wait, but he ignored their protests and pushed past them. Searching through the empty chambers, he found himself outside a door through which muffled voices echoed.

Hereward hammered his fist three times on the wood, and the voices snapped off. For a long moment, there was no sound. Then footsteps padded towards the door and it eased open a crack.

Alexios Comnenos' eyes widened in surprise when he saw the Mercian. The commander of the Roman army was naked to the waist, his cheeks flushed and his long black hair curling into ringlets with sweat. His enemies still called him boy, though he had seen twenty-four summers. Still young for such a powerful position, but he had been a better general and warrior than all of them when he was only just starting to grow hairs on his chest, and he had more than grown into the power heaped on him by the emperor. The warriors who fought at his side respected him above all others.

Before Alexios could utter a word, Hereward pushed past him to tell him the news about Varin where no one could overhear them. For long seasons they had been allies, bound by secrets and plots, and they had entrusted each other with their lives. The commander began to complain, but his words drained away as the Mercian ground to a halt. There was no longer any use in pretending.

In the bed, a startled woman peered back, the silk and furs pulled tight to her neck to hide her nakedness. She was older than Alexios – five years, the

Mercian knew – and her delicate aristocratic features were pretty, her lips full, her mahogany hair tumbling in curls around her pale face. Hereward had seen her before on many occasions. Why would he not? She was Maria of Alania, the emperor's wife.

He stared in surprise for a moment, then bowed his head in deference. 'I am sorry to disturb your peace,' he murmured, though no words would do justice to that moment. He turned his back upon the bed. He heard the rustle of silk as the woman slipped out from under her covers, and then the sound of bare feet upon marble as she darted into the next chamber.

'Are you mad?' he whispered. 'If the emperor finds his wife here he will cut off your balls. And then he will cut off your head. And now that you have made me an ally in your crime, he will cut off my head too.'

Alexios shrugged and poured himself a goblet of wine. 'A man will risk anything for love.'

'There are women aplenty in this city. The greatest beauties in all—'

'Not like her.' Alexios spun back, his eyes dark with emotion.

Hereward felt surprised by the intensity he saw there. He had fought alongside the Roman for many a year, and the commander had always seemed serious, a cool-headed general. On the battlefield, he was like ice in his planning. Never had the Mercian seen him like this.

'How long have you been risking your neck?'

'How long have I been in love with Maria?' Alexios

corrected, each word cracking. 'From the first moment we met.'

'You are throwing meat to starving wolves.'

'I have no choice. I cannot turn away from this.'

Maria stepped out of the dark of the adjoining chamber, now composed and covered in an amber dress of fine Syrian silk that all but glowed like the sun. 'As a captain of the Varangian Guard, you have sworn an oath to the emperor,' she began, fixing her gaze on the Mercian. She spoke English fluently, but it was edged with the thick accent of her Georgian homeland. 'But you are loyal to your friends, yes? To Alexios?'

'I have seen nothing here this night that is worthy of mention.'

She nodded and smiled, plucking up a comb to attack the tangle of her hair. Now they were all bound by this secret.

Hereward thought how strange this honest love must be for her. Her life had been nothing but a series of arrangements to maintain the balance of power. Her father, King George, had sent her to the court at Constantinople to further her education, but she had found herself, at fourteen years, married off to Michael Doukas before that guileless boy had ascended to the throne. With her son, Constantine, she had fled to a Petrion monastery when Nikephoros had deposed Michael and sent him away to become a monk.

'She is a beauty, is she not?' Alexios' eyes sparkled as he watched Maria comb her hair.

'Aye,' Hereward agreed, but he saw much more.

Like many of the women he had encountered in Constantinople, Maria of Alania had ambition to match even the most hardened of Roman aristocrats. After the life of an empress, she would never settle for a meagre existence in a monastery, anyone could have seen that. And so it was. His thoughts flew back to the time of mourning that settled on the city when Nikephoros' wife had died and it seemed that every woman in Constantinople was battling for his hand and the power that came with it. The Doukai had given Maria the help she needed to compete, even against her former mother-in-law Eudokia and her daughter Zoe. And like Alexios, the old goat Nikephoros had been dazzled by this woman's beauty, and, no doubt, his desire to stop the Doukai plotting against him.

'How is your son?' Hereward asked. 'Is he well?'

Maria's eyes flashed, and a silent understanding flew between them. Nikephoros had so far refused to name Constantine as his heir. If he had, he might have bought Maria's loyalty. But now she knew, as all who passed through the court knew, that her days yet to come were built upon shifting sand. After an instant she found her smile again. 'He thrives like the tallest and most beautiful flower in the garden.'

Turning back to Alexios, Hereward whispered, 'The empress is a fine catch, any man can see that. But you must keep your mind on the battle ahead.'

'Maria will not tear me away from the path we forge together. I am no callow youth. I know full well the import of all the matters we have discussed.'

'We must talk about what I saw in the east, and the Blood Eagle, and the threat rising in the west,' Hereward pressed. 'The days we have left are fewer now. Hope is fading. Soon it will be time for us to make our choice.'

Alexios nodded, but before he could speak the door swung open. It was Alexios' mother, Anna Dalassene. Tall and slender, in a dress of brightest crimson, she was a woman who commanded attention. The beauty of her youth had not been diminished. Her black hair, now streaked with silver, tumbled down her back. She held her head up imperiously, as if she ruled that city in all but name. And once, Hereward knew, she had almost had her fingers upon the throne until plots and powerful men had prised her grip away.

Her gaze moved slowly, heavy with the wine that she loved so much, and then it fell upon Maria. Hereward stiffened. When roused, Anna's fury knew no match, and here was her much-loved son, the plaything of an older and more powerful woman, a rival even.

But Anna only smiled and nodded. 'Maria,' she said. 'How beautiful you always look.'

Maria glided across the chamber, and touched the other woman's forearm in greeting. 'My beauty pales beside your own,' she purred.

Hereward studied the two women together, the quick looks, the smiles, the way they held themselves close. No rivals these, but friends who shared secrets, and a friendship that was itself a secret, for he had seen no sign of it at court.

Maria flashed a smile of parting at Alexios. With a nod to Hereward and Anna, she eased out of the door into the quiet house beyond.

'Wash yourself, and dress. We have urgent business,' Anna commanded her son. Turning to the Mercian, she added, 'You have heard news of the Normans in the west, readying to attack?'

'From Alric. The churches are filled with Romans. Word travels fast when folk worry.'

'We cannot leave these matters to the emperor.' She poured herself a goblet of wine. 'He is old, too fearful in his long years, too slow. But we still have time. The Turks are not ready to make their move. Not yet the risk that we will be caught fast between the blacksmith's tongs, ready to be smashed upon the anvil.'

When Alexios slipped into the other chamber to follow his mother's commands, Hereward lowered his voice. 'You know of this business with the emperor's wife?'

Anna's lips curled into a faint smile. 'My son is still young, and this is what young men do. They get carried away by their hearts and forget their heads.'

'With Maria, he could lose his head.' Hereward studied the aristocrat as she crossed the room to peer at the dishevelled bed. He furrowed his brow, trying, and failing, to understand what ran through her mind. For he had learned that for Anna Dalassene there was always some advantage to be gained from even the smallest thing. Much as she valued her children, and Alexios in particular, she was not averse to using them in whatever plot she weaved.

'And Alexios' wife, Irene . . . ?'

'She knows nothing of this, of course.' Anna lazily waved an arm, almost slopping wine upon the flagstones. 'You know as well as I that my son's marriage to the granddaughter of the Caesar John Doukas was merely to keep the Doukai close, and happy. They can be a dangerous family, filled with passion and long-held grudges.'

Hereward nodded. He had long since accepted the manipulations of the powerful Roman families constantly jostling for advancement. Here love meant nothing; only power.

'Besides,' Anna said, 'Maria has the emperor's ear. She can whisper honeyed words as they lie in their bed stained with the sweat of their lovemaking. And perhaps, with those words, Maria can guide her husband to look fondly upon Alexios, and upon his wishes.'

Hereward smiled to himself. He admired this woman. She had sharper wits than almost any man at court. No wonder she had found shared interest with Maria of Alania. In England, the new bastard king was forcing women to their knees, putting men above them in all things. But here in this strange, reeking city, women could look a man in the eye, and, if they were brave and cunning enough, wield as much power.

When Anna turned back to him, her face had darkened. 'We have found ourselves in a stew, have we not, Hereward of the English? Constantinople seethes with plots and all of them are coming to a head at once. Because all here know that the night is drawing in fast, and if the throne is to be seized, it must be done before the sun is gone. Caught as we are between the Normans and the Turks, the hours of peace are fading fast within these walls. Karas Verinus readies himself to put that devil-child upon the throne. I can see it in every part of him at court, in his smiles and his calm words and the swagger that grows by the day.' She threw back the last of her wine with fury. 'And the Nepotes know they must make their move before Karas if they are to stand any chance of taking the crown.'

Hereward prowled the chamber, one hand upon his sword. Anna Dalassene was right. He rarely slept easy these days. 'Karas is a dangerous man, but he is a plain one. He is a warrior. You will know when he is ready to raise his axe. No, it is the Nepotes that trouble me. They are all smiles and words of kindness until they turn like cornered dogs. We must be ready for them, above all.'

Alexios stepped back into the chamber, humming to himself as he pulled on his cloak. Anna gave him a weary look. But when she glanced back at Hereward the Mercian was surprised to see the worry etched in her face. 'If all goes wrong, there will be bloodshed and death to a degree that none of us have known before in our lifetime, not even you, with all your battles in England,' she said. 'And it is likely that few of us will see a new dawn breaking over the empire. Not I, not my sons. Nor you and your loyal spear-brothers.'

Far away across the city, the stillness of the night was broken by a dim pounding. That steady beat grew louder by the moment, as others took it up, until it rolled like thunder.

Alexios' features hardened. 'The watch-drums.'

Hereward dashed out of the house with the other two close behind. In the chill, they ran through the dark streets as men and women began to emerge from their homes, faces creased with fear. Warriors were already milling along the eastern walls when the trio clambered up the stone steps where the drums boomed their warning beat.

Doom-doom-doom.

Hereward saw what had driven the night-watch to alarm. The sky was ablaze. Across the narrow stretch of water, beyond the city's eastern borders, fires too numerous to count had turned the lowering clouds a bright orange. Thick smoke drifted across the narrow sea.

His nostrils wrinkled at the acrid stench, and his thoughts rolled back across the years to another night when he had stood there, watching flames rise up into the night. Then the foe was the army of the Norman adventurer Roussel de Bailleul. But this was much worse. It seemed at that moment that the whole world was burning.

'You took the Blood Eagle too late,' Anna breathed.

Alexios drew himself up. 'The Turks are almost at the walls. They are setting our villages alight. This is a sign. They mean to attack, and soon.'

'Emperor Michael should never have given up any lands we owned to the Seljuks.' Anna fixed her gaze on those rolling waves of amber light on the underside of the clouds. 'Not even to keep the peace. It only brought the Turks closer. And now . . . now . . .'

'It is not too late,' Hereward said before she could give voice to her fading hope.

'No. But it is close.' The low voice rolled out like the groaning of a long-closed door.

Anna and Alexios jerked round. Two figures had ghosted close to them. The man who had spoken was swathed in black from head to foot, a scarf he had wrapped around his head, long robes that swept the stones. His shaped beard was black too, as were his eyes. At his belt a silver dagger gleamed. Hereward nodded to Salih ibn Ziyad. It had been long years since this man had saved the Mercian's life in the hot lands of Afrique, and in that time Hereward had learned that Salih was as deadly as he was wise.

Beside him was a girl, as skittish as a pony, though just as lethal as the man with whom she walked, the Mercian knew. She was Ariadne Verina, the niece of the bastard Karas, but she was nothing like her uncle. Hereward watched her darting eyes, and the tics that flickered across her features. There was a hint of madness there, born of the terrible treatment she had endured at the hands of her father Victor.

Salih greeted Anna and Alexios, then said, 'The Turks will never rest until they have taken Constantinople, any man could see that. The Romans have brought this fate upon themselves.'

'There is still time to fight,' Hereward replied.

'Perhaps.'

'We will fight, all of us, and we will win. I, al-Kahina, slayer of devils, vow this.' Ariadne's voice was low and throaty, the voice of a much older woman. She believed herself possessed by the spirit of Meghigda, the queen of the Imazighen of Afrique, whom Salih once served. Perhaps she was. Or perhaps this was the way she dealt with the miseries life had meted out to her. But Hereward saw both Anna and Alexios flinch, unnerved by that sound coming out of the mouth of a young girl.

'You must not underestimate the Seljuks,' Salih said. 'Long before I reached the homeland of the Imazighen, I walked this earth far and wide, and I learned much of these Turks, of their ways, and their days long gone, and their dreams of days yet to come. They have the fire of God in them, and it burns brightly. That is where they gain the strength to fight on through all hardship.'

'We all have the fire of God in us,' Alexios insisted.

Salih ibn Ziyad peered across the water, the flames dancing in his eyes. 'They are born of a great race of warriors who roamed the lands of the far east long ago. Horsemen. Worshippers of the spirits of the wind and the trees and the plain. Conquest is in their blood. Then, in the time of their fathers, they chose another path, that of the prophet Muhammad. His teachings have given them strength, and purpose. This is a potent brew, Roman. Ignore it at your peril.'

91

Alexios grunted, the words seemingly weighing on him.

'Then help us fight,' Hereward urged. 'You have spent your days schooling this girl, I know. Guiding her as you did Meghigda. But there is work here for you . . .' He eyed Ariadne. 'For both of you. If you know these Turks as well as you say, you may have knowledge that could help us.'

'You speak now for the emperor?' Salih said with a sly smile.

'We, all of us, face a terrible fate,' the Mercian continued. 'If not from the Turks, then from the Normans in the west. And if not from them, then from those within these walls who would drown us in a sea of blood to get their fingers upon the crown. Join us. There is a way ahead, I swear it.'

Salih walked away along the wall towards the steps. The girl followed him silently. As the night swallowed them up, the wise man's words floated back. 'The way ahead is to flee Constantinople before it is too late. If you do not, you will burn here with the rest of these poor souls.'

CHAPTER EIGHT

The torch over the door sizzled. Along the narrow street, the shadows swelled away from the wavering flame as a figure with a strange rolling gait hurried out of the dark. Ragener the Hawk ignored the pounding of the watch-drums. He rarely ventured out into the streets. He was sick of the cries of startled women, of men cowering away from him for fear that he was some devil who had come to drag their miserable souls down to hell. But the night cloaked him and gave him some thin peace.

His face was ruined. His nose was missing, slit off during a fight in some filthy back alley. What remained of his hair clung to his scalp in patches, the rest burned off or torn away. Both ears too had been lost. His bottom lip had been carved in two so his speech often sounded as though he had a mouth filled with pebbles. One eye was milky. The rest of his features were a mass of scar tissue. His most recent loss, his greatest perhaps, was his left hand, lopped off by the man he thought of as that bastard Hereward.

Aye, he was a monster to the eye, a half-man,

whittled down by battle during his time as a sea wolf, preying on those too dim-witted to protect themselves when they were upon the whale road. He had not deserved any of the misery that fate had dealt out to him, he thought with bitterness.

But he would gain his revenge.

Yet this evening he had little choice but to leave his lonely chamber in the house of Karas Verinus. Wheezing, Ragener hammered his good fist upon the door. The sign of the brothel, the alabaster rose affixed to the wood, jumped at the impact.

When the door swung open, an aged eunuch with rouged cheeks and lips glanced up and down the street, then beckoned him in. Ragener could smell the vinegar reek of the fear-sweat on him.

'You made haste. That is good,' the eunuch burbled, wringing his hands as he spoke.

Ragener pushed past him into the perfumed hall. The grunts and rhythmic bangs of lovemaking echoed through the walls. 'You have told no one?'

'Not a soul. Only I know.'

'Good.' Ragener fingered his knife under his tunic. At least that was only one throat he would have to slit. 'Lead on.'

Grasping a fat candle in a brass holder, the eunuch lurched along a narrow corridor past numerous closed doors. The air was thick with musk. At the rear of the house, the brothel-keeper came to a halt before a door carved with swirls of intertwining ivy. In his shaking hand, the candle sent the shadows leaping around the walls. Ragener cocked his head.

Only silence reached the holes where his ears had been.

'Well?' he demanded. When the eunuch made a low mewling noise, the Hawk shoved him back and growled, 'Wait here. Do not dare leave. Do not let anyone enter.'

Stepping into the room, Ragener closed the door firmly behind him. For a moment, anger contorted his ruined features. 'You will be the end of me,' he growled, as much to himself as anyone.

On the bed sat Justin Verinus, cross-legged. When Ragener had first met him, near eight years gone, he had been a boy, but even as a man he had lost none of the innocence in his features. Beneath a thatch of russet hair, Justin's face was pale and uncannily still, as if he were at sleep. His wide, dark eyes stared. Ragener had long since stopped looking into them. The unlined face told him this was a child, but those eyes promised an old man, twisted by the years.

He shivered.

Justin was sitting in a pool of blood that had seeped through the covers and was dripping on to the flag-stones. That steady beat was the only sound in the chamber. The remains of one of the whores lay over the end of the bed, her auburn hair hanging down on to the cold floor. Another woman, or what had been one, sprawled at Ragener's feet, one arm reaching out for the door. Their bodies had been opened up, at neck, and gut, and groin.

The sea wolf paid the corpses no attention. He had seen too many of them in recent times. 'Where are your wits?' he sighed. 'You are to be emperor soon . . . perhaps within days. Do you think the people will settle for a butcher to rule them? Why can you not contain your foul urges, if only for a little while? Once you sit upon the throne, you can do whatever you will, kill anyone, and none will be the wiser.' He swept out an arm across the bloody chamber. 'But if this were to reach the ears of the populace, all that has been planned for you would be gone. And you would be hanged in the forum of Theodosius, a feast for the ravens.'

Justin only stared, that sickening, unblinking stare, as if Ragener were speaking in some foreign tongue. The blood dripped in that steady beat, marking the moments of his life's passing.

Unable to contain himself any longer, Ragener felt bitterness well up in him and fill his mouth with acid. 'Why have I been so cursed?' he cried, reaching out his good hand in a plea to God. How many times had he cleaned up the filth left by this monster? This was his life now. No brave warrior. No swordsman carving out his destiny. He had become a midwife for a moonchild.

He clenched his fist, steeling himself. 'My reward will come,' he snarled. 'I have not sacrificed so much to see my days ebb away in this manner. When you are emperor . . . when Karas is the power standing behind your shoulder, then I shall be raised up. All will bow to me. And all who have ever offended me will face my wrath.' The sea wolf narrowed his eyes, looking at Justin, through him and the walls and across the miles and the seasons. He was back on the ship, drifting under a hot sun, reliving that moment when the axe swept down to take his hand. The memory of the pain only made his hunger stronger. 'And Hereward will be the first to lose his head.'

Blinking away the vision, he turned his attention to the ragged bodies. 'Now help me. We must be done with this by dawn.'

CHAPTER NINE

A rainbow dappled the whitewashed wall. Shimmering flecks of coloured light danced as the young man turned in the shaft of sunlight. His *loros*, the ceremonial garb that only the imperial families wore, was aglow with more riches than many in Constantinople saw in a lifetime. His shoulders strained against the weight. Rubies, emeralds, sapphires and pearls studded the silk, which had been embroidered with golden thread and decorated with enamel plaques.

From the twisted branches of the old tree in the courtyard, Ariadne Verina peered through the arch into the house where Leo Nepos was trying on the fine garment. She stared, entranced, as she had been from the moment she first met him.

The tree hid her well. There was nowhere in that sprawling city that was denied her. Crawling through drains barely wider than her shoulders, creeping across the amber-tiled roofs, clambering over walls, slipping into houses while the occupants slept. Her father had called her a rat, usually before he had laid the back of his hand across her face. But that was where she found her freedom.

The white-haired tailor knelt at the young man's feet, adjusting the *loros* so that it swept less than a finger's width above the marble floor. He looked up, his face glowing at the magnificence of his handiwork. 'Even the emperor himself would be proud to wear such a wonder.'

Leo Nepos raised his head, no doubt wishing he was anywhere but there, Ariadne thought. He had been a strange child, quiet and introspective. And now, on the cusp of manhood, his implacable features had grown even more unreadable. He did cut a handsome figure, though. Ariadne smiled. Tall and strong and slender.

'And what is the occasion for this fine garment?'

'Keep at your work,' Leo snapped. 'I am not wasting all of my morning standing here while you sew.'

Chastened, the tailor bowed his head back to his work.

Ariadne leaned down so she could study Leo's face through the archway. So sullen. She tried to recall the last time she had seen him smile. Clenching her tiny fists, she stifled her rising anger. This was his damned kin's fault, the hated Nepotes. They saw value only in power, not in honour, or love, or tenderness. And with each day that passed they were shaping Leo more firmly in their own image.

'Get away from me!'

In the hall, the tailor sprawled across the floor, his

arm flying across his face. Leo's sword flashed towards the whimpering man's neck.

For a moment, Ariadne thought he was going to run his victim through there and then. But anguished cries drowned out Leo's snarl of fury. His mother Simonis and his sister Juliana darted forward, grabbing his arms to drag him away.

'Sheathe your sword now,' the older woman demanded, her face like flint. Elegant in a scarlet silk dress, she had lost none of the beauty of her youth, though like Anna Dalassene's her black hair was now streaked with silver.

With a scowl, Leo lowered his blade.

Juliana knelt beside the frightened man. Her slender fingers brushed his face and hair. Her smile shone as she whispered soothing words. Ariadne glowered. How easily men fell for her deceit.

'My brother feels the weight of the demands of his coming celebration, tailor,' Juliana was saying. 'He does not normally growl like a cornered dog.' Still smiling, she turned to Leo and urged, 'Make your apologies to the man you have wronged, brother.' When no reply was forthcoming, her eyes flashed above that smile and she said with a crack in her voice, 'Speak now.'

'I was wrong to treat you so badly,' Leo muttered, and gave a curt bow. 'We will finish our business another day.'

As Juliana ushered the tailor out, Simonis loomed over her son. 'Would you throw away all that we have planned?'

'I am tired of that fawning old fool. I am tired of all this waiting. I am ready.'

'Soon you will have all that you ever wanted. The crown, the power. You will be the pride of the Nepotes.'

Leo softened. This was what he had always wanted, Ariadne knew, more even than the crown and the power. He had lived his life in the shadow of his elder brother, Maximos. But now that Maximos had left Constantinople, his family paid him heed. Aye, because he was useful, Ariadne thought with a grimace. Among all the Nepotes, Leo was now the only one who could carry the family's ambition on to the throne. And from the sound of it they would be making their move soon. Why else would they be preparing such a grand *loros*?

'Go, take off your finery,' Simonis said, her voice gentle now. 'Your father grows as restless as you. We must reassure him that we are almost ready.'

Ariadne watched Leo follow his mother out of the hall. If she could spirit him away from there, she would. There was still hope. Now that she was more than Ariadne Verina, now that she was al-Kahina, slayer of devils, she would find that strength she had hitherto lacked. Meghigda had always protected the innocent, and she, Ariadne, would continue her work, for she was Meghigda, Meghigda the strong, not Ariadne the weak and broken and abused. And Leo was a true innocent, she firmly believed that.

She could save him.

Filled with determination, she began to claw her

way up to the higher branches so that she could leap on to the roof. Salih would soon be missing her, and if he found she was here in the hall of the Nepotes, risking her neck, he would give her the edge of his tongue.

Before she had gone too high, she heard urgent voices nearing and clambered back to her hiding place to spy some more.

One of the voices was Juliana's, the other belonged to a man. A moment later, Wulfrun of the Varangian Guard marched out into the courtyard, his helm under his arm. His expression was dark. When Juliana skipped to his side, Ariadne curled up as tight as she could, now terrified that she would be discovered.

Under the tree's shade, Juliana guided Wulfrun to a stone bench next to the trunk. With reluctance, he sat. Ariadne covered her mouth, choking her breath into her chest. If either of them looked up, they would see her in an instant.

'Do not fret so,' Juliana was saying. She was smiling, trying to manipulate this man she professed to love as she did every other man. Wulfrun's head was bowed, his shoulders stiff, but Juliana pressed her side against his and leaned in so that her breath warmed his cheek. Feeling her blood boil, Ariadne realized how much she detested this deceitful woman.

'You are in danger. I do not know how much longer I can protect you.' Wulfrun's face was drawn. He seemed to have the weight of the world upon him.

'Constantinople will not fall,' Juliana replied brightly.

'You live in the dream that has afflicted this city, this empire, for too long. Once you Romans were strong, but no longer. Now your enemies are stronger, and they move against you by the day. And the emperor is pulled this way and that by the buzzing of the flies that surround him, but does nothing.'

Juliana hesitated for a moment. 'Soon the emperor will not be a problem.'

Wulfrun's eyes narrowed. 'What say you?'

Ariadne watched the woman wrestle with her thoughts as one by one the masks of deceit fell away. Finally an open, honest face remained – the first time it had been seen in many a moon, Ariadne wagered – and it was troubled. 'Soon we will move upon the throne.'

'Why do you tell me this? You know I have given my oath to protect the emperor.'

'And you have given your oath to protect me. Which one matters most?' Juliana's voice hardened. 'You know we are no angels, we Nepotes. You know we plot to seize the throne.'

'As long as you gave no voice to it, I could pretend it was not true.'

'We have no choice but to act soon. Karas Verinus is preparing to seize the throne – he told me himself. And the moment the crown is placed upon the brow of his mad nephew Justin, the order will be given to slaughter the Nepotes.' Her voice cracked. 'Do you want me dead?'

Wulfrun lurched to his feet, his fists bunching in frustration. 'Plots everywhere! What afflicts you

103

Romans? The enemies lie without, yet you would tear each other to pieces.'

'I will say it again, Wulfrun. Do you want me dead?' Juliana pushed up her chin. Ariadne could see that her eyes were glistening with tears. Of fear, perhaps. 'This is no longer about plots and power, about war and the empire. It is about living to see a new day. Against a man like Karas Verinus, seizing the throne is the last hope we have.'

'You use words well,' Wulfrun growled, 'and caresses and tears too. But I will not be twisted by you. I have had my fill of it, do you hear? Your family is like a sickness. You blacken all who fall within your view. I have seen what you and your mother and father have done to Leo. There was once a hope that he might escape the misery you inflict upon all, aye, and upon yourselves, but that was when he was a boy. Since then you have all shaped him, crushed the innocence from him, prepared him to be your instrument for power: a sword, not a brother or a son. What hope now for him?'

Ariadne stiffened, hearing her own thoughts echoed back at her.

Rising, Juliana reached out her arms to comfort him, but he turned away. 'Sometimes I think this is my curse for all my sins,' he said. 'To offer love, but receive only pain in return, until the life drains from me and my days are ended with a knife in the back in the middle of one of your plots.'

'How can you say such a thing?'

Wulfrun whirled. 'I have turned a blind eye for so

long, there are days when I am lost in darkness. But I have heard the talk all over the city . . .' He swallowed. 'The talk of you and other men. I have tried to see only good in you, Juliana, and it has been the hardest battle I have ever fought. But I have reached the end of that road. I cannot tell if you use me or not, but here, with death drawing nearer, I can no longer live this way. I would not see myself as weak.'

Juliana's cheeks reddened. 'These rumours you have heard, all of them are lies . . .'

Wulfrun held up his hand to silence her. 'No more,' he said wearily.

'When Falkon Cephalas had your head upon the block, I helped save your life when I should have run to preserve my own neck.' Her voice trembled. 'If I did not care for you, would I have risked all?'

'For each moment when I thought you could truly love, there have been a hundred others when I have been sent running like a one-eyed farmer's dog to further the cause of the Nepotes.'

Juliana grasped the guardsman's arm and spun him towards her. 'You are a warrior, Wulfrun, and I thought you understood this world is a battlefield. There are no heroes, like the ones they tell of in the old stories. Nor are there devils. There is only living to see the next day, and how we do it—'

'There is honour.' Filled with fire, Wulfrun pushed his face closer to hers. 'There is goodness in a man's heart.'

Juliana placed a hand on his chest, as if to hold him back from attacking her. Her voice softened. 'We have all done things that we would not tell to another. You too, I would wager.'

A shadow crossed Wulfrun's face.

'I have done more than most, I cannot deny that,' she continued. 'From the moment we let go of our mother's skirts, we Nepotes are taught what we must do to gain power. We sacrifice the chance to live the life of a farmer. But what we might gain . . . oh, Wulfrun, what we might gain. This is who I am. Juliana Nepa. Power is my birthright, and I will do whatever it takes to hold it in my hands.'

For a moment, Wulfrun looked as if he had been slapped across the face, Ariadne thought.

'And yet . . . at the same time, I love. I love my mother and father, and Leo. And I love you, Wulfrun. I have always loved you. No lies here. No twisting.' Juliana smiled. 'No coursing with a one-eyed farmer's dog. I speak from the heart.'

Ariadne watched the tremors in Wulfrun's features as he struggled to accept what he was hearing.

'Then be my wife,' he said after a while.

Juliana nodded slowly. 'I will.'

Wulfrun gaped, speechless. Ariadne could see that he had reconciled himself to ending this mockery of a love that he had endured for so long. She leaned down further, risking discovery. But she was gripped by what she was hearing, and wanted to see Juliana's face more clearly. She wanted to know if this was another of the woman's manipulations. But no – she seemed to be speaking truly. She loved him. He was her instrument of achieving power. He was the man she held dearest. What a strange world this was, Ariadne thought.

Juliana's eyes gleamed with a cold fire. 'I will wed you. But not until Leo sits upon the throne.'

Wulfrun shook his head. 'If Karas Verinus moves against you, I will kill him with my own hands.'

'He will destroy you, Wulfrun, as he has destroyed so many others. No, the only hope I have is to see the Nepotes ruling the empire.'

'But . . . I have sworn an oath to the emperor.'

'And you have sworn an oath to me,' she repeated. 'Now is the time to choose. Stand with the Nepotes or lose me for ever.'

Ariadne watched Wulfrun waver, and her heart went out to him. To be forced to make such a choice, a man of honour like this commander of the Guard. Why, it must be like a sword plunging into his chest.

Juliana pressed her lips on Wulfrun's mouth in a deep kiss. When she pulled back, she breathed, 'There will be one other reward for you: vengeance. As long as I have known you, you have carried in your heart the pain of your father's death. Who caused that death?'

'Hereward.'

'Hereward,' she repeated. 'And now, finally, it is time to make him pay. My father has sent out word for a good man with an axe, one who can keep us safe until we make our move. And one who will take the heads of our enemies when that day dawns. Aid me now and Hereward will be the first to fall. I give you my vow.'

In that moment, Ariadne felt overwhelmed by a portent of doom, one that swallowed Wulfrun, the Nepotes, perhaps all of them. There could be no good ending to this.

As silent as a ghost, she hauled herself up through the branches until she could leap to the roof. Her feet made not even a whisper when she landed. Creeping across the creaking tiles, she lay on her belly on the side that overlooked the street and watched Wulfrun leave. Then she crawled to the end and dropped on to the lower roof over the kitchen.

When she was on the ground, she sat in the shadows of the alley beside the house. 'Meghigda,' she prayed, closing her eyes, 'come to me. Show me the path I must take.' But in her heart, she knew. She had to save Leo. If he took the throne, he would be lost to her for ever. And if she ventured near him, the Nepotes would kill her, one of the loathed Verini.

As the shadows lengthened, she felt the fire of al-Kahina start to burn inside her. 'I am the slayer of devils,' she murmured. 'And I will slay all who cross my path.'

Finally, when dusk fell, she crept out of the alley. Barely had she taken a step when hard fingers closed around her arm. She whirled, spitting, but any epithet died in her throat as she looked up into the cold face of a mountain of a man. He wore a helm, as if he were on a field of battle, and twin coals burned in the eyelets. His mail-shirt was rusted and stained with blood, and his cloak was in tatters.

'A thief?' he growled.

'I am no thief, just a poor beggar,' she lied, aware of his size and his strength. 'Who are you?'

The warrior leaned down so he could search her face. Ariadne glimpsed a worrying look of madness and blood-lust in his eyes.

'My name is Varin,' he said. 'They call me the Blood Eagle.' He looked past her, along the street. 'Is this the house of the Nepotes?'

Ariadne frowned. 'It is. What business do you have there?'

He levelled his cold, unblinking stare at the torch now flickering above the door and said, 'I have been told they need a good man with an axe.'

CHAPTER TEN

The long table groaned under the weight of the food. At the far end, a bald head bobbed in a halo of sunlight shimmering through the refectory window. The hall was empty apart from the solitary diner, the stillness broken by a smacking of lips and a sucking and swallowing that sounded like a man marching across a quagmire.

The monk was a mountain. His jowls flowed like melted candle wax, his shuddering rolls of fat barely contained by a cream tunic as large as a soldier's tent. His chubby hands danced from bowl to bowl in constant motion, thrusting the morsels into his mouth with barely time to chew and swallow each one.

Neophytos Nepos was at feast.

Alric's mouth watered as he breathed in the aromas swirling from that sumptuous meal. He had not eaten at the Yule celebration the previous night and he marvelled at the display before him. Fresh-baked bread – the fine, white kind, not the hard thistle bread that the poor ate. *Apaki*, pork, grilled over coals and basted with wine and honey. Roast kid stuffed with garlic, leeks and onions and coated with the tangy fish sauce, *garon*, that the Romans loved so much. *Afrato*s, beaten egg white topped with chopped chicken cooked in wine and fish sauce. Crab and lobster and squid. Orache and kohlrabi glistening with olive oil. *Mizithra* cheese curdled with fig juice. Food was one of the few pleasures remaining to Neophytos, and he indulged it to the full. And the kitchen, in turn, indulged him, knowing the power his kin wielded.

So consumed by his meal was he that the eunuch had no idea Alric had entered the refectory. Only when he paused from his eating to swill down a cup of the honey and milk *meligalia* did he look up.

'Join me,' he said in his reedy voice.

'I have already broken my fast,' Alric lied.

'There is hardly any meat on you,' the eunuch sniffed.

Alric rounded the table, trying not to look as hungry as he felt. 'Outside our gates, the poor fight over scraps of bread tossed out by our brothers. While there is such need, how can you feast so?'

'Victor Verinus took my balls with his knife. God would not begrudge me some joy in my flavourless life.'

'And now his brother Karas has the emperor's ear,' Alric replied, moving the conversation on to the matter that interested him most. 'You are not worried that he will come for you too?'

'I am a poor servant of the Lord. Such a powerful general would have no interest in me.' Neophytos pushed a handful of *apaki* into his mouth and chewed slowly as he watched his visitor.

Alric circled him. They always eyed each other like two dogs marking out their territories, Alric had come to realize. As one of the Nepotes, the eunuch was his family's eyes and ears within the church, for within this Christian city as much power lay here as in the emperor's court. Even a crowned head must bow before God, and God's representatives upon earth. And Neophytos no doubt knew that Alric was Hereward's eyes and ears too.

'Karas was drinking wine late into the night with Falkon Cephalas at a tavern in Caenopolis, I am told,' Alric mused. He studied the fat on the eunuch's neck for any sign of a tremor to indicate that this news troubled him, but Neophytos only proceeded to tear off a squid's tentacle. 'That they make common cause would be troubling for the Nepotes, I would wager?'

'My kin have other matters to concern them. I hear there may be much joy soon.'

'Oh?'

'A wedding. Between Juliana and Wulfrun of the Guard. Or so I hear tell.' He turned his piercing pale-blue eyes upon Alric. 'How fares your master Hereward in the Guard these days?'

'God is my master.'

'Of course. Forgive me. I would not think to suggest otherwise.' He chewed on the tentacle, swallowed and belched. 'Hereward. The man who fought a king. And lost. Still, he kept his head upon his shoulders. I would

112

think he gives thanks to God each day for that small mercy.'

Alric bristled, even though he knew Neophytos was only trying to rile him. Unable to contain himself, he blurted, 'You misjudge Hereward. He is no mere warrior, good with axe and spear and sword. His wits are sharper than any blade.'

'Aye. He had wits enough to flee England like a whipped cur.' The eunuch tore off a knob of bread and used it to scoop up a chunk of *mizithra*.

'Wits enough to study his enemies, learn their skills and turn them against them. In the fenlands of England, he saw how fire could be used as a weapon that would drive men mad with fear. In Flanders, he learned of the spear-pits, hidden by branches, where an unwary foe will fall and impale himself upon the spikes. You see only a wild fighting man, but he is always watching.'

Neophytos smirked, just a flash, like the sign of a viper before it struck. 'Only God sees all. And Hereward is but a man. Here in Constantinople there are enemies no man sees. Until it is too late.'

Alric flinched. But before he could decipher what lay hidden in the eunuch's words, loud voices rang out in the monastery.

'What is this?' Neophytos frowned. A shadow crossed his face. 'Is it the Turks? They are attacking now?' His voice drained away to a whisper. 'Too soon. Too soon.'

Too soon for the Nepotes' plans, Alric thought. He hid a petty smile at the other man's discomfort. 'Let

113

us see.' Without waiting for the eunuch to haul his bulk away from the table, he hurried in the direction of the clamour.

A crowd of monks swarmed around two men in the hall by the monastery door, wailing and praying with hands thrown to the heavens. One of the newcomers was tall and thin as a sapling, his wiry hair matted with sweat. Dirt streaked the front of his tunic and turned his hands black. Tears carved paths through the grime on his cheeks.

The other man was filthier still. He was old, shrunken and twisted, more bones than meat, with a mass of wild hair that had been plastered against his head. Grey clay caked him from head to foot, his ranging eyes white and wide amid the muck. Clawed fingers clutched at what appeared to be a shroud binding his body.

'A miracle! A miracle!' one of the monks exclaimed as he caught at Alric's arm.

'Brother, we have been blessed. Here, in Constantinople, God is at work,' another cried, clutching his head.

Alric spotted Neophytos lumbering along the corridor, wheezing from the exertion. When the eunuch reached the edge of the crowd, Alric demanded, 'Tell me what has driven you to such heights.'

Palladius, a young monk with one milky eye, held out his hands towards the clay-slaked Roman. 'This man, brother, this man has been raised from the dead. Our Lord has spoken! Give praise to the Lord!'

''Tis true.' The tall Roman stared at the old man,

dazed. 'I dig the holes for the dead at the boneyard by the gate of the Neorion. Ten years now, dig, dig, dig.' He swallowed, his mouth dry. 'This morning . . . at sunrise . . . I saw . . . I saw . . .'

'Tell him,' Palladius urged. 'Tell him as you told me, so that he may know the wonder.'

Swallowing again, the digger scrubbed his hand through his hair. 'As God is my witness, I saw this man claw his way out of a fresh grave. Fingers first, like a new bloom. Then a hand, and an arm, and then he dragged himself out. Blinking, he was, as though he was seeing the sun for the first time. And he said . . . and he said . . .'

' "God has raised me"!' Palladius cried, throwing his hands high.

The gravedigger nodded in agreement.

'Is this true?' Alric grabbed the filthy old man's shoulders. 'You were dead and now you have risen?'

The old man's gaze, wandering and distant, slowly drew back to Alric's face and he nodded. 'I was dead,' he croaked. 'And God has given me life.'

'A miracle!' Palladius proclaimed.

For a moment, the old man worked his mouth as if trying to recall how to form words, and then he roared, 'And God has spoken to me!'

Silence crashed down across the circle of monks. For an instant, they gaped, and then they reeled back. 'Blasphemy,' someone stuttered.

Alric fixed a stern gaze on the old man. 'What say you? Choose your words well, for you are among men of God here. No lies.'

'In the silence of the grave, God spoke to me,' the clay-stained man said.

As one, the monks crossed themselves.

'The Lord spoke to me!' the old man shrieked.

One of the churchmen crashed to his knees, gibbering.

'And he speaks to me still. He raised me from the dead so I could spread his word among all folk here, in this place.'

Palladius steadied himself, struggling to drive the quaver from his voice. 'Then tell us.'

Shaking his head slowly, the old man raised his arm and pointed at Alric. 'I will only speak through him.'

'Through me?' Alric furrowed his brow.

'God has chosen you,' the old man said, in awe. 'God has chosen you, and me, and together we will spread his word.'

Alric felt the weight of all the monks' stares fall upon him. Every man stepped back, so he was isolated with the filthy revenant. He tried to protest, pointing at some of the senior monks, but the old man waved a dismissive hand at them. Swallowing, Alric relented. 'Speak, then. What is God's message?'

The old man looked around the ashen faces. 'Aye, I will speak, for his message must be heard loud in every home. And it is this: doom is coming to Constantinople,' he croaked. 'Doom for all of us.'

CHAPTER ELEVEN

The monastery corridor thundered with the sound of marching feet. Monks threw themselves against the walls as the Varangian guardsmen surged across the flagstones. Swept up in that flood of black and crimson, leather and steel, two men skipped to keep up. One was Falkon Cephalas, the other the emperor. His face as white as his hair, the latter looked a day past death.

Hereward strode at the head of the band, his Dane-axe at the ready for any sign of trouble, as it always was when Nikephoros ventured out in public. To his left, only a step behind him, Wulfrun's implacable gaze was fixed on the way ahead.

'Out of the way,' the commander boomed when one of the churchmen strayed into his path.

Not a moment had been wasted when word reached the palace of this new prophet who foretold disaster for the empire and all who lived within it. The news had been delivered by the Patriarch Kosmas himself, who had received direct communication from the abbot at the monastery of St George. There could be no doubting the truth. God's own disciples had sealed it. Blanching at the fate uttered by this miraculous being, the emperor had insisted upon hearing the terrible pronouncement for himself.

When they reached the door, Wulfrun growled at Hereward to wait. He feared a trap, the Mercian knew, a scheme to lure the emperor out of his safe haven to where he could be slain for one of the many grudges the swelling army of plotters held against him.

Yet as the commander marched into the room, the Mercian thought how distracted he seemed. He had not complained even once at Hereward's insistence that the spear-brothers form the core of this band guarding the emperor instead of Wulfrun's own chosen men. Some weight had descended upon him in the past day. And he now eyed Hereward with even greater suspicion, if that were possible.

Glancing back, the Mercian locked eyes with Kraki, then Guthrinc. A silent communication flashed among them. They were ready for whatever lay ahead.

Behind them Nikephoros was trembling, his hands clutching insistently at the fabric of his tunic. Falkon Cephalas, though, remained as unreadable as ever. He glanced at Hereward, then looked away before his eyes could be studied.

Once more the door swung open. With a grunt, Wulfrun beckoned.

The Varangian Guard escorted the emperor and his chief adviser inside, where the abbot and the monastery's senior brothers shuffled around with fearful expressions. When they saw Nikephoros, they bowed their heads, no doubt terrified that he would demand answers that only God could give.

'Leave us now,' Falkon Cephalas insisted, seizing the authority. He swept his arms to usher the churchmen out.

As they filed from the chamber, Hereward glimpsed two lonely figures at the far end of the room. A wild-haired bag of bones in a filthy shroud squatted on a stool, watching the proceedings from under hooded brows. Alric stood behind him.

With a deep breath, the monk drew himself upright. But the Mercian could see the unease etched in his friend's face. His worry became clearer still when his gaze fixed on Hereward. So many questions lay there. Hereward nodded to him, offering strength.

Edging forward, the emperor frowned to try to hide his own anxiety. In a show of deference, he pressed his hands together. 'Who are you, prophet?' he enquired, his voice barely more than a whisper. 'What is your name?'

'Megistus,' the old man murmured as if remembering. 'That was my name when I was first alive and it is my name now.'

'And it is true? God has raised you from the dead?'

'It is true.'

Nikephoros swallowed. 'Oh, to be alive now, when God works his miracles around us,' he said without much conviction. Steeling himself, he paused for a moment and then asked, 'God has sent me a message?'

'For your ears. For the ears of all who dwell here.'

Megistus shuddered, his eyelids fluttering. Craning his head back, he looked to Alric for help. The monk placed a steadying hand upon his shoulder. 'I am still weak,' the old man croaked. 'But God has sent this virtuous man to be my strength. With his aid, I will deliver the Lord's words to all who will listen.' He patted the monk's hand.

'For God's sake, one of you loose your tongue,' the emperor snapped, looking from the old man to Alric.

The air itself seemed to withdraw from the room. Not a man moved. Covering his eyes, Megistus lowered his head. 'I see . . . blood, running through the streets. A river of it . . . an ocean. Drowning all Constantinople. Aye, drowning all the empire. The sun is going down, and the never-ending night is drawing in.' He moistened his lips. 'And I see the crown . . . the jewelled crown you wear upon your brow . . . drenched in yet more blood.'

Nikephoros reeled back, his hand flying to his mouth.

'He stokes the fires of your fears.' Falkon had appeared at his master's elbow. His lip curled in disbelief. 'What do you desire, old man? Gold?'

'He wants naught.' Alric's voice was barely more than a whisper. 'Only to be God's tool upon this earth. Listen, heed, or walk away and face the judgement he tells of as surely as night follows day.'

Hereward felt a tug of pride at his friend's bravery. Alric had taken a stand against the most powerful in the empire. The heart of an Englishman beat in his chest.

Roughly thrusting his adviser aside, the emperor barked, 'Tell me more. I must know. Who spills this blood? When does this doom fall?'

'Soon,' Megistus replied. 'God whispers in my ear, he shows me these things, but I know no more than what the Lord utters. Not even that these things will come to pass, or whether there is something within your power to avert them.'

'God has sent a warning.' Alric's voice grew more confident with each word. 'The Lord is not cruel. He would not send this message to you if there was no hope of changing the path.'

Nikephoros dabbed at the sweat on his forehead, nodding furiously. He seemed pleased by Alric's words. Hereward smiled to himself. The monk had done well. No one now could accuse him, or the old man, of treason. This was a warning, not a threat.

'I hear the cries of women and the sobbing of infants. I see good men put to the sword.' The old man's eyes rolled up so only the whites were visible. 'The best of the empire dying. I see our enemies storming the gates . . . the walls . . . the great, unshakeable walls . . . falling. In the east a fire burns, as bright as the sun. In the west, a sword carves the sky open.'

'The Normans and the Turks,' the emperor croaked.

'But there are also enemies within these walls,' Megistus whispered. 'Friends who hide daggers behind their backs. Be watchful, O emperor, for they will strike while your eyes turn east and west.'

Hereward saw Wulfrun stiffen. His commander

must surely be thinking of his love, Juliana, and those cunning Nepotes.

'The sands run out faster than you think.' The prophet bowed his head, growing weaker. 'Even now, as we talk, the vipers slither from their nest. You must act soon, O emperor, sooner than soon, or all this will come to pass.' Megistus slumped on his stool and Alric caught him.

'Is he . . . ?' Nikephoros stammered.

'He lives, but he is weak,' the monk replied as he supported the old man. 'But he has more words within him, have no doubt of that.'

Nikephoros snapped round to Falkon. 'Bring the prophet and this monk to the palace. God speaks through this vessel and I would have God at my side at all times. We will make no decision without the prophet's consent, for fear . . . for fear . . .' He choked down the rest of his words and whirled away. 'And let no man speak of what was said in this room,' he boomed, 'or I will have that bastard's head.'

Hereward gave a tight smile. There could be no hope of that. This would be all over the city before sunset. And then the anxious chatter would turn to fear, and to panic, and what then? Would the plotters bide their time, as they had been, waiting for the best moment to seize the throne? Or had their hands been forced?

Wulfrun stared at him as if he knew what the Mercian was thinking. This prophecy may itself have brought about the carnage it foretold.

122

CHAPTER TWELVE

The crowd clogged the street outside the palace. Paupers in rags with their alms bowls raised high. Merchants waving purses stuffed with gold as if that were enough to buy them salvation. Servants and slaves, whores and butchers and ironworkers. Their wails of terror, their desperate pleas and prayers, rang up to the heavens.

'This is madness,' Kraki shouted above the clamour.

Guthrinc drew himself up to peer across the heads of the throng. 'Barely a day since the prophet clawed his way out of the grave and now the whole city knows what he has to say.'

'Nay, the whole empire,' Sighard exclaimed.

Hereward surveyed the turmoil with a shake of his head. 'This is a Christian city. There are more churches here than moneylenders, so they say. No wonder they are fearful if they think the Lord has warned them of their doom. What say you, Hengist?'

Mad Hengist danced around them, his crimson cape whirling. Pale eyes stared from his rodent face at horizons none of them could see. 'Today we are all mad. This is God's work.'

The others nodded. Watching his kin slaughtered by the Normans had driven him mad, some might say. But where others saw lunacy, the spear-brothers heard only wisdom.

Hiroc the Three-fingered and Derman the Ghost skirted the edge of the crowd to join them. 'There is no way through this,' Hiroc grumbled, wiping the sweat from his brow. 'This is worse than William the Bastard's army.'

Sighard laughed. 'You did not try hard enough, Three Fingers,' he shouted, pointing.

The crowd was parting as if Moses commanded it. Five men thrashed cudgels this way and that, cracking heads and shoulder blades until the way ahead was cleared.

In their wake walked Juliana Nepa, her chin held high as if there were only calm around her. At her heels came the rest of the Nepotes: Leo scowling at the common herd, one hand upon the hilt of his sword, Simonis, as elegant as her daughter, and Kalamdios, drooling and twitching, held aloft on his wooden chair by four slaves. And at the rear, towering over them all, was Varin, glowering through the eye-holes of his helm, his Dane-axe held high as a warning to anyone who dared venture too close.

'That . . .' Kraki said, gaping. 'That must surely be the Blood Eagle? He stands with the Nepotes now?'

Hereward nodded. 'Herrig the Rat has been watching the house for me, night and day. News reached my ears the moment Varin appeared at their door.'

'The Nepotes and the Blood Eagle,' Sighard said,

124

turning up his nose. 'They know their own kind, these wild dogs.'

'This cannot be good news for the emperor,' Kraki grunted. 'The Nepotes alone were threat enough.'

'Nor us,' Sighard said, 'when we are called upon to defend him.'

Hereward smiled. 'Look closer. The Nepotes are not here because of their lust for power. They are afrit, like every mud-spattered ceorl. They want good news from the mouth of the prophet. Hope.'

Hiroc narrowed his eyes at his leader. 'And you are not afrit? Through the lips of that old man, God has warned that all of us face Judgement Day.'

Kraki shook his axe. 'If we are to die, we die,' he said, stealing the words from Hereward's lips. 'We will end our days with a battle-cry and our enemies' blood upon the wind.'

Hereward eyed his spear-brothers. They had fought so many battles against forces that many had said could never be defeated, they imagined this was merely one more. None of them could see the reality of the overwhelming threat arrayed against them. So much to gain if they could win. But a defeat would be the end of them all.

'Where are your alms cups? Where are your prayers? Would you seek to enter this house blessed by God with only sour faces to buy your way in?'

At the wry voice, Hereward turned to see Deda the Knight, standing in the shade of a wall. His long black hair gleamed, his pale Norman skin now well tanned by this eastern sun.

Grinning, the Mercian clapped a hand on his friend's arm. 'How goes this new work, brother?'

Kraki snorted. 'So high he flies, it is a wonder he even remembers the warriors who saved his neck back in those sodden fens.'

'I remember clearly,' Deda replied with the ghost of an ironic smile, 'and as I recall, it was I who saved your necks.'

The Viking glowered, but Hereward could see that his eyes were sparkling. Wherever they were, whatever heights they reached, none of them would forget the bonds that were forged during the harsh struggles of those last days in England.

'Come,' Deda said, beckoning, 'unless you would like to take up your arms and fight your way into the palace, like the Nepotes.'

As the Norman skirted the surging crowd with Hereward at his side and the spear-brothers trailing behind, the Mercian nodded appreciatively. He had come to trust this warrior who had once been his enemy. Deda was a man of honour. No hunger for power or gold blackened his heart. He found joy in places where others saw only misery. Hereward had always thought that, if he could, Deda would have given up everything to be a farmer, sharing the simple pleasures of life with his wife Rowena.

Yet now he had indeed risen high. The emperor himself listened to Deda's words of wisdom during the councils of war and defence. As an adviser he was privy to the secret discussions that shaped the empire. Seasons had passed before Deda had eased his way into the heart of the government. But once Nikephoros knew that this warrior had once had the ear of the victorious William the Bastard, the emperor had seen value in his words of wisdom.

Hereward smiled to himself. If only Nikephoros knew that William would have gladly choked the life from the Norman knight. Now Deda could perhaps place one finger on the empire's rudder. And if necessary he could counter the influence of that plotting dog Karas Verinus, or at least keep an eye upon his movements.

'What news?' the Mercian whispered, when he was sure they could not be overheard.

'The emperor is heeding the words of the prophet.' Another smile flickered on Deda's lips. 'But then what wise man would ignore God's advice? Falkon Cephalas is once more building his guard to keep this city's army of plotters under his watchful eye. This time, let us hope the cure is not worse than the sickness.'

Hereward grunted. How could he forget how Falkon had become a power that almost rivalled the emperor himself, with his rogues threatening the lives of any who stood in the adviser's way? That murderous guard had been the death of one of the spear-brothers, the gentle Turold, and had threatened even Hereward himself.

'Nikephoros is a vain man, and no great leader,' he said, 'but if there is one thing he watches with care, it is any threat to his own neck. He will not let Falkon Cephalas get out of hand.'

'There is talk, too, that the emperor may send riders to the east to request the aid of the Caesar, John Doukas. The empire has honoured him with the title, and though the years are heavy on him he still commands some power to shape.'

'Even though he betrayed the empire?'

'Men are called traitors until they are of some use. Then they are merely friends.'

'Then Nikephoros is finally ready to make war on the Turks.'

Deda shrugged. 'Except Karas Verinus presses to attack the Normans first. He sees Robert Guiscard as the greater threat.'

Hereward frowned. 'The same Karas Verinus who advised leaving the Normans well alone until the army is ready to take a stand against such a force of seasoned fighting men?'

'It would seem he has had a change of heart. But only within the last day.'

The Mercian pondered on this news as Deda led the way round to the back of the palace where a door in the wall led into the kitchen gardens. Since Nikephoros had made the palace his home, this entrance had been barred on the inside, to keep out enemies real and imagined. The Norman rapped on it twice, and the door swung open.

Framed in the archway stood his wife, Rowena. Her hands and apron were dusted with flour, and white streaked her headdress. Once Deda had gained his position of trust, it had been easy to find her work in the palace kitchens.

She smiled at her husband, but her dark eyes glinted with a sharp wit when she narrowed them at the spear-brothers. 'I smell trouble,' she said.

'And you would know it well,' Guthrinc said with a bow. 'Have you told your Roman friends of our time in England?'

'There is time enough for that,' Rowena said with mock haughtiness. She ushered the warriors in and Deda helped her bar the door behind them.

'Wulfrun waits within,' the knight told Hereward. 'He would speak to you about the part the Varangian Guard will play in the emperor's plans.' He eyed the spear-brothers. 'Though he called for you alone. And you know he grumbles like an old woman on a cold winter night when he sees these rogues trailing at your heel.'

'Then we had best make ourselves scarce,' Guthrinc boomed with a clap of his hands. 'I smell honey cake. And I would wager there is some good Roman wine close enough.'

Rowena pretended to scowl, then beckoned the spear-brothers to follow her across the garden to where the kitchens steamed and smoked.

'You do not need my advice,' Deda said, leaning in to the Mercian, 'but I would watch Wulfrun. He seems a changed man. We both know he has long carried a grudge, but now I am not sure he can be trusted at all.'

'I will keep both eyes on him. But Wulfrun is a simple man. He can be guided along the right path.'

Hereward could see Deda was unsure, but took his

129

leave nevertheless and made his way into the palace, where the sound of the crowd in the street outside throbbed even through the thick stone walls.

CHAPTER THIRTEEN

The cloying scent of incense drifted among the shafts of sunlight. Along the corridor, whispered prayers floated, and hands that were easier as fists were now pressed together in prayer.

Hereward marvelled at how the sanctity of a church had now settled on the palace. As he passed the nobles who had been granted access to Megistus, he saw either beatific expressions filled with hope that the doom could be averted, or features crumpled by dread at what was to come. A few showed hungry eyes.

The emperor was a fool to think he could ever have kept the prophet a secret, not when every man and woman in Constantinople craved salvation. Or the power and standing that came from an audience with God's chosen one.

Outside the half-open door of the chamber that had been set aside for the revenant, the Mercian paused to watch. Still filthy in his rags, the old man rocked on his stool. Alric stood behind him, his shoulders hunched in weariness. Hereward felt a pang of concern for his friend.

The parade of desperate nobles had been ceaseless. And now it was the turn of the Nepotes. Juliana knelt before the godly man, her golden hair almost brushing the flagstones. Her mother stood beside her, head bowed in reverence. Kalamdios lolled in his chair with Leo at his shoulder.

Hereward snorted. It would take more than a few words to expunge the stain on their souls.

Turning away from his eavesdropping, he carried on along the corridor. He knew the substance of the Nepotes' weasel words without having to hear them. Feigned grace, pronouncements of charity and supplication, all mingled with coded musings designed to draw from the prophet any news that might aid their own advancement. *When is the right time to act? How great is the risk?* Never for a moment would they think that God opposed their rise to power.

The whispers fell behind him as he climbed a short flight of steps. Here was the chamber where the emperor conducted his most important discussions, ones that he could not risk being overheard. Two of the Varangian Guard kept watch at the door, their axes held against their leather breastplates. They nodded to the Mercian as he eased in.

Hereward was greeted by a full-throated tirade. Nikephoros paced along the far side of the room, near the windows that overlooked the Bosphorus. Red-faced, spittle flying, he shook his fists as he demanded a plan that would save his neck, Constantinople's riches, and the empire, no doubt in that order. Even at that distance, Hereward could smell the fear on him.

'Robert Guiscard has long since built his excuse to attack us,' the emperor was saying. 'He says he has taken up the cause of that bastard Michael Doukas.'

'His daughter was betrothed to Michael's son,' someone muttered hesitantly.

'Aye, that Norman dog thought he could buy his way to our riches with a marriage,' Nikephoros spat back. 'But it has been two years since Michael wore this crown. Two years!'

Wulfrun leaned in to Hereward, glaring. 'I sent word long ago.'

'There is an army of fearful folk laying siege to the palace, if you have not looked out of the window.'

'When I find the loose tongue that spoke of the prophet, I will cut it out myself.' The commander turned back to the group of men standing in a crescent in front of the emperor.

Hereward looked around the chamber. Advisers and senators nodded and pursed their lips in a show of contemplation. These were Nikephoros' most trusted men, too grand a circle for Deda to be admitted. But Falkon Cephalas was there, as he always seemed to be these days, just a hand's breadth away from the throne of power. And towering over them all was Karas Verinus, his implacable gaze fixed upon Nikephoros. His face was cold, but his eyes held the murderous fire of a man who would happily have stepped forward and snapped the emperor over his knee.

'Can you not hear my words? The prophet has spoken and there is no time to waste,' Nikephoros all but shouted, hammering one grey, wrinkled fist into his palm. 'Where is the fucking wisdom here?'

'But the army is not ready for an attack,' someone ventured.

The emperor glared.

'We are short of good men. There is so little gold . . .' The man was beginning to babble under Nikephoros' icy stare. 'We cannot afford to keep seasoned warriors sitting in their huts and tents when there is no need for them, cleaning their axes and telling old battle-stories. We agreed we would buy them when there was need—'

'We need them now,' the emperor roared. 'If we could talk the Turks into joining us to attack the Normans, as we did before, we would. But they see no gain now from such an alliance. They bide their time and wait for us to falter so they can seize what is ours.'

'The Immortals are ready.' Karas did not raise his voice, but his words carried such force that all the men there looked towards him.

'At last. I knew I could count on you, Karas,' Nikephoros said, nodding. 'Speak. I would know your thoughts.'

'The Immortals are good Roman men. They fight because of the fire in their heart, and their love for you, not for gold. Under the command of Tiberius Grabas, they have never been stronger.' Karas pushed his way past the elders to stand in front of the emperor. 'And their ranks have never been so many. We have no need of an army of filthy barbarians with such warriors riding under our standard. Swift, they are, and they strike like God's lightning. Set them free to attack Robert Guiscard. The Norman bastard will not be prepared. He will not know what fate is bearing down upon him until he falls beneath the swords of Rome.'

'The Normans are not fools.'

Heads jerked round as Hereward spoke.

'Still your tongue,' Wulfrun hissed, grabbing the Mercian's arm. 'Are you mad?'

Hereward shrugged the commander off and stepped forward. 'And they are not weak.'

The emperor squinted over the heads of his advisers. 'Who speaks?'

'Hereward of the English.'

Nikephoros nodded. 'Aye. You know those Norman bastards better than most. What say you?'

The Mercian sensed Karas' gaze upon him. The general would not take kindly to having his words challenged, even less so before the eyes of the emperor. 'Our spies have told us the Normans are sixteen thousand strong, and they are armed with the best weapons in the world. Their army is not made up of mud-soaked ceorls wielding wood and stones, you must trust me on that. They have knights too, many of them, with double-edged swords, and crossbows that can put a bolt right through a man's chest and out of the back. Aye, I will say it . . . they are the best fighting men in the world, if not the fiercest. You Romans know this. That is why you pay them more gold than most to have them join your army.'

'You think the emperor's army is not up to this challenge?' Karas' voice was steady, his stare piercing.

'Warrior to warrior . . . aye, that could be true, but I would not wager any coin upon it. To be sure of defeating the Normans, you need more. A fortress of tree and water and bog, as we had in Ely. If there had been no treachery in that final battle, we would have crushed the Bastard's army. But here you do not have such a stronghold. There will be six Normans to every Roman who rides under the Immortals' standard, and the battle will give the lie to the name of your men. It will be a slaughter.'

'I would imagine from your words that you do not think much of Romans,' Karas said.

Hereward sensed Wulfrun looming at his back, silently urging him to walk away from this confrontation. 'Romans, English, Normans . . . who is best . . . this means nothing to me. I care only about good men losing their lives for no gain.'

'So, we heed the words of barbarians now?' Karas kept his stare fixed on Hereward.

'Aye,' someone else agreed in a sneering tone, trying to curry favour. 'We pay these barbarians to fight for us and to die for us, not to hear their witless words.'

A ghost of a smile flickered on the general's lips.

Hereward stiffened. He was sick of these Romans, with their plots and their cunning and the way they used words as weapons, twisting everything to get what they wanted.

'Hereward stands here because he knows the

Norman ways better than most,' the emperor said, but the Mercian could hear that his voice was wavering. Nikephoros would not make a stand on such a thing as this, where there was no advantage to himself. And Karas would keep his pride, and good men would see their days ended.

The door creaked open at his back. He turned to see Alexios marching in. The young warrior was pink-cheeked, his hair plastered to his head with sweat. Breathless, he looked around the room and said, 'Would that I had been here for the start of this council, but I was summoned to the gate of Rhesios, for no good reason, it seems.' His gaze settled briefly on Karas before moving on to the emperor. 'But it is good that I found my way to this door, for I have much to say on this matter. Hereward speaks true.'

A sudden silence fell on the room. Karas' features hardened. Hereward guessed Alexios had been listening at the door. As he spoke, he seemed to be fully aware of all that had been discussed.

'Faced by enemies on two fronts, we need all the strength in our army that we can call upon,' Alexios continued. 'To attack the Normans now, while we are unprepared . . . Aye, the Immortals are a force that would make any enemy tremble. Aye, they are swift. And if all goes well upon the day, they may draw out a glorious victory.' The young general looked around the room once more, but then fixed his attention fully on Nikephoros. 'But there will be deaths, and many of them. If they fail . . .'

'They will not fail,' Karas said.

'If they fail, the Normans will know that our defences are thin and they will ride straight for Constantinople. And what then? Will we arm the women and children and set them on the walls? And if the Immortals claw a bloody victory but are left ragged, what then for our war with the Turks?'

'But the prophet said there could be no delay,' the emperor protested. His voice had grown reedy.

'Would you rush to the doom that he has prophesied?'

'What, then?' Nikephoros began to pluck anxiously at his sleeve.

'There is much that is within our power,' Alexios said. His calm, commanding tone seemed to soothe the emperor a little. 'All that I would counsel is that we move with a steady step, to the limits of our powers and no further. We take no risks in search of cheap glory.' He stared at Karas, a challenge that everyone in the chamber recognized. The seasoned general had been humiliated by this man young enough to be his grandson.

Though Karas remained apparently emotionless, Hereward knew that inside he would be simmering, and that was when he was at his most dangerous.

The emperor jabbed a finger first at Alexios and then at Karas. 'You are both wise heads, whatever the years that lie between you, and you know the might of our army better than any. By the time the sun sets, you will give me a plan that you have both agreed on, or you will feel the edge of my displeasure.'

Alexios nodded his agreement. Karas said nothing.

Grabbing Hereward's arm, Wulfrun leaned in until his hot breath burned the Mercian's ear. 'You have caused enough trouble here. Take your leave. Wait in the guardhouse. I would have speech with you.'

Hereward saved his smile of satisfaction until he had stepped out of the door. If he had poked a stick into a wasps' nest, so be it. He could not sit idly by while the empire stumbled even deeper into distress, not when the lives of his spear-brothers were at risk.

The guardhouse at the rear of the palace was empty. At that hour, some warriors of the Guard would be sharpening their blades on whetstones as they waited to replace the band that kept watch upon the emperor. But since the prophet had put dread into the heart of everyone in the city, there was no rest for any man skilled with a weapon. The bulk of the Varangian Guard roamed the walls, the streets, the fora, searching for threats everywhere.

Pulling off his helm, Hereward set it upon a stool. He would wait here for Wulfrun to give him a tongue-lashing, both of them knowing it would do no good.

The door swung open at his back, and as he turned Hereward saw that a man he did not recognize had arrived, swathed in a cloak to mask his identity. When he looked up, the shadows within the hood fell away to reveal a face only God could love. Ragener the Hawk glowered at him with his one good eye, wheezing through the holes where his nose had been.

'You must be quicker than that if you would stick a knife in my back,' Hereward cautioned.

'He is here,' the sea wolf said.

A shadow loomed across the threshold, and then Karas pushed his way into the chamber. Ragener swung the door shut behind him.

Hereward nodded, understanding. 'My words were too strong a brew for you.'

'I have watched you, English.' Karas' voice was low and steady, but his gaze was filled with contempt. 'Clawing your way up out of the mud, eyes fixed upon the sun. Your hunger put iron in you as you pulled your way up to the heights. How high did you think you could climb? To the very top?'

Hereward narrowed his eyes, waiting for the general to make his move. Karas was not a man who coped well with any challenge to his word.

'You think you are the equal of a Roman.' Karas began to prowl along the wall, his gaze fixed upon the Mercian. 'But you are nothing. A barbarian, little more than a beast of the field.'

'This day has been long coming,' Ragener muttered, barely able to contain his glee. 'A judgement, at last.'

Karas' fingers had closed around the hilt of his sword. His breath was short, as if he could barely contain his simmering anger. 'I have heard tell of England. No stone houses, only wood.' He raised his arms up and spread them to the glory that was Constantinople. 'A land of rags and ashes and fires to keep the night at bay. A land of men who can only beg for scraps, or die in battle. Barbarians. You are not fit to live with civilized men, English.'

Hereward felt only contempt for the Roman and his petty insults. 'I have heard men say such things.

Before they looked up my length of steel, with the last of their breath drifting away in the wind.'

Karas continued to prowl around his prey. He was savouring this moment, waiting for his chance to strike. 'You think highly of yourself.' The general's face hardened, his eyes glittering. 'Because you dared to challenge a king. And lost. Aye, I have watched you over these past years as you raised your eyes up and dreamed of being our equal, of gaining power, perhaps, or gold, some standing that would give you value. I wondered if you would ever become a threat.' He waved a dismissive hand at Ragener. 'He says you are like a hungry wolf. That you are only biding your time. Yet I see only a barbarian, with yearnings that far exceed his wits or his skills. You are no threat. And if you had kept your lips sealed you would have been able to pass your days thinking you could be something better.'

Hereward held his gaze. 'We English bow our heads only to God. And we never keep our mouths shut.'

'And that is your undoing. This day, English, you have sealed your fate.' Karas slowly drew his sword.

Unsheathing Brainbiter, Hereward levelled it at his opponent. Karas was bigger than him, and no doubt stronger, despite his years. But the Mercian felt no fear. He had faced worse.

'Kill him,' Ragener urged. 'Cut him to pieces. Make him pay for what he did to me.'

The door swung open, almost bowling the sea wolf over. Alexios and Wulfrun stepped in. From the relief etched in the younger man's face, he had come searching for his friend, fearing that an angry Karas had come to avenge his humiliation. Wulfrun seemed only mildly disappointed that Hereward was still alive.

With irritation, Karas eyed the new arrivals, then sheathed his sword. 'Your fate is sealed, English, and that of your brothers too. All of you are a stain upon the glory that is Constantinople. If not this day, then soon. Death waits in silence, you know that well. No man hears it when it stalks him. Go about your business. But know that when you least expect it, your days yet to come will be stolen from you.'

Without another word, he strode from the chamber. Ragener hurried after him.

Hereward sheathed his sword. Alexios and Wulfrun were both watching him with grim expressions, as if he were already a dead man. And perhaps he was.

CHAPTER FOURTEEN

The woman fell, screaming, in the centre of the crowded street. As she disappeared beneath the heaving bodies packing the Mese, men turned from bellowing their complaints to throwing wild punches. The violence surged along the throng like fire in a summer forest. Stalls crashed over, merchants clawing the hungry away to protect their wares.

Ariadne felt Leo grab her shoulders and pull her back into the safety of an alley. She gasped as the riot thundered out of control. The rabble-rousers and the preachers who had whipped up the crowd into this frenzy fled in fear, stunned by the speed of the escalation.

For too long now, Constantinople had been on the edge. Fear coursed everywhere: fear of the enemies beyond the walls, of the prophet's dire warnings that had rung out for days now. And all on top of the anger that had been mounting for seasons at the shortage of grain, the coin that seemed to buy less and less, the emperor's failure to solve any problem, however small.

And then, that morning, whispers had rushed through the crowd that the Turks had closed off the trade routes to the east. Now there would only be more want, more hunger, more suffering. The empire was falling to its knees.

'We should leave,' Leo shouted above the din.

'Wait,' Ariadne shouted back.

The fighting began to move away. The dazed citizens and dismayed merchants picked themselves up. Peering out of the alley, Ariadne nodded to a filthy boy crouching on the other side of the street. With a grin, the lad darted to a group of children cowering in another alley.

Within a moment, they were scurrying among the legs of the wealthy men and women hurrying along the Mese. The children were fast, like rats, leaping and weaving, eyes bright with anticipation. Some paused when they saw an opportunity, putting on a sad face and reaching out an upturned hand, pleading for alms, or bread. Others slipped along furtively, unnoticed, eyeing fat purses. Ariadne nodded with approval. When these were sure they had room to escape, their hands would flash. A knife to cut a string, or just a wrench to free a loop, and they would be gone again, with cries of alarm ringing at their backs.

'You are mistress of an army of beggars and thieves now.' Leo turned up his nose as he watched a boy and girl dart away in the confusion. They were both filthy, as thin as blades, but they were laughing as if this were the greatest game of all.

'If I did not aid them, they would be dead. These are the abandoned. Those without mothers and fathers, who have crawled to Constantinople in search of a better life. Those thrown out to breathe their last by kin who can no longer afford to feed them. The stolen ones, the beaten ones, the unloved.'

'What do you see in these street-rats?'

'I see myself. And you too, if you had not been high-born.' Ariadne pushed up her chin. 'Al-Kahina cared for children. And I am al-Kahina now.' She felt a pang of regret that there were so few places they could meet. She pushed Leo deeper into the reeking alley, away from prying eyes. 'Tell me your thoughts,' she said.

'One day, when I rule the empire, you will be my empress. *Augusta.*' Leo let the word lie upon his tongue, enjoying the feel of it.

Yet he looked so serious, Ariadne thought. Always so serious. Even the faintest of smiles was like a gift these days.

'You know your kin will never agree to that.' She reached out a comforting hand, but he felt like stone under her fingers. 'One of the Verini, the most hated of all God's creatures, sitting aside one of the Nepotes at the head of the empire?' She laughed sadly. 'My throat would be slit the moment my back was turned.'

'I will be emperor. I will wear that crown upon my brow.' His eyes glittered with defiance. 'My sister and mother will do as I say.'

Ariadne looked into his eyes. He truly believed his

145

words. She could not bring herself to shatter his conviction. Letting her fingers slip to his hand, she squeezed tightly. 'You are not like your kin, Leo. I have known that ever since I laid eyes upon you,' she murmured. 'Your blood is not your destiny. You do not have to walk this path to the throne . . .'

Leo flashed such a fierce glare that her words died in her throat. 'And what would I be then? Nothing. I may as well run with your street-rats.'

Ariadne bowed her head. She could see the weight of his mother's and sister's hand upon his shoulder in everything he did. 'Your family are making you something you are not—'

'My family are everything.'

'In search of power, they will force you to commit some act that will taint your soul. This hunger for the crown, Leo, I am afraid it will doom you.'

'I am already doomed.' His voice was hollow, his eyes haunted. He bowed his head. 'My soul is already stained. No, the crown is the only thing I have left. Mother . . . Father . . . Juliana . . . they cannot deny me then. I will have given them the thing they desire most.'

His voice was so brittle, Ariadne felt her heart rush out to him. But she could see now that words alone would not move him.

'Gods, you make me sweat keeping up with you.'

They both started as the voice rumbled through the gloom. Ariadne watched the Blood Eagle emerge into the half-light.

'You are not my keeper.' Leo's eyes blazed.

146

'Aye, I am now,' Varin said.

Behind him, blonde hair glowed in the shadows. Juliana followed, her nose turned up in disgust as she held her skirt up above the filth. Before she was seen, Ariadne scrambled back along the alley to crouch behind a cluster of broken amphorae.

'Heed me, for I will say this only once,' Juliana said when she reached Leo. 'The Blood Eagle will stay by your side at all times. We have enemies aplenty in this city.'

'I have a sword—'

Juliana cuffed Leo around the ear. He scowled back at her, but dropped his head in deference none the less. 'Are you still a child? Folk carry on with their lives, but while they look away and think themselves safe, death circles, drawing closer with each day. One does not see death coming.'

'I will watch over you,' Varin said. 'Death is an old friend of mine.'

Ariadne watched Leo cast a sullen glance along the alley, searching for her. She sighed, frustrated. She could not risk letting him know where she hid.

'Then let us have no more of this.' Juliana shoved Leo back towards the street. She turned to the Blood Eagle, smiling. 'The Nepotes have been blessed by your service, Varin. We could not have wished for a better warrior to guide us through danger. Hereward will come to regret saving your life and bringing you back to Constantinople.'

CHAPTER FIFTEEN

Lightning danced along the eastern horizon. As the night sky turned white, a distant storm rolled across the hills of Bithynia.

Hereward leaned on the ledge of the window, watching the play of light and dark. Below him, orange-tiled rooftops stretched out to the sea wall and the Bosphorus beyond. His neck was prickling, a sensation that usually only came to him on the eve of battle. There was an odd mood to the city this night, like the one seasoned sailors shared just before a mighty wave struck their vessel.

'On nights like this, I think of my husband.'

In the shadows on the edge of a circle of moonlight, Anna Dalassene lay on a long, low bed-seat. After England's clime, Hereward found the night warm, but she had furs heaped across her legs. The wine had got the better of her, as it seemed to do so often these days. She was a hard woman. But when she was deep in her cups, he saw a different Anna. A well of sadness was buried beneath that flinty surface, one dug during a life of struggle for those she held close.

'I have heard only good of John Comnenos. A brave warrior on the field of battle, and a strong leader.'

'Aye, you are much alike in that respect. But you show me a kindness, and there is no need. You know as well as I that John was not brave when it was most needed.'

Hereward shrugged. 'I have heard the tales. But like all tales in this city, there are many sides and the truth is hard to see.'

'There is only one truth that matters. John refused to take the throne when his brother Isaac set the crown aside because . . .' she turned up her nose, 'God was looking on him unfavourably.'

'To be emperor . . . that is a great burden.'

'And would you have turned away when the throne was offered to you? Would you have thought the burden too great?' Anna narrowed her eyes at him. 'Would you, Hereward, have denied the power that could have brought safety and joy in this hard life to your kin, to your friends? To your spear-brothers?'

Hereward did not answer.

'No, John was weak, and he sacrificed all of us to his cowardice. He became a monk, did you know that? And he died kneeling before God.' Anna slopped wine from her goblet. Hereward could see her hand shaking. 'I am despised here, I know that. Folk think me consumed by a hunger for power. The woman who will do aught to sit her son upon the throne. But Constantinople is as much a field of battle as any you have fought upon. You must know that?'

'I learned that lesson soon enough. The moment I set foot upon the quay after crossing the Marmara Sea. But here the weapons are tongues and poison and a knife in the dark. You do not see death until you are halfway to heaven.'

Anna sucked in a deep breath. 'Then you do know. In Constantinople you are victorious or you are defeated. Walk away from the throne and you show your back to your enemies. I have enemies everywhere. Men who would gladly slit my throat while I sleep, and the throats of all my children, and my friends, and anyone who showed me any kindness. I care little for myself. I have no hunger for power. But I would see my children safe. And if the only way to do that is to set Alexios upon the throne, then I will make that happen.' In those last five words, her voice became like stone.

Across the water, thunder rumbled and the sky turned white again. 'Winning is only the first step. Keeping a grip upon the throne, that will be the hardest fight.'

Throwing off the furs, Anna eased herself up and glided across the floor to his side. When she settled on the other side of the ledge, Hereward could smell her scent: honey, and lime, and some unfamiliar spice.

'You have heard my tale of woe, yet I know little about the days gone by that forged you,' she said.

'They are best left where they are.'

'Your spear-brothers rut like stags in the Vlanga, but I have never seen you with a woman, or a boy,' she said, watching the storm. 'They say you live only for

150

battle. That seems, to me, only part of a man. Are you then a half-formed thing?'

Hereward could feel Anna's probing eyes upon him. Inside, he clenched. These were things he rarely spoke of, yet were rarely out of his thoughts. He felt warmth towards Anna, and God knows she could still turn a man's head. But he had only truly loved one woman, and she still lived in his heart. 'I had a wife, once.'

'You left her behind in England?'

'She is dead.'

'Oh.' Anna looked out to sea. 'And did she give you a child?'

'She did. A boy.' The Mercian hesitated. It seemed that he dwelled upon his son more and more with each passing season. And yet with each thought came an ache that he could not dispel. When he saw the lad in his head, the child had no face. He did not have a name. 'When he was a babe, I sent him to be raised by monks.'

'For his safety?'

'Aye. The Normans would have ended his days if they knew the leader of the rebels had a child who could carry on that fight once his father had been defeated. And . . .' He hesitated, but he was already swimming in the dark ocean of memory and what might have been. For that moment, Anna, Constantinople, everything was forgotten, and he was back walking through the rain-soaked fens, thinking of the road he would have travelled if the English had won. 'To be safe from me.'

'You?' The voice floated to him across the waves.

'Aye. I should never have become a father. I have a devil inside me. Bloody deeds, those are my legacy. Even when I was a boy. The ravens have always followed me.'

'But now you are wiser.'

Hereward looked at the woman. Her eyes gleamed in pools of shadow. 'That devil is with me always, I know that now. I cannot shackle him. I am still the same monster I was as a boy. But I have made my peace with him.'

Anna smiled. 'We all have our devils.'

'Alric has taught me that we cannot see God's plan. If I can bend my devil to do some good, then that may well be my path. But make no mistake, I am still a devil. I will still do terrible things.'

Anna's smile faded at whatever she saw in his face. He was well used to that by now. 'Then we will walk this road together, both of us, whipping our devils before us.'

'Let us hope that our devils have enough of hell about them to keep us alive until we have gained what we desire.'

Down at the waterside loud voices echoed, drunken sailors returning to their berth. Even as the city simmered, life went on. 'These are dangerous waters. None of us can tell which way the currents will drag us,' Anna said. 'I look into days yet to come, and wonder. Do we make the right choices, even now? Will this road lead us straight to our doom?' She eyed Hereward over the lip of her goblet. 'For all our striving, fate may already have decided our ending.'

'Aye.'

'You are not afraid?'

'No. I have faith.'

'In God.'

'In my wits, and my sword. And my spear-brothers.'

'I would hope that is enough.' Anna slurred her words, and her eyes were wine-misted. 'And yet none of us can see God's plan, as you say. What if you were saved in Ely only to be brought here to the heart of Christendom to answer for your crimes? What if death was laughing at you that day? While you thought you had escaped, to find new hope in the east, death was taunting you with a false promise while bringing you to the doom that had been set aside. The hand of hope snatched away causes even greater pain. What if that is the punishment God has decreed for the crimes you say you have committed?' Anna shuddered and wrapped her arms around her.

'If God says that is to be my fate, so be it.' How many times had this crossed his mind? And yet there was nothing to gain from being racked with doubt. A warrior made his plans for victory, and when they went awry, he made new ones.

'I am cold,' Anna murmured, talking to herself. 'Cold in my heart.'

Hereward strode across the chamber and returned with one of the furs. He laid it across her legs.

Smiling as if she was unused to such a kindness, she pulled the fur tight around her. 'We are alike, you and I, in so many ways.' Her voice was low, barely a

153

whisper. Weighing her thoughts, she watched him from beneath heavy lids and then reached out to rest her cool hand on the back of his. 'Come to my bed,' she said. 'For a night, if that is what you wish. For longer, if you will.'

Hereward let her hand rest upon his skin as he chose his words. 'I met my wife when I was little more than a youth, in Flanders, when I had been driven out of England for the first time. Her name was Turfrida. My devil was alive in me in those days, but even so she found a place for me in her heart. When I sailed away from Flanders she came with me, and left her kin behind. When I fought for the English she stood by me, and she had more fire in her heart than any warrior. Would that I had had a thousand of her upon those walls in Ely. She is dead . . .' slowly he withdrew his hand and placed it upon his breast, 'but she lives on. Turfrida was my wife then, and she is my wife now. There will be no other woman for me.'

He thought that Anna might fly into a rage at being rejected. He did not want to lose the most powerful ally he had, but he could say no other. Yet when he peered into her face he saw that her eyes were glistening. With the back of her hand, she wiped her cheek. 'Would that all my sons grow to be as you.'

Baffled by her words, the Mercian frowned. 'You wish them to be devils?'

Anna shook her head sadly. 'Do you not desire comfort as old age turns your hair white and your

154

muscles weak? Do you not wish to stave off the lone-
liness of those last years?'

'A good warrior does not die old.'

Before Anna could respond, the door swung
open. The Mercian heard a girlish exclamation.
'Oh.'

Here was Alexios' wife, Irene: slight, hair long and
gleaming black, eyes huge and dark. She was barely
more than a girl, and if not for her fine dress would
not have looked out of place among Ariadne Verina's
lost children. Her face was creased with worry. Irene
was one of the Doukai, Hereward knew. The marriage
had been arranged to ease the tensions that always
simmered between that family and the Comnenoi, not
least to placate the brooding presence of the Caesar
John Doukas. Even hidden away on his estate in the
east, he still kept a close eye on his family's fortunes,
and still plotted.

'I . . . I would not have troubled you if I had known
you were here,' she said, her voice tremulous. 'But I
was told Alexios was here. Do you know where
I might find him?'

Now Hereward understood the concern he saw in
the girl's face. As with so many of these arranged
alliances among the empire's aristocrats, there was
little love between husband and wife in this case. But
in the few times he had seen Irene at court, she had
always worked hard to pretend theirs was a true
marriage. Alexios could barely bring himself to look
at her. Irene was a proud girl, as one would expect of
one of the Doukai. Every cold look or silent dismissal

from her husband in public must come like a slap to the cheek.

Anna put on a honeyed smile. 'I have not seen my son all even. But he has risen high, as you know, and in this time when the empire faces war his wits and his words are needed more than ever. I would wager that even now he advises Nikephoros on the path ahead.'

'He is not with the emperor,' Irene snapped. 'I have been to the palace . . .' She caught herself, seeing Anna's eyes flash and recognizing she had been too forceful. 'You must speak true. I will search the palace again.'

Her words had barely died away when voices echoed from the corridor outside. Hereward could hear that one of them was Alexios, arguing with an older man. Irene's expression brightened. But when Alexios swept into the chamber, herding Anna's aged adviser Genesios ahead of him, her face fell. Behind her husband walked Maria of Alania, the emperor's wife.

Hereward watched the flickering emotions on Irene's face, quick loathing becoming hurt, then a smile that had clearly been well practised over time. She knew full well what lay between her husband and this older woman, though it had never been given voice. She knew as all wives would know.

Maria shifted with discomfort.

For a moment, Hereward feared the uneasy silence would never be broken. But then Irene bowed her head and muttered a greeting to the emperor's wife.

Hereward felt sorry that she had to endure such a confrontation. But she was strong, standing her ground and hiding her feelings well, apart from a faint flush to her cheeks.

'Irene. Your beauty never fades,' Maria said.

'We have important business,' Alexios interjected, resting a hand on his wife's arm. He glanced at Maria and added, 'The emperor's business. But I will come to you as soon as we are done here.'

Irene gritted her teeth, but then found another smile and nodded. Slipping away, she paused briefly as the door closed and glanced back. Hereward caught sight of a face like thunder before she was gone.

'What is this?' Anna said, trying to keep her voice steady. She looked from Alexios to Maria and then to Genesios. The old man's face was crumpled with distress.

'We had no choice,' Alexios said. 'You know we would not have taken such a risk . . . coming here . . . if not . . .' He glared at the adviser.

'He found us,' Maria said. 'Together.' Though her face had become like stone, Hereward saw the fear in her eyes.

'I will never tell,' Genesios cried.

'We can take no risks,' Maria protested. 'If Nikephoros discovers my betrayal, our heads will be gone by dawn.'

'Mother, tell her,' Alexios said. 'There is no man more loyal than Genesios.'

'I saw him with Karas Verinus, their heads bowed

together,' Maria protested. 'Karas would use this knowledge to destroy all of us. Then he would be free to sate his hunger for the throne.'

'We spoke of the coming war with the Normans,' the old man wailed. 'I would never betray the Comnenoi. My heart is filled only with love for you all.' Dropping to his knees, he closed his eyes, pressed his hands together and mouthed a silent prayer.

'My son speaks true,' Anna said. She crossed the chamber to confront the other woman. 'No servant has been more faithful. Genesios' wise words guided me when Alexios was a babe in my arms. His teachings shaped my son's wits and made them as sharp as they are now. And when the Doukai drove me out of Constantinople and I had no friends anywhere, and little hope, Genesios stood by me. Only Genesios.' She rested a calming hand on the old man's shoulder. Relief flooded his face. 'No man has served us better,' Anna continued. 'No man ever will.'

As Anna passed behind the kneeling man, Hereward saw a flash of steel. The hidden blade whisked across Genesios' throat. Choking, the old man flapped feeble hands at the gush of crimson. An instant of disbelief froze in his eyes. A moment later he had crashed forward into the spreading pool.

Gaping in horror, a mute Alexios reached out one wavering hand towards the man who had been like a father to him. Maria nodded, her face impassive. Both women knew there was no other choice.

Hereward was uneasy. If Anna felt any regret for the brutal slaying and for the harsh blow dealt to her

158

son, he could not see it. She kept her back to him as she swayed towards the door.

'Throw the body into the sea,' she said without turning. 'No one will tie this to us. And from this day on, take more care. This death is now upon both your souls.'

And then she was gone.

CHAPTER SIXTEEN

Black against the pink-streaked sky, the gulls wheeled past the great dome of Hagia Sophia. Their plaintive shrieks echoed over the silent city. Now the storm of the previous night had blown itself out, the breeze from the plains was cool.

Three men waited in the shadows against the western wall, not far from the towering gate of Rhesios. Though there were few prying eyes in that first light, they kept their heads down. Their voices were lost beneath the whine of the wind in the rooftops of the clustering houses.

Easing back the hood he used to hide his ruined features, Ragener the Hawk peered up into the face of his master. Nearby, Justin kicked pebbles into the road.

'I am placing my faith in you,' Karas Verinus rumbled. 'This is what you have desired since you joined my service. Do not let me down.'

The sea wolf swallowed, no doubt caught between excitement that his fortunes would soon be great, and unease at the magnitude of the task ahead of him.

Karas felt only contempt for this weak-willed cur, but there was no other he could trust to be his right hand.

'I will do as you ask,' the Hawk replied when he could speak, 'and I will do it well. You will not regret giving me this chance to prove myself.'

'Let us pray that is true, for your sake.' The general craned his neck to study the top of the vast wall. For the first time in living memory, no guards watched the western approach to the city. His coin had been well spent. Nothing could be left to chance, certainly no whispers that he had sent his man – a man as recognizable as this one – out on some secret task.

Tethered to the wall-post, a chestnut mare raised plumes of dust as it stamped its hooves. Not too large, it had been selected specifically for the sea wolf, who was more at home on a heaving deck than a bucking horse, Karas had noted with disdain. 'Your ride,' he said with a nod. 'It will serve you?'

Uneasily, Ragener walked up to his mount. As he glanced back to show his approval, his gaze skittered to Justin who was now prowling around the street, seemingly oblivious of Karas' desire for secrecy. The Hawk hurried back and whispered, 'Watch him while I am gone. He needs to be shackled or he will bring all your plans crashing down.'

Karas sniffed. 'There have been worse emperors than Justin, in Constantinople and in Rome.'

Ragener widened his eyes, scarcely able to believe there could be anyone worse than this murderous youth.

'Our emperor Justinian sent his army to Cherson with orders to drown some of the inhabitants with stones bound to their feet, and to roast the others alive,' Karas said. The sea wolf's face remained blank, so he shook his head and continued, 'Diocletian tortured and executed good Christian men and women by the hundreds in the Circus Maximus and the Colosseum, while the citizens of Rome looked on and bayed for blood.' When he noticed the Hawk's frown, he asked, 'Have you had no learning?'

Ragener squirmed. 'My father was a farmer. I learned of the seasons, and the harvest.'

'And the lore of your land? Of the empire? Of Rome, and Constantinople, and of the great men who carved riches from this earth?'

The ruined man shook his head slowly.

'If you do not know the days gone by, how can you chart a path into the days yet to come? What is gone makes what is to come, always.' Karas hawked phlegm and spat into the dust, seeing from the other man's baffled face that he was wasting his time with such talk. 'Emperors must not be afraid to release rivers of blood,' he said, almost to himself. 'Strength is all. This is the lesson we must learn.'

The general watched Justin and felt a pang of doubt. Even after all he had said, he knew his charge would be a devil to herd away from trouble. But the Verini were destined to rule the empire. He had been told so by his father after the third beating of that summer's day. His father had thrashed him to teach him what strength would be needed for the great battle ahead.

'The guards will be here soon. You must be away,' he grunted.

Ragener clambered on to the back of his horse and steered it out through the narrow gap where the gate had been left ajar. Karas watched him sway along the long road that would soon be swarming with the filthy and bedraggled, fleeing from the fighting in the west or hungry for the gold they foolishly believed Constantinople would rain down on them. His disgust edged towards despair. Once he had commanded mighty armies and now look at him. His success was in the hands of a half-man who had never fought in a single battle.

Not for the first time, he felt the weight of his years start to press down upon his shoulders. Here lay a fear that he could not easily defeat, that his best days lay behind him and all that waited on the road ahead was weakness, infirmity and death.

As he always did, Karas fanned the flames of anger in his heart to burn those sour thoughts away. Striding across the road, he snarled one hand in the back of Justin's tunic and spun the startled youth round. In a flash, he hammered his huge fist into the young man's face, again, and again, driving his nephew down into the dust. He felt the blood seep under his knuckles.

Leaning down, he glared into Justin's swollen eyes. 'You will not give in to your weaknesses,' he growled. 'You will not murder, or rape, or drink blood, or whatever other foul tastes your father instilled in you. You will do nothing to cause the throne to be snatched away from me, not at this late hour. Do you hear me?'

Justin's bewildered gaze slowly hardened as he peered back at his uncle. With the back of his hand he smeared the blood, still holding Karas' stare. For a moment, the general thought the younger man was about to challenge him there and then, and Karas would have had no choice but to break his neck. But then Justin nodded.

'Good,' Karas snapped. 'We are in agreement. Today we begin our march upon the throne. The road is short. Walk with me, and soon you will have all the power your heart desires.'

He strode off along the street towards the heart of Constantinople, but with each step he could feel Justin's baleful stare upon his back. The youth was a danger to all who walked with him. Karas narrowed his eyes as he watched those gulls swirling around the church's great dome. He was no fool. He had no friends, and from now on he would have to watch his back too.

CHAPTER SEVENTEEN

His mother's face loomed over him in the dark. Hereward could still feel his father's blows and the heat of his anger as he waited for her soothing words. Her assurance that he could survive these agonies if only he could keep strong, keep the fire burning in his chest. But this time her face darkened.

Beware the wolf in the night, she told him. *Beware.* The whisper rustled around his head. *Death is coming for you, Hereward. Death waits in silence. It is coming. It is here!*

The Mercian found himself rushing up through a world as black as pitch. A moment later he jerked into the dawn chill of his chamber. Kraki was shaking him roughly.

'Gather your axe and your shield,' the Viking growled. 'It is war.'

Hereward squinted as he stepped out into the grey light of the Vlanga. All around the ancient quarter, his fellow guardsmen flooded from the small, white-washed houses they had been given when they joined the emperor's elite band. Some were bleary-eyed, still carrying the weight of wine-addled heads, slipping on helms and fastening cloaks as they hurried. Others strode purposefully, their freshly painted shields bright with their sigils, ready for battle as though they had not just been roused from their beds.

Kraki waited with Guthrinc on the other side of the street. The two men were grinning and pointing at Sighard, who was still trying to dress himself as he stumbled up. He looked bewildered from lack of sleep.

'What is this?' Hereward asked as he joined them.

'At first light some messenger from the emperor was racing up and down as if he had a snake in his breeches,' Kraki grumbled. 'You were sleeping like the dead.'

'The Normans are coming.' Guthrinc scrubbed fingers through his thatch of hair. 'It is time to fight or die, it seems.'

Hereward shook away the last remnants of his troubling dream. 'The decision had been made,' he complained. 'To attack the Normans with this feeble army is madness. The emperor has barely had time to scrape together more gold to pay for new fighting men.'

'Be that as it may,' Kraki said. 'The order has been given. They have probably found false courage in the depths of their wine, or they have been driven mad. But we are paid to do as we are told.'

As he watched the flow of guardsmen, the Mercian simmered. Karas had found some path that led to his getting his own way. 'I will not send you out to die for no reason.'

166

'Disobey the emperor and we will die here,' Kraki replied, 'and our heads will sit on poles. And what will that little black-haired girl think then, eh?' he said, turning to Sighard and giving a gap-toothed grin. 'No kisses when the crows have feasted on your face.'

Sighard's cheeks coloured. He made a show of ramming his helm on his head so he did not have to continue with this line of conversation. 'War will be good for you,' he grumbled instead. 'You have so little to do with your hours that you dwell on my comings and goings.'

'We never tire of it,' Guthrinc said with a grin and a wink at Hereward. 'Like watching a deer walk on a frozen lake.'

Beneath his helmet brow, Sighard glowered.

The other spear-brothers trundled up. Derman and Hiroc walked in pensive silence, fastening their armour. Mad Hengist and Herrig the Rat gambolled around each other like children at play, laughing. Hereward led his men into the flow of guardsmen. The warriors – English and Danes and Rus – drew themselves up as sleep sloughed off them. By the time they reached the Vlanga Cross, the force once more looked as fearsome as their reputation suggested.

The stone cross was well worn by the elements, raised on a platform where wandering preachers could spread the word of God to the heathen warriors of the Vlanga in days long gone. Beyond it was the stump of a ruined tower that hailed from the earliest days of Constantinople, so the legends told. Worn steps ran around the outside of the shattered heap of stones, and here the men of the Vlanga would hang their dying enemies as sacrifices to the blood-and-fire gods of the northern wastes, the stories said. Now it was the place where the Varangian Guard gathered whenever they were called to arms.

Under the silver vault of the heavens the warriors waited, wintry eyes and fierce beards revealing their true wild nature. Silence lay across them.

Wulfrun climbed on to the tower's stone steps so he could be seen by every man there. Hereward could read nothing from the commander's face – it was as grim as always. But a few steps down, Ricbert crouched, watching over the men, and the sly grin that he usually sported was nowhere to be seen.

'This is not good news,' Guthrinc grunted, seeing the same signs.

'The Normans,' Hiroc muttered. 'It must be.'

'Or the Turks,' Derman said in his whispery voice. 'They have closed off the trade routes to the east. We few must ride off to face the barbarian horde or the empire will fall to its knees in starvation.' He shrugged. 'That is the end of us, then.'

'Dismal bastard,' Kraki grunted.

Wulfrun looked out over the raised heads. 'Our axes are needed once more. The Duke of Apulia, Robert Guiscard, has ventured across the whale road to the edge of the empire. This is no invasion. He has brought only a small army with him, enough to test our courage. It is a warning we must heed. Once he has set up camp upon our land, it is only a matter of time before he marches upon Constantinople with every man under his command.'

For a moment, Wulfrun let his words settle upon the men. The shrieks of the gulls filled the dawn.

'We have one chance within our grasp. To ride hard, this day, while the Normans stake their tents and sharpen their axes. To catch them before they are prepared. To annihilate them while they are still few. To let their blood stain our land – aye, and Robert Guiscard's too if we can get our hands upon him – so that they will know never to challenge us again. One chance to turn this tide. Do we seize it? I say we do.'

A rumble of approval ran through the Varangian Guard. Axes and spears were raised up, their sharpened blades glinting in the dawn light.

Kraki nodded at this news. 'I will take a small band of Normans over the other choice.'

Wulfrun let their mutterings ebb away. 'Know that the Normans call Robert Guiscard *Viscardus*,' he continued. 'The cunning. The fox. He is no fool. He knows news of his arrival would reach us like the wind. This may be a trap to lure our fiercest warriors out from behind the city walls where we can be destroyed. We will not know the truth until we look our enemy in the eye.'

'Ah,' Guthrinc said, dropping a hand on Kraki's shoulder. 'Fate gives, fate takes away.' The Viking scowled.

Hereward studied Wulfrun's demeanour. His words made sense. Attacking the Normans now would also buy time to build the army up to the strength necessary to take a stand when the city came under siege. But the risks were great.

Wulfrun reached out one hand to where a hook-nosed man stood watching. 'Tiberius Grabas will lead the Athanatoi into battle, but you Varangians will be in the forefront of the fighting, as you always are.'

That was good, Hereward thought. The Athanatoi were no longer raw, or arrogant. In the seasons since the Mercian had first ridden with them, the Immortals had become seasoned through battle. Their skill on horseback, their tactics under Tiberius' command, both were unmatched. If only the Romans had a whole army to equal this elite force.

Wulfrun looked across his men, proud of what he saw. 'Death waits in silence,' he boomed.

Hereward shuddered, hearing his mother's words spoken to him by a man who would happily see him dead. His neck prickled as he felt a premonition of his own end.

It is coming. It is here!

'Death waits everywhere,' the Guard roared back.

Once the echoes had died away, the guardsmen checked their weapons and adjusted their armour. Some muttered prayers and crossed themselves as they waited for their orders. Wulfrun jumped down from the steps and marched over.

'You will lead the Varangian Guard into battle,' he told Hereward. 'I must stay here at the emperor's side. Take your spear-brothers. You have a bond even stronger than the one which joins all who serve in the

Guard, and you will need all the help you can get in the coming fight.'

'You spoke truth. If we are swift enough, we can strike before the Norman scouts return with news of our coming. Surprise will be on our side.'

For the first time, Wulfrun's mask fell away to reveal a glimmer of worry beneath. 'Let us pray it is enough. God knows, our army is far from ready for war with the Normans. And the Turks are cunning. I am fearful that if they learn we are fighting in the west with all we have, they will seize the moment to attack Constantinople. We put one of their war-bands to the axe only two days gone. There were only twenty of them, but they were on the banks of the Bosphorus, ready to cross. They are getting bolder by the day.'

As Wulfrun turned back to his men, a murmur rose up among the gathered warriors. Hereward watched Alexios pushing his way through the crowd, encouraging every man he passed. He was a good leader, knew the right words for the right time. The fighting men liked him.

When he reached Hereward, he announced, 'I will ride with you.'

'Good. The men will fight harder still if they know you are beneath the standard.' The Mercian could already see relief on the faces of his spear-brothers. Alexios' skill in battle had become almost legendary. He would give them a much-needed advantage over the Normans.

'The emperor's war council has been meeting through the night.' Alexios lowered his voice so only

Hereward could hear. 'Karas Verinus feels his hand has been made stronger by this Norman advance. He argued for this war-band to ride out and the emperor agreed.'

'I would wager that he found much joy in the knowledge that the two men who fought against him were now riding into battle, while he sits safely behind the walls at the emperor's right hand.'

'Karas spoke with passion to make sure only the best men were sent.' Alexios paused. 'The best men. The greatest threat to his plans.'

CHAPTER EIGHTEEN

Gold lines shimmered on the wide expanse of milky marble. Along them, rival armies of counters stared each other down. Two men hunched over the *tavla* board engraved in the surface of the street for any passing players to use, oblivious of the stream of passers-by enjoying the morning sun. One of the players rolled the dice, frowning as he studied the result.

Two other men had paused on their journey to see the game unfold.

'I do not like these games.' Falkon's face was as still as a millpond. Karas recognized that he had never seen any honest emotion play out on those features. Every smile, every frown, every tiny crease, appeared studied.

'There are more than enough in life,' Karas agreed. 'Oft times we do not know the other player. That makes winning hard. But there are some who have a God-given ability to succeed. I have studied you, Falkon Cephalas. I would wager you are one of them, eh?'

'I am a simple man, here only to serve the emperor.'

Falkon watched the players ponder, move their pieces, ponder some more. Karas watched Falkon. He could plumb the depths of a man's soul. That was one of the strengths that had allowed him to carve out his own empire. But he could not read this adviser at all.

Returning his attention to the game, Karas smiled to himself. 'There is much to learn from *tavla*. Each player needs both luck and strategy. Luck may define the outcome of a single contest. But over time, over many games, over many years, the player best versed in strategy will always win. The game of life is long, Falkon, and it favours the best of us.'

The emperor's adviser contemplated the counters, saying nothing.

'Our merchants are as cunning as foxes,' Karas continued. 'Their gold buys space on more ships, a fleet of them, perhaps every ship in the east, to find a way past the Turks who block our trade routes. I hear a new supply of silk has been unloaded at the quayside. I would see the quality for myself. Walk with me.'

The late morning was warm. The Mese, the busiest thoroughfare in the city, thronged with life. Time and again, the two men paused to avoid people rushing by them. In the merchants' stores that lined both sides of the avenue, anything anyone ever wanted could be found, so it was said. When Karas looked across the bobbing heads pressing into the shadowy interiors to buy the goods on offer, he thought how many folk still prospered despite the difficulties that afflicted Constantinople. But soon there would be a reckoning.

'These are dark times for the empire,' he said. 'When I was a boy learning to be a warrior, dropping my sword, being knocked on my arse, I spent the hours before sunset learning all I could about our history. We were great in those days, Falkon. The Romans of the east held their heads high. They were feared, they were admired. Constantinople was a beacon in the night that cloaks this world. And we could be that way again. We should be. It is our destiny.'

'There are many who feel that way.' Falkon pressed his palms together.

'The emperor is a strong warrior, a wise man,' the general continued, choosing his words carefully. 'But he is assailed every day, every hour, by small troubles and large. His gaze flutters like a sparrow over the land, and he has no time to see anything for what it is. No time to find the path that leads out of this mire on to the high ground. He needs help, Falkon.'

'And that is why he has chosen good men like you and me to hold high the light and guide his way.'

Karas nodded. He could tell the other man was choosing his words with care too, and he liked what he heard. He had been right to make this move. 'And now we hear whispers that the emperor's wife is spreading her legs for Alexios Comnenos. All the court is alive with this talk.'

'I have heard it. I pay no heed to it. Some will see lust in an odd look, an arch of the neck . . .'

'But if it were true . . .'

'If it were true, it only serves to draw more power from the emperor. If he cannot keep his wife, how can he keep an empire?'

Karas smiled to himself. For all his understated words, Falkon knew the dangers here. A proud man like Nikephoros would not be able to control his ire. He would wreak havoc to save face, and this was no time for turmoil. The results would be too unpredictable. 'We each see different threats ahead,' he said. 'Or perhaps we see the same threats from different sides. But if we work together we can share our knowledge. We can find the answers that escape each of us alone. And thereby we can better aid the emperor.'

Falkon said nothing.

'Your wisdom . . . your army of eyes and ears you have spread out across the city . . . aye, I know they are there,' Karas said. 'My sword. My fist. *My* army of men with strong arms. Together, we can restore the empire to glory.'

After a moment's thought, Falkon nodded. 'No man could question that wisdom. We will be allies, Karas Verinus.'

'Only good will come of this, you can be certain of that. Our enemy in the west will now be confronted. The biggest threat will be the enemies within these walls.'

'My eyes and ears watch all plotters.'

'There are only two who should worry us. With Alexios Comnenos riding with our army, the

176

Comnenoi – and that witch Anna Dalassene – are less of a threat. I can deal with them. That leaves only the Nepotes.'

'And what whispers reach your ears?'

'The whore of a daughter, Juliana Nepa, offered me her body in exchange for my support. They plot to bring the emperor down, have no doubt of that. They would place the boy, Leo, upon the throne, but it is Simonis and Juliana who would stand behind his shoulder, whispering in his ear, guiding his hand. The empire would be ruined in no time.'

'And, of course, all men know of the long feud between the Nepotes and the Verini,' Falkon said, as if only just remembering this fact. 'I would think Emperor Leo would not waste any time making sure you were no threat to his rule.'

'I have lived my life with a sword in my hand. Protecting my own neck is not something that troubles me. But the Verini will not be the only ones to fall if the Nepotes lay their bloody hands upon the crown. Those who had the old emperor's ear . . . the Nepotes would see them as a threat to be quickly removed.'

'We all think of ourselves as men of learning, with wits sharpened by the wisdom of years. The danger always is that we think we know more than those who would stand against us,' Falkon mused. 'It is an easy mistake to make, a burnishing of our pride that warms our hearts and makes us walk tall. We are all guilty of it, even men as humble as ourselves. I see now that I have not given the Nepotes enough of my time. It would be wise to watch them—'

'Closely.'

'Indeed, closely. I have men in their employ . . . rogues, mostly, who take the Nepotes' gold and would be part of any army that tried to seize the throne. No doubt they hear whispers . . . words spoken without thought . . . I will have them tell me all they find in that house.'

'And you will tell me.'

'Of course, Karas Verinus,' Falkon said with a bow. 'We are of one mind here. We will know what the Nepotes plan almost before they have thought of it themselves, and we will be ready to act before they have sharpened a blade.'

'I knew I was wise to come to you, Falkon Cephalas.' In the shadows of an alley, Karas glimpsed a familiar face, pale and mysterious. Justin was watching him, beckoning with a jerk of his head. 'I must take my leave now. There is much to do. But this talk has warmed my heart.'

Falkon bowed once again and disappeared into the flow of bodies. Karas slipped into the alley. 'What now?' he growled. 'More of your mess to clean up?'

'Maria has sent word that the emperor should be brought to the palace on a matter of urgency,' Justin replied in his whispery voice.

'Where is he?'

'Hunting with his falcon and those old men he calls friends, away in Deuteron.' He stared, unblinking. 'Anna waits with Maria.'

Karas furrowed his brow. 'The two of them?

178

Together?' What business could these women share? They were rivals.

He allowed Justin to lead him through the streets to the palace, where members of the court were already gathering. News of Maria's plea had travelled fast, igniting curiosity. His thoughts racing, he climbed the steps to the throne room two at a time.

The chamber was awash with whispers as the aristocracy gossiped about what was to come. As Karas looked around the throng, he knew instantly that the two women had planned this audience. If they had wanted to meet the emperor in private, they could have done so without word leaking out.

Maria and Anna stood together, isolated from the growing crowd, looking like mother and daughter. They had posed themselves like beatific statues in the Hagia Sophia, faces raised and turned towards the light streaming through the window, eyes half closed, hands pressed together, faint smiles on their lips.

Karas smirked. How clever they thought they were. Now he could divine the spark of this plot.

The aristocrats fell silent as a voice barked the arrival of the emperor. Karas turned as the door swung open and the emperor's personal guards, Boril and Germanos, strode in. The two murderous bastards were never far from their master's side these days, ready to hack down anyone who dared even look with hate in their eyes. Breathless, Nikephoros lurched behind them. Karas thought how the bewilderment on his face magnified his age.

'What is amiss?' the emperor called.

Still smiling sweetly, Maria held out one arm to him. 'I have great news,' she said.

Boril guided the old man to the throne and the emperor slumped into it. 'Tell me,' he croaked, his darting eyes showing puzzlement at the crowd and the sense of occasion.

Maria stepped next to the throne, beckoning Anna to stand beside her. 'We have talked long and hard, the two of us, and agreement has been reached,' Maria announced. 'From this day forth, I will take Alexios Comnenos under my care. I will treat him as if he were my own true-born son, a brother to my own Constantine.'

A gasp echoed from the gathered courtiers, followed by a rustle of insistent whispers.

Maria bowed her head as if overcome with emotion. 'He will have my protection, and my motherly love, and, one day, a share of all that I own.'

Karas stifled an incredulous laugh. Motherly love? Maria was barely five years older than Alexios.

Blinking stupidly, the emperor gaped at his wife.

'I see God's light shining out of him,' Maria continued, 'and I know this is the path I must follow. Only I can keep him safe, as God wishes.'

Nikephoros looked to Anna, his mouth working but no words coming out. 'Is this your wish?' he asked eventually.

Anna nodded. 'I want only what is best for my son. No greater care could be given him than that offered by Maria.'

Nikephoros looked around the chamber. Karas saw

his dilemma. How could he deny such an impassioned plea in front of so many witnesses? 'So be it,' the emperor said.

Karas watched his face, the narrowing of his eyes as he looked from Maria to Anna, the tightness of his lips. The old man was no longer the warrior he used to be, but his wits had not lost their sharpness, and his cunning had only grown. The emperor suspected there was more to this than he had been told, Karas could see, and that doubt would be like a worm in his heart.

As the nobles cheered the news, Karas steered Justin away. 'They have moved fast, those women, to protect Alexios and their own necks,' he murmured. 'The emperor has saved face, for now any whispers can only concern the affection of a mother for her son.' He nodded, pleased that his own plans had not been knocked awry.

'But Anna Dalassene . . . what does she gain?' the boy whispered.

'They both gain. If Nikephoros falls, Maria will have the Comnenoi behind her when she seats her idiot son Constantine upon the throne. And for now, Anna has gained the protection of the crown for Alexios, or so she thinks, and has forged a deeper alliance with Maria.'

Karas allowed himself a grin. He had seen that fleeting look on Nikephoros' face, the hardening of his eyes. Aye, the two women thought they were clever, but cracks were forming, and when the time came he would be ready to prise them apart.

CHAPTER NINETEEN

The sun was high overhead and the warm wind gritty with dust from the hazy west. As the gate of Rhesios ground open, a column of mounted warriors rode out of Constantinople. The ground throbbed with the rolling rumble of hooves, drowning out the exhortations from the line of guards watching from the towering white wall. Tears stung their eyes. At the head of the army shone the standard, a golden double-headed eagle against a red background, a memory of greatness that would, perhaps, shout greatness once again.

In their silver armour burning in the noon light, the Immortals could draw the eye for only a moment. But the Varangian Guard rode beside them like their shadow, a pool of black edged with crimson.

Hereward and the spear-brothers were at the head of the line of horsemen. The Mercian eyed his men. Guthrinc looked thoughtful, ready for what lay ahead, Kraki sullen. Sighard kept throwing concerned glances behind him, no doubt thinking of the woman he was leaving behind. Hengist was unusually still and silent, his gaze turned up to the gulls arcing across the clear blue sky.

As the city fell behind them, Kraki turned to Hereward and grunted, 'Like old times, eh? Apart from the horses. However much I ride, I will never get used to being on the back of one of these beasts. Give me the solid ground beneath my feet.' He spat into the dirt.

'Sometimes I think we are cursed to war against Normans until we have made amends for the failures of days gone by.' Hereward squinted through the billowing dust towards the high land ahead. His chest felt tight, his shoulders heavy, and he knew those signs well. He sensed a threat moving around him in the shadows, unseen. Karas Verinus in Constantinople, and the Nepotes too. Though he could not divine their plans, he could feel them steering him towards some fate he could not yet imagine.

And then there was what he believed to be the greater threat, the unknown, looming somewhere ahead like a storm at sea. He could taste the danger.

The dream of his mother still hung over him, so heavy at times that he felt as if he were suffocating. He had started to think that it was not merely a warning, but a premonition of his own death.

'Those days are long gone,' Guthrinc said lightly. 'No bellies will get filled by thinking on last year's harvest.'

Mad Hengist looked towards the horizon. For now his eyes, and his head, were clear. 'Our bellies are full,' he murmured. 'We have earned more gold and glory than ever we could have dreamed . . . earned it by following you, Hereward. We owe you all that we have. And Guthrinc speaks true – there is no need to think on what has slipped away into the mists.' He gave a tight-lipped, humourless smile. 'But the Normans . . . ? They are not something we should fear. Aye, I could find some joy in ridding the world of a few more of that warlike breed.'

Hereward nodded. 'We will fight, as we always have, whatever enemies stand in front of us, or at our backs. And there is always something to fight for.' He noticed Kraki looking at him. The Viking narrowed his eyes.

'You have a plan.'

'I always have a plan.'

'And when will you be sharing it?'

'When the time is ripe.' Hereward urged his horse to pull away from the spear-brothers. He had much to think on and he needed his head clear of witterings.

The commander of the Immortals, Tiberius Gabras, took the lead and the column made its way along the great west road which stretched through the passes in the chill highlands down towards the western sea. And there they would find the camp of Robert Guiscard and his force of fighting men probing into the hinterlands. Those warriors would be fresh. It was only a short journey across the whale road from Apulia and Sicily. But the Athanatoi and the Varangian Guard would have spent days on horseback. Hereward hoped that would not be the deciding factor in the coming battle.

As the sun slipped down to the edge of the hills, the Roman army found themselves skirting a growing stream of people fleeing from Guiscard's army towards Constantinople, their meagre possessions piled on creaking carts or strapped to the backs of mules. Since the Normans had fought their way into Apulia, crushing, murdering and burning villages as they had done in England, the flow had been near ceaseless. But now these were Romans from the villages along the western coast, all of them with tales of slaughter and misery upon their lips.

Hereward felt pity when he saw their anguished expressions and heard their desperate pleas for food. His thoughts flew back to all the suffering he had witnessed in England after William the Bastard's invasion. When he glanced back at the spear-brothers and glimpsed their dark faces he knew they too could never forget. All they could do was exhort the refugees to keep the fire in their bellies until they reached the city. The army's own provisions in the carts trundling at the rear of the column could not be spared. But Hereward felt his own resolve stiffen in the face of their despair.

Camp was made at the foot of the high hills. They supped on rough wine and hard bread dipped in sweet olive oil. Moving among the campfires, Hereward and Tiberius selected the best hunters among their number, men good with bows and spears who would be tasked with riding down meat for meals in the coming days.

At first light, the army set off into the highlands,

leaving behind the grassy plain to pass through thickly forested slopes filled with the scent of resin and damp vegetation. Hereward let his thoughts drift in that shadowy world of dark-green leaf and brown dust. A warm breeze stirred the branches. Soon they were in a rockier, wind-blasted landscape. The air grew chill, and the riders dragged their woollen cloaks around them, their cheeks pinkening.

Clouds the colour of steel banked up overhead, and the wind gusted intermittent showers into the men hunched over the necks of their horses. Kraki, often derided for wearing his northern furs even in the heat of the Constantinople summer, laughed long and loud every time he saw one of the others shivering.

A day later, as they plunged into a wooded valley deep enough to keep the wind howling high above them in the treetops, they heard cries echoing from the gloom somewhere ahead. Hereward took a handful of his men forward to investigate.

In the mud and grass at the side of the road, a cart leaned over almost on its side, its axle shattered when it had veered off the hard surface. Bales had spilled out from the back, some of them splitting open. A red-faced merchant spitting with fury was lashing a cowering boy with the whip he used to steer his horse.

Hereward felt such a surge of anger he shocked himself. Deep inside his head his devil roared, and the blood thundered through his temples.

'Leave him,' he bellowed, but the merchant was so caught up in his rage that he was oblivious even of an army riding up beside him.

Jumping down from his mount, Hereward strode off the road. As his vision closed in around him, he saw not a merchant chastising his helper, but his father Asketil pounding his fists on his own younger self.

Without slowing his step, he snarled his hand in the back of the merchant's tunic and yanked him round. He caught a glimpse of a startled expression, heard the beginning of a choked plea, but he could no longer control himself. His fist hammered into the man's face. Blood spurted. For a moment all his senses left him.

When the rumble of sound returned, filled with strange shouts and the screaming of a boy, he became aware that his sword was in his hand and he was about to thrust it into the merchant's gut.

Hands grasped his arms and shoulders and hauled him back. Kraki's voice thrummed in his ears before Brainbiter was wrenched from his hand. Though he struggled, the spear-brothers held him fast and gradually his devil slipped back into the depths.

Hereward shook his head to clear it. Between sobs, the boy was pleading, 'Do not kill him. He is a good man.' The lad was so small a strong wind might blow him away. His sandy hair was a mass of curls, his cheeks red and tear-stained. He held out an imploring hand.

The Mercian bowed his head, feeling a cold knot in his gut. When he looked up, Alexios floated in front of him, his brow furrowed. 'What is wrong, brother?'

Hereward glanced down at his bloody hands. A

chill crept into his bones. 'You may let me go,' he murmured. 'I am done.'

Reluctantly Alexios and the spear-brothers stepped back. Hereward felt shamed when he saw their wary stares. Taking back his blade and sheathing it, he said to the merchant, 'You have your life. Use it well. Do not hurt this boy again.'

The merchant muttered something, but his mangled lips made the words unintelligible.

'It is not his fault.' The boy wiped away the snot on his upper lip. 'The Normans murdered his wife. His grief has made him a different man. We are fleeing with all we had.' He glanced down at the broken cart and added in a low voice, 'I steered it off the road. I have brought ruin to him.'

Hereward had thought his guilt could get no stronger, but now his chest felt so tight it would burst. He looked back at the merchant. 'You were wrong to whip the boy, but now I have wronged you more.'

When he had made arrangements with Alexios for the merchant to be given one of the army's carts, he rode ahead of the column, alone, aware of his spear-brothers' eyes upon his back, unsure what they thought of him, no longer knowing what he thought of himself.

Three nights later they had crossed the high ground and were making their way down the westward slopes towards the coast. They were six days out of Constantinople. Now, so near to their enemy, they took more care, leaving the great road to wend their way through deep, tree-shrouded valleys where flies droned through dappled patches of light.

Ahead of the main column, the scouts roamed far and wide. Herrig the Rat led the band. He was far from his home among the vermin in the watercourses and bogs of the fenlands, but he had earned the respect of the Guard, though few would spend much time drinking with him, unsettled by his odd stare and the strange cackling that had come from too many seasons in the wilderness away from other men. And, too, by the chinking Norman finger bones that hung on a leather thong around his neck. But when he was tracking spoor, following the pattern of broken grass, or spying shadows moving more than a day's march away, even the fiercest warrior held his breath in awe. Only God or the Devil could have granted him such powers.

That evening they made camp in a clearing in the forest about halfway down the slope of the final foothill before the coastal plain. When the wind was from the west, they could smell the salt of the whale road. The tents spread deep into the trees on every side, where the insects clicked and the scent of resin was strong.

Under a clear, star-sprinkled sky, the warriors feasted on cold rations: cheese, olives, venison. No fires were allowed for fear the smoke would carry to the enemy, and no singing rang up to the heavens.

His belly full, Hereward walked among the men with Kraki and Tiberius at his side. He kept his eyes ahead, ignoring the wary looks from those men who did not know him well and were troubled by his attack upon the merchant. The night was balmy, but he sensed no relaxation. The warriors stared deep into the dark, their faces taut, every one aware that the next day's battle would be hard. Many would not return to Constantinople.

'You Romans think this a winter chill.' Kraki wiped the sweat from his brow. 'You would think you had entered hell if you spent a cold season in Eoferwic. The winds cut sharper than a Damascan blade.'

'I have heard tell of your barbarian lands,' Tiberius replied, his eyes sly. 'If there is no woman to keep you warm at night, you sleep with sheep.'

'Better sheep than the small boys you Romans love,' Kraki grunted.

When Tiberius stepped away to piss against a tree, Hereward said, 'Sighard came to me earlier. He thinks he wants to wed this girl who has taken his days.'

'Aye, he is besotted,' Kraki said. 'What did you tell him? To dunk his head in a water barrel?'

'And you would not have wed Acha, given half the chance?'

The Viking looked away into the night. 'That was never to be.'

'He is young, true, but he deserves some reward.' Hereward imagined the face of Turfrida.

'Those women who idle their days in the Vlanga are hungry for the gold and the glory of the Varangian Guard. Any man will do. You know that.' Kraki hawked up phelgm and spat. 'Spare him the sword in his heart that will be his only reward for that coupling.'

Hereward heard a fatherly note of concern in those

words, though the Viking would undoubtedly deny he cared even a jot about the youngest of the spear-brothers. 'I will ponder on it,' he said.

Keen whispers rippled back through the resting men, and when Hereward saw they were accompanied by broad grins he knew Herrig the Rat had returned.

Sure enough, the English scout strode up through the tents. His hand-picked band followed close at his heels, struggling with someone in their midst that the Mercian could not see.

'Your man is good,' Tiberius said with a satisfied smile when he returned and saw that the scouts had a captive.

'Aye, though you would not tell it to look at him.'

When the scouting band found Hereward, Herrig gave a gap-toothed grin. 'A gift for you.'

Two of the others hurled their captive forward. He sprawled at Hereward's feet and looked up with hate-filled eyes.

It was a Norman soldier; the Mercian recognized the shaved head. His face was bruised, his lips caked with blood.

'We have cleared all of Robert Guiscard's scouts that we could find. No word will reach the fox of our approach.' Herrig snickered. 'I brought this one back so you could put him to the question. But when you are done with him, let me have his hand.'

The Norman scout showed a defiant face, but a flash of fear lit his eyes. He had spent enough time in Herrig's company to know what was to come.

'I will not speak,' he said through gritted teeth.

'You will. Do not ask for mercy. There will be none.' Hereward turned and walked in the direction of his tent. Without looking back, he flicked his fingers. 'Bring him.'

The scout closed his eyes and muttered a desperate prayer before hands grabbed him and dragged him towards his fate.

CHAPTER TWENTY

A silver wave washed out of the forest on to the grassy slopes running down to the shore. The ground throbbed with the sound of hooves. The Immortals and the Varangian Guard were sweeping out of their camp, ready for battle after their silent night.

Ahead, the dawn light edged glistening strands along the rolling breakers. Like a disturbed anthill, the camp of Robert Guiscard and his army swarmed with activity along the edge of the beach.

At the point where the land flattened, Tiberius Grabas raised one hand and the rumble slowly ebbed away as his force came to a halt. The wind had dropped, but the air felt warm and heavy, threatening storms to come.

Hereward watched Alexios and Tiberius guide their horses along the line to where he waited at the head of the Varangian Guard. The Athanatoi lined the flanks, ready to torment the Normans from either side while the Guard drove like a spear into their heart.

Alexios' and Tiberius' armour caught the first rays of the sun. The commander of the Immortals had drawn his sword already, but the younger Roman seemed as calm as if he were at hunt, Hereward thought. Their horses were skittish, as if they sensed what was to come.

'They knew we were coming before dawn.' Tiberius nodded towards the enemy. 'This close, we could not hide the sound of an army approaching.'

'Aye. But fate has been kind to let us reach this point undiscovered.'

Before his death the previous night, the Norman scout had told Hereward everything he wanted to know. Robert Guiscard had no knowledge of the army bearing down on him. He must have been waiting in vain for his scouts to return from the hinterland, but Herrig the Rat had done a good job of ensuring that none of them would ever be seen again.

The Mercian watched Guiscard's men readying themselves. They were fast, well organized. He weighed their numbers and the location that Herrig had described to him in detail, turning over the strategy that he had discussed with the Roman commander deep into the night. In his arrogance, Robert Guiscard had camped his army in a bowl. High land, heavily wooded, rose up on three sides. The fourth was the whale road. Guiscard was trapped. His warriors could only retreat into the waves, where the waters would eventually run red with their blood. A few no doubt would escape to the ships at anchor just offshore, the ropes straining against the swell. All they could do then was flee back to Apulia, their tails between their legs.

'We are evenly matched,' Alexios noted. 'Clearly, more men have joined Guiscard's army since we left Constantinople.'

'Then it is good we have the upper hand,' Tiberius said.

Hereward could see the unease in his eyes. They all knew victory here could change everything. If Guiscard was crushed the moment he set foot upon Roman land, he would not be so quick to risk an attack in days yet to come. No one could doubt that he lusted after the power that resided in the crown, and all the wealth that would be his if he found a way to seat his daughter beside a new emperor on the throne in Constantinople. But the duke's own empire was already large, and if his forces were weakened in battle with the Romans it was unlikely he would be able to hold on to Apulia and Sicily.

Aye, victory could change everything, Hereward thought, just as defeat could set them all on course for disaster. Emboldened by success, how long before Robert Guiscard decided to march upon a weakened Constantinople? And who would be left to stand in his way?

Tiberius sucked in a deep, calming breath, then swept his eyes along the ranks of gleaming armour of the Immortals and the brooding warriors of the Guard. He nodded. 'It is time.'

Hereward gritted his teeth, summoning up his devil from deep within him. Here it had a part to play, not tormenting innocents.

A raven flashed across his vision. 'Death waits in silence,' it said to him in a croaking old man's voice.

Somewhere on the edge of that great black sea, his long-dead allies were cheering him on. All the warriors of the Varangian Guard would be hearing the voices of their own dead now, he knew. Those voices would rustle through their skulls. The fire in their breasts would roar into a blaze that could burn down all before them. The battle-rage would come, and it could only be sated by the blood of their enemies.

'Death waits in silence,' the raven called to him again, before it took wing into the shimmering dawn light.

For a moment, the world seemed to hold its breath. Every man was fixed in place, eyes narrowing so that all they saw was the enemy.

The wind moaned. The surf crashed. The gulls cried.

The command rang out.

The world heaved into life, the air booming with the thunder of hooves and full-throated battle-cries. As the Roman army surged out of the grasslands and into the salt wastes, the Immortals skirted the edges along the solid ground that Herrig and his band had already scouted.

Hereward punched his fist into the air and roared. As one the Varangian Guard slid off their mounts, breaking into a lope the moment their feet touched the ground. Axes swung, balancing the rolling gait. The Mercian heard the rasp of breath all around, like the sound of a waking wolf. But then the wind roared in his ears, and the blood pounded, and all the sounds of the world were snatched away.

Through pools of brine, the pace never slowed. The hungry gaze never shifted from the prey. Hereward wondered how it must feel to be their enemies and to see this monstrous sight bearing down upon them. A smudge of black and crimson reaching across the breadth of sight, resolving itself into a savage pack filled with glittering eyes, wild beards and hair, yet joined in a single purpose.

Destruction.

Doom.

The ground flew beneath his feet. Glistening diamonds of spray danced all around.

Ahead, the Normans waited, unmoving, a wall of iron. Grey they were in their hauberks and helms, with their double-edged swords drawn, and their axes raised. Faces carved from granite, eyes like frozen lakes.

Closer the Roman army drew, and closer still.

And then the wave broke. Hereward hacked his Dane-axe down. An arc of sparks blazed as the Norman in front of him parried the strike with his own axe.

The sun fell away, and the sky, and the world became dark in the turmoil of battle raging all around. Bodies crashed against him, elbows and knees fighting for advantage. Blades whisked everywhere. Screams ripped through the thump of blood. Cascades of rubies showered down, splattering faces, staining armour.

Hereward narrowed his eyes, his vision closing in on that single face in front of him, a patchwork of scars running the length of the left side. Lips pulled back from teeth in a snarl. So close they were, face to face in a dance of death, that Hereward felt a hot blast of breath upon his face.

His eyes never left his enemy's, and in that moment they knew each other, knew the values they shared, their strengths and weaknesses, their fears and hopes.

The Norman warrior swung his short-handled axe towards the Mercian, thrusting it forward in an attempt to hook his foe. Hereward leapt aside before the scarred man could wrench the weapon back, tearing open flesh.

Rolling on his heels, the Mercian heaved his axe down once more. The Norman jerked back, cursing. But the fighting men roiling behind him blocked his escape. Brought up sharp, he turned his face away. The blade missed his cheek by a whisker and tore across his shoulder, rending links on his hauberk. With a howl, the warrior renewed his attack, more venomous than ever.

Hereward felt a calm settle on him. He was ready, as was his devil. The Norman had allowed his pain to rule his mind, a fatal error.

As the scarred man lurched forward, axe raised, the Mercian rammed the haft of his axe into his foe's face. Lips burst, teeth shattered. Stunned, the warrior reeled. Before he could find his wits, Hereward crashed the axe into his shoulder, driving him to his knees.

Wrenching the weapon back, the Mercian saw he had cut deep into the Norman's ribs. Blood gouted. The man could not survive. Thrusting one boot into his chest, Hereward drove him into the wet ground and moved on to the next.

How long the battle raged the Mercian could not tell. Every moment seemed to last an age. The faces of his fallen enemies blurred. How many had he slain? His right arm ached and blood stained him from head to toe.

As space opened up about him, his devil began to settle back, sated. He looked around. His feet dragged through a sucking bog of gore and shit and piss. Bodies littered the shoreline, at times three or four deep. As many dead Varangians as Normans, it seemed. They were evenly matched.

Wiping the blood from his eyes, Hereward glanced towards the flanks where the Immortals harried the enemy. Herrig had warned there would be little space to use the cavalry effectively, and the Mercian could see that was true. The riders churned as they lashed their swords down.

But the Normans had positioned their archers on the edges of their army, ready for just such an attack. Arrows whined, and the horses reared up in agony as the riders fought to keep them under control. Some went down, the Romans falling to the swords of their enemies.

A cry rang out, and Hereward whirled to see Kraki standing over the bloody body of a Norman who, no doubt, had been ready to end the Mercian's days while his back was turned. The Viking pointed to his eyes, his head, and then at Hereward.

Drawing himself up, the Mercian looked to the Immortals once more. Now he could see that for all the skill of their archers, the Normans on the flanks were being whittled down. Perhaps there was hope, and the two armies would not hack each other down into the bloody mire until there was only one man left standing.

Yet barely had the thought crossed his mind before a battle-cry rang out at his back.

Spinning round, he squinted into the dawn light. Warriors on horseback were streaming out of the trees, perhaps two hundred of them. His heart pounded. Somehow the Normans had called down allies. This force had been waiting for the moment when they were most needed to turn the tide of battle.

Glancing around at his spear-brothers, he saw their faces stiffen as they recognized the hopelessness of this fight now they were so outnumbered.

'Hold,' Kraki called, pointing at a Norman warrior nearby. Hereward followed his gaze, and saw the same look of horror on their enemy's face. The Normans did not recognize the newcomers either – they thought they were allies of the Romans.

Along the shoreline, swords and axes fell as warriors craned their necks to watch the approaching force.

This new army carried no standard at its head. Narrowing his eyes, Hereward saw that only a few wore armour, and then only leather. Most had no helms, and what shields he could see were faded.

Who were they?

CHAPTER TWENTY-ONE

'To the standard!' Hereward roared, thrusting his axe into the air. As his Varangians turned towards him, he was already bounding through the coarse grass on the edge of the salt wastes.

The unknown war-band wheeled along the shore-line into the rear of the Immortals' right flank. They were heading for the Roman standard. Whoever they were, it was clear they supported the Norman force. Their weapons might be old and poor, but they fought as if they cared nothing for their lives. Hereward watched as the Romans finally found their wits and urged their mounts towards a narrow channel that would give them space to regroup.

Yet the Athanatoi were caught between hammer and anvil. Realizing they had found allies, the Normans discovered new fire in their hearts and renewed their attack.

Caught in the confusion, the Roman warriors began to fall one by one, each man crushed into the ground by the hooves of the wildly milling horses. The unknown men were single-minded. They drove on through the churning mass. Hereward's eyes narrowed. Aye, pulling towards the front where the banner of Alexios Comnenos fluttered in the breeze. He cursed, understanding. One of the great rivals for power in the empire was about to be slaughtered and no one would suspect any plot. Another Roman hero fallen in battle. This was the work of some treacherous bastard in Constantinople.

Ahead, the storm of steel blasted towards the mercilessly pounding waves. The Immortals there were trapped between the mysterious attackers and the Normans. Their horses roiled in confusion as their riders fought to restore order.

Arrows lashed through the air, punching into shields, faces, flanks. At the back, the newcomers hacked like butchers readying meat for the pot.

These new enemies were no seasoned warriors, Hereward could see as he neared. No more than rough men who had clawed their fingers round weapons they were too slow to learn how to use, they wished only to overwhelm their prey by force of numbers. That gave some hope.

A Norman loomed on the edge of the Mercian's vision. With barely a thought, he heaved his axe in an arc. His shoulder jolted as the weapon smashed into the man's face. Not a step was missed.

Hereward caught a glimpse of Alexios in the centre of the maelstrom as he hacked his sword this way and that. The spear of rogues and cut-throats drove towards him. There was no way out.

Feet pounded at his back and he sensed his men

drawing closer at his command. Kraki appeared to his right, Guthrinc to his left.

'Save Alexios,' Hereward snarled. 'He is the one they want.'

Plucking the bow from his back, Guthrinc nocked an arrow and let fly in a heartbeat. The shaft rammed into the cheek of one of the rough men. He pitched off his mount and disappeared under the hooves. Those near him glanced round in shock.

The deafening roar of battle swallowed him. The dawn light seemed to ebb away as the shadows of the surging horses crashed down. Then there was only the madness of battle spinning all around.

Snarling his hand in the tunic of the nearest rogue, Hereward yanked the startled rider off his mount. As he went down, so did the Dane-axe. One blow was all it took, and then he moved on to the next. Nearby his spear-brothers dispatched their foes with the same ease. The blade of black and crimson began to cut deep into the heart of the new force.

Some of the riders still thought their height gave them an advantage. Their weapons rained down, but so weak were their blows they bounced harmlessly off raised shields. How could they compete with skills learned on the field of battle, Hereward thought? The viciousness, the intensity, the cunning blows that ripped. The flick of an axe that split tendons at the back of the knee, or the ankle. A lost hand, as good as a killing blow. A rake across a poorly armoured belly, spilling guts.

As they took their time to die in the bog of their

own blood and filth, they could think on their over-confidence. They had dared to challenge true warriors and they had paid the price.

When he unseated another rider, he glimpsed Alexios once more through the forest of raised arms and weapons and scowling faces. The young Roman was still holding his own, but arrows were whistling around his head and it was only a matter of time.

If it were at all possible, the din grew louder still, with battle-cries soaring above it. The rest of Robert Guiscard's army was racing along the beach to join their unknown allies. Hereward cursed. They were outnumbered, soon to be surrounded. Hope was ebbing.

The cut-throats seemed to draw strength from this turn in the tide. Wheeling around, several of them somehow managed to act in unison. Swords and axes came down as one. Hereward glimpsed the danger – one blow in many could slip through defences.

'Shield wall,' he bellowed.

With one mind formed over long years of battle, the spear-brothers swept together. Shields locked in the blink of an eye. To the front. Overhead. Impenetrable. Blows slammed against wood. Horses' flanks crashed against them on every side, buffeting them like a ship in a storm. But they held firm.

And yet, crouched in the heat and the reek of sweat behind the shields, Hereward knew they had only bought themselves a little time.

'We forgot one thing.' Guthrinc eyed the gaps that opened and closed between the shields.

'The spears,' Derman said.

Hereward gritted his teeth. 'We do not need spears with these curs.' Driving himself upright above the shields, he rammed his axe up. His rapid movement startled the enemies who towered over him and they reeled back. But not fast enough. His blade ripped a face in two. Blood gushed down.

A moment after the Mercian ducked back, Guthrinc jerked his giant frame up and tore through another man.

'Keep moving,' Hereward growled.

The shield wall edged forward step by step. The cowardly dogs were keeping their distance as they turned their attention back to easier targets. Yet soon the spear-brothers slammed against an unyielding barrier and Hereward knew they could go no further.

Alexios and the surviving warriors of the Immortals' right flank were pressed tightly together. Robert Guiscard's men and the new force were crushed against them, picking them off one by one.

'They will be dead before we carve our way through there,' Kraki snarled.

'That is the least of our worries.' Derman pointed back along the shoreline. A sea of enemies stretched away. The Varangian Guard were just as embattled as Alexios' band.

'This is going to be a slaughter,' Hiroc the Three-fingered breathed.

And so the emperor will be left defenceless, Hereward thought as he finally understood the intentions of the one who had sent these cut-throats to kill them.

Hengist laughed and laughed, his insane joy spiralling up to the swooping gulls.

Like night falling, Hereward sensed his men becoming resigned to their fate. They had fought too many near-hopeless battles before not to recognize that this was worse than all of them.

'Wait,' Guthrinc said suddenly. Craning his neck, he squinted into the distance. His eyes were sharper than any man's there.

'What do you see?' The Mercian felt his chest swell when he saw his friend's spreading grin.

'Ready your arms,' Guthrinc said. Blood speckled his face and sweat dripped from his chin. 'We still have a fight on our hands. A tough one, aye, but a fight.'

The thunder of pounding hooves boomed against the clamour of battle. From where he hacked this way and that at their enemies, Hereward could not see what was approaching. A moment later, he was dazzled by reflected light shining off the Immortals' armour, as if the sun had come down from the heavens.

Tiberius was roaring, his face a mask of righteous fury, his sword thrust ahead of him to signal the charge. Though they had seemed to be retreating from the assault of the Norman archers, the Athanatoi's left flank now rammed a path through their enemies.

'We have one chance,' Hereward bellowed. 'Let us use it well.'

There were not enough Immortals surviving to turn the tide of the battle, any man could see that. But Tiberius' desperate attack had shattered the enemy ranks. Cowards to a man, they surged away from the fate bearing down on them. A corridor opened up to the heart of the fighting. But though Hereward craned his neck, he could not see Alexios anywhere.

A moment later he caught sight of the young warrior on foot, his back against the cliffs that edged that end of the bay. Three towering Normans faced him, waiting for their moment as Alexios swung his sword back and forth to keep them back. His helm was gone and blood streaked his face from a gash across his temple.

Whirling, Hereward seized the shoulders of one of the Varangians nearby. Shouting into the man's face, Hereward commanded, 'Take the rest of our men and flee to the horses. This battle is done. Our only chance is to retreat and save the necks of those who survive.'

'And what of you?' the other man shouted.

'I will bring Alexios. Go!'

As the warrior compelled his fellow guardsmen to storm from the fight, Hereward spun back. His spear-brothers were still clustered around him, their weapons levelled, ready to fight off any attack. They would never obey any order to abandon him, he knew that. Together, they bolted towards Alexios.

Like a pack of ravening wolves, the spear-brothers fell on the three Normans. The enemy died in an instant. Hereward caught Alexios as he staggered. Weak from blood loss, he seemed on the brink of collapse.

'You have my thanks,' the Roman gasped.

'We are not safe yet.'

Looking back, the Mercian saw that the corridor through the fighting had closed. The war-band had regrouped and turned their attention back to their quarry. Hungry grins leapt to the lips of the nearest when they saw that only a handful of defenders stood with Alexios.

The Normans too were crowding closer. Hereward and the spear-brothers, with Alexios in their midst, backed to the rocks.

The Mercian looked past the sea of enemies. Tiberius had lost sight of them. Hereward shouted out to him, but his voice was drowned by the cries of their foes, and then Tiberius turned his horse around and rejoined the Immortals, who were retreating to lick their wounds.

'Let us see how many we can take before we step into Valhalla.' Kraki gripped his axe with both hands.

'There is no way out?' Alexios gasped, his eyes rolling. 'I have cost you your lives . . .'

'We fight, as we always have,' Hereward interrupted. 'Today or tomorrow, a warrior always dies on the field of battle.'

'I would rather die tomorrow, if asked,' Hiroc grumbled.

'We could fly!' Mad Hengist threw his arms into the sky.

The cut-throats began to move forward.

Sighard followed Hengist's gaze. 'Hengist speaks true!'

A way up the rocks lay at their backs, steep and vertiginous but still accessible.

'We will be dead before we are all up there,' Hiroc gasped.

'Then climb fast,' Hereward barked.

As one, the spear-brothers sheathed their swords and threw their shields over their backs. Herrig the Rat bounded up the lowest rocks first, and waited to assist the others. Hands helped Hengist to follow, and together the two men hauled Alexios up to join them.

Their enemies roared their fury when they saw what the spear-brothers were doing. Raising their axes, Hereward, Kraki and Guthrinc prepared to fight them off as the others swarmed up what at first had seemed like a sheer wall, clinging on to handholds to reach the ledge above, where clumps of yellowing grass revealed an easier route.

Once the last of them had been hauled up, Kraki and Guthrinc argued about who should go next, until Guthrinc relented.

Three enemies raced their horses forward, trying to pin the remaining two Varangians against the rocks. Hereward lashed out with his axe. The blade raked across the flank of the first horse and the leg of its rider. The beast reared up, its scream merging with the howls of its master. It crashed into the other two mounts, unseating its rider, who plunged to the ground.

Kraki hacked down, then spat on the body. That was enough to make the others more cautious, and they hung back to wait for their companions, now galloping to join them.

'I am harder to kill than you,' the Viking grunted. 'You go next.'

'If you try to stay I will kill you myself.'

After a moment, the Mercian heard Kraki turn and scramble to safety.

Furious that they might be losing their prey, the nearest cut-throats leapt from their horses. Hereward watched them rush towards him. If he turned to climb, they would plant their weapons in his back. His moment had passed. He felt no fear, only an abiding calm.

But then an arrow whined through the air and thumped into the chest of the closest attacker. A gift from Guthrinc, Hereward knew. As the man fell, stones large and small rained down on the advancing band. Skulls cracked, blood gouted.

Hereward seized his moment, and began to claw his way up the rock face.

Running feet pounded behind him, and he twisted aside just in time. An axe clanged against the rock where he had hung, showering sparks.

Wrenching round, the Mercian glimpsed the man about to swing his weapon again. With a snarl, he slammed one boot into his opponent's face. As the man reeled back, Hereward pulled himself up out of reach.

A few arrows rattled against the rocks on either side, but they were half-hearted efforts. He clambered on, the encouragements of his spear-brothers ringing in his ears, until he felt Guthrinc's huge hands haul him up on to the grassy ledge. The others squatted around on their haunches, their eyes on him, waiting for his command. Alexios sat against the rock, his skin like snow, but his eyes gleamed a little brighter.

'You are well enough to go on?'

Alexios nodded.

Turning, Hereward looked down on the carnage. Bodies littered the shoreline. Red streams ran down the beach to turn the surf pink. The remnants of the battered, bloody Norman army trudged back to their camp where a lone figure stood looking up at the cliffs. Robert Guiscard, it must be, Hereward thought. Though the figure was distant, the Mercian could see the tall, slender man whisk his sword in the direction of the spear-brothers. A salute or a warning?

As he turned away from the battlefield, axes and swords punched the air and cheers rang out. His men had every right to celebrate. Though their ranks had been torn apart, they had won this day.

Hereward spat a mouthful of blood. Another victory stolen from them by treachery. He watched the last of the Roman army gallop away up the slopes of the bay.

'We lost half our number.' He could hear the bitterness in his voice.

Sighard crawled on his belly and peered over the lip to the swarming army of cut-throats below. About a hundred of the mysterious enemies still survived. 'Who are they?' he asked.

Hereward watched some of the rogues begin to

climb the rocks. At that moment, a group of the war-band broke away and rode hard back across the salt wastes towards the slopes leading down to the bay. 'They are going to ride us down.'

Weary, Hiroc bowed his head. 'How can we escape them? We have no horses. We are far from Constantinople. And if the Norman bastards come looking for us too . . .'

Hooking a hand under the other man's arm, the Mercian dragged him to his feet. 'We have not fought so hard and lost so many brothers to give up now.' He looked around at his men. They were drained, bedraggled, and nursing wounds, but one by one they stood up and nodded their assent.

'What, then?' Hiroc asked. 'Those dogs will be here in no time.'

'We run,' Hereward told him. 'Run!'

213

CHAPTER TWENTY-TWO

'This is no place for the pride of the Nepotes.'

On the table, the flame on the candle stub guttered. Dancing shadows twisted the Blood Eagle's features into the face of a monster.

Leo pushed himself up from the puddle of wine and squinted at the man who towered over him. 'Leave me be,' he snarled. His words were those of a petulant child but the wine slurred them.

'You are fortunate to have good friends.'

Ariadne felt Varin's eyes settle upon her and she shuddered. She had reached deep inside herself to find the strength to bring the cold-faced warrior here, not knowing if he would kill her the moment he laid eyes on her. But Leo could not be left alone in this den of thieves and murderers, where figures hovered in the shadows beyond the candlelight, eyes glinting like knives, hands never far from hidden weapons. It would only have been a matter of time before they decided to rob him, or worse, she thought, kneading her hands.

And there was one here more dangerous by far than

all these cut-throats. Ariadne searched the gloom, but though she saw no one she could sense that wolf circling just out of sight, waiting for his moment to pounce.

The tavern was notorious, one of the worst in all Constantinople, so whispers said. Nestled against the Kontoskalion Gate a stone's throw from the harbour, it was a place where sailors passed the hours between voyages, drunk, or gambling, or fighting. When she had crept in, Ariadne had heard many strange tongues, from traders from North Afrique and Syria; some Rus too. Thieves hunched on stools in the dark at the back of the low-ceilinged room, plotting which merchant would next lose his purse in the crowded marketplace. And murderers hid there, she had been warned, escaping justice, with their blades still as sharp, their blood still as cold.

'Come, we will get you back to your bed. A few hours' sleep will prepare you for all the morrow's cursing of this night, when your head is filled with pebbles and your mouth as dry as Afrique's sands.' Varin laid a hand on his charge's shoulder, but Leo threw it off.

'I said leave me be,' the youth snapped. 'I am one of the Nepotes. I do not answer to the likes of you.' He wiped his mouth with the back of his hand and eyed Ariadne. 'And you . . . I cannot trust you either, it seems.'

'I would never see you come to harm—'

'How did you find me? Do you follow me night and day?'

'Friends watch over those who cannot look after themselves,' Varin growled, answering for her.

Ariadne stepped forward. 'Why do you come here? Why leave your home and the ones who love you—'

Leo barked a bitter, drunken laugh.

'Do you wish to die?' the girl pressed. 'You know there are many in this city who would see the Nepotes dead. Aye, and two who want it more than any others, who would see all their rivals for power with their throats slit.' She felt a force stir within her, either in her heart or in her head, and when she next spoke she heard the voice of the only woman she had known in her short life who had not been beaten down. 'Two, aye, and God has cursed me to share the same blood,' al-Kahina/Ariadne said.

'Enough talk. She speaks true – it is not safe here.' Varin hooked his arm under the protesting youth's shoulders and dragged him to his feet.

Struggling, Leo kicked over the table. His goblet and the dregs of his wine splashed across the puddled flagstones. 'Leave me!' he bellowed.

Barely had the words left his lips when a lithe figure darted from the shadows. At first, Ariadne thought it was the one she feared more than all others, but it was only a rogue, his clothes and face filthy with the dirt of the road. Candlelight glinted off a blade, a short, curved knife like the ones the dark-skinned sailors from Afrique carried at their waists.

Ariadne cried out. Varin was encumbered by his drunken charge and she was too far away to intervene. But the Blood Eagle only grunted. As the attacker stabbed his blade towards Leo's chest, the Viking flicked the fallen table up with the tip of his boot. The wood cracked the shins of the attacker and he howled, stumbling over the obstacle.

Varin tossed Leo to one side. The youth crashed on to the wine-soaked floor in an unceremonious heap. The axe swept up faster than Ariadne had ever seen a blade move, and then thundered down, splitting the rogue's head in two.

Ariadne felt acid rush into her mouth. Her kin revelled in brutality and she had seen many a death in her few short years. This one had been administered with such cold efficiency she felt stunned. Varin yanked out his axe and turned towards the darkened tavern as if he had just brought down a tree for kindling.

A rumble of shock had erupted when the axe came down. Now only a blanket of silence suffocated the chamber.

'My axe is ready for all of you,' the Blood Eagle announced in a calm, measured tone.

For a moment, Varin, Ariadne and Leo could have been alone in all the world. Not a breath rustled out. Then a figure hovered on the edge of the circle of illumination, weighing what lay before it. When the man took one more step forward, the light wavered across his face. The features seemed as frozen as a wintry lake, with two black-coal eyes staring from the depths.

Ariadne stiffened. He never could resist the smell of blood.

217

Justin Verinus surveyed the drunken man in front of him. 'This is the pride of the Nepotes?'

The girl who hid in the dark behind al-Kahina shivered. As she roamed the city each day, she could not help but hear the whispers of this being's true nature, rippling out from the brothels and inns. *Not man, but beast*, they repeated over again. *Not man, but devil.* Knowing him as she did, she could not fault those words.

'Stay back, brother,' she commanded. 'This is not your business.'

Justin cocked his head, puzzled by her strange cadence. 'But it is my business,' he replied in a whispery voice. 'All of Constantinople . . . all of the empire . . . is my business, or will be soon enough.'

Waving his axe towards the bloody remains, Varin demanded, 'Your man?'

'I have never laid eyes upon him before this moment.' Justin stared, unblinking, as ever unreadable.

Leo scrambled to his feet, swaying drunkenly. 'He lies!' The youth jabbed a finger at his rival. 'Every attempt upon my life has been at his behest.' He fumbled on the floor for his goblet. When he came up, Varin plucked the vessel from his hand and tossed it away. Leo glared at him, but then he sneered as he turned back to Justin. 'He fears me. He knows that the crown will be mine, not his—'

'Still your tongue.' Varin's words cracked like a lash.

Ariadne recoiled. It was too late. Leo had already admitted to treason in a tavern filled with witnesses

218

who would no doubt kill each other to claim the emperor's gold for reporting this plot.

The Blood Eagle must have known this too, for he turned back to the shadows and announced, 'If one man here stirs my wrath, I will return. I will find you. And when I am done, there will not be enough of you left to choke a dog.' Nodding to Ariadne, he said in a quiet voice, 'The hour is late. We must be gone.'

Leo began to protest, but the words were half-hearted. His hunted expression showed that he knew what he had done.

Once they were at the door, Ariadne turned back. Justin still stood in the wavering candlelight, staring at them. Drawing her knife, she pointed it at him. 'I saved your neck once, brother, and once is enough to set you on a new road. You did not choose to walk it. Know I am al-Kahina, slayer of devils, and blood or not, if you harm a hair on this man's head I will cut out your heart myself.'

In the warm night, Ariadne realized her hand was shaking. Al-Kahina was no longer with her.

'You have a warrior's heart,' Varin grunted to her. He shook Leo as if he were filled with rags. 'And you are a jolt-head for not seeing the ruby in all that filth under your nose.'

For a while, the streets sped by until they were sure Justin or any of his cut-throats were not following them. Leo had grown more sober with each step, and when they paused to catch their breath he said to the Blood Eagle, 'If I were emperor, I would make you the commander of the Guard.'

Varin grunted. 'You have much to learn. I will not always be by your side to keep you safe.'

'Then teach me,' Leo gushed. 'Teach me, like my brother . . . like Maximos . . .' The name seemed to stick in his throat. Tears welled in his eyes, and then terrible sobs racked his body and he slid down the wall to sit with his head in his hands.

Ariadne felt her heart ache with pity. She dropped beside him, resting one hand on his shoulder. 'What is wrong? You are alive—'

'I killed Maximos!' Leo blurted, his eyes raw. 'With the sword he gave me. I stabbed him.'

Ariadne felt ice-water rush through her. She could see from his drawn face that he was not lying. 'Why?' she murmured. 'He loved you.'

At that, Leo began to sob again. When he had drained every tear, he said, 'Maximos was turning his back upon the Nepotes . . . his own blood. He was done with us . . . with all our plans, for the throne, for everything.'

'Kalamdios and Simonis . . . and Juliana . . . they told you to do it?'

'Maximos' leaving was a betrayal, and the Nepotes will not be betrayed.' His voice hardened and Ariadne sensed he was repeating something that had been told to him so many times that it had become almost a part of him. She felt a deep dread of what was to come for him, for both of them.

Leaning down, Varin snatched a handful of the youth's tunic and dragged him to his feet. He shook him once, hard, cracking his head against the stone. Leo cried out and scowled at the Viking.

'Heed my words,' the Blood Eagle rumbled, lowering his huge head so he could peer into Leo's eyes, their noses barely a hand's width apart. 'Every man walks a hard road. Sometimes it leads into shadow. Sometimes it leads to hell. But the gods would not damn a man without giving him a fighting chance. Walk that road and you will come to a place where roads cross. You will have a choice. Take that other road, even if it is strewn with rocks and leads to shadow.'

'It is too late!'

Varin shook his head. 'Not for you, little brother. Not yet. There is still time. Soon you will come to the crossroads. Turn away. Turn away. For if you choose to stride on you will be lost for ever.' His voice held a surprising gentleness. Letting go of the tunic, he rested his hand on Leo's shoulder. In that moment, Ariadne thought she could see deep into the Blood Eagle's own hidden life, and she was sure this lesson had been played out once before. Only that time, Varin had been the one hearing the advice. And he had not heeded it.

Leo hung his head.

Varin stepped away and led Ariadne to one side. For the first time, she thought she glimpsed something in his face beyond the frozen wastes of his home.

'You cannot save him,' he said quietly, but firmly. 'He can only save himself.'

'I cannot stand by,' she breathed. She felt her eyes burn.

Varin stared at her for a long moment, and she

squirmed under the intensity of that gaze. Yet his voice was gentle, and seemed filled with care for her. 'I would not see you dragged along that same road to hell. Take care, little one. Take care.'

CHAPTER TWENTY-THREE

The rain lashed down. In the clearings beyond the trees, there was only a wall of water, misty and impenetrable. The forest rumbled with the deafening sound of the deluge, so loud, so relentless, it seemed there had never been silence.

Even the canopy of branches and leaves offered little protection as the English warriors trudged on with their heads bowed into the gusting torrent, unable to see more than a few spear-lengths ahead. Tunics were sodden, boots too, hair flat and dripping. No square of skin was dry, and the nine warriors could not remember a time when it ever had been. The air reeked of damp and mud and rot, the colours leaching away to misty grey and mud-brown.

'Keep moving,' Hereward exhorted. They were weary, he knew, and they had endured taking it in turns to carry the wounded Alexios.

Wiping the water from his eyes, he squinted ahead and cursed under his breath. Their enemies would be upon them before they saw or heard anything. But they could not afford to find shelter, even though every man was fighting the chill that was eating its way into his bones.

If they wanted to live, they had to keep moving.

At first, everything had seemed well. Once they had left the clifftops overlooking Robert Guiscard's camp, they had raced through tracks made by deer in the dense undergrowth. The Normans had let them be, returning to lick their wounds. Though they had not driven the bastards back into the sea as they had hoped, Hereward thought they might have done enough to stop the Duke of Apulia from making a rash move against Constantinople. That would buy more time to build the army.

But that war-band, it was a starving dog on the trail of a rabbit. Once the riders had found their way up the slopes and along the clifftops, the forests had rung with the whoops and howls of their hunting. Now no one could be in any doubt that they wanted the head of Alexios, and perhaps Hereward himself.

If only they could have looped round to find the Immortals and the rest of the Varangian Guard. Tiberius would not ride away until he was sure that there had been no survivors. But now even that thin hope had faded.

Through the night they had scrambled, into increasingly wild country, hoping the horses would not be able to follow. But at some point the rogues must have abandoned their mounts, for the hunting calls never diminished.

At dawn, the rains had come.

Hereward glanced round at his men. Weariness had

carved lines into their faces. Yet not one of them complained, not even Hiroc, who found something to grumble about in even the greatest victory. The Mercian was proud of them for that. But could they last longer than their pursuers before exhaustion claimed them? That was the question that haunted him.

A hand caught his arm. It was Kraki, the Viking's beard and hair and furs so bedraggled he looked as if he had taken a dunk in the lake. He nodded towards Derman, who was limping badly, his face a mask of pain.

'Turned his ankle on a root as we ran through the dark,' Kraki said, his voice low. 'He cannot walk much further. We must carry him too.'

'And slow us down more?' Hereward looked back at Alexios. The Roman had recovered somewhat from his exhaustion, but he was still weak. Sighard and Hengist were helping him along. 'It is time. We must make a stand.'

'We cannot fight them. They have the numbers.'

'If not now, then in a day, when we are weaker still? No, we fight.'

Hereward turned and commanded his men to stop. They collapsed against tree-trunks, throwing back their streaming faces and sucking in soothing breaths.

Looking round, the Mercian saw this place was as good as any. True, the drumming of the rain would mask the arrival of the ones hunting them. But they were near the top of high ground where the trees were at their thickest. Riven with rushing streams, the slopes ran away into the haze of the downpour, the ground churning into a sea of mud.

'Do not rest yet,' he said. 'We have hard work ahead of us.'

For long hours, the spear-brothers laboured. When they were done, they slumped around the broad trunk of a spreading oak, filthy from head to toe. White eyes peered through the masks of mud, looking to Hereward for his command. The Mercian allowed them only a short time to rest, and then he whisked his hand to right and left and the warriors melted into the trees. This was how it had been in the fenlands of England. A fortress of wood and water that had given them an advantage over the invading army.

Hereward ghosted from tree to tree down the slope. The rain swallowed him. Amid the thunderous pounding of the torrent, he crouched behind a juniper. The fire in his chest burned hotter. His head roared with the rush of blood. Anger came fast. More treachery threatening to steal away what little he had gained for his loyal spear-brothers. He would not, could not, see them suffer more than they already had.

Sliding Brainbiter out of its sheath, he waited.

Soon after, they came. Shadows appearing in the sheets of rain, like graveyard revenants. One here, one there, others trailing behind. The dark smudges took shape, forming into men. Axes in hand, heads bent, listening. Each step was measured, cautious, and they kept their silence. They knew their enemies were near.

Hereward flitted through the trees from his cover, keeping low. He followed a route that would not easily catch the eye of any of the approaching war-band. Creeping in from the left flank, he crouched in the tangled roots of an old oak and watched one of the outliers straggle nearer. Tall and skeletal and wrapped in a sodden cloak, the man slipped in the mud with every other step, keeping one eye on his feet as he danced around the fast-running rivulets of rainwater.

He did not see the Mercian coming.

Slipping out from his hiding place, Hereward gripped his sword with both hands and rammed it into the enemy's side. The din of the downpour drowned out the man's cry. The Mercian had bounded away before his slain foe had pitched face forward into the mud.

The war-band trudged past him, oblivious of his presence. There were eighty of them, he guessed, too many for the spear-brothers to defeat in open battle. Yet even in the face of that revelation, he felt calm. The whispers of his devil drove out all doubts.

A pool had appeared in a hollow running along the slope, deepening by the moment. Hereward eased into the icy water, feeling nothing. Lowering himself until his eyes were just above the surface, he peered through the sheet of rain that had turned the pool into a boiling cauldron. When he was sure all his enemies were ahead of him, he waded on.

Behind one of the stragglers, he clawed his way out on to the muddy slope and rose up. If his quarry had peered back, he would have been confronted by a terrible sight. A face streaked with mud, eyes cold and unfeeling, teeth bared, more a beast than a man.

Hereward thrust his sword through the rogue's back with such force that the victim's feet lifted off the ground. Clamping his hand over the dying man's mouth, the Mercian dragged him back and eased him into the swelling pool. Face down, the body drifted away, trailing a splash of colour in that grey and brown world.

Blinking away the streaming rainwater, Hereward moved silently up the slope. Brainbiter drank one life, then another, and another. No one heard, no one looked back, and with each death his devil cried louder, for more, more, to appease the hunger that could never be assuaged. But he knew it was only a matter of time before he was discovered and he was ready for it when it came.

A body fell. A head snapped round to flick water from eyes. A cry rose up, leaping from mouth to mouth.

Hereward did not wait. He had done as much as he could. Now all their lives were in the hands of fate.

His feet slipping in the sea of mud, the Mercian scrambled deep into the trees. The war-band was racing wildly after him. Legs skidded out from under them. Bodies careered down the slope. The cursing rang out so loud that Hereward could hear it even above the pounding of the rain.

He grinned, pleased that he had caused such confusion. In a fight like this, warriors needed to keep their lines, shoulder to shoulder. Running like a rabbit would only lead to an early death.

Weaving among the trees, Hereward led the war-band on a madman's dance. All eyes would be on him. They had forgotten he was not alone here.

An arrow whistled past his head. Looking round, he saw it had thumped into the chest of a rogue closing on his back. Guthrinc's eye never failed.

Two more shafts lashed out, two more fell. The bowman's quiver would soon be empty, but he had used his arrows well.

With a great leap, Hereward cleared a mat of branches and leaves and darted a little further up the slope before turning to face his enemies. He watched them come, his features cold.

As the war-band drew out of the mist of rain, they came to a halt. Grins sparked on their faces. They could see they were many and here was only one rabbit, and a weary one at that.

The Mercian laid the blade of Brainbiter across his left palm and tapped it a couple of times, showing he was ready for what was to come. A few frowns crumpled brows. In the face of their overwhelming force, they had expected terror, not this calm.

'Who is your master?' Hereward called.

'Little good that knowledge will do you, dog,' one of the men shouted back. 'Your days are done.'

Hereward grinned like a wolf. 'Come, then. I will take a few of you with me to hell.'

Laughter rang out, but the Mercian was pleased to hear that some of it was laced with unease. He showed his back to them and walked up the hill.

The laughter turned incredulous, and then the

command echoed and the force moved as one. Hereward broke into a run, making sure not to show the changing nature of his grin. Only when the screams tore through the thunderous rainfall did he stop and turn.

Along the line of the advancing war-band, the dying now cried out for salvation. Bloodstained hands reached up to the heavens. The survivors reeled back in horror.

The shallow pits his men had dug along the hillside and then disguised with branches and leaves had done their work well. Each one was now filled with men impaled on the stakes hidden beneath. If time had been on the spear-brothers' side, the pits would have been deeper, the spikes smeared with shit so that even a scratch would bring death, as he had learned in his wandering in Flanders. But this would suffice.

Twenty more at least were now out of the fight. Hereward nodded, pleased. As howls of anger rose up, he shook his sword in mockery and ran on. The war-band thundered after him.

Further up the slope, the spear-brothers waited for him. Axes at the ready, they stood in a line, ready to fight and perhaps to die, though no one would have guessed it from their grins. Only their cold eyes showed how grim their position was. Yet even Alexios and Derman had found the strength to stand with them.

Pushing his way into the heart of the line, Hereward roared, 'We are at the gates of hell, brothers. Let us drag our enemies through with us.'

As the war-band rushed out of the gusting rain, he

felt a shadow flash across him. His raven was here, he was sure. If this was the moment his premonitions had been warning him of, he was ready.

Wave upon wave of rogues crashed upon the rocks of the English defence. The axes slashed down, splitting heads, carving open shoulders and necks and chests. With gritted teeth, the spear-brothers battled through a mist of blood that turned them red from head to toe.

As he kicked another wounded man down the hill, Hereward wondered what was driving these cut-throats to fight on with such fury – lust for gold or fear of what fate awaited them if they failed? But their strategy was clear, as it had been by the shore. Overwhelm by force of numbers.

And though the English had the advantage of height and weapons and armour, the Mercian could see that sooner or later that plan would work. He sensed his brothers flagging. Their arms were growing heavy, their strikes weaker. With each blow, it took them a moment longer to wrench their axes out of flesh. And soon that moment would be long enough for one of their enemies to thrust a sword past their defences.

'Go.' Hereward squinted through the blood dripping into his eye-sockets. 'I will hold them off here.'

'And run through that mud up the hill?' Guthrinc retorted. 'No. My thanks, but I would rather stand here.'

'Less talk,' Kraki roared. 'You are buzzing in my ear like a fly!'

When Derman stumbled back with a gash across

his arm, Hereward felt sure their time had come. But then he heard a drumbeat, distant at first then growing louder, louder even than the rain.

The war-band heard it too. The attack slowed. Brows furrowed in hesitation.

The drumbeat grew louder still, and then through the wall of rain rode armed men, a host of them coming from all directions between the trees.

'The Immortals,' Hiroc exclaimed. 'Those bastards did not leave us to die alone after all.'

The Athanatoi fell upon the cut-throats, who scattered wildly. But fighting or running, they were no match for armoured knights on horseback. What the hooves did not claim, the swords did. And when the Varangian Guard swept through the forest, no one remained to sate their axes.

One of the riders guided his horse up the hill to where the spear-brothers waited. 'We have searched high and low for you,' Tiberius Grabas called through the pounding of the rain.

'You did not need to rush,' Kraki shouted back. 'We were almost done here.'

The spear-brothers laughed, which only made Tiberius scowl more. He had never learned to understand this strange humour.

'Ah, they only wanted Alexios,' Hiroc grumbled. 'The rest of us . . . we were just lucky.'

Hereward tipped his face back to let the rain wash the blood away. But then a thought came to him and he set off down the slope, with the querying calls of his men ringing at his back.

At the stake pits, he came to a halt and walked along the line. Most of the men were already dead, their blood drained into a slurry at the bottom, but one still clung on to life.

Hereward crouched at the edge of the pit and peered down at him. 'There is no saving you,' he said as the man croaked a plea. 'Your wounds are too great.' He heard the spear-brothers run up behind him, but he kept his eyes on the dying man. 'Loosen your tongue and I will spare you these agonies. Send you to heaven in peace.'

'Anything,' the last of the war-band gasped, his head sagging.

'Who commanded you to attack us?'

For a long moment, there was only silence. Hereward feared the man had died. But then he said, 'A man with a face that no woman would ever look upon. Nose gone. Scars . . . lips . . .'

'Ragener,' Sighard exclaimed.

'That bastard,' Kraki snarled. 'Then Karas Verinus is behind this. That dog only does his bidding.'

Hereward stood up, feeling his resolve harden. Karas had made the decision to see them all doomed. Looking down at the wounded man, he said, 'Give up your sins. You will have a good death.'

CHAPTER TWENTY-FOUR

The scream rang out through the forest.

From the shelter of a vast, overhanging rock, two riders peered down to where the war-band had marched into the dense forest, convinced their prey was close at hand.

'What is the meaning of that?' one of them asked.

'It means we have lost,' the other replied from the depths of his hood. He searched the tree-line, praying that he would see his allies swarm out, holding Hereward's bloody head high and dragging Alexios' corpse behind them.

Ragener felt despair crush his heart. All the fears that had burdened him on the long ride from Constantinople had been realized. He had hoped that once this business was finished, Karas Verinus could no longer doubt his loyalty or his worth. Now his only hope was that he could keep his head on his shoulders.

Francio grunted as if he had expected no less. He was the general of that rag-swathed war-band and looked no more the part than any of his men. His leather breastplate was cracked and worn and seemed to have been stolen from a man twice his size. His breeches were filthy with mud, as were his face and hands, and his hair hung in greasy ringlets. He stank as if he had shit himself. True, the sword at his side had gold embedded in its hilt, also stolen no doubt, but the blade was badly notched and looked as though it would shatter in any battle.

Ragener clenched the fingers of his good hand, trying to push aside his contempt for this man and all who served under him. It was their fault he had failed. Their weakness that had betrayed him.

When he had first entered the secluded valley where they had made their camp, Ragener had thought he had found a band of thieves who would slit his throat and leave him for dead. But no, this was the army Karas Verinus had been building ready for the day when he would make his move on the throne.

Karas was clever. He knew he could not bring his own well-trained warriors from his estate in the east. Nikephoros was suspicious of anyone who showed their power in Constantinople. Nor could he pay gold for axes-for-hire when the empire's own army was buying every roaming fighting man that could be found.

But these curs . . . he could not call them warriors . . . Ragener simmered as he recalled how they had mocked him for his shortcomings. Half-a-man, they called him. If they had not been so many, he would have slit all *their* throats in their sleep. But once he had told them what Karas required, they had ridden west immediately, choosing the wilderness rather than the great road, skirting any villages where there might be prying eyes, and finding a narrow, dangerous pass in the highland that only Francio seemed to know.

And then they had made camp near the western shore, close to Robert Guiscard's force but still hidden, waiting for the Immortals and the Varangian Guard to arrive, as Karas had said they would. The general had held back the messenger's news of the Norman army from the emperor's council just long enough to give Ragener a head start.

'We must be away,' the sea wolf growled, though his ragged lips took the edge off his words. 'First, to our camp. The wounded must be put to the axe. There must be no sign here that leads back to Karas Verinus.'

'As we agreed.' Francio hesitated. He nodded towards the forest. 'But what of the wounded in there?'

'If I know that dog Hereward, there will be none of your men left alive.'

'The emperor would have Karas' head if he knew such a slaughter had been wrought upon some of his greatest warriors when the empire is staring into the face of doom.'

Ragener's eyes darted towards the other man. 'Do not think you can claw more gold with threats. Still your tongue. You know what Karas will do if you betray him.'

Francio fell silent.

Ragener watched the forest, still hoping. He

understood his master's plan. It mattered little if all these rogues were slaughtered. Karas could find two more to replace every one that fell. When the time came and the truth of his plot was revealed, he would need but numbers, not men skilled in battle.

Only one thing made this business bearable. Hereward might have won a small victory here, but he would reap the whirlwind. Karas Verinus would only be driven to greater fury.

With a loud curse, Ragener dug his heels in his horse's flank and rode off to slaughter.

CHAPTER TWENTY-FIVE

The dawn sun turned the plain into a ruddy sea. A cloud billowed on the Via Egnatia, which carved through that wide, flat land to the purple hills, misty on the horizon. One by one, the guards above the Golden Gate turned and watched it roll towards the city. The sound of drumming hooves rose up, and after a moment the wind drew back the bank of dust to reveal a column of riders. Helms and axes glinted.

Eyes narrowing, the guards gripped the edges of Constantinople's western wall and peered through the thin light. Though this war-band was not large and their pace was slow, fear of the Norman invasion had driven deep into their hearts. They would take no chances.

But as the column neared, they glimpsed familiar crimson cloaks flapping in the breeze, the colour dulled by the mud of the road. At the front of the column of shimmering knights the great standard of the empire fluttered. Word leapt from lips to lips and then swept deep into the waking city. The heroes of the empire had survived.

When the warriors passed through the gates and into the shadow of the houses clustered near the walls, the guards looked down on heads bowed with weariness, blood-spattered tunics, and filthy makeshift bandages tied round raw wounds. Some clutched the necks of their mounts. Others looked as if they would slip to the ground at any moment. Many were being supported by their brothers.

Bedraggled, beaten, the Varangian Guard was home.

The Athanatoi too were fewer in number than when they had ridden west, their armour dented from the blows of numerous weapons.

If this was victory, it looked very much like defeat.

Hereward rode in at the head of the Varangian Guard, his spear-brothers close behind him. When he looked up, he saw the rising worry in the faces of the men on the walls, and he knew this sickness would sweep across a city already cowed by fears that its days were numbered. The fires would be fanned and would quite possibly burn Constantinople to the ground.

Thrusting one fist into the air, he bellowed, 'Victory!'

His men caught up the proclamation. Their full-throated bellow reached up to the top of the walls, and the Immortals too managed to raise a rolling cheer. Hereward was pleased when he saw relief fill those watching faces. There would be time enough later for talk of what went wrong.

He jumped down from his horse and waited for

Alexios to limp up to him. On the long ride home, the Roman's wound had mostly healed, but he still looked too pale.

'We cannot waste a moment,' Hereward whispered. 'You must tell the emperor of Karas Verinus' treachery.'

'It is our word against his.'

'Aye, but I would wager that dog Ragener would loosen his tongue if he thought another part of him was about to be lost.'

Alexios raised his head, his defiance growing. 'You are right. This is our chance to bring that bastard to his knees. He has gone too far, sending Romans to slaughter in service to his own lust for power. He must pay.'

While the boys assisting the wall-guards scrambled to lead the horses to water, the Varangians and the Immortals bellowed for meat and wine. Hereward and Alexios climbed back on to their mounts and, leaving the others behind, rode along the Mese into the city.

As they passed through the forum of the Ox, already starting to buzz with citizens, Hereward furrowed his brow. He saw eyes dart towards them, narrow and suspicious. In the forum of Constantine, he caught sight of small groups of armed men, their faces hard and scarred, their clothes shabby. He sensed their eyes following him and Alexios as they rode by.

'Something is amiss,' he murmured.

'There is a strange mood in the city,' Alexios agreed,

frowning. 'Are they so scared their spirits have been broken? Where are the cheers for the returning heroes? They must know who we are.'

As they approached the Milion, with the dome of Hagia Sophia looming behind it, the money-changers in Argyroprateia kept their heads down. More knots of armed men waited in the shadow of the hippodrome.

'You have seen them before?' Hereward asked quietly, nodding to one of the groups.

Alexios shook his head.

When the two men hurried into the sun-drenched hall of the Great Palace, Hereward found it alive with the emperor's advisers and other officials, readying themselves for the day's business. He saw heads swivel towards the new arrivals, but no greetings were uttered. On the far side, Falkon Cephalas walked with another man, his hands clasped behind his back as he listened intently. He, at least, nodded to them.

'So. You yet live.'

Hereward turned to see Wulfrun walking towards him. The Guard commander's face was unreadable, as always. Juliana Nepa walked beside him, her golden hair bright in the shafts of sunlight. She smiled at Hereward and Alexios.

The Mercian stiffened. She was cunning, that one. Who there could ever think badly of her? 'It takes more than an army of Normans to kill us,' he replied.

'We thought the worst.' Wulfrun looked from Hereward to Alexios and back. He seemed untroubled by the notion. 'Word was sent that you were cornered, with no hope of escape.'

'Word from one of Karas Verinus' men, no doubt.' Wulfrun nodded.

'He spoke too soon.'

'Though who could fault him?' Alexios added. 'Karas was certain of the outcome long before the battle was joined.'

Wulfrun narrowed his eyes, questioning, but it was Juliana who stepped forward. 'You say the general has been plotting?'

'In that, he is a match for the Nepotes,' Hereward said.

'Hold your tongue,' Wulfrun snapped. His eyes were filled with a cold warning.

When Juliana glanced past them, her face hardening, Hereward turned to see Karas Verinus striding down the steps, no doubt from the chamber where he had been advising on the matter of war on two fronts and the enemies waiting beyond the walls.

'His lies will soon be done,' Alexios said in a low voice.

Karas marched across the hall, his back straight, his head high. Yet he could not resist a look towards the two new arrivals, the mud and the blood making them stand out among the finely dressed advisers. The general tried to keep his face calm, Hereward could see. But he could not prevent a flash when his eyes fell upon them. The Mercian felt as if he had looked into a furnace. Karas seethed with anger that Alexios and his English enemies had not been destroyed. But more than that, Hereward glimpsed a hint of a greater threat to come.

'We should wait no longer,' he murmured to Alexios. The Roman commander nodded and led the way south through the palace complex to the Chrysotriklinos.

When they pushed their way into the octagonal throne room, they found it swarming with members of the court. Hereward could see from their faces that they had already received news of the war-band that had arrived at the Golden Gate, but they were unsure who yet lived and who had been lost.

Their faces racked with worry, their hands clenched, Anna and Maria waited by one of the sixteen windows. Hereward watched the relief flood them when they saw the new arrivals. Anna threw her arms around her son and embraced him. Maria surely wished to do the same, but wisdom prevailed. The emperor's wife only smiled. 'I am pleased that you are well, my son.'

The Mercian looked to the throne, where Nikephoros appeared a wizened husk of a man, but his implacable gaze lay heavy on them. If he felt jealousy, he hid it well, yet there was no warmth there.

'Take care.' Anna leaned in and whispered so that no one could overhear. 'In the two weeks you were gone, Constantinople has changed.'

Before she could say more, the emperor said, 'Step forward. Let me lay eyes upon these heroes.'

Hereward frowned. Nikephoros had formed the last word as if he had a mouthful of pebbles.

'Word reached us that you were dead,' the emperor said, when they approached.

'Many tried to make that true,' Alexios replied with a bow. Hereward heard the deference his young ally had put into his voice. 'But we stood firm. Though we lost many good men, we split the Norman army and drove what was left into the sea. Robert Guiscard will not be attacking Constantinople soon.'

Nikephoros seemed pleased. 'He knows our power, then.'

'He knows it well.'

A ripple of relief ran among the gathered aristocrats.

'That is good news,' the emperor continued. 'But the word that reached us said you were surrounded. You were about to be crushed. How did you survive? Did God aid you?'

Choosing his words, Alexios replied, 'Aye, God has smiled upon us. But we bring grim news. A trap was set for us, a trap made here in Constantinople.' He let his voice rise above the sudden worried whispers that rustled through the court.

'A trap, you say.'

'Another war-band attacked us from behind while we fought the Normans. Many men fell to their axes. We were lucky to escape with our lives.'

Nikephoros leaned forward in his throne. 'And you accuse a Roman of this treachery?'

'The treachery is theirs!'

Hereward spun round. Ragener was pushing his way through the crowd, throwing off his hood. In his

244

scarred face, his milky eye all but glowed, and he was wheezing through the holes where his nose had been. The men and women nearby reeled back from the sight of him.

Alexios bristled, reaching for his sword. 'You. Faithless dog.'

As the young Roman began to draw his weapon, Hereward grabbed his arm and held him back. Leaning in, the Mercian whispered, 'Do nothing that will make them think any worse of us.'

With reluctance, Alexios let his blade slip back into its sheath. Glowering at the sea wolf from under heavy brows, he relaxed his shoulders and stepped back.

'Let him speak,' the emperor ordered.

Hereward was puzzled. A cur like Ragener to be allowed to command the floor in the throne room?

Ragener seemed to find new courage in the emperor's approval. Looking around the chamber to gauge his audience, he thrust another man forward. 'They lie. Here is one of our scouts, just returned from the west. Whatever they might say, he knows the truth of how these necks were saved.'

Hereward snorted in disgust. Now he understood. Karas Verinus had acted faster than he had expected. The general would not tolerate word getting out of his involvement in this traitorous attack. Nor could he allow his enemies time to lick their wounds now that he had revealed how far he was prepared to go to destroy all who stood in his way.

'We have heard from our own good men that these warriors were surrounded by greater numbers. Only death awaited them. And yet here they are,' Ragener went on. 'There can be only one answer. They have betrayed the emperor. They offered up aid and succour to the Normans to buy their lives.'

'Is this true?' Nikephoros asked. Hereward heard no surprise in the emperor's voice. Karas had already presented this news. This was a show for the court, nothing more. And perhaps, too, it was the emperor's own revenge for his cuckolding. If so, he had chosen his time well.

The scout nodded, but his darting eyes showed his unease. 'I saw them talking to the Normans, to Robert Guiscard. And then they were allowed to ride free.'

'He lies,' Alexios shouted, furious. 'Call for Tiberius Grabas. Call for any of our brothers.'

'Even their own brothers do not know the truth,' Ragener yelled over him. 'These two went behind their backs to save their own necks. Are they now conspiring with our enemies? Are they sending messages of our army's weaknesses? Will we find the gates left open one night when the Normans ride to our walls?'

Hereward felt all eyes turn towards him. It mattered not that these were lies. In the seething cauldron that was Constantinople, suspicion was often enough to destroy.

Fighting the urge to respond, the Mercian instead leaned in to Alexios and whispered. The Roman nodded and said loudly, 'Our brothers know full well what happened – we never left their sides. Ask Tiberius Grabas. Or any of the Athanatoi, or the loyal Varangian Guard. Or do you think those great heroes

246

of the empire are traitors too?' he added, baring his teeth at Ragener.

For a moment the emperor hesitated. 'Two stories. Both ring true. But who should be believed? I must think on this, and listen to wise words. Send for Falkon Cephalas.'

Alexios' shoulders slumped, but he kept his chin high. Hereward watched Nikephoros' eyes move from Alexios to Maria and back. His wrath at the humiliation he suspected had left him open to Karas' snake-tongue.

Hereward walked tall out of the Chrysotriklinos with the young Roman at his side, but he could feel the weight of the eyes on his back. Once outside, the two men hurried to a tavern by the harbour of Theodosius, where they would not be recognized.

Now Hereward understood the true nature of those armed men he had seen in the fora. Karas Verinus had already started to move his force into the city. The general would not sit back and wait for Hereward and Alexios to argue their innocence. They had already lost the protection of the emperor. He, Alexios, Anna and the rest of the Comnenoi, all of them were in danger.

The shadows cloaked them. In a corner at the rear, they perched on their stools, cupping their goblets, heads bowed but eyes always flickering towards the door.

'What next for us?' Alexios asked in a low voice. 'Falkon Cephalas will not be our champion, of that we can be sure.'

'Keep faith. Nothing is certain. Power shifts here like the swell upon the whale road.'

'I cannot be so sanguine. You heard my mother – everything changed in Constantinople while we were fighting in the west. Karas seized his moment, when his greatest rivals were looking away.'

Hereward nodded. 'Aye, it is only a matter of time. Karas has the emperor's ear now. There is little you can say . . .' Hereward caught himself. Alexios' shoulders were already hunched from the burden of his worries. Nothing could be gained from telling him his love for Maria had only made things worse. 'But still, we must not give up hope.'

'We should never have left.'

'We had no choice, you know that.'

Alexios shook his head, the strain carving lines in his forehead. 'Karas will persuade the emperor to execute us for treason. It matters not what Tiberius Grabas or any of the others say. The matter has surely been decided. Or he will send his army of cut-throats to slay us while we sleep, or walk with friends. Our only hope is to flee.'

'And go where? I have had seasons of running and I am sick of it. My spear-brothers . . .' Hereward choked down his rising anger. He would not risk seeing this taint spreading to Guthrinc and Kraki and the others. Karas Verinus would be prepared to end the days of anyone who dared walk with the men he despised most. 'Your fellow nobles think us nothing more than barbarians, less than the dirt beneath their

248

feet. But our place has been earned here, by sweat and blood. We will not give up.'

'Then you would stand, and die?'

'If need be.'

Alexios poured wine into his cup. 'We had grown too confident. Once the Comnenoi returned to Constantinople . . . once my mother was accepted back at the court and I became commander of the western armies . . . we thought our struggle was over. But our enemies were more cunning. Karas Verinus watched and waited for his moment and then he took it.' Abruptly, Alexios hurled his cup across the tavern in a rage. The Mercian saw the sudden glances that flashed their way. They would do well not to draw more attention.

'We are not yet dead,' Hereward said, resting a hand on his friend's shoulder. 'We must find a way out of this trap. The emperor has not made his decision. For now, there are only accusations, only whispers.'

'Whispers grow louder as they leap from tongue to tongue. And soon enough, they become axes. This is how Constantinople works. You must know that by now.' Alexios wiped the sweat from his brow with the back of a trembling hand. On the field of battle, no braver warrior fought. But the young Roman knew full well his enemies here were more brutal than any honourable fighting men. Hereward could not disagree. For all their learning, their silk tunics and marble statues, the Romans could be the true barbarians.

'Then we have only one road left open to us,' he said quietly.

Alexios frowned at him.

'We must ask that God judge us.'

CHAPTER TWENTY-SIX

Candles flickered throughout the Nea Ekklesia. That constellation of lights, seemingly greater than in the heavens above, burnished the gold on every wall and every surface so that all of the New Church was ablaze.

'And if God says we are guilty?' Alexios hissed, his eyes darting askance.

'You doubt God?' Hereward looked up at the great dome above, the one dedicated to the Christ. Four more domes surrounded it, each one belonging to a saint. 'There is nothing like this in England,' he murmured to himself. 'Gold buys even a new road to heaven.'

Alexios scowled at him. 'Have your wits fled? Our heads could be in the dust before one of these candles burns out.'

The Mercian shrugged, to the other man's annoyance. 'It is out of our hands now.'

Bowing their heads to God's Table, they crossed themselves. Hereward felt calm. No anger burned in his breast at the injustices that had been heaped upon them, the lies, the betrayals. He was ready.

At their backs in the belly of the church, Constantinople's nobles waited. No doubt they held their breath, hoping for a greater thrill than anything they might have found in the hippodrome that night. The Nepotes were there. Four slaves had carried Kalamdios on his chair and set him at the front, where he could mewl and drool and enjoy the hatred in his black heart. Simonis stood at his side, stately, smiling, one hand draped across her husband's shoulder. Juliana watched intently, the sunlight to Wulfrun's shadow beside her. Was the Guard commander praying for vengeance, the Mercian wondered? The youth, Leo, was there too, sullen and distracted.

And on the other side of the church, Karas Verinus brooded. He would not have expected this plea, they were sure. Hereward allowed himself a grin at the discomfort he had caused his tormentor by disrupting his plans.

The reedy chant of the eunuch announcing the emperor's arrival echoed through the church. The doors swung open and Nikephoros stepped in, a white insect creeping across the flagstones. Boril and Germanos flanked him, hands resting on their sword-hilts.

Once the ruler had taken his place at the front of the congregation, the small door behind the altar opened and the prophet shambled in. Alric walked close at his heels, resting his one hand supportively on the feeble old man's shoulder.

A hush fell across the church, as if everyone there was in the presence of the Lord himself.

Hereward locked eyes with the monk. If he could have found a way to speak to his friend he would have, but Alric spent all day and night locked away with Megistus, an honour and a burden in equal measure. The monk's features looked drawn, his eyes red-rimmed with weariness. Hereward felt a pang of pity. But his friend still forced a smile and nodded.

Footsteps approached from the rear of the church and a small figure passed the Mercian's left side and rounded the altar. Falkon Cephalas looked back across the congregation and said, 'You bear witness today upon this judgement. These two, Alexios Comnenos and Hereward of the English, have thrown themselves upon God's mercy. They will abide by the pronouncement we hear this day.'

Beside him, Hereward sensed Alexios plucking uneasily at his tunic. The Mercian jabbed his elbow into the other man's ribs.

Falkon turned to the prophet. 'Has God moved you to speak?'

'He has,' Megistus said. He took a shaky step forward and peered through rheumy eyes at Hereward and Alexios. 'These two? Yes, yes, I see it now.'

'They have been accused of betraying the empire . . . of conspiring with our enemy. How does God judge them?'

'God brought me back from my grave to warn all here of doom, for Constantinople, for the empire,' Megistus croaked. The candles lit two lamps in his eyes as he looked around the church. 'Doom has been turned away from Constantinople . . . for now.'

Relief rushed through the court. Someone cried out in thanks.

'Silence,' Falkon commanded.

'Doom has been turned away . . . by these two men.' Megistus' voice rose and he pointed a trembling finger at the two accused. 'Ruin may return . . . the streets may yet run with blood . . . if all care is not taken. But for now these two men have heeded God's warning. Their swords have cleaved one enemy in two. Wounds must be licked before that army marches again.'

Alexios sucked in a deep, juddering breath of relief.

'Then how did they escape?' Falkon pressed. 'We have heard they were surrounded on all sides by enemies, too many to fight.'

Megistus hesitated, swaying. His eyes rolled shut and his mouth worked but no words came out. Then, in a small voice, 'It was God's will.'

Hereward could feel the weight of eyes at his back, not least those of the emperor. The court had been denied their blood, but they could not deny the prophet's judgement.

Falkon Cephalas bowed his head, folding his hands together across his belly. He let silence reign for a moment before announcing, 'Then it is agreed. These men are innocent.'

'Hold,' Megistus cried, lurching around the altar. 'There was treachery, aye, but not by these two. Another here betrayed the empire.'

Alexios glanced at Hereward, his eyes wide, and then he turned and stared at Karas Verinus. The general's face was like stone.

'He speaks truth.' Karas raised one hand to command attention away from the prophet. 'And this will be my shame until my dying day.'

The court erupted in confused chatter. The emperor stared, baffled. 'You, Karas?' he called.

'Not I, but the dog in my employ. I sent him west, with gold, to buy more men upon the road. If needed, they would march in support of the Athanatoi and the Varangian Guard.'

Karas looked around until his gaze fell upon a hooded figure at the rear of the church. Hereward smiled coldly. Ragener the Hawk was receiving full payment for his loyalty to his cruel master.

The general pointed at the sea wolf. 'He is the traitor. He took my gold, and then he took more from the Duke of Apulia to try to turn the tide of the battle. Roman blood was spilled because of him.' Karas boomed the last sentence with such force that the congregation spun round as one. Faces twisted with rage. Voices roared for the ruined man's death.

Hereward could see Ragener waving his hand and shouting in protest, but his words were drowned out by the congregation's fury. His features crumpled and the Mercian thought he saw bitter realization there: a man so ruined, one who was little more than a beggar, could have no voice among the most powerful people in Constantinople. And Karas knew that too.

Wrenching open the door, Ragener bolted from the church. The court surged after him in a frenzy of furious yelling.

Hereward felt no pity for the sea wolf. He had

brought this upon his own head the moment he had chosen to ally himself with a man who cared for nothing but his own lust for power. His days would soon be ended, and God would be his judge for all the torment he had inflicted on good men and women.

The Mercian looked back across the altar, hoping to see that Alric found some peace in the sea wolf's fate. But Falkon Cephalas was already ushering the monk and Megistus out of the small door and away.

Alexios sagged with relief. 'You are a man of great faith to stay so calm.'

'Aye, I have faith,' Hereward replied with a taut smile. He searched the church for Karas Verinus, but the general was already gone. 'Do not think this business is over. All we have done is save our necks from the executioner's axe at dawn. No, our doom may be even closer. Nikephoros still suspects us. Not even if the Lord himself raised us up on the wings of angels would he look on us kindly again.'

Alexios lowered his eyes, understanding the meaning of Hereward's words.

'And do you think Karas Verinus will walk away now? He has shown his true face here, attacking us from the front, and he has suffered another blow. Now he will come for us from the shadows. Today. Tomorrow. A week hence. But he will come, have no doubt of that. We can never rest easy again.'

CHAPTER TWENTY-SEVEN

In the lamplight, the black eyes of the three men glittered with cold glee. Each wind-leathered face was a patchwork of scars. One was missing an eye. Another had lost four teeth, turning his grin into a grimace. Their tunics and breeches were little more than rags, reeking of human filth. But the levelled swords, they were sharp enough.

Hereward looked from one face to the other. His own blade was still sheathed, and they would be upon him before he had the chance to draw it. The streets on the edge of the Vlanga were deserted at this time of night. There was little point in calling for aid.

'Karas Verinus did not wait long to quench his lust for my blood,' he said. Scant hours had passed since the Lord had judged him innocent of treachery. Since then it seemed that all the city had been convulsed in the search for Ragener the sea wolf.

'You will not be mourned,' the one-eyed man grunted.

'No,' Hereward agreed. 'I am not a good man. I

have the devil in me. But what I lack in God's spirit, I more than make up for with cunning.'

The one-eyed man snorted. Barely had the sound left his lips before his throat opened up. The crimson rush glimmered in the lamplight as he pawed at the wound.

His two allies gaped stupidly, their thoughts lumbering like a drunken man's. One of them gargled something, a curse, a prayer, and spat a gobbet of blood as he pitched forward. A pool formed around him where he lay.

The surviving rogue looked from the two bodies to Hereward, still unable to comprehend, even when the two knives swept towards him from the dark.

'You are cunning and you are wise,' Salih ibn Ziyad said, a pool of shadow in his black robes. He emerged from the night and crouched to wipe his curved blade upon the tunic of one of the dead men. 'Wise to call upon us to be your defenders.'

Dipping down to clean her own weapon, Ariadne added, 'You would have us watch you day and night for all time?'

'Not even the two of you could do that.' Hereward placed a boot on one of the fallen men and rocked the body gently. 'They will come now like the waves upon the shore. They will not rest until I am dead. You will buy me time, that is all.'

'Time for what?' Ariadne asked. 'To flee?'

'I cannot leave. If I go, your uncle will take out his wrath upon my men.'

'Then kill him before he kills you.'

Hereward smiled as Ariadne stood up. In that moment, he thought he truly could see Meghigda inside her, instead of the madness born of suffering that afflicted her. 'I have been known to be good with a sword, true. But even I could not battle my way through the army that surrounds Karas Verinus now.'

Salih sheathed his dagger, his eyes continually searching the night. 'Death waits in silence, that is your proclamation, yes? And I have been known to be good at cloaking myself in silence. Even Karas Verinus could not escape me.'

'I do not doubt it. But the general is a clever man and he has sown his seeds well. If he dies, you can be sure the emperor will soon find reason to blame me, or Alexios, or both of us, and we will follow Karas into hell.'

'You must keep hope,' Ariadne said, clutching his arm. Her eyes were wide, her voice thick with emotion. 'Heed the words of al-Kahina. In the end, hope is all we have.'

'You read the words in the heavens, and in the winds, and in the voice of birds. What does your wisdom tell you, Salih ibn Ziyad?'

'Death is close.'

'Death is always close.'

'You do not fear it,' Salih stated.

Hereward peered across the dark street, into the night, into years gone by. 'I have seen enough of it. I have dealt more than my fair share. There comes a time for every warrior when that cup overflows. You make friends with the end. You yearn for the ones you have lost along the road, and sometimes you wish too much to see them again.'

'What of the living? Would you abandon them?'

Hereward laughed without humour. 'Do not mis-judge me. I am not ready to rush into the grave. There is much still to achieve. If nothing else, I would not hand my enemies victory. There is little honour among any of them; they are not deserving of success. And my spear-brothers, the men who have followed me for so long . . . I would see them rewarded for their loyalty.' He started to say more, but then he let the soughing of the wind snatch his words away. After a moment's stillness, he added, 'But my heart tells me you speak true. Death is out there, I smell it. The rot on the wind. It fills my dreams, aye, and my waking visions too. It may be that it is already too late, and victory is no longer in my hands. If I am taken before my plans have ripened, I ask one thing.'

'Speak.'

'Do not mourn me. Tell my spear-brothers not to grieve for me. By rights, I should have died when England fell, at Ely, and the days since have been a gift.' He nodded, recalling Anna's words. 'I am at peace with that. But you must fight on in my stead. You must find the reward that my brothers deserve. Do you swear?'

'You have my word,' Salih replied without hesitation. 'You have earned that at least.'

So much lay between them that would always remain unspoken. They had been enemies and they had been allies, but through it all they had recognized that they spoke the common tongue of honour. A shared moment of silence fell upon them.

Hereward looked down at Ariadne and into her wide, haunted eyes. 'I hear your words and what lies at the heart of them,' she said. 'And I am afraid.'

CHAPTER TWENTY-EIGHT

Alric paced the chamber that had been his home for the better part of three weeks. The dry air reeked of vinegar-sweat and his stomach rumbled. Why had the night's meal not yet been delivered, he thought bitterly? That was the only moment in each day to which he could look forward.

'I have had my fill of this,' Megistus moaned from the corner. His tunic was wet. He had pissed himself again.

'You know full well we reached an agreement.'

The old man looked up with his rheumy eyes. 'You lied to me.'

'Never.'

'You did not tell me how much would be demanded of me!' His voice rose to a cry.

Glancing round, Alric waved his hands frantically to silence him. At that time of night, voices carried far along the empty corridors. 'Hush.'

Megistus began to mewl, rocking from side to side as he plucked at the filthy wool of his tunic. His anxiety mounting, the monk grabbed the man's shoulders and shook him a little too hard. 'Have you lost your wits? Think, think. What if the guards hear your cries? The emperor?' He leaned in and hissed, 'If they find they have been so deceived, what then, for you?' *And me*, he thought. 'No gold for you. It will be the grave, and in truth this time.'

The old man's head flopped forward and he began to shake with juddering sobs. Weariness had taken its toll. He had barely been allowed to sleep since Palladius had brought him into the monastery, coated from head to foot in what they had said was the clay of the grave. At times, it had seemed that every noble in Constantinople was insisting upon an audience with the prophet to hear the Lord's plans for them, and for the empire. They had not even been allowed to leave the stifling chamber, almost as if they were captives, not God's instruments. Eating there, sleeping there, day after day of questions and pleas and tears.

Crouching, Alric eased his grip on Megistus' shoulders until it felt comforting. 'You have done your work well,' he whispered. 'Never in our wildest dreams did any of us expect so much would be demanded of you.'

His words did little to soothe the old man. Megistus sucked in a deep breath and croaked, 'I am sick to my belly. So weary my thoughts tumble and turn and I no longer know what I say. What if the wrong words fall out? What if I reveal the lie? They will kill me!'

'You will be well rewarded, better even than we promised,' Alric assured him.

'I would be done with this. I beg of you. Give me what you owe me now and I will ask for no more. I want to go back to my life, and my home. I was filled with greed before . . . I did not know . . .' He began to babble.

'Come.' Alric helped him to his feet. 'You will feel better when you have slept a little. We will talk more of this at first light.'

He led the old man on a meandering path to the bed that had been set up for him in the corner of the chamber. He understood the toll that had been taken on this 'prophet'; had feared it would be this way from the very start. 'We are almost done here,' he murmured. 'Hold firm for a while longer and you can rest as much as you want, and live like a king.'

Megistus' eyes were fluttering and his breath was shallow. So tired was he, it seemed he would sleep where he fell, Alric thought. He laid the old man down on the low wooden bed, and within a moment rumbling snores echoed around the bare stone chamber. Stepping back, the monk gave a sigh of relief, but he knew this would not be the end of it. He had bought himself only a little time. Megistus had reached the end of his tether; all the signs were there. His complaints would only grow louder.

But Alric could not risk the old man's fraying so much that he could not contain his protests. Too much was at stake. All of their lives, for one.

Stepping away, he closed his eyes and pressed his face into his hands. He had been afraid from the moment he had set out on this road. Now not a moment passed when he did not feel sick with worry that he would be discovered.

Shaking the wool from his head, he tried to imagine what he would do if things got worse on the morrow. Should he flee? But then he would have to leave Megistus to his fate and his conscience would never allow that. No, his only hope was to use the tongue that God had given him to persuade the old man to carry on, and he would pray that that would be enough.

As he trudged to his own bed on the other side of the chamber, he jerked round at a long, low creak, like the moan of a grieving widow. He had heard it enough times to know what it was: the sound of a door being quickly closed.

His heart began to pound. Had someone overheard their conversation?

Rushing to the chamber door, he peered out into the ink-black corridor. At the far end, the flame in a lamp guttered as the last of its oil was consumed. Nothing moved. But a ghost of a presence hung in the air. His senses prickled. It lingered for just a moment, and then the light winked out and darkness swallowed everything.

CHAPTER TWENTY-NINE

The two naked women glided through the baths. Heads turned towards them, stares drawn, no doubt, by the confidence they exuded. Few there could believe they were mother and daughter, for Simonis' beauty was undimmed by age. Juliana smiled, pleased by the attention. Soon all eyes would be upon them wherever they went.

'Look,' she whispered to her mother behind her hand. 'There is some filth that not even the waters of the baths can wash away.'

Soaking in the warm waters were Anna Dalassene and Maria, the emperor's wife, or Alexios' whore, depending upon which rumour was circulating. Their laughter tinkled out among the echoes.

The air was warm and sweetly scented with sandalwood and lime, wisps of steam drifting through shafts of sunlight breaking through the high windows. As the women passed the alabaster statues, Juliana swayed her hips, revelling in those stares too – Virgil, Julius Caesar, Demosthenes, Plato and more, men who had made their mark on history. She liked to feel their eyes upon her naked body. Long ago these monuments to the great had been rescued from the grand baths of Zeuxippus when that place had been turned into a prison. But still they thrived, silent and unyielding, still their power was known.

Juliana and Simonis waited until their procession caught the eyes of Anna and Maria and then they walked over and came to a halt beside the bath, each with one hand upon a shapely hip. Juliana choked down a giggle when she saw the sour looks flash across the other women's faces. *Oh, how they hate us*, she thought. *And with good reason.*

'We are honoured to see you here,' Simonis said. 'Such a rare sight.' She was smiling, but Juliana knew her mother used that look as a dagger and the other women knew it too. 'And how is your son, Alexios?' She extended a long finger to Anna, then moved it to Maria, then back and forth. 'Your son? Your son? One son, two mothers! Do you fight to kiss his cheek at night?' She let her heavy-lashed eyes fall upon Maria for just a moment too long.

Maria blushed.

'How lonely you must be,' Juliana said to Anna with a sad pout, knowing full well her innocent expression only added poison to her words. 'No husband in your cold bed, and now all your sons are gone too. What is left for you? Sewing with the old wives?'

'I am good with needles, 'tis true,' Anna replied, smiling back, 'and I never prick myself. But it is said you have had pricks aplenty, perhaps more than any woman in the city – nay, in the empire. You must take care.'

Juliana bowed her head, her smile fixed, but as she turned away her face hardened. 'In a few short days I would happily loose her blood myself,' she hissed as she and her mother swayed on their way.

Her eyes sparkling, Simonis whispered, 'Why sully your fair hand? Leave her to Varin. He will give her the wings of an angel to fly her to the lofty heights of which she has always dreamed.'

They both laughed at that.

Once they had dried themselves and had the slaves rub scented oils into their skin, they left the baths and walked to the Augustaion to buy spices from the portico of Achilles. The merchants laughed and flirted with them, showing their white teeth in their dark faces, but Juliana heard barely a word. She felt her blood throb with excitement. As the days grew warmer and the mullein flowers bloomed with the first sweet scent of spring, the hours seemed to be rushing towards her.

When they returned to the house to find Wulfrun waiting, she threw her arms around his neck, barely able to contain herself. He looked taken aback by this unseemly display, but she made him take off his helm and led him to the court at the back to sit under their tree. She was surprised to feel the stiffness in his shoulders, and glanced back into the house. Simonis flashed a knowing look before disappearing towards the cookhouse.

'Why did you wish to see me?' Wulfrun asked.

Juliana bowed her head, choosing her words carefully. The time of leading him by the nose had long since passed. 'You love me?'

'You know that I do.' But the sag of his shoulders that punctuated his admission seemed to suggest this was a burden beyond all others. She nodded, understanding his unspoken thoughts.

'I know I have asked much of you in the name of our love, and I will ask more before we are done. But these days of requests are almost over and then we can be at peace, together.' Juliana took his hand. 'You have seen the worst of me, and you know . . . you know more than you say. I understand. I am quick to deceive. But I do not lie when I say my feelings for you are true. I have never loved another, Wulfrun, and I love you with all my heart.'

'Then do not ask of me what I know you are about to ask. Spare me.'

'I cannot.' She bit her lip. 'All our work has been leading to this moment. All the strife, all the struggle and the misery and the hardship. Season upon season of it. But it will be worth it all once Leo has the crown upon his brow. We will want for nothing. Every man, woman and child in the empire will bow their heads to the Nepotes.'

Wulfrun looked down at his hands. 'It is time, then?'

Juliana nodded.

'What of Karas Verinus?'

'Karas is brute strength, nothing more.' She could feel her voice hardening as she spoke. For all the ruin that had been inflicted on her kin across the years, her feelings for the Verini had moved beyond hatred into something that burned like a furnace. She thought of her father when he was young and strong, before the blade had sliced into his head. She remembered the indignities to which both she and her mother had been forced to submit. She seethed at the aching hardship they had endured when all their wealth and power had been stolen. 'But we are more cunning,' she continued, once she had calmed herself. 'We know all of Karas' plans, as well as he knows them himself.'

'How?'

Juliana only smiled. 'When Karas moves upon the throne, we will take him by surprise. He thinks us beaten, and that is good for he pays us no heed. But we have our force ready, hidden in the city. One word and they will rise up. All this time, we and not the Comnenoi have been his true enemy, if only he could see it.'

Wulfrun leaned back against the tree. Juliana could see he was fighting with himself.

'I hate to see you this way,' she urged him. 'You are an honourable man. But now it is time for you to make that choice I told you of before, between honour—'

'And you?'

'Good times will soon be here, and we can put all this struggle and strife behind us. We can be together, Wulfrun, as we were always meant to be. You and I, with the empire at our feet.'

'I never wanted the empire. Power, glory, gold, no. Only you. Only you.'

'Hereward must be killed.'

Wulfrun stared down at the patches of sunlight dappling the flagstones. Juliana felt puzzled. He seemed to sag like an emptied water-skin.

'What is he to you?' he asked.

'I would have thought the notion would have set you alight! After all he did to you . . .' Juliana exclaimed.

'What is he to you?'

Juliana sighed. 'Hereward must die so you can order the Varangian Guard to support the Nepotes. He would never agree to that.'

'Because he is more honourable than me?'

Juliana caught her breath. When Wulfrun looked up, his expression was fierce. It was only a fleeting moment before he hid it again, but she had seen the torment there. 'Because he does not see us . . . see me . . . as you see me. With Hereward gone, no one will stand in your way. The Varangian Guard will abandon Nikephoros and swear their allegiance to the Nepotes. This is my gift to you,' she murmured, caressing his cheek. 'Once Hereward is dead, your days gone by will no longer haunt you. You will be free of those shackles. Only days yet to come, Wulfrun, only days yet to come. Does that not fill your heart with joy?'

'You ask too much of me.'

Juliana grasped his hand. 'You do not have to plunge a blade into Hereward yourself. Only look the other way.'

'How will he die?'

'We have made our plans well. And when we are

ready, soon, we will tell you.' Juliana reached out her other hand, pleading. 'This is for the best, you know that is true. The empire is on its knees, dying by the day. This is the time to act, Wulfrun, to find a strong leader. If we fail, all will be lost.'

Wulfrun bowed his head, crushed by the decision that had been forced upon him. After a moment, he croaked, 'I have made my choice, and may God have mercy upon me. When you call me, I will be ready.'

Juliana beamed, barely able to contain her excitement. 'Only good days lie ahead. You will see.'

She led him back to the courtyard entrance and kissed him once on the cheek, deliberately avoiding the haunted look that sat in his face. When he was gone, she could not resist a smile. She ran through the house to the chamber where her family waited.

'Wulfrun is with us,' she announced.

Simonis clapped her hands together. Kalamdios rocked his head, his mouth making strange noises of assent. Only Leo seemed unmoved.

'I will be ready,' the youth said. 'When I wear the crown, all will be changed.'

Varin loomed in the doorway, with another, smaller figure hovering behind him. 'My axe is also ready,' the Blood Eagle declared. 'It yearns to drink Hereward's blood.'

'If he only knew that the moment he brought you back to Constantinople, he set in motion his own doom,' Simonis said.

'Every man is the architect of his own victory, and his own demise,' Varin replied. He stepped aside so the other man could enter. Falkon Cephalas bowed.

'I have more news on Karas Verinus' plans.'

'And he still suspects nothing?' Simonis enquired.

'He thinks me loyal to him, yes,' Falkon said, with a nod to Varin. 'And thus he too is an architect of his own demise.'

CHAPTER THIRTY

In the hearth, the fire had died down. The embers glowed red in the grey swirl of ashes. As the ruddy light ebbed, the shadows closed in across the feasting hall. The air was fragrant with the scent of woodsmoke and the succulent juices of the lamb that had been roasting over the flames earlier that night. Snores sawed through the dark from the unconscious warriors face down upon the ale-puddled table or sprawled on the floor where they had slipped off their stools. All was still.

With heavy-lidded eyes, Kraki peered through the mead-haze. This could be England. This could be the great hall in Eoferwic, with the snows piled high against the timbers and the bitter wind soughing through the thatch. But it was the Vlanga, and a place made for those whose hearts ached for their lost homeland and all they had left behind. At times there was comfort to be found in the familiar surroundings. Some days, though, it felt like a blade in the belly.

In the faint glow by the hearth, Kraki thought he saw a figure standing, a woman. He squinted. It was

Acha, he was sure. The only woman he had ever cared about. He had sent her away to save her life. She deserved better than days of running and fighting and, no doubt, an early death. Yet there was not a night when he did not yearn for her.

Kraki snorted. The mead had made him weak, a farmer. She was a woman, nothing more. When he had first picked up the axe his father had given him, he had accepted the warrior's life. Fire and blood, blood and fire. And death. Death was always close. These Varangians knew a thing or two.

Death waits in silence.

Yearning for some woman, mewling like a child in his head, that was not the warrior's way.

And yet, and yet . . .

The trail of smoke whisked and Kraki felt a blast of cooler air. The door had opened.

'Who is there?' he slurred.

From the dark walked another figure, a man this time.

Kraki nodded. 'Where have you been?'

'Making plans.' Hereward sat at the long feasting table opposite his friend.

Kraki could see the Mercian was not himself. No doubt one of his regular brooding moods. 'Drink,' he said, fumbling for a fallen goblet. 'You need to learn to find joy in life. All this sourness will turn your blood to vinegar.'

'I have no thirst.' Hereward gently pushed the goblet away. 'The feast went well. That is good. You have earned this.' He glanced at Guthrinc, whose breath

275

was rumbling against the wood of the table nearby. He looked across the rest of the spear-brothers too, to be sure they were all asleep. 'I would have speech with you.'

Kraki reached for one of the few jugs that remained upright on the table and poured himself another drink. 'You are going to put the spear to my joy now, I can hear it in your voice,' he said, wiping his mouth with the back of his hand.

'I have had dreams, of my ending.' The Mercian stared away into the dark, remembering. 'Dreams while I sleep, dreams while I wake. My raven comes to me to warn me.'

'Dreams.' Kraki snorted dismissively.

'Portents.'

'You will outlive us all.'

Hereward smiled, though the Viking sensed an odd twist to it. His friend looked tired. Lines had appeared that he had not seen before.

'Aye, that may be true. But a wise leader would make plans.'

Kraki nodded. He could not deny that.

'If I fall, you must lead the spear-brothers.'

The Viking fluttered a dismissive hand and gave a drunken chuckle.

'You must agree to this.'

'There are better men here. Guthrinc—'

'When we met, in Eoferwic, you led Earl Tostig's huscarls. He trusted you with his life, and Tostig was not a man to risk his own neck. Aye, you were a bastard among bastards who would have gutted me with a smile, but you knew how to win in any battle. And now, here in this city, our brothers need a leader who knows how to win.'

'You talk like a man who has had a bellyful of ale. Enough of this.'

Hereward leaned across the table, his face hardening. 'Agree.'

'If it will still your damn tongue, aye, I agree,' Kraki snapped.

The Mercian was satisfied. Nodding, he leaned back. 'There is more.'

Kraki cursed and searched around for any remaining ale.

Grasping the Viking's wrist, Hereward insisted, 'Heed me. When I fall, if I fall, do not mourn me. That is the hour of most danger. You will need to be ready to fight, to save all your necks, not mewling like babes.'

'You think we would shed tears for a bastard like you?'

Hereward nodded again, pleased. He was silent for a moment, but then found more words, drawing them up from deep within him. 'Make sure my son in England is safe.'

Kraki's hand hovered over his goblet. How long had it been since he heard his friend mention the boy? 'You would want me to send word to the monks at Crowland Abbey?'

'Aye. When he is older. A year, perhaps two. If he is still there.'

'And tell him about his father?'

The Mercian shook his head. 'Better he grows up not knowing who I am, or that he shares this cursed blood of mine.'

'Done. Now leave me in peace to enjoy my drink.'

Grinning, the Mercian pushed back from the table and walked towards the door.

As he found some dregs in another goblet and drained them, Kraki felt the back of his neck prickle. He knew Hereward must be standing there, watching him. An urge to say farewell rushed through him. But when he looked up, his friend was gone.

CHAPTER THIRTY-ONE

Moonlight silvered the ripples crossing the green pool. Around its edge the two men wandered, past the soaring columns and the statues of old emperors, under the portico to the lion's head where the fresh spring water trickled out. The tinkling reverberated around the fountain house. During the day, the crescent-shaped monument would be filled with citizens drinking or raucous wedding parties, but at that time of night the two visitors could enjoy the peace.

Karas Verinus turned and admired the view across Constantinople. Perched there atop the Third Hill, the Great Nymphaeum gave him clear sight of the city and all its wealth and power and beauty, all that would be his in just a few short days. The moon had near turned night to day. The white stone of the great buildings glowed, with the dome of Hagia Sophia dominating all. Lamps flickered here and there like fireflies in the fields of his youth. Karas nodded, pleased with what he saw.

Here, in this sanctuary that had been consecrated

to the water nymphs, men and women who worshipped the old gods came to drink deep of the spring waters that they believed were a source of magic. He picked up two cups and handed one to Justin. The youth stared at it blankly.

'Drink,' Karas urged, holding his own cup under the stream. 'Drink and raise your cup to the power that rules the heavens.'

With a shrug, Justin took a cup of the cold water and swilled it back.

'On my first day in Constantinople, I came here and looked across the city, as we do now,' Karas continued as he searched the view for familiar landmarks. 'I took a cup of this water and made my oath.'

'What oath?'

'The same one you are now going to make.' The general looked down at his charge. Justin seemed younger than his years, so it was easy to think of him as a boy. But Justin was a man, with as many summers to his name as Karas had when he first came here. The general scrutinized those unsettling black eyes. He had had his doubts about Justin – what man would not? But he had the blood of the Verini in him. For better or worse, Justin was the hope of days yet to come.

For a moment, Karas rested one hand on Justin's shoulder, a silent communication of acceptance. Then he said, 'You are ready?'

'I am. I have always been ready.'

'You know what will be demanded of you?'

Justin nodded.

'The Verini have waited for this for long years. When I was a boy, my father told me that it was the destiny of our blood to wear the crown of the empire. Our enemies have always conspired to keep us away from the throne. I . . . betrayed by all at court when I had slaughtered a sea of Turks at Manzikert, made to carry the stain of that defeat by the cowards who had really caused it. My brother, murdered when he believed his hands were almost upon the prize. And you . . . now it is your turn to avenge us both.'

Justin pushed up his head. The moon shone from his eyes.

Karas was pleased by what he saw there. 'Then tomorrow we take our first step into a new age. This has been long in coming. True, the prophet threw my plans awry. His warnings of doom, the ride to war, the near-revolt here within the walls . . . but now all bends before our will once more.'

'And what of Ragener? Could he still not cause upset?'

'By rights, that ragged dog should be long dead.' Karas gritted his teeth, pushing his simmering anger down inside him. 'But he is a coward at heart. He will lie low like a rat in a drain. He would never dare defy me. Worry not. He will be found, and his days ended. Now, raise your cup.'

Justin held up his offering, the water shimmering.

'Soon you must leave the city and wait until you are summoned,' the general continued. 'Our enemies here will want to strike at me through you. If I have no heir, the throne will be hard for me to gain and keep alone, they know that.'

'I will make ready to leave.'

Karas raised his own cup. 'Then this is our oath, before the eyes of God. Our enemies will be crushed. Their blood will run like rivers in the streets. And when all is done, the crown will sit upon the brow of one of the Verini. So do we swear!'

CHAPTER THIRTY-TWO

'Come, now, or lose your friend for ever.'

Hereward jerked his head up from the slow, meditative strokes of the whetstone along the edge of Brainbiter. In the doorway, the lamplight limned Wulfrun. Ricbert stood at his shoulder. Beyond them, the sound of running feet echoed across the courtyard of the Boukoleon palace.

'What friend?'

'The monk Alric. And the prophet too. They have been taken from their sanctuary.' The commander and his aide turned away from the door. The cool night air rushed in over the bags of sand the Guard used for cleaning mail, and the whetstones and the hammers.

Hereward cursed under his breath. This was a moment he had long expected, and dreaded. He hoped he was ready for it. Sheathing his sword, he hurried out and caught up with Wulfrun and his escort of seven guardsmen. 'Who has taken him?' he demanded.

'Some traitor who does not want the emperor to

have God on his side.' Flames flickered in the eye-holes of Wulfrun's helm. As he held that gaze for a long moment, Hereward thought the commander was on the brink of saying more, but he turned away. 'Would you waste what little time we have asking questions, or do you want to aid your friend?'

'Where?'

'We know little . . . who has taken them, or how they escaped the palace guards,' Wulfrun said. 'But my messenger said they were travelling north, towards the gate of the Neorion.'

'And the harbour beyond.'

'With a ship and a fair wind, they can be far from the city by sunrise.'

As the Mercian followed the knot of warriors out of the palace gate and into the tangle of streets, he steeled himself for what was to come. The guardsmen loped through the streets faster than any man could ride, darting along narrow rat-runs and reeking alleys as they passed in the shadow of the church of Urbicius and into the Pisan quarter. At that late hour, the city was still.

'This is the perfect time to spirit away the emperor's prizes and leave him weakened,' Wulfrun growled. '*God has abandoned you.* I can hear the cries of Nikephoros' enemies even now.'

'The prophet's voice has changed the course of things here,' one of the other Varangians grunted. 'Many must be angry that their plans have been shaken.'

As they neared the towering gate of the Neorion,

284

the moon broke through the clouds. The road became a white wake punching through the wall's shadow.

Once they had passed through the gate, Wulfrun held up a hand to bring the band to a halt. The air was scented with cinnamon from one of the store-houses clustered around the basin. Through a gap in the jumble of buildings, Hereward watched the moon-light glinting off the waters of the Golden Horn. During the day, the Neorion harbour throbbed with life. Sailors and merchants ferried a stream of goods from the ships into storage, ready to be sent out across the river. The air sang with the sound of hammers from the boat-makers who lined the water's edge.

Now only the wind whistled among the buildings.

Wulfrun hissed an order to his men that Hereward could not hear. One stayed behind, a red-bearded Rus named Tabor, fierce in battle but duller-witted than any other guardsman. The others divided into two bands and disappeared in opposite directions along the shadow of the wall. Wulfrun did not wait for questions. He bounded down the road, flicking his fingers for Hereward and Tabor to follow.

Drawing Brainbiter, the Mercian hurried along behind. The moon showed them the way. Storehouses loomed on either side, aged timbers cracked and stained by the elements. The road zigzagged down the slope among them. Whatever might lie ahead was hidden by the constant twists and turns. As Hereward crept on, his nose wrinkled at the changing scents: the sharp tang of unfamiliar spices, the vinegary reek of spilled wine, the sweet aroma of olive oil.

But then he could smell the sea upon the wind, and hear the lapping of the waves against the quayside. He saw Wulfrun crouch beside Tabor in the lee of the final warehouse and then beckon to him. Under the moon, the crescent of the harbour was brightly lit.

Squatting, the Mercian glanced along the waterfront. The skeletons of hulls were drawn up by the workshops, the hammers of the boat-makers discarded alongside them. Rats scurried over heaps of ballast stones and piles of fresh timber next to rows of vast clay amphorae reeking of pitch. On the swell, ships of varying size and design from the four corners of the world strained against their creaking tethers.

Hereward looked to Wulfrun. The commander raised a finger to his lips and pointed along the flagstones at the water's edge. A body lay there, leaking blood from a slash across the throat. Further along the sea wall, another corpse sprawled.

Keeping low, Wulfrun crept through the shadows by the workshops until he found the cover of a ballast heap. When Hereward and Tabor crawled beside him, the commander pointed once more, this time out into the harbour. A lamp swung on a small boat being rowed away from the quay. The dancing light revealed three cloaked men in it, one of them at oar.

'The prophet and the monk and one man to guard them,' Tabor rumbled. 'Where is the other?'

Nodding to the two dead men, Wulfrun whispered, 'We cannot be certain there is only one more. We must take no risks until we know how many enemies await us.'

Tabor nodded. 'You speak wise words. We wait until we have more warriors at our back.'

'And while we wait here, my friend could be lost,' Hereward snapped.

Wulfrun scrambled back from the heap. 'Stay here until I bring more men.' When Hereward glanced up, the commander had already disappeared into the shadows.

'This is strange business,' Tabor muttered. 'I cannot make head or tail of it.'

A red glow swayed on a ship at the far end of the moored vessels. The firepot had been lit ready for a night journey across the whale road. The small boat was rowing towards it.

Tabor had seen it too. 'We are too late.'

Hereward knew what he had to do. Standing up, he said, 'Stay here. There is nothing to gain by risking two lives.'

'Have you lost your wits?' Tabor growled. 'You have so many enemies your life already hangs by a thread, and the lives of those who stand with you too. Why risk your neck here?'

'I cannot stand by and watch my friend taken. Once they have got what they want from him, they will not let him live, you know that.' Hereward leapt down the heap, calling, 'Stay here. When the commander returns, let him know where I have gone.' After an instant's hesitation, he added, 'And if I do not come back, tell my spear-brothers . . .'

'I will tell all Constantinople that you died a glorious death,' the Rus called back, 'and a foolish one.'

Hereward scrambled over the sea wall and into a boat barely big enough for two men, little sturdier than the hide and timber vessels the fenland folk used for fishing back in England. He felt unsettled to be back upon the water, but he soon found his balance. Dropping on to the rower's bench, he grasped the oars and prepared to give chase.

For one moment, he heard Tabor's words echo in his head – *This is strange business* – but he pushed them aside. Everything was strange now, in this city of shadows, and there would not be an end to it soon.

The night sky was now brilliantly clear and ablaze with stars. The moon cast a milky path across the black waters. Every vessel was as brightly lit as if it were day. Hereward lowered his head. He would have to take care if he were not to be seen.

Heaving on the oars with all his strength, he felt the boat sweep towards the moored ships. His quarry was ahead, the distance between them shortening by the moment. It was too late to turn back now.

Hereward choked down his doubts. He had set his course; in truth had set it long ago. Perhaps even the day he had led his brothers away from England. If fate chose to ruin his plans, so be it. His life was no longer his own.

Keeping his head low, he watched the three men drag themselves up on to the deck of the ship. It was long and narrow, like the knarrs the northmen used for trade, with a square-rigged sail to speed it across the waves. He was only a whisper behind.

Guiding the boat into the shadows cast on the water so he would not be seen, he loosened his shoulders. Slow strokes. No splashes. Silent, silent.

Once he was alongside, he stood up, balancing against the sudden rocking, and then hauled himself aboard. Cloaked in preparation for the ocean chill, rows of sailors perched on their benches, their backs to him. They were waiting for the order to row out of the harbour and away.

The three new arrivals turned as one the moment the Mercian stepped down on the boards. Two of them recoiled, sailors by the look of them. Their faces were beaten to the texture of leather by the wind and sun.

The third was Justin Verinus, Karas Verinus' murderous beast of a nephew.

The pale-faced youth stared blankly. 'How did you know I was leaving Constantinople this night?' His whispery voice was almost lost beneath the lapping against the hull. He drew his blade.

Hereward looked past him. The sailors were rising from their benches. Their cloaks slipped from them.

Justin glanced round at the sound of movement as the men found their balance on the rocking deck. His mouth fell in shock. These were not sailors, not his men. They were warriors. Swords and axes were already in their hands. Mail-shirts gleamed in the moonlight. Some on the flanks had bows, the nocked arrows pointing towards him.

On the edge of his vision, Hereward caught sight of the two sailors who had accompanied the Verinus bastard edging away from their charge. Their faces were ashen. They knew what was coming. Every man there knew. Stumbling, they dropped over the side to their boat. The Mercian heard their oars splashing as they rowed away as fast as they could.

Hereward drew Brainbiter, levelling it at Justin Verinus, then the fighting men. The blade glinted in the moonlight, but he knew all there could see it was a poor defence against a war-band.

And then the ranks of warriors parted. A towering figure clambered across the benches and the oars and the rope. No one spoke. No one moved. Hereward felt a cold deep in his bones. This was the moment he had long known was coming, the moment when fate would decide his days yet to come.

Drawing himself up to his full height, Varin, the Blood Eagle, pointed his axe at the Mercian.

'You have been betrayed,' he boomed. 'The leader you trusted has led you into a trap. Are you so blind that you cannot see those closest to you want you dead? Is this the great warrior? No, I see a cur before me, too jolt-headed to know it is chasing its own tail. Step forward, Hereward of the English. Your misery ends this day.'

CHAPTER THIRTY-THREE

Ariadne hauled herself up the mooring rope. Seawater sluiced from her sodden clothes. The swim from the quayside had been cold and she shuddered as she pulled herself on to the deck.

On the adjacent ship, the battle between Hereward and Varin raged under a moon so bright it was as clear as day. The fight was so furious! She felt terror course through her as she realized the Englishman was close to being overwhelmed. And even if he could defeat his enemy, the war-band would be upon him in an instant to hack him to pieces.

There was no hope.

How did it come to this, she thought, choking back a sob? She burned with shame at the way she had failed Hereward. And now he would die.

From the moment he had left the Boukoleon palace, she had followed him, as Salih had bid her do. But he had been led into this trap before she had recognized it for what it was. Before she could act.

Sparks flashed across the gulf of night as the two seasoned warriors clashed weapons. Ariadne jolted with each blow as if she were there fighting beside them.

Turning, she searched the shadows of her vessel until she saw the figure standing in the prow, watching the battle on the neighbouring ship. It was the one she had seen at the harbour just before he had rowed out here.

Leo Nepos.

Staggering across the rolling deck, she grabbed his arm. 'Save him,' she pleaded.

Leo jerked round in surprise. 'I am here to bear witness on the day the Nepotes won the crown.' He pushed up his chin. 'Today, Justin Verinus will die, and Hereward of the English too. And then the road to the throne is clear.' He turned back to the battle.

Feeling dazed, Ariadne followed his gaze, and saw Justin cowering aft, by the swinging firepot, away from the flashing blades. But Ariadne found her eyes drawn once more to Hereward. He seemed to know his days were ending. There was no fire in him. The Blood Eagle parried his strikes with ease. His axe came closer to his opponent's flesh with each moment. She could hear his snarl, and the grunting of both men. She winced at the screech of steel on steel.

'You can stop this,' she pleaded again. 'Hereward does not need to die. Nor does my brother. He can be sent away . . .' She felt her heart sink. Where was Salih? She could not change the outcome of this night on her own.

'If your brother lives, he will always be a threat to us.' Leo was unable to take his eyes off the battle.

Slipping on the deck, Hereward went down hard. With a roar, the Blood Eagle swung his axe.

Ariadne cried out, but Varin had been a moment too slow. Rolling to one side, the Mercian pushed himself to his feet. Alerted by her cry, he met her eyes across the swell and yelled, 'Stay back.' Even as the words left his lips the Blood Eagle came at him again.

How had the Nepotes learned that her brother would be leaving Constantinople this night, at this place, so they could set their trap?

'Justin Verinus will die,' Leo repeated, his voice firm. 'And once I am certain that he and Hereward are dead, I will carry the news back to my mother and father and sister and we will rejoice.'

Ariadne felt the blood throb in her head. Al-Kahina was calling to her, taking hold. 'I cannot let this stand.'

Leo glared at her. 'Then we are done. The next time I lay eyes upon you, you will be my enemy.'

Through the haze of the warrior-queen, Ariadne felt as if a blade had stabbed into her heart. But she would not back down.

Barely had the look of hatred crossed Leo's face when she saw Justin move on the other ship. He was seizing his moment. Snarling his hands in his cloak to protect them, he grabbed the firepot and hurled it along the deck.

Cries of alarm rang out from the war-band as the

red-hot coals skidded along the boards. Hereward and Varin wrenched round in their life-or-death struggle, seemingly oblivious. In the confusion, Justin hurled himself over the side.

Leaning over the gunwale, Ariadne searched the inky waters for her brother until the moonlight picked him out. 'Justin,' she yelled. 'Swim towards me.'

His arms flailed, splashing – he was not a good swimmer – but somehow he crossed the short distance. Feeling the strength of al-Kahina inside her, she reached down and helped him clamber aboard. Sodden, he collapsed on to the boards gasping for breath.

Leo had drawn his sword. 'Good,' he snarled. 'Now I can claim this victory for my own.'

Justin staggered to his feet. Ariadne saw a smirk creep on to his lips. He was not scared. In fact, he seemed to relish this confrontation.

'No more,' she shouted. 'This is madness.' She stepped between them. 'I will not let you kill my brother,' she said to Leo, baring her teeth. Looking directly at Justin, she added, 'And I will not let you kill the one I love.'

For a moment she stared across the water, distracted by the rising panic on the other ship. The flames were roaring up from the hot coals. They cast a hellish light over the scattering war-band. Some tried to stamp out the fire, but it must have caught on sailcloth for the flames only leapt higher. Terrified cries rang out.

When she turned back, Justin was staring at her with eyes that seemed to contain no life.

As fast as a snake, his fist slammed against her cheek. She felt a burst of pain and she flew back on to the deck. Tasting blood in her mouth, she shook her head. Justin cared nothing for her. He had never cared. Now he had drawn his own sword and was readying to attack his rival.

Beyond him, smoke billowed out across the black harbour waters. As Ariadne clambered back to her feet, she caught sight of the warriors opposite ripping off their mail and helms as they hurled themselves over the side. She gaped. The heat must be like a furnace, the smoke choking, yet still Hereward and Varin fought on.

She found she could not tear her eyes away from that monumental battle upon the blazing ship. Even Leo and Justin were gripped, their swords hanging in their hands.

Everything seemed to slow. All sound drained away. She felt as though she were in a dream and there was only that moment, for ever. Hereward and Varin, lit by the flames. The Blood Eagle's mad grin. His axe sweeping up, shimmering in the ruddy glow.

Hereward fell. In that instant, she thought she saw him look towards her, or perhaps it was part of that terrible dream. His face, even then, showed only courage and acceptance.

The axe came down.

Ariadne screamed.

Exhausted, Varin drew himself up and raised his

axe high. He roared his triumph into the night, even above the din of the flames, a howl that sounded like a beast at hunt.

Ariadne felt her rush of despair turn to anger. 'I am al-Kahina,' she snarled. 'I am al-Kahina. I am al-Kahina.' A vow, a prayer. She would not see another loss this night.

When she turned to Leo and Justin, they seemed struck by whatever they saw in her face. Yet they were still determined to kill each other, she could see it.

In a flood of rage, she flung herself at the two men as their swords came up. She crashed into them, spun round. The world whirled. A hilt crashed against her forehead. She felt a momentary blackness and then she was falling, with another body tangled in hers.

Down they plunged into the icy waters, and down further, until the darkness and the cold swallowed them. For an instant, she felt the urge to let go, to drift away, let all the miseries end. But then, with her lungs burning, she kicked up until she broke the surface.

Once her mind settled, she felt panic once more, and wrenched around, searching for whoever had fallen with her. But she was alone on the swell. Craning her neck up, she saw Leo peering over the side of the ship. How filled with loathing he seemed when he saw her. She turned her head away from that heartbreaking stare, and when she looked back he was gone.

Though she splashed around and dived down several times, Ariadne could find no sign of her brother. Whether he was alive or dead, she did not know. But she could feel the cold creeping deep into her bones and she knew she needed to reach the shore soon if she were to live. Her heart heavy, she swam back through the rolling cloud of smoke and the reek of burning, crawled up the stone steps from the water, and collapsed on the quayside. She was shaking from exertion and shock. Through slit eyes, she made out a crowd of nervous onlookers drawn by the blazing ship and the smoke. They feared the Turks or the Normans. None of them knew what a tragedy had unfolded this night.

Ariadne closed her eyes, feeling only despair.

When she opened them again a few moments later, she saw movement further down the harbour. Varin was striding along the edge of the quay, carrying Hereward's limp body in his arms. A few of the warriors from the burning ship had clambered up the steps to follow him, soaked and shivering.

For a moment she lay there, gathering her strength, until she heard the sound of running feet moving through the storehouses to the harbour. Varin and the body were gone, but Wulfrun was racing from the shadows with a band of Varangians. They ground to a halt, staring at the burning ship. She had seen the commander leave. Why had it taken him so long to bring reinforcements? Unless, she thought, he had been in no rush to save the hero of the English.

Pushing herself up, Ariadne blinked away hot tears. 'He is dead,' she yelled in anger. 'Hereward is dead.'

Another Varangian, a broad, red-haired warrior,

stepped out from behind a heap of ballast stones where he must have been watching the fight aboard the ship.

''Tis true,' he said. 'I saw it with my own eyes. You are too late. Hereward is dead.'

CHAPTER THIRTY-FOUR

The owl swooped above the rows of graves. Its mournful hoot echoed through the stillness of the cemetery pressed hard against the wall beside the gate of St John de Cornibus. The lamp of the full moon carved deep shadows from the markers and mausoleums across the bright boneyard. Beyond, the houses of the Venetian quarter were silhouetted against the star-sprinkled sky.

The chink of steel upon stones rang out. Two men, beggars in threadbare tunics, toiled in a new grave, breaking the hard-packed ground with borrowed picks and turning out the rocky earth into a pile beside it. Every now and then they would pause to wipe sweat from their brows with the backs of their hands, smearing streaks of brown dirt.

Arms folded, another man towered over them, observing their labours. 'Good,' Varin grunted. 'Keep digging.' Though his arms ached from the battle, it was a good exhaustion, the kind felt after a job well done. At his feet, the rough-hewn coffin leaked blood into the dust. Ropes had been tied around the top and bottom, ready for it to be lowered into the grave.

Varin looked around. The cemetery was a lonely place. Haunted, some said. Silence lay heavy upon it. Yet in the distance he could hear cries, of alarm, or anger, or rebellion or fear, the sound of a city on the edge.

Rubbing the small of his back, one of the men pushed himself upright and leaned on his wooden shovel. 'Why give him a burial? I have never known the like. 'Tis easier to toss the dead over the wall, into the sea. Let the fishes finish them off.'

The other paused with his pick mid-strike and waited for the Blood Eagle's reply.

'Our masters are wiser than you,' Varin said. 'Here Hereward will lie in an unmarked grave. His friends will never know whether he is alive or dead. None will be able to mourn for him. And in time he will be forgotten.'

The gravedigger sniffed. 'Men die all the time.'

'Not a man like this.' Tapping one boot against the coffin to emphasize his words, the Blood Eagle added, 'A man who is second in command of the Varangian Guard found drifting in the Bosphorus, this cannot easily be forgotten. Justice will be demanded. Vengeance.'

'You fear his friends, then. That they will come for you.'

Varin prowled around the hole. 'I fear no man. Nor death either. No, this is by order of your masters. They have plans that must continue apace. They would rather the city hear whispers of Hereward's death, and doubt, and wonder, and no one know whether truth or lie. A man with questions looks one way for answers and sees not what is happening in the other.'

The gravedigger scratched his head. Varin could see these thoughts demanded too much of him. When the man made to open his mouth again, the Blood Eagle held up his hand. 'Still your tongue. You are being paid to dig, not talk.'

Muttering under his breath, the man returned to his labours.

Soon after, the grave was done. The diggers crawled out, wheezing. Varin allowed them to slake their thirst from a hide before they grasped the ropes on the coffin. Staggering against the weight, they lowered the box into the hole. Blood dripped into the dark.

The coffin dropped to the bottom of the grave with a thump, and the men let the ropes down on top of it. They began to refill the pit as fast as they could. The job done, they stepped back to examine their handiwork – a faint mound of freshly turned earth with no marker to show who lay beneath.

'Done,' one of the gravediggers said.

'Done,' the Blood Eagle repeated.

Then he took his axe and ended their days, as the Nepotes had insisted, and tossed their bodies over the wall into the sea.

CHAPTER THIRTY-FIVE

The ashes in the hearth were cold. Kraki stared at them, remembering Hereward coming to him as if in a dream, to talk of death and what must be done in days yet to come. How could he call himself friend? He had made light of the Mercian's fears, had all but laughed in his face. And he had not said farewell. His eyes dropped to the goblet of wine that sat untouched on the table in front of him.

On the benches around the feasting table, the spear-brothers sat with their eyes fixed on horizons only each man could see. Alexios stood by the seat that Hereward normally occupied, his face drawn as if he had not had a moment's sleep. In front of the door, Wulfrun and Ricbert stood like sentinels. They had not moved since they had delivered the news. Kraki had never known a mood so grim, not even after England had fallen.

'What now for us?' Sighard asked into the silence.

'We do not whine like children, that is first above all things,' Kraki growled.

'Aye,' Guthrinc agreed, nodding slowly. 'Hereward

believed he should have died in Ely when England fell. He has been counting every day since as a gift from God. He knew this time was coming.'

'But he was our leader.' Sighard looked around the stony faces. 'Without him—'

'Without him, we will be the men he has taught us to be.' Kraki glared at the younger warrior.

Drawing himself up, Alexios paced around the table, becoming more determined with each step. In his expression, Kraki could see the celebrated general who had commanded great armies.

'Hereward is not gone,' Alexios began, his voice commanding attention. 'Not while he lives in our hearts. You are right to mourn. Warriors could not have asked for a better leader. This long battle that has been fought since you left England's shores was the one Hereward wanted, to lead you to a place where you could find peace, and reward for all your sacrifices. The standard has fallen, but now it is up to one of you to grasp it and lead the others on in the days yet to come. Who will shoulder this burden?'

Silence fell across the spear-brothers. Then, after a moment, all eyes settled upon Kraki.

'It is too soon to decide that,' the Viking muttered, though he could hear Hereward's words echoing in his head. He did not want this responsibility. His anger hardened in his chest and he pushed himself up, looking to Wulfrun. 'Tabor witnessed all. Varin the Blood Eagle murdered Hereward. I demand justice.'

'There will be justice,' the commander of the Guard

replied. 'But we must be sure. Tabor is slow-witted. He cannot be certain what he saw.'

Kraki felt his rage surge, a better feeling than the paralysing grief. He stormed across the hall, stabbing a finger at Wulfrun. 'You are trying to protect the Nepotes. That woman of yours. If Varin killed Hereward, he did so by order of that bastard kin. There is no honour in you.' He spat on the boards at the other man's feet.

Wulfrun raised his axe, Kraki a fist.

Alexios stepped between them. 'We do not turn on each other,' he commanded. Grabbing Kraki by the shoulders, he added, 'Hereward was my friend too. I will make sure there is justice.'

Kraki fought against the seething rage within him, and after a moment he nodded. Turning away, he cast a sullen look at Wulfrun and pointed. 'But do not trust a word he says.'

'His grief eats away at him,' Alexios said to Wulfrun. 'You must give him this day.'

Wulfrun nodded, spun on his heel and strode out, with Ricbert close behind.

Sitting back at his bench, Kraki bowed his head over his goblet, calming himself. 'Someone needs to tell the monk,' he murmured.

'I will tell him,' Alexios said. 'Perhaps he will have some words of comfort for you.'

Kraki snorted. Once Alexios had left, he tugged a leather pouch out of his furs and tossed it into the middle of the table.

'What is that?' Sighard asked.

'Gold. All that I have saved since I joined the Guard.' The Viking looked around the faces of the spear-brothers. 'It is a reward, for anyone who can tell me where Hereward lies.'

'You are a fool. You waste your hard-earned gold,' Hiroc the Three-fingered grumbled.

Rising, Kraki hammered a fist upon the table. 'I cannot rest until I find his body. I will bring it home for a hero's funeral and we will sing it into Valhalla.'

Mad Hengist began to dance, laughing. 'He is the bear-killer, the giant-killer. In England, they whispered Hereward could never die.' Pausing, he stared at the Viking, then pointed. 'The sword must be brought back.'

Kraki could feel the eyes of the others upon him. Some were pitying, he knew that. But he had spoken truly: he could not rest until he had achieved his aim. He owed it to his friend. 'The word will go out from this hall. A fortune to the man or woman who leads me to him.'

'And what then?' Guthrinc asked in a quiet voice. 'We wail and mourn and tear at our hair?'

Kraki pulled his axe up from the bench and laid it on the table. 'Then we will have our vengeance.'

CHAPTER THIRTY-SIX

Alric limped from the palace chapel. Long hours of prayer had driven spikes of pain into his knees and his throat felt like the sands of Afrique from the incense that had swathed him all day. But he felt at peace, and that was good. No one could begrudge a man in mourning some time away from the stifling chamber of the prophet. It was the emperor himself who had given him permission to petition the Lord for Hereward's soul. If truth be told, he felt that one more hour with Megistus, overseeing the constant procession of nobles looking for salvation, would have driven him mad.

Though only two days had passed, the news of Hereward's death had spread far and wide. Alric was surprised by how many had been saddened, not only his spear-brothers but all the Varangians who had fought alongside him on the field of battle, and the members of the government who were grateful for his wise counsel. Even Nikephoros, who, for all his weaknesses, still had the heart of a warrior and recognized the courage of one of his own.

Fighting men knew things that other mortals did not, Hereward had always told him. And they saw things hidden to most eyes. At times, Hereward had seemed to despise himself more than his enemies. Alric grinned. What he would have given to see his friend told he was held in such high regard by both high-born and low.

At the door of the chamber that had become his new home, he felt his mood darken once more. 'They have fed you well, I hope,' he called as he stepped inside. 'Sometimes the slaves are so in awe, they forget you need to eat like other men.'

Megistus roamed along the far wall of the chamber, tugging at his greasy grey locks. His eyes burned under his wild brows. Alric flinched. He thought he saw a glimmer of madness there.

They had underestimated the toll that would be taken on the old man, that was certain. No one could have guessed how the demands on him would spiral once the great fear had gripped Constantinople. Too many begging hands, too many whining pleas and prayers.

Hurrying over, the monk caught Megistus' shoulders, easing him back to his stool. 'You must rest,' he murmured.

'Let me return to my home,' the old man whined. 'I have done no wrong.'

'Do you not remember how long we spoke beside your hearth, and all that was said? You agreed you would see this business through to the end. And then you would be well rewarded. You swore an oath, Megistus.'

'No,' the old man moaned. 'No.' His eyes rolled, and when he looked up Alric felt as if he was not recognized. 'I can take no more. My bones are old and weary. I will die here, I know, never again to see the sun. I will die.' His crackling voice rose to a shriek.

Alric shook the old man to calm him, and then, when he realized this was only making things worse, he dropped to his knees and leaned in so their faces were only a finger's width apart. He flinched at the old man's foetid breath.

Megistus' gaze swam and then settled on the man in front of him.

'What did I tell you?' Alric whispered, pushing the frustration out of his voice. 'If you raise the guards' ire, they will take you from here and put your neck on the block.'

The old man's eyes widened in terror.

'All will be well,' the monk whispered. He pressed a finger to Megistus' lips. 'But your tongue must remain still. As quiet as a mouse, until you are spoken to.'

The old man nodded, too fast. Alric felt a pang of guilt for making him afraid.

Heavy footsteps echoed along the corridor and came to a stop outside the cell. The monk stood and stepped calmly away from Megistus as the door opened. Looking up, he saw the face of Karas Verinus and felt the chill flood through him. In all the time Megistus had offered up his prophecies, Karas had never asked one question of him. Perhaps he feared

308

that God would reveal the secrets he kept hidden in his heart. Whatever his reason for seeking a private audience now, his timing could not have been worse. Alric swallowed.

'The prophet is resting,' he said.

'The prophet is a liar.'

Alric's heart thumped when he saw that Karas was now standing with his back to the door. The general had one hand upon the hilt of his sword, his icy stare seemingly weighing whether to use the blade on Alric.

'What is this?' Alric tried to keep the waver out of his voice.

'I know the truth, monk.'

Alric backed towards Megistus. 'I will call the guards.'

'There are no guards.' Karas looked Megistus up and down. 'A filthy beggar.'

'God has chosen him—'

'Do you not fear the judgement of the Lord, monk? Blasphemy slips so easily from your lips.'

Alric felt a chill run deep into his bones. ''Twas you outside the door the other night. You heard—'

'I heard, monk,' Karas replied, 'but I am no fool. It only gave substance to what I already believed. I had long wondered who stood to gain from this deceit. And still I wonder. Was this the plan of Hereward, or Alexios Comnenos?'

Alric sagged. There was no point in denying it.

Karas took a step closer. 'Who gains, monk? It is not God who speaks through this beggar's mouth, but a man who knows he can twist even an emperor to his will.'

'What can you do?' Alric said, his face hardening. 'Who will believe you if you speak this way beyond this chamber? All of Constantinople knows that God speaks here.'

'You speak true,' Karas said. 'And I bow to your wisdom.'

With the speed of a striking viper, he lashed out. The hilt of his sword crashed across Alric's forehead and the monk spun to the flagstones. Blinking away the blood and the tears that clouded his vision, he saw the tip of the blade flash towards his throat. A warning.

Megistus threw himself from his stool and scrabbled towards the door. He was too slow. Karas snarled one huge hand in the neck of the old man's tunic and hauled him clear of the ground. Mewling like a babe, the old man flailed, but he was too weak to break free. With his other hand, the general raised his sword until the tip rested against that scrawny neck.

Karas smiled, cold and cruel. 'Whoever controls God, controls the empire.'

CHAPTER THIRTY-SEVEN

'Can no one be trusted?' Nikephoros ranged around the chamber, flexing his fingers as if choking a small child. 'I am surrounded by bastards. You are sure of this?'

Karas held the emperor's gaze. 'I heard it from the lips of Tabor of the Varangian Guard. Hereward was slain by the Blood Eagle, at the behest of the Nepotes.' He shrugged. 'Some grudge, long in the making.'

'A plot, no doubt. Against me,' Nikephoros raged.

'There are plots and there are plots,' Karas continued in a calm voice. 'Most will never amount to anything.'

'I want the Nepotes punished. All of them. I want their heads.' Spittle flew from Nikephoros' lips.

'We must take great care,' Falkon said, stepping forward. 'The city rumbles on the edge of open rebellion. Not against your rule, no,' he added quickly as Nikephoros' eyes blazed. 'But out of fear. We are beset by enemies, great and powerful ones with armies that could crush us. Bread is in short supply. Our own army is weakened. And the prophet's words have fanned these flames into a fire that could burn down all Constantinople.'

Nikephoros leaned against the wall and rested one hand across his eyes. Karas considered for a moment that he might be about to faint at this litany of misery.

'All your people want is to feel safe within these walls . . . these walls that they have been told will keep out any threat,' Falkon continued, one arm outstretched. 'But if they see noble head after noble head rolling, if they feel there is a sickness of revolt in the court itself, they will lose all faith in the ones who lead them. And then they will know there is no safe place anywhere. That road can lead to one place only.'

'What, then?' the emperor asked in desperation. 'For God's sake, find me a path through this wilderness.'

'There is one way,' Karas ventured. He kept his voice measured, but this was the moment for which he had waited. 'Falkon Cephalas, your eyes and ears in the city tell you the Nepotes are no threat?'

'This is true. They are weakened, and afraid they cannot command the support of the court, or the church, not with the prophet speaking out so boldly. They will not move against the crown.'

'Then only one true threat remains,' Karas said. 'The Comnenoi.'

The emperor narrowed his eyes at the general. 'You have proof that they plot against me?'

'You know as well as I that Anna Dalassene has always coveted the throne.'

'Wanting is not reason enough to act.'

'Only treachery could have allowed Alexios Comnenos to escape from the Normans. He denies it, and his running dogs bark at his command, but there can be no other explanation. Whatever the prophet said.' Karas folded his hands behind his back. He was sick too, sick of these politics. A sword in his hand, that would solve all his problems, but he could afford to bide his time now he was so close. 'But if that is not enough, my own eyes and ears in the city have found evidence that the Comnenoi are preparing to make a move against you. And now the prophet has said the same.'

Nikephoros recoiled as if he had been burned. 'Is this true?'

'This very morn,' Karas said. 'I heard it with my own ears. God has spoken.'

'I must hear it for myself,' the emperor gasped, hurrying towards the door.

'It is too late.'

Hearing the weight in Karas' words, Nikephoros whirled.

'A sickness has come over Megistus. He is close to death.'

The emperor blanched.

'The monks care for him even as we speak. But I fear the worst.'

Stumbling across the chamber, Nikephoros sagged into a chair. Karas saw his shoulders crumple with despair. The emperor was a man on the edge, his mood swinging by the moment. 'God is abandoning us.'

Karas strode in front of him, peering down at the

313

bag of bones. 'Are we not the centre of all Christendom? No, God's work here is done, that is all. The prophet has offered up his final account, and now he can return to the grave. The Comnenoi must be destroyed.'

The emperor nodded slowly. 'It is God's plan.'

Karas held Falkon's gaze, smiling. 'And if we are wise, we will not anger the people. Punish the Comnenoi and all other plotters will be too afraid to act. One example is all that is needed, only one, and when folk hear it is the man who has betrayed us to our enemies, they will cheer us. We are keeping them safe, as they wish above all else.'

Falkon bowed his head in deference. 'What do you suggest?'

'We do not need to execute anyone,' Karas replied. 'Arrest Alexios and his brother Isaac, and then blind them. And send his mother back to the convent at Petrion. That will suffice.'

'What of my wife?' Nikephoros eased his shaking body out of the chair as he eyed the other two men uneasily. 'Now she has made Alexios her own son—'

'This may be for the best.' Karas let the words hang. He looked deep into the emperor's eyes and held his gaze, a silent communication flowing between them.

Nikephoros understood. His cheeks coloured and his face hardened. 'Yes,' he all but spat. 'It is God's plan. Seize Alexios, and blind him.'

CHAPTER THIRTY-EIGHT

'Is this true?' Anna's eyes blazed, but behind her mask of anger Deda glimpsed true terror.

'The word has gone out from the palace. From the emperor himself. I sought you out as soon as I heard.' The knight glanced from his wife Rowena, who had first heard the news, to Alexios and Isaac. The younger of the Comnenos brothers looked dazed at this rapid turn of events. Alexios, though, drew himself up, ready.

Through the windows, gulls wheeled across a blue sky. But their shrieks faded behind shouts of alarm and the clatter of boots and steel rising up from the thronging streets.

Anna whirled, panic breaking through her forced composure. 'Leave!' she all but screamed at her sons.

'But where should we go—' Isaac began.

Anna threw herself across the chamber, dragging her sons towards the door. 'Run! Alexios! Isaac! Run!'

As the shouts drew nearer, the two men shook themselves into action. Darting to the door, Alexios peered out into the corridor and gave a nod that all was clear.

'We will take horses at the gate of Rhesios and ride west,' he said, glancing back at his mother. He flashed a smile, hoping to soothe her.

'I will help them.' Even in that sun-drenched chamber, Salih ibn Ziyad seemed to be cloaked in shadow. He had been standing in a corner, so silent and still Deda had almost forgotten the wise man was there. Ariadne crouched at his feet, like a dog about to attack. 'Take the Great West Road and you will have to fight every step of the way. I will show you a quicker route, away from prying eyes.'

Alexios and Isaac turned back and hugged their mother goodbye. 'We will return. All will be well,' Alexios murmured.

Deda watched Anna raise her head and clear her face of any emotion. But her eyes flooded with tears, betraying her.

'Come with us,' Isaac urged.

His mother shook her head. 'There is work for me here,' she replied, her voice now commanding. She was hoping to buy her sons time to escape, a mother's sacrifice, Deda thought as he studied her face. If Alexios and Isaac knew what she intended, they would not be able to leave, and then all would be lost. He felt a wave of concern.

'Hurry,' the knight urged before they could read the truth in Anna's words. 'You have no time to waste.'

Once the others had gone, Anna fell back into a chair and held her head in her hands. 'This has come too soon. We are not ready.'

'We knew Karas Verinus would not wait until the stars were aligned for the Comnenoi.'

Anna nodded slowly. 'If only . . . A week more. A day. Our plans have been long in the making, yet they have come to naught,' she said in a quiet voice. 'Now all we can hope is that the Comnenoi can live until dawn.'

For a long moment, the words hung in the air. No one could deny them. Feeling uncomfortable, Rowena brushed the flour from her apron and said, 'I must return to the kitchens before I am missed.' The knight nodded to his wife, pleased that she would be away from danger.

Anna nodded. 'You may well have saved my sons. I will always be in your debt.' Turning to Deda, she added, 'It would be wise if you were not seen with me. My presence will taint even the purest soul in the eyes of the emperor and his allies.'

'It would not be honourable to abandon you in your time of need,' the knight replied with a bow. 'You should have a sword to protect you.' Still bowing, he unsheathed his blade and balanced it on the palms of his hand, offering his service to her.

'No,' she replied, her voice softening at his promise of sacrifice. 'You have a good heart, Deda, and great courage, and I would not see that wasted on me. Stay with your wife. In the days to come, she will need your protection as much as I. This business is only the beginning of Karas' attempt upon the throne, and of his vengeance. I know *his* foul heart. He will not rest until he has brought doom to his enemies, and to his enemies' kin, and to all who walked with them. Watch your own back.'

'Where will you go?' Rowena asked.

Anna thought for a moment, and when her eyes sparkled Deda glimpsed her old defiance returning. 'There is only one place in this city where I will be safe.'

CHAPTER THIRTY-NINE

Deda and Anna hurried out into the sun and crossed the street to the shade on the other side. As they slipped into the crowd of baffled onlookers trying to make sense of the din drawing nearer by the moment, they ducked down, catching their breath. The knight watched Anna's face harden as she began to calculate her options for survival.

'Not a moment too soon,' she whispered.

The emperor's men surged up the street and crashed into the building where the Comnenoi had been only moments earlier.

'We should find a hiding place for you,' Deda urged, trying to steer Anna into the maze of narrow streets at their backs.

Anna smiled and shook her head. 'No, hiding is the last thing I should do. Now we must buy time for Alexios and Isaac to escape. I will bring the whole of the emperor's wrath upon me, if that is what it takes.'

Deda felt only respect for her courage, but his neck prickled with fear at what was to come. With his hand never straying far from the hilt of his sword, his eyes searching every doorway and alley, he followed her through the streets. Past the hippodrome they hurried, and the church of St Euphemia, until Anna plunged into the crowds thronging the forum of Constantine.

Keeping his head down, Deda looked around the square. It was brimming with life. Some were conducting business, haggling and haranguing; some rushed by with their arms laden with goods. Others dawdled and chatted. He felt a pang of worry that in the bustle he might not be able to draw his sword at need.

Within moments, he caught sight of knots of the emperor's men pushing through the assembled crowds.

'When they come for me, step away and hurry back to Rowena,' Anna whispered, leaning in. 'Whatever threats they make. They will not harm me here among the people.'

Though he did not agree, Deda nodded his assent. A moment later, Anna found the steps at the foot of the forum's monument and clambered up them so she could be seen above the crowd. 'My sons are no traitors,' she shouted. 'They are heroes of the empire.' Her sharp voice carved through the babble of voices, and as heads turned and silence fell it reached to a band of the emperor's men. As they rushed forward, Deda stepped away from her, but kept his sword hand ready.

Anna showed no fear as the men surrounded her. Deda watched, poised to rush to her rescue should it be necessary. His promise be damned. He could not stand by and see her harmed. He counted six of the emperor's men, and no doubt many more nearby. How many could he take out? Yet they looked unsure if they should brandish their weapons. They had probably never captured a woman before, and certainly not one of Anna's standing.

Peering over her captors' heads, Anna called, 'You all know my sons, Alexios and Isaac. They are heroes of the empire, are they not?'

A ripple of agreement ran through the crowd, growing louder. Soon men and women were yelling for Anna Dalassene to be left alone. The emperor's men lowered their eyes, growing ever more uneasy in the presence of the mob around them, but they kept the circle tight. Finally, one of them whispered to another, who raced off.

'You will wait here,' one of the group commanded.

Anna only smiled.

Looking around, Deda could see that Anna's ploy had worked. The crowd thickened as the raucous voices grew louder.

After a few moments, the bodies separated and Falkon Cephalas pushed his way through, with the man who had run off. Falkon waved his hand and the circle of the emperor's men opened.

'The emperor has requested your attendance,' he said.

'The emperor has requested my attendance,' Anna repeated, her voice dripping with sarcasm. 'There are troubles here, Falkon, and great ones. My sons are loyal to the emperor, every man and woman here knows that.'

'I am told they have fled the city,' Falkon replied. 'Is that the behaviour of innocents?'

'They are saving themselves. This day we have learned of a plot by the enemies of the Comnenoi . . . ones who can only be enemies of the empire. A plot to blind them both!'

More angry voices punctuated her words. Anna had the crowd in her hand. She drove them into battle on her behalf like a seasoned general.

'Yes, they have fled the city,' she continued, 'but only so they may continue to offer loyal service to our emperor.'

'And why did you not go with them if you fear for your family?' Falkon asked.

'Because I have put my faith in God, Falkon. Would you deny me that?'

Her words whipped the crowd to even greater frenzy. Bodies buffeted the small circle of guards. Falkon looked around, calculating the threat.

'Let me pray!' Anna cried. 'Let me petition God for protection for my sons, for myself, for all the Comnenoi.'

So loud was the response that Deda knew Falkon had no choice but to agree. With a low bow, he swept his arm in the direction of the Hagia Sophia.

Pressing her palms together, lifting her chin and peering through heavily lidded eyes, Anna began to walk. The circle of armed men dogged her steps, the cheering crowd swarming all around.

Matching her pace, Deda pushed through the milling crowd to keep up. He kept his head down to avoid drawing attention to himself, but he could not help a smile at Anna's performance as he watched her turn her face up to the heavens, her mouth an O of beatific ecstasy. As she glided across the forum and along the Mese to the Milion monument, the cheering crowds reached out to her.

When she began to cross the square to the Hagia Sophia, Deda spun round at loud cries. Royal guards from the Scholae Palatinae wearing their familiar golden torcs were racing up, demanding that Anna be brought back to the palace.

Anna must have heard, for although she didn't look round, she walked faster. At the same time, she bowed her head as if crushed beneath the weight of her grief. The crowd's cheers grew louder still.

Dwarfed by the grand entrance to the Hagia Sophia, she paused at those three arches under the great stone buttresses and muttered something to the keepers. With a flourish they threw the door open. Deda stiffened. The royal guards were lashing out on all sides to force a path through the crowd. There was still time for them to drag her back to face Nikephoros' wrath.

'Help me,' Anna cried. 'Please, God, help me.'

Though she had called out to the Lord, the crowd seemed to take it upon themselves to be his agents upon the earth. Yelling and shaking their fists, the people flooded into the path of the Scholae Palatinae. They were thirty deep, Deda saw, and from their angry resistance it was clear they were not about to budge. He squeezed through the bodies to the entrance to watch Anna's final display.

Crossing herself, she swept through the church to the inner sanctuary and bowed twice to God. On the third bow, she grasped the iron rings upon the closed doors of the sanctuary and slid to her knees. Her voice soaring up into the vault overhead, she cried, 'Let not my blood be spilled. Let no man dare harm me in this house of God, for the Lord will protect me. Unless my hands are cut off, I will not leave this holy place except on one condition: that I receive the emperor's cross as guarantee of safety.'

The crowd roared, and Deda nodded. Anna had escaped the emperor's clutches. Nikephoros had underestimated her, and now she had bought the Comnenoi their last chance.

CHAPTER FORTY

Bands of armed men stormed along the sun-
drenched Mese, the great street leading west from
the heart of the city. They barged aside any who
crossed their path, tearing off hoods to peer into faces,
demanding information at the point of a blade. The
emperor's men swarmed everywhere. Soon there
would be no safe place anywhere in Constantinople.

Ariadne crouched in a shadowed alley and waited
as a group of the soldiers hurried by. Once she was sure
they had all passed, she held up a hand to signal to the
others. She felt haunted by the failure of the previous
night, though Salih had repeatedly insisted that she
should not blame herself for Hereward's death; there
was nothing she could have done. But of one thing they
could all be sure – she would not fail again.

Alexios and Isaac crept along the alley, with Salih
close behind. Ariadne pointed the way down a narrow
rat-run between the rear of the merchants' stores and
the rows of workshops. Though it disappeared into
shadow, she knew it would lead them away from the
crowds.

'What fools we were.' Ariadne heard the bitterness in Isaac's voice as he squeezed along the path. 'We should have known Karas would come for us again once his plan in the west had failed. Even if he had seized the throne, he could never have rested while the Comnenoi were here to challenge him.'

'You know this city better than I,' Alexios whispered to Ariadne. He took her hand and looked into her eyes. 'Without your help, we would never have escaped alive. We will always be in your debt.'

Ariadne nodded, but it was not enough. When she closed her eyes, all she could see was Hereward falling beneath the Blood Eagle's axe. She blinked away the vision and led the way along the narrow path.

Through the hidden byways of the city they hurried, clambering over spoil heaps, sneaking past workshops ringing with hammers, ghosting through tranquil gardens, always keeping far away from any area thronging with life. The day drew on. The sun slipped towards the horizon. At the forum of Arcadius, beyond the Vlanga to the west, she took a north-west turn along the quieter road through Xerolophos. That would lead them to the gate of Rhesios in the city wall on the slopes of the Seventh Hill.

Ariadne watched the others march along the dusty road. Alexios and Isaac were sweating, but their determination kept the weariness at bay. Salih was a pool of shadow, cool and calm. They kept their voices low when they talked, but she heard hope in their tones, which pleased her. That emotion seemed in short supply.

As the cistern of Mocius rose up on their left, they heard the sound of many feet approaching and scrambled off the road to hide. A war-band thirty strong strode towards the city. The men were filthy, wearing little more than rags, but they carried swords and axes that seemed to shine like new.

Once they had passed, Alexios growled, 'Karas Verinus' men, no doubt. He builds his army by the day, ready to seize the throne.'

'How long before that bastard makes his move?' Isaac asked, watching the war-band march into the dusty distance.

Alexios exchanged a glance with his brother. 'These are desperate days. Time is short.'

'Do not think about staying and fighting.' Salih's face was like stone, his voice gravelly. 'You command no strength in the city. But while you are gone you will have allies here fighting for you. Do not doubt that.'

Alexios nodded. As Salih led them back to the road, Ariadne was proud that she had chosen to follow him.

Soon after, the western wall loomed, a thick band of black against the reddening sky. As they neared, it soared up high over their heads, as broad as five men lying head to toe. The empire's standard, a golden double-headed eagle on a red background, fluttered in the late-afternoon breeze. Ariadne craned her neck, but could see no movement. The guards would be in their chamber atop the wall, out of the merciless sun but able to see anyone approaching across the western plain.

The horses were tethered in the growing gloom next to the gate, fed and watered and ready to carry messengers into the city. Ariadne watched Alexios and Isaac sneak up to them, taking care not to cause alarm. They were good horsemen and took two mounts without any disturbance.

Ariadne waited at the foot of the stone steps while Salih crept up to the guards' chamber. Death waits in silence, the Varangians said, and there was no one more silent than her master. He returned scant moments later, wiping the silver blade he carried at his waist. Ariadne met his eyes, acknowledging the necessity. She felt uneasy that good Romans had died, but they were desperate now.

Alexios and Isaac hurried to crank the gate open before reinforcements arrived. Once the two men had mounted, Ariadne reached up to take Alexios' hand. 'God goes with you,' she murmured.

'Your mother will be kept safe, as long as I live, and Maria too. You have my word on that,' Salih said.

Alexios looked down at Salih and Ariadne and nodded his thanks. 'We are at our lowest ebb, but this tide will turn, never fear.' Ariadne heard defiance in his voice.

She frowned as something passed between Alexios and Salih, a hint, perhaps, of hope they both shared but neither dared voice, or perhaps a shadow of some secret to which she was not privy.

She watched the Comnenoi gallop towards the fat red orb of the setting sun until a cloud of their dust swallowed them up.

'They are brave, but for now their time is over.' Salih ibn Ziyad turned away and hurried back along the road towards the darkness gathering above the city. 'And soon, perhaps, it will be time for us to follow them.'

Ariadne felt a pang of worry. She could not abandon Leo. 'What say you?'

'Karas Verinus has removed his greatest rival. Now only the Nepotes remain. They will fight like starving dogs, but soon they too will be gone. Then he will be free to seize the crown. But a man like Karas Verinus will not approach the throne like a thief in the night. These streets will run red with blood. We must be ready.'

CHAPTER FORTY-ONE

The torch flared as the door opened. A wash of light shimmered across the stone walls and a blast of dank air reeking of wet straw rushed out of the dark.

'There.' The guard jerked his head along the tunnel. 'At the end.' He grunted, bored, and shuffled back to his chamber to return to his bread and olives.

Deda took the torch from the wall, the pitch spitting. He glanced at Rowena and forced a weak smile. It was worse than they had thought. Behind them, Guthrinc stooped, the top of his head brushing the dungeon tunnel's roof. Four days had passed since Anna had sought sanctuary in the Hagia Sophia, and the knight wondered how she was. But this matter was more pressing.

Rats scurried ahead of them as they made their way through the gloom deep beneath the Great Palace. In the cell at the end of the passage, the pale figure they had come to see recoiled from the light, throwing one arm across his eyes.

'They treat you well?' Deda felt a wave of pity.

Alric rested his head against the wall and forced a grin that failed to mask his exhaustion. 'The last time I was held captive, they cut off my fingers,' he replied, holding up his stump. 'Holding on to my pieces . . . to me, that is well.'

'No beatings?' Guthrinc asked.

Alric shook his head.

'That is good. I thought I might have to crack heads.' He leaned down and offered the monk the lip of a water-skin. 'Fresh. Slake your thirst.'

As he drank, Deda nodded to Rowena. While she hurried to the door to keep watch, the knight crouched beside the monk and whispered, 'We must not be seen here. Karas is looking for any excuse to remove all likely enemies from the field of battle.'

Alric leaned forward. The knight saw his eyes widen with eagerness. 'Can you free me?'

Shaking his head, Deda replied, 'For the price of a little coin, the guard let us in to see you. But Karas has eyes everywhere and we would be seized before we had left the palace.' He felt guilty for shattering the other man's hopes.

The monk sagged back against the wall. 'I do not know how much time I have left to me.'

'We have heard the lies,' Guthrinc said, stooping. 'All Constantinople has heard.'

'That I gave poison to the prophet,' the monk replied with bitterness, 'and now he hangs on the edge of death. If he survives, I will face questions, ordeals . . . and if he dies, I will follow him.'

'Karas is cunning,' Deda murmured. 'Step by step,

he bends all Constantinople to his will. The prophet cannot speak out against him.'

'As Hereward planned,' the monk interjected.

Guthrinc frowned, puzzled by this news, but before he could say anything Deda continued, 'His enemies are falling. The Comnenoi are in hiding. He tightens his grip upon the government by the day, buys the favour of advisers, whispers in the emperor's ear. Soon he will make his move upon the throne.'

'And then my days are done,' Alric said, his smile tight. 'And all our days, no doubt.'

'Keep a fire in your heart,' Rowena called from the door.

Deda watched the giant Englishman crouch to reassure the monk. 'We will not let one of our own rot down here. Not one of us will rest until you are free.'

'I will keep faith, as always.' Alric's voice did not waver.

When Deda glanced back, the last thing he saw was the monk's smile receding into the gloom. And then the dark swept in.

As the trio left the lower levels and climbed the stone steps back to palace life, a large shadow loomed across the sunlit doorway above. Deda sensed the others stiffen.

Neophytos the eunuch furrowed his brow when they emerged into the light. 'Are you lost? I would think there is little for you in the bowels of this place.'

Deda bowed. The monk seemed to be growing larger by the day. He did not like this man, with his snake-tongue and his insincere smile. 'And you are far from your cell at the monastery. I would think you would be praying for your kin with all that is happening in Constantinople.'

The eunuch bowed back, the fat rolling under his tunic. 'God has already smiled upon my kin. The Nepotes are blessed.'

As they walked away, the knight could feel Neophytos' eyes heavy upon his back.

'His smile was too confident,' Guthrinc muttered. 'By rights, the Nepotes should be afraid of what Karas does next.'

'The Nepotes are the least of our worries,' Deda replied as they stepped out into the sun-drenched courtyard. It had an old oak in the centre, with a stone bench shaded under its spreading branches. Around the edges, mullein flowers filled the air with their sweet scent. 'Let them and Karas tear chunks out of each other like starving dogs. I fear for Alric.'

'You gave him hope and that is good,' Rowena said. Deda thought how careworn she looked. He felt a note of sadness that in all these years he had not been able to give her a better life. 'But the truth is harder,' she continued. 'We have few allies left in this city. Who do we turn to next? Who will listen to us now that the Comnenoi are gone?'

'I will speak to Wulfrun,' Guthrinc said. 'He still has the ear of those who stand at the emperor's shoulder.'

Deda leaned against the oak, his arms folded as he reflected. 'Karas may have one more task left for Alric

– to speak for the prophet and tell the city that the rule of the Verini is God-sent.'

'If that is true, we may have more time to buy his freedom,' Guthrinc said. 'But I would not wager his life upon that thin hope.'

'Agreed,' the knight replied, the shadows of leaves dappling his face. 'Then we have little choice.'

For the rest of the day, Deda waited in the Vlanga, listening to the rumours the spear-brothers had heard from the other guardsmen. Once night had fallen, he crept back to the Great Palace and Rowena let him into the kitchens. In an instant, her smile faded as she read his taut expression. 'You still feel the same way?'

The knight nodded. 'I cannot turn my back, you know that.'

'No, you are an honourable man.'

'But I must do this alone—'

Rowena scowled, silencing him.

Deda took her hand. 'I would never put your life at risk.'

'In England, I could have suffered in silence in my village and watched the Normans kill my kin, my neighbours, crush everything I held dear. Yet I followed the rebels under Hereward's standard, knowing full well that my days could end at any moment. We are one, you and I. We know there are times when all must be risked, for if not, what would we have? Dust and ashes.' She kissed him on the cheek and whispered, 'Do not worry about me. I am with you. Follow your heart, my husband, and I will be at your side.'

Deda heard the fire in her voice. He let himself sink into her eyes and her smile for a moment, feeling that he had made no better choice in his life than the one to join with her. 'Then if our days end, they end,' he said. 'We will be together, and we will know that we always fought with honour.' Raising her hand to his lips, he kissed it. 'Come, then. We are as one.'

Emboldened, he turned and hurried from the kitchen and along the dark palace corridors. Rowena followed, her skirt swishing across the flagstones.

The palace was still at that hour. Occasionally bursts of laughter echoed dimly and distant singing rose up through the shadows from the quarters where the Varangian Guard idled away their time until their blades were needed. Deda and Rowena moved as carefully and quietly as they could. If the Guard was called, there would be no hope for either of them, and then no hope for Alric.

Down the steps they crept, and down to the dank dark where the reek of shit and piss and filthy straw drifted through the air. At the entrance to the corridor that led to the cells, Deda held up his hand to bring his wife to a halt. Ahead, a candle flame danced.

He felt Rowena rest her fingertips upon his shoulder, her touch wishing him luck, and then he pulled away. He drew his sword deftly and eased forward, sliding one foot in front of the other. Ahead, voices murmured. Two men by the sound of it, as he had anticipated.

Slipping his sword hand behind his back, he stepped up to the circle of wavering light. He had not encountered these guards before. One squatted on a stool against the wall, looking fat and dull-witted, and probably drunk too from the way his eyes moved slowly from his cup to the new arrival. The other was tall and rangy, his face scowling, his hand never wavering far from the short sword at his waist. Jumping to his feet, he blocked the way to the chamber beyond.

'What is your business?' he snarled.

With the speed of a striking snake, Deda whipped his sword round so that the point now rested just above the man's breastbone. As his drunken partner jerked alert, the knight curled one foot round a leg of his stool and yanked it away. The fat man crashed back and slumped unconscious to the floor.

'One of your captives leaves with me,' Deda said, his smile taking the edge off his words. But he nudged the tip of his blade into the tall man's flesh for emphasis. He watched the guard's eyes narrow as he calculated he was not paid enough to risk his neck. The man nodded.

Deda felt a touch of relief. He had no wish to kill an innocent man.

The fat man on the floor groaned and clutched at his head, while the other guard trudged through the arch at the rear of the chamber with the knight's sword at his back.

'That one,' Deda said, waving a hand at Alric's cell. When the guard turned to him, frowning, the knight snapped, 'Open the door.'

With a shrug, the tall man threw the door wide. The cell was empty.

For a moment, Deda stared. He felt his confusion turn to dismay. 'Where is the monk?' he asked.

'He has been taken,' the guard replied, caring little. 'I would not expect him to see the dawn.'

CHAPTER FORTY-TWO

The line of torches trailed out of the New Church into the night. Laughter rose up, and excited chatter, as the procession of nobles emerged from their prayers. It was the edge of spring and the night was balmy. Bats flittered over the rooftops and the scent of new vegetation drifted on the warm breeze. The devout gathered in the square in front of the Nea Ekklesia, waiting for the slaves to rush out with amphorae of spiced wine to fill goblets, and to offer chunks of roast lamb and cheese. Eyes were bright, and faces too. This was a celebration, and not just of the Lord above.

Crouching in the dark, Ariadne watched the Nepotes and their allies in their struggle for power mill around the wide space. News had swept through the city earlier that day that the Turkish horde had moved even closer to the city. There had been too much worry, too much sweat and fear and doubt. The people had all but exhausted themselves. Yet she could see no sign here of the doom that everyone said hung over Constantinople. Whatever these nobles had been praying for, it was not salvation.

Creeping forward, Ariadne searched the night clustering hard around the church. Beyond, the lights of the Great Palace and the Chrysotriklinos twinkled, but there in the shadows groups of armed men waited. They kept watch to ensure the Nepotes' safety, no doubt, but Ariadne had never seen so many.

For a while, she watched them enjoy their celebration, and then she spotted Leo. She felt a bittersweet mix of feelings: joy, but also sadness at the way they had parted at the harbour. He stood aside from the others, with Varin towering over him. They seemed deep in conversation, Leo's face dark and troubled, and after a moment the Blood Eagle rested a hand upon the young man's shoulder. Ariadne frowned, unable to understand what was passing between them.

Anxious, she waited until Leo broke off the conversation and wandered away to the edge of the circle of light cast by the torches. Here was her chance. As she sneaked close to him, al-Kahina called to her, but Ariadne pushed her voice away. She could not look away from Leo. How sad he looked, how burdened.

'Leo,' she whispered from the shadows under a sweet chestnut tree.

As he turned, recognizing her voice, he looked around to make sure he was not being watched. Varin had disappeared into the throng, and those nearest were lost to their conversation and their wine.

'Will you hear me out?' She saw his face hardening.

'Away. I told you – I am done with you,' he said in a hushed voice.

'There is still time to heal this wound,' she said quietly. 'We are alike, you and I. We should not fight.'

At her words, he softened a little. 'No, this is not a night for fighting.' He glanced over the heads of the nobles. 'It is a time for joy, for two days hence the seasons change and a new age dawns over the empire.'

'Is this not a secret that should be kept close to you?' she asked, happy that he had trusted her.

But he only snorted. 'What can you do? What can anyone do?'

'What of Karas Verinus?'

'Karas Verinus does not yet know he has lost.' Leo glanced away suddenly, and Ariadne could see there was something he was not telling her.

'What is it?'

Leo shook his head. 'Why are you here?'

'To beg you not to go through with this bloody plot.'

Laughing, Leo shook his head in bafflement. 'Can you not see me seated upon the throne, with the crown upon my brow and my *loros* shining in the sunlight?'

Yet Ariadne felt sure she heard an edge of bitterness in those words. 'I see you dead!' she said, too loud. Heads turned towards them.

'Why do you care so?'

'Why?' Her shoulders sagged. 'Your kin dreams of power, of glory, but only death can lie at the end of this road you are upon. And I do not wish to see you dead. My heart would break.' At that moment, she hated herself for revealing the emotion she had kept locked away for so long. She felt exposed, and as weak as she was when her father treated her worse than a dog.

Though she expected mockery, Leo only nodded. 'I have heard those words of death once this night already.'

Ariadne looked behind him until her gaze settled on the scarred visage of Varin, the Blood Eagle, away in the crowd. The warrior seemed to have become more of a father than Kalamdios. How strange that was, she thought. A man who unleashed slaughter was more caring than Leo's own blood. 'Then heed him.'

'I hear him, and I hear your words too. Do not think that I am not moved by them. But we can never escape the pull of days gone by. What we did when we were different folk affects us for the rest of our time.'

'I cannot believe that. We all can find another road.'

Shaking his head, Leo hesitated, and as he looked down Ariadne saw his hand trembling. For a moment, his face softened further and she glimpsed the boy she remembered from when they first met, all those seasons ago. She saw a deep sadness there. 'There could never be any hope for us,' he said in a quiet voice. 'You were right when you said that to me. My kin will not allow it.'

'Then run away with me! Let us leave Constantinople . . .' Her voice drained away and she felt a pain like a knife to the heart when she saw her enthusiasm was not mirrored in his face.

'You could never understand. Your kin betrayed you, and you escaped their shadow. But I . . . I am bound to mine as if I were fettered. Here . . .' he touched his head, 'and here.' His heart. 'However much I hate what they have made me do, I can never walk away. I am one of the Nepotes, now and for all time. My blood is theirs. We are one. What they want, I must want, and I could not deny that even if it meant my own death. Now leave. We will not speak again.' Leo turned his back on her and walked away, but his voice floated back. 'Pray for me. Pray for us all.'

CHAPTER FORTY-THREE

The Hagia Sophia towered over the city. With its vast dome and its ornate mosaics and alabaster statues, and gold glimmering everywhere, every man and woman in Constantinople recognized it as a monument to God's glory. In their minds, the Lord lived here and kept the empire safe.

Rowena thought how comforting that must be as she pushed through the sea of bodies washing up to the door. Every street, every alley surged with life, up to the Basilica Cistern, and the Milion mile-post, and even the north wall of the hippodrome. The din of voices rang off the stone walls of the great buildings all around. The morning sun lit faces hopeful, angry, jeering, laughing, all of them seeking distraction from the grind of life that only seemed to be getting worse.

'The people see this as an act of rebellion against an emperor who is failing to protect them. It cheers them.' Rowena heard Anna Dalassene's voice float out from the cool dark of the church as the matriarch came to greet her.

'There will be real rebellion soon enough, and when the blood flows, they will look back upon this one fondly,' Rowena replied as she stood on the threshold marvelling at the crowd. Stepping inside, she breathed deeply of the sweet incense. There was a calm here that she had not felt for days.

Rowena set down a basket of bread covered with a linen cloth, food for the hungry woman seeking sanctuary and the only reason she had been allowed entry to the Hagia Sophia. She felt exhausted. The spear-brothers had searched high and low for Alric. Questions had been asked, but it seemed not a soul knew what had happened to him. There was no hint of execution, no sign that even Karas Verinus knew of his whereabouts. But she would bow her head before God's Table here in the great church and would pray for his safety.

And she would pray for the spear-brothers too. In their hooded eyes and drawn faces she could see the depth of their pain at losing their leader. Hereward had been the best of them. She felt her own grief as sharp as vinegar. She owed the Mercian everything, including her life – if he had not aided her in the fenlands, the Norman bastards would surely have taken her head – and her husband, for he had brought her to Deda and all the joy he had given her. Would they now lose Hereward's confessor and friend Alric too? Never.

'Nikephoros will not let this challenge stand,' she said.

'This was not the way I wished it to go. But what

choice did I have?' Anna walked back along the nave to escape the roaring of the crowd. Rowena followed. Clerics knelt at prayer, mumbling over relic boxes, or whispered together in corners.

'Holy Wisdom, that is the meaning of the name of this church,' Anna said, looking up. 'The Wisdom of God. Would that I had some.'

Rowena thought Anna looked strong for all her ordeal, though her eyes seemed heavy with exhaustion. She followed the other woman's gaze to take in the vaulting above the nave, high overhead. The sumptuous mosaics glowed as if they were set with jewels in the sunlight blazing through the myriad windows around the great dome. Never had she seen such magnificence. It made the churches of England look like beggars' huts.

'Whispers reach our ears that the Nepotes will make their move on the morrow,' she murmured so that she would not be overheard.

Anna looked about at the busy church. Rowena saw her features grow taut. 'What hope, then?'

'There are some of us prepared to resist, as you know, and we do what we can. Word goes out to allies near and far, but only silence returns.'

'And Karas, when will he strike?'

'Our eyes and ears tell us he has sent word to Justin to return to the city, but—' Rowena choked off the words as the roar of the crowd rolled through the entrance.

Anna's furrowed brow smoothed and she smiled. 'Come.'

Rowena followed her as she glided serenely to the door. A wake cut through the swell of yelling people. The matriarch pressed her hands together as if in prayer and watched its progress. Rowena saw a triumphant smile flicker across her lips.

A moment later, she gasped. 'The emperor.'

'The power of the crowd. Even royalty must heed it.'

Rowena could see Nikephoros, surrounded by his advisers and Varangian Guard, making his way towards the great church. He had a face like thunder, furious no doubt at being wrong-footed by the matriarch of the Comnenoi. The group came to a halt at the foot of the steps and Falkon Cephalas walked forward.

'Anna Dalassene, you have sought sanctuary in this sacred place,' he called, 'and all men, even emperors whose power is given by the hand of the Lord, respect the might of God.'

Anna bowed. 'We are both humbled in his presence.'

In the shadow of the church's great door, Rowena smiled. The other woman had positioned herself as an equal to the man who now stood below her.

'I seek only the safety of my kin, who have shown nothing but loyalty to you and the empire. The accusations against them are nothing but lies,' Anna continued. 'Will you give me your word that the Comnenoi will not be harmed?'

Turning back, Falkon conferred with Nikephoros. When he returned to the steps, the adviser announced, 'It is agreed.'

But Anna was not done. 'Swear this oath to me now,' she cried. Rowena marvelled at the other woman's audacity.

The crowd caught her words and echoed them back, full-throated. The boom became a cheer that rang up to the Hagia Sophia's dome. Nikephoros shifted uncomfortably. Glancing round, he saw that all eyes were upon him, every man and woman willing him on.

Rowena could sense Anna smiling inwardly. When the accusations of betrayal were first mounted, she might have feared this throng would tear her limb from limb, but these, the ordinary people, had proved to be her greatest ally. Nikephoros could not deny such a number, not when he had such a frail grip on power.

The emperor waved his hand. The Patriarch, who had been walking beside him, raised aloft the cross he held, one as long as a spear, Nikephoros' own. It was large enough to be seen by all the crowd. When the cross was lowered once more, Nikephoros placed his hand upon it.

'I so swear,' he muttered, glowering at her from under his eyebrows when he was sure no one else could see.

'Louder,' Anna shouted over the emperor's head. 'Let us proclaim this oath to God himself, and to all the citizens of Constantinople.'

Another cheer rang out, drowning out whatever curse Nikephoros let fall from his lips.

'I so swear,' the emperor boomed. Rowena thought she could hear fury in those few words.

Then Nikephoros spun on his heel and marched towards the Great Palace with his group of the faithful close around him. Falkon, however, waited behind.

Once the crowd sensed the drama was done and began to drift away, he climbed the steps and bowed to Anna. 'Only one thing remains to be said. The emperor insists you leave this place and take refuge in the convent of Petrion. You know it well.'

Anna nodded.

'For your own protection, of course. The emperor cannot guarantee your safety in Constantinople, where there are so many loyal to him who might still think you a traitor. Is this agreed?'

'It is.'

'And in good time Maria will join you there, for her own safety too. You will be well treated. Your kin may visit, and bring you food. The guards will look on you with kindness.'

Guards, Rowena thought. Anna would be a captive in everything but name. And yet Rowena could see she had no intention of resisting. And why should she? In a day's time, the world may well have changed for good.

When Falkon Cephalas had left, the two women walked slowly back through the shafts of sunlight into the belly of the church.

'And so Nikephoros thinks he has sucked the poison out of this wound,' Anna said. 'He is safe. The Comnenoi have been crippled. And while the emperor looks to me, he does not search for treason in those who once enjoyed my favour.' She eyed Rowena, smiling.

Rowena bowed in thanks. She had long been suspicious of this woman and her lust for power. But Anna matched her flint with kindness for those who were her friends.

Rowena moved closer, her words hushed. 'Nikephoros and Karas may no longer be a threat to you, but never forget there is no safe place anywhere in this city.'

For a moment Anna frowned, and then she looked past Rowena's shoulder and knew what the other woman meant.

A smile playing on his lips, the hated Nepotes church spy Neophytos was watching her like a hawk.

CHAPTER FORTY-FOUR

'This is the place?' Kraki growled.

When the moon drifted out from behind the clouds, the blanket of shadow unfolded across the cemetery. The Viking scanned the rows of graves, the markers, the dunes of brown dust and yellowing grass and weeds. It was as dismal a place as any boneyard he had ever seen.

'Aye, I saw it with my own eyes,' the boy insisted. His black hair stood up on his head like a cock's comb and he never seemed far from a mocking grin. Perhaps nine summers lay on him, but he had a tongue as sharp as someone twice his age. Kraki had not been sure he could trust those sly eyes, and still doubted it, but he was now clutching at straws. For all the gold he had offered, no one else in the entire city had come forward with news of where Hereward's body lay.

The lad pointed to a mound with no marker. 'There.'

The Viking held up his torch and grunted. All the spear-brothers thought him mad, except Hengist, who *was* mad. They told him Hereward's remains would have been tossed into the sea, but there were more ships and boats out there than folk in the forum of Constantine on a sunny day, and the only bodies that had snarled in their nets since Hereward died were a couple of beggarly-looking fellows in clothes that had been tattered even before they entered the sea. Bringing the Mercian home was all that mattered to Kraki. It was a matter of honour, for no warrior abandoned an ally. A friend.

'Shall I dig?' Sighard asked hesitantly.

Kraki nodded and set the torch into the dirt. At least someone had agreed to accompany him this night, more out of pity than anything, the Viking suspected. But he thought how bereft Sighard looked, and how anxious. This would be hard work for even a cold-hearted bastard like himself.

The gritty ground crunched as Sighard plunged in the wooden spade. At the end of the grave, the boy stood with his arms folded, a wry expression on his face. Narrowing his eyes, the Viking tugged the leather pouch of gold from his belt and tossed it over. The coin clanked at the boy's feet. The lad looked down at it hungrily, but he did not stoop to pick it up.

'If my friend lies in the grave, take it,' Kraki said. 'If I find you have tried to cheat me, your arse will burn like the sun.'

Licking his lips, the boy eyed the pouch, and then shook his head. 'I cannot take it.'

Kraki snorted, thinking this was some ploy to demand more. But the lad only kicked the pouch back across the grave, then turned on his heel and fled.

Sighard leaned on his spade and watched the boy disappear into the night. 'We are in the pits of madness when even beggars turn their nose up at good coin.'

'Dig,' Kraki said.

As Sighard returned to turning over the loose soil, Kraki realized he was shaking. So many questions had he asked, in every tavern and workshop and forum, it seemed, but however much he wanted what he sought he still dreaded this moment.

The spade dipped and turned, dipped and turned. Sighard wiped away the sweat springing to his brow. And then Kraki heard the crunch of wood upon wood.

Sighard stared at him. Kraki stared into the grave. For a long moment the two of them stood, frozen, and then the Viking sighed and nodded.

Dropping down, Sighard scrabbled away the rest of the soil with his bare hands until he had uncovered the box. Cracking his knuckles, he tucked his fingertips under the edge and tore off the lid. The reek of rot rushed out and both of them recoiled.

When Kraki leaned back in, he prayed silently to himself that he would see some other dead face staring sightlessly back at him. He thought of Hengist's words, that Hereward was a giant-killer, a hero who would never die.

And then the two warriors' eyes settled on the bloody body.

Kraki collapsed to his knees, burying his face in the dust so that Sighard could not see his emotions. A shudder rushed through him.

Tears streaming down his face, Sighard raised his face to the sky. 'What do we do now?' he croaked.

Kraki pushed himself up, letting the anger rise within him. 'Now, we fight.'

Fat drops of rain began to fall, dappling the dust around the graves. In the distance, the heavens rumbled. Kraki cocked his head, narrowing his eyes.

'Thunder,' Sighard said.

The Viking shook his head. The dim sound of a horn rolled out from the ebbing rumble. A warning from the walls. As the two spear-brothers looked at each other, the sound swept towards them, caught up by other horns until it seemed the whole world was blaring an alarm.

CHAPTER FORTY-FIVE

1 April 1081

Black clouds swept in, flooding the plain beyond the western wall with a deep dark. The rain began to drum along the stone. Thunder crashed high in the heavens. Yet beneath the storm, the world throbbed. Away in the night, hooves pounded the ground, another storm, one of steel, drawing ever nearer. Pressing the horn to his lips, the herald pushed back his head and blasted the alarm again.

Deda looked out from the wall, praying for lightning to reveal what was coming. He could understand the grim faces of the spear-brothers standing next to him. They could be forgiven for thinking that fate had turned against them. The Verini and the Nepotes were already preparing to bring down war within the walls, and now this.

'An army, a good-sized one by the sound of it,' Guthrinc murmured. The English stood apart from the Varangians, who had been summoned to the wall by Karas Verinus to welcome his murderous nephew

Justin home from wherever he had been travelling, and to guard him as he made his way back into Constantinople; the privilege of the emperor's military adviser.

Deda's eyes flickered towards Karas as he stood beside Wulfrun. The knight had expected to see a look of triumph upon the general's face. Surely this force could only be men that Justin had gathered, ready for the battle for the throne. But Karas looked as confused as every man there.

The army rumbled closer still. The world shook. Deda felt his heart sink. Already that night he had endured disappointment in his search for Alric. He had bribed one of the slaves at Karas' hall, but the monk was not being held there, nor had he been seen at all. Desperate now, he had hoped the spear-brothers would help him. But Kraki and Sighard were nowhere to be found, and the others were already following Karas' orders.

'Give us light,' Wulfrun bellowed under the roar of the storm.

Several Varangians thrust pitch-dipped arrows into the flames of a torch, then nocked their bows and sent them into the heavens. As the shafts plunged down, the gloom fled from the light and the landscape came alive. As one, the guardsmen jerked alert, gaping and pointing. A torrent of warriors on horseback raced towards the city. Helms and armour flared briefly in the dancing flames, gone in an instant as the night engulfed them once more.

'How many are there?' Ricbert gasped.

Karas rested both hands on the wall and leaned out, peering into the dark. The rain lashed his leathery face. 'More important, who are they?'

More flaming arrows blazed through the night sky.

In the moment before they winked out, it was Karas' turn to gape. Deda saw it too: the double-headed eagle standard of Constantinople at the head of the column of warriors rushing towards them. These were the empire's fighting men. But why were they arriving this night, he wondered? And why was Karas so concerned?

As the general's face hardened, heads snapped round to a new arrival making his way along the wall from the steps. The old man was wrapped in a fine emerald cloak decorated with a filigree of gold thread, his hair tonsured to show his devotion to God. Deda blinked away the rainwater, doubting his own eyes, but this could be none other than John Doukas, who bore the honorary title of Caesar and had ruled the empire as regent when the last emperor Michael Doukas was but a boy. Yet the Caesar had long been out of favour in the court, for treasonous plotting more than anything, and had been in near-exile at his estate in the east.

'What brings you here?' Karas barked, still reeling from the sight.

'Karas Verinus, my old friend,' John said. Though the greeting was warm, Deda knew these two men had long been suspicious of each other. 'Why, I am here to welcome the return of the son of my other good friend Anna Dalassene.'

The knight watched the general look back out into the night, realization dawning upon him.

'I hear tell Alexios Comnenos has won over the commanders of two of our armies in the Thracian countryside,' the Caesar continued in a faintly mocking tone. 'Why, that must be the sound of them approaching now.'

Karas glowered. 'You support the Comnenoi now? I remember the day when you would have gladly seen all of them dead.'

'Allies are not always friends, as you well know. Who best serves the needs of the Doukai in the court in days yet to come? Nikephoros? You? I think not.'

Deda braced himself against the gale blasting the top of the walls. The rain lashed down, but the two old men seemed oblivious.

'The walls will hold firm,' the general spat.

'Unless a man awash with gold robbed from a tax collector showered coin upon the guards to make sure the gates were open. And then his army could ride unhindered into the heart of Constantinople.'

Karas held the other man's eyes. In that long moment, Deda thought that if the general could have choked the life from the man before him he would have done.

'Constantinople seethes with plots, Karas Verinus,' the Caesar continued. Deda watched his lips tighten into a supercilious smile. 'Some are barely hidden. But the cleverest among us keep their plans far from the light.'

357

Deda could not hide his grin. Karas, a bastard among all bastards, had been outmanoeuvred by Anna Dalassene. She was more cunning than he had ever guessed.

'Then this is a battle to the death,' the general snarled, no longer making any pretence at loyalty. 'I will rouse my army. And we will see who is fit to take this throne.'

Deda felt shocked. He could scarce believe it. This was the moment they had all dreaded – a war upon the streets of Constantinople.

The Caesar gave a slight bow in response, which only seemed to anger Karas more. As the general stalked away, he grabbed a messenger and commanded, 'Bring Justin to me when he arrives.' And then the gusting rain folded around him and he was gone.

The onrushing army crashed into the wavering circle of light from the torches above the gate. Deda glimpsed Alexios and Isaac at the head, determined to seize their moment.

Wulfrun was running along the wall, his voice booming above the storm. 'To the palace. We must defend the emperor.'

As the Varangian Guard raced towards the steps, Guthrinc glanced at Deda. The knight had never seen him so worried. 'Please. Find Kraki,' he called. 'At the boneyard near the gate of St John de Cornibus. Before we all die fighting for an emperor we despise.'

The thunder cracked. Lightning flashed. The pounding rain drowned out any other words. And then came the rumble of hooves and the tramp of marching feet as Alexios and his army surged through the gates to war.

CHAPTER FORTY-SIX

The woman hurried with purpose through the crowds, thrusting aside any who stumbled into her path. Juliana Nepa's blonde hair was plastered to her head by the driving rain, but her face was flushed with passion, her eyes afire. She felt so much excitement she could barely contain herself.

In this night torn by screams, with people milling in terror in the streets, she saw only opportunity. Now was the time to act. The walls had been breached, everyone knew, though no one could rightly say by whom. And now it was rumoured that Karas' own army was massing for a battle that would rip Constantinople asunder.

Juliana felt the euphoria rush through her. How long had her family waited for this moment to seize the throne? In the chaos, the Nepotes' own force would be rising up to crush Karas' army, if her mother and father had already given the order. And she had no doubt that the moment news reached them of this new army that would have been done.

Fate had gifted them an even greater chance than

they had ever dared imagine. Though the Nepotes had not planned to make their move upon the throne until the morrow, no better moment would ever present itself. As the ground shifted under their feet, weaker men would have bemoaned their lot, but not the Nepotes. They would seize this day.

Ahead, the door to the hall of the Nepotes glowed under the wavering light of the torch above the jamb. Juliana breathed a sigh of relief. Running a hand through her sodden hair, she composed herself. Now the Nepotes would be seen as the saviours of the empire. When the force that Varin had amassed brought order, no one would question their intentions. After this madness, the people would want a strong leader on the throne.

Leo would be emperor by dawn.

Pushing the door open, Juliana darted inside. 'Mother!' she called into the depths of the house. 'The hour has come early. Bring Leo. Varin, gather your men. We must march on the palace now.'

As she hurried into the next chamber, she thought of preparations that would be required for the coronation. Leo would need to be dressed in his ceremonial jewelled *loros*. Neophytos must be alerted so he could prepare himself to be the new Patriarch. Sour voices would be raised in the church, of course, but Cosmas would step down once he had seen what riches awaited him in his days yet to come. She and her mother must don their finest dresses, one gold with black embroidery, one black with gold embroidery, ready for the moment when they stood behind the throne and watched the crown being lowered upon Leo's brow.

The moment when, finally, after all these years, they would have won.

And then she could marry Wulfrun, and there would at last be time for love, and all those tender exchanges that had been set aside in the plotting and struggles of recent years. Peace, finally. Peace for all of them.

Her thoughts tumbled into one another. So much to do. But there would be time enough for preparation as Varin led his army of rogues to the palace. Nikephoros would not stand a chance, not with his Varangian Guard scattered across Constantinople trying to bring order. No one would mourn the passing of that wizened bag of bones.

As the torrent of calculation finally ebbed away and the echoes of her footsteps faded, Juliana frowned. The house was silent.

'Where is everyone?' she demanded.

The words rolled out through the chambers like distant thunder. The house was empty.

Juliana cursed. Her mother and father and Leo must have left for the palace already. Perhaps it had already fallen to Varin and his men. They should have waited for her! Hitching up her skirts, she spun on her heel and hurried back to the door.

She would not be denied her moment of glory, not after all the sacrifices and the suffering.

Though she was loath to go back into the tumult and the bloodshed with no one to protect her, she steeled herself and stepped outside. But as she passed the entrance to the shadowed garden, she glimpsed movement. Her heart skipped a beat.

'Mother?' she said once more. But she knew it was not Simonis. Leo, then. Hiding. She had always feared he was a coward at heart.

Her eyes glittering, she marched out into the night.

Juliana's nostrils wrinkled. The breeze smelled oddly musky. As she grew accustomed to the dark, she realized there was something amiss. The tree, *her* tree, the one she had sat under since she was a girl . . . its silhouette now looked strange. She felt the hair on the nape of her neck prickle, but she could not stop herself from stepping forward.

At that moment, the full moon broke through the storm-clouds and a beam of silver light streamed down as if God had chosen to illuminate the scene especially for her.

Juliana recoiled. She felt the acid rise in her mouth and thought for a moment that she would vomit.

Hanging in the branches of the trees, her father had been freed from the prison of his body and preserved on the brink of taking flight to the heavens. Kalamdios was naked. His head lolled to one side. His eyes were open and staring, his swollen tongue protruding from his lips. His arms were outstretched, his feet crossed at the ankles. Pink wings glistened behind him, his lungs, torn out through broken ribs and unfolded. Black blood pooled on the earth beneath.

Reeling from shock, Juliana suddenly felt very afraid. When hot tears burned her eyes, her senses flooded back and she spun, desperate to scramble away from that terrible vision.

But there was no escape.

Caught on the small olive tree in the shadows by the side of the door, unnoticed when she entered the garden, was another blood eagle. Her mother. Simonis, too, was naked. Her dead eyes were white in the gloom. There was something almost of beauty in the way she had been presented. The curve of her arms, her hips, the line of her legs, all showed grace, like a swan taking flight. If Juliana had not been sickened to the point of madness, she would have thought that this had been a work of love.

As the fog of shock began to drift away, Juliana felt a rush of fear for her own life. She scrambled back to the house, almost stumbling in her desperation. But she knew she was not alone, even before she jerked her head up to see the figure blocking her escape.

Silhouetted in the doorway was a giant figure holding an axe. Varin. And in the silence that enveloped her, Juliana could hear the drip, drip, drip of blood on to the marble floor.

His face showed no emotion, his gaze strangely reminiscent of the saints in the mosaics in the Hagia Sophia. Caught in that fierce attention, she froze. But then he spoke and the spell was broken.

'Hereward sends his greetings.'

The Blood Eagle loomed over her and now his eyes were like fire.

Chapter Forty-Seven

A lric stopped struggling with his bonds to listen to the screams and the clash of steel upon steel echoing through the stone. The fighting away in the night was drawing closer by the moment. He had no idea what could be happening, but he feared the worst.

Glancing around his cell in the thin light from a single oil lamp, he cursed his lot. It was not so filthy as that foul hole beneath the Great Palace, and he should give thanks to God that he still lived, but he would not die here while the city burned around him. Though he strained his arms against the bonds that bound his wrists to his ankles, they were as tight as ever. He could not even cry out for help through the cloth tied across his mouth.

But then hurrying footsteps echoed outside the cramped chamber and he jerked himself upright. When the door was flung open, he breathed in the sweet-scented blast of incense. This time he heard none of the chanting of the monks, only sounds of fury.

In the doorway, the huge bulk of Neophytos loomed. Beyond him, Alric glimpsed the sumptuous mosaics running just below the vast dome of the Hagia Sophia, the tiles shimmering in the flickering torchlight.

The eunuch did not look so confident now. There was none of the grinning and the mockery that had taunted Alric when the corpulent monk had bribed the guards to allow him to be taken away from the cell beneath the palace. Now fear gripped the other man, and he appeared to be trembling.

Wheezing from the exertion, Neophytos leaned down and yanked the rag from Alric's mouth. 'Do not think to cry out,' he said between breaths. 'No one will heed you.'

This hiding place had been chosen well, the eunuch had told him when he had first been dragged here. He was high up in the church, off one of the walkways that circled beneath the dome. With Anna Dalassene seeking sanctuary far below, the guards had kept the Hagia Sophia near deserted.

'What is happening?' Alric demanded. 'The fighting—'

'Silence.'

Alric narrowed his eyes. 'The time has come, then. The Nepotes are rising. Or you would not be here to take me to the prophet so that we can proclaim that you and your filthy kin have been chosen by the Lord.'

'Still your tongue, I say,' Neophytos snapped in his reedy voice. He cocked his head, listening. Alric watched his expression and realized that perhaps the outcome of this matter was not as certain as the Nepotes had once believed.

Neophytos grabbed Alric's tunic and began to drag him to the door. 'You will do as you are told,' he said. 'When my kin have seized the prophet from Karas Verinus' hands we will be ready.'

Alric laughed at the uncertain tone he heard in the other man's voice. But before he could goad the eunuch further, he was blinded by a spray of warm crimson.

Gasping, he blinked away the gore. Neophytos stood clutching at his throat, a gurgling sound bubbling from his mouth. Blood frothed between his fingers. Alric could only gape as the eunuch's eyes rolled back, white, and the sickening mewling died in his throat. Like a mountain being shaken by God's wrath, he slipped to one side and crashed to the flagstones.

A knife glinted in the torchlight. The blade was clutched in the hand of a figure half-crouched in the doorway. Shaking the blood from his eyes, he recognized the form. Ragener, the half-man.

Crumpling his ruined features, the Hawk spat on the dead man at his feet. 'I followed this cur thinking he would lead me to Leo Nepos, so I could slay him myself and prove to Karas once and for all that I am worthy of his trust. But no, he has led me only to you. The source of so much of my misery.'

Alric felt a chill when he saw the grin creep across the sea wolf's face. Madness glinted in his eyes.

Ragener cocked his head on one side, but his ragged grimace twisted his mocking smile. 'No kind words? Yet we are so alike, you and I. Almost like brothers.'

'I have nothing in common with you, and if I did, I would slit my own throat.'

Ragener held up the stump of his right arm. 'See? God has judged us equally.'

Alric felt his rage simmering. 'God did not judge me. This hand was taken by a friend who saved my life, after you had cut off my fingers.'

'My life has been blighted by fate,' the Hawk cried. 'This is no fault of my own. No, it is men like you and Hereward who caused my suffering, for no good reason. But your master is food for the maggots now. And soon you will follow. But I will still be here. I will be the victorious one.'

Dashing forward, Ragener slashed with the knife. Alric flinched. He felt a flood of relief when he realized the blade had only sliced through his bonds. As he rubbed his aching wrists, the Hawk waved the knife at him. 'Stand.'

But this was surely no gift of freedom. The sea wolf no doubt wanted to deliver him back to Karas Verinus to earn the general's favour. Anger bubbled up inside him. How many times had he and his brothers suffered at the hands of men like this, men without honour? He was sick of it.

The anger became rage, erupting out of him. With a roar, Alric dropped his head and hurled himself forward. Drawing on strength he never knew he had, the monk rammed Ragener out of the chamber, across the narrow walkway that circled the dome and into the low rail. His roar thundered across the ringing space beneath the dome, drowning out the sea wolf's pathetic squealing.

Ragener's one good arm flailed, the knife falling to the floor.

In the haze of his fury, Alric's wits fled him. Only when Ragener flipped over the rail did he jerk to his senses.

Screaming, the sea wolf grabbed the monk's tunic, dragging him half over the stone wall. Alric felt fire burn in his joints as he clung desperately to the rail with his good hand. But he could feel his fingers trembling from the strain, his grip weakening. The Hawk's weight was too great, pulling him over into the void, and he could not break that grip without loosing the hand that anchored him.

Tears of frustration stung his eyes. He peered down past the shrieking Ragener, past the glittering gold, cold statues, to the flagstones so far below. There, a tiny figure, a woman, Anna, craned her neck up at him, her mouth open. She was crying out, he was sure, but her voice was drowned by Ragener's furious cursing.

To die like this, shattered on that floor, after all his struggles. He felt bitter at the unfairness.

'Pull me up,' Ragener screamed. 'Or you will be damned.' Alric saw fear burning in the sea wolf's scarred face.

'I have killed once before. I have betrayed God for the sake of my friends. My soul is already tainted. There is no going back for me.' Alric half closed his eyes and muttered a prayer. He was ready.

On the edge of his vision, movement flashed.

A sword hacked down. The blade sliced through Ragener's wrist. And then the sea wolf was falling, tumbling, turning, growing smaller as his shriek spiralled up. And then the sickening crack, and silence.

Alric reeled back, so dazed by his brush with death he thought he would faint.

Words reached him through the mist, a voice he had half convinced himself he would never hear again.

'See. You have two hands again. I work miracles.'

Glancing down, he saw Ragener's hand still frozen in a death-grasp in the folds of his tunic. His dumbfounded laughter turned to a juddering sob of relief. After a moment, he looked up.

Hereward loomed over him.

His friend's face swam before his eyes and for a moment he could almost believe this was a ghost.

Hereward, risen from the dead.

Finally.

Alric felt such a flood of relief that their plan had worked, he fainted into the Mercian's arms.

CHAPTER FORTY-EIGHT

'The city is at war.' In the nave, Hereward's voice echoed through the vast empty space of the Hagia Sophia. 'Stay safe here with Anna Dalassene.'

'You will need help,' Alric protested. The Mercian watched his friend's eyes flicker to dead Ragener and the spray of blood across the flagstones surrounding the shattered body. Through the walls, the clamour of battle throbbed ever closer.

'With God's will, Hereward will have all the aid he needs,' Anna said softly, resting one hand on the monk's shoulder. 'We have work to do here.'

'It seems there is much I do not know.' Alric narrowed his eyes and Hereward felt a pang of guilt for not taking his friend into his confidence, in spite of all they had been through together.

'Do not be stung. This plan has been years in the making. No man, and only one woman, was privy to all of it, except me. You and Varin had a part. The prophet, the death I feigned to hide away from my enemies. Only Anna knew the whole. But I vow I will tell you all. If we live through this night.'

He glanced towards the door, hoping he still had an unimpeded path to the palace. His mind was racing after so long lying low, plotting, allowing only fragments of his ultimate aim to be seen by each of his co-conspirators so that no one ally could reveal all if they were captured and tortured, by Nikephoros, by Karas, by any one of the myriad other enemies that seemed to shadow his path across this earth.

'You did well,' Anna said. 'The whole of the city believed you dead.'

'I only pray that Kraki and the other spear-brothers will forgive me,' he replied, 'but I could take no risks. This plot would only succeed if all thought I no longer had any part to play.'

'Aye, you have done well,' Alric added pointedly. 'Since we first met you have always learned the ways of your enemies and turned them back upon them. But who would ever have thought you had such a talent for deceit.'

'In a pit of vipers, the one who wins is the greatest viper of all.' Hereward tried to smile, but he could not help being stung by the bitterness in his friend's voice. In this game, only winning counted. Too many people were relying upon him. 'Now is not the time to explain. Time is against us. Find the Patriarch,' he commanded, 'and make ready.'

Drawing his great sword, he ran out into the raging night. Pausing on the steps, he took in the chaos before him: some soldiers fighting, others carrying armfuls of loot, citizens fleeing for their lives.

If God had smiled upon them, Alexios and Isaac

would have won the support of the armies in the west and they would now be carving a path through whatever resistance Nikephoros could throw at them, and the remnants of Karas' force of axes-for-hire and cutthroats. There was no way through this without bloodshed, and only God knew who would survive to see the dawn. If he was not one of them, so be it. Death had become a friend to him in recent days.

Forcing his way across the square, Hereward reached the palace and raced through the deserted corridors. The guards had all fled. The kitchens were silent, the torches along the walls illuminating a jumble of fallen fruit, scattered olives and spilled wine, smashed pots and shattered amphorae. He presumed they must have been cast aside when what few servants would have been there at that time of night had fled.

The palace appeared abandoned, empty, but he knew better. Putting his thumb and forefinger in his mouth, he whistled. Three short bursts, one long. A sign that he had last used in the rain-soaked fenlands of England. He felt a momentary sense of sadness as he remembered his homeland.

An answering whistle sang back to him. Moments later came the sound of something heavy being dragged across the flagstones, and a figure rose up among the stores in the shadows on the far side of the kitchen. Rowena slipped out into the flickering light.

'The hour has come?'

Hereward nodded.

He watched her hesitant smile appear. She seemed torn between excitement and apprehension. But then she nodded eagerly and said, 'My heart has near burst at keeping these secrets.'

'My trust was always well placed.'

Gathering up her flour-streaked skirt, Rowena swept away.

'Take care,' Hereward cautioned. 'The night is filled with enemies.'

At the door to the kitchen gardens, Rowena paused and glanced back. 'For England,' she murmured. And then she was gone.

CHAPTER FORTY-NINE

The night was torn by screams, a hundred, a thousand, all merging into one howl of despair. Along the narrow streets, a torrent of bodies flowed away from the worst of the fighting. Men, women and children buffeted each other, clawing their way past their neighbours, their faces ragged with terror.

Keeping a firm grip on the sack he held in his left hand, Kraki pushed aside anyone who blocked his way.

'This is madness,' Sighard yelled above the din.

'Feel the blood thunder in your heart. This is life. Now bring me our enemies. I am ready for them.'

The Viking tried to push aside his churning emotions. At first confusion had enveloped him when he had stared down into that grave and realized it was not Hereward who was interred there. Then he had felt anger that he had been lied to by someone, he was not yet sure who. Then worry that Hereward might yet be dead, his body lost in the sea. But now, as he ran, he was beginning to feel a sense of hope, that something beyond his ken was unfolding in front of him.

Yet as the two men crossed the second hill towards the Mese, they ground to a halt, aghast.

'You are right,' Kraki growled. 'This is madness.'

In the swell of fighting in the forum of Constantinople, they saw Roman warriors, and Constantinople's standard. But these men were running wild. The Viking watched them knock down merchants in front of their wives to rob them of purses stuffed with coin. Others smashed open doors and looted riches. The blood of innocents streamed across the flagstones. The city was being ransacked by those who should have been its saviours.

On the two men ran, heading east.

Sighard had feared they would never find their brothers in the surging field of battle, but Kraki knew better. No warriors had greater courage. Guthrinc and the others would always be in the thick of any fighting, no doubt honouring their oath and defending the main route to the palace. Rounding a corner, he saw the torches that lit the hippodrome ahead and knew that he was right.

In the shade of the Milion monument at the eastern end of the Mese, a line of Varangians held fast as wave after wave of fighting men crashed against their shields. Kraki could see that the attackers were not Roman troops, and for that he thanked the gods. No, undisciplined and dressed in rags, these must be Karas Verinus' men.

Roaring their battle-cries, he and Sighard flung themselves into the fighting. Kraki felt the fire in his heart swell as, still holding tight to the sack, he hacked and slashed, splitting heads and severing limbs.

'Now you come,' Guthrinc bellowed as the two warriors carved a path through the enemy ranks, 'once all the hard work has been done.'

'We are here to save your necks,' Kraki snarled back. 'I will hear your thanks once we are done.'

The line of spear-brothers opened, and Kraki and Sighard leapt the dead and the dying to slip among their friends.

Unseasoned as they were, Karas' men began to hold back, waiting for an advantage. Kraki eased himself into line beside Guthrinc. It felt good to be back with his comrades and he joined in the chorus of insults with which they taunted the enemy.

Kraki looked along the row of his brothers and decided to seize the lull. 'We found Hereward's grave. His body was not in it,' he shouted. Even as he heard his own words, he still felt unsure. Could he begin to hope? Dare he?

Kraki heard gasps of disbelief, then questions, too many, all tumbling over each other. Shaking his head, he said with a grimace, 'I know no more than that.'

But his reticence did not seem to hold back the rush of emotion. 'Hereward!' the spear-brothers roared with one voice, fists and weapons pumping the air. A battle-cry, an outpouring of relief or jubilation, the Viking could not be sure.

'He has risen,' Mad Hengist exulted, throwing his hands towards the heavens.

'A plot, more like.' Guthrinc grinned at him. 'He is

a cunning dog. When all think him dead, he can make his plans unnoticed.'

'Aye. And when I find that Mercian bastard, I will carve out of his flesh every secret he has kept from me.' Snarling with pent-up rage, Kraki lunged at one of their foes who had strayed too close. His blade ripped open the man's chest and he fell back, howling, among his allies. Stepping back, Kraki weighed the sack he clutched in his left hand and felt the glow of relief. Hearing Guthrinc's words, he could believe Hereward was alive. Only that sly Mercian dog would concoct such a deception.

'And what part do we play in this?' Hiroc complained. 'Are we fodder for Alexios' enemies, dying to buy him time?'

Kraki turned to glower at the man on the other side of him. 'You think Hereward would cut us adrift? I will have words with you when your wits return.'

Barely had he finished speaking when a voice rang out from the deserted square behind them. Looking back, the Viking saw Rowena and Deda beckoning furiously.

'Come,' the knight shouted.

'Hereward needs you all,' Rowena yelled.

As one Kraki and his spear-brothers turned and ran in the direction of the palace. Reaching the grand entrance, they re-formed and turned once more to face the enemy. But to Kraki it seemed that Karas Verinus' men were taking their time to follow, no doubt relieved that they no longer had to fight their way to their destination.

But as the Viking moved to speak to Rowena, a giant figure loomed out of the shadows – a warrior brandishing an axe. It was Varin.

Kraki cursed. That treacherous bastard, here, now! He hefted his own blade.

'Stay your hand.' Rowena reached out and grabbed Kraki's arm to hold him back. 'The Blood Eagle stands with us. He has always stood with us.'

CHAPTER FIFTY

Under the sputtering torch, Hereward watched his shadow waver. Even now, the metallic taste of the mushroom still lingered in his mouth. His raven had already led him along the shore of the great black ocean, and he had met with the dead and listened carefully to the words that were whispered there. Now the flames were licking up from his heart, and the battle-fury was growing. He was ready, and his devil was ready, and together they would raise all hell.

Through the walls, the sounds of battle echoed. The Mercian closed his eyes, imagining the clash of steel upon steel, seeing the blood. On the one side, Alexios' army, on the other, Karas Verinus' men, both of them fighting to the last for that blood-stained crown. But there would be no need to worry about the Nepotes' warriors now, not if Varin had done his duty.

Hereward gave a lupine smile.

Footsteps thundered along the flagstones, drawing nearer. A moment later, the spear-brothers crashed into the chamber. They were breathless, gore-spattered. It looked as though they had fought every step of the way here.

The Mercian held up a hand in greeting. Though he felt joy at seeing his brothers again, a wave of guilt washed through him for having deceived them so. He could not fault the confusion and anger he saw amid the relief in their faces.

Kraki was glowering at him. 'You are a bastard for letting us think you were dead.' He looked to have been in the thick of battle, as did they all. His face was speckled with blood and gore dripped from his axe.

'Why did you not trust us?' Sighard asked, wiping crimson spatters from his eyes.

'Trust had naught to do with it. Knowing my plan would have put all your lives at risk,' Hereward replied, raising his voice. 'I know I must make amends to you all. But that is business for another time. Now we have a battle to win.'

Footsteps swept closer, and Alexios emerged into the chamber, his expression grim. 'Half my men are looting,' he spat. Hereward could see his simmering anger. 'I will punish every one who has betrayed the faith of the people.'

Hereward looked up at the young nobleman. He was dressed for battle in mail-shirt and helm, with his shield upon his arm and his sword in his hand. His eyes gleamed with defiance. 'This battle is not yet won, Alexios. We have much still to do.' He beckoned to Kraki. 'Come with us. Karas lurks here somewhere, with a handful of warriors, enough to cause trouble.

We must find Nikephoros before we lose what little we have gained through surprise.' He nodded to the other spear-brothers. 'Stay here. Make sure no one else comes through that door.'

Hereward spun away, with Alexios and Kraki close behind. They hurried along the corridor into the depths of the palace.

'If our luck has fled, Wulfrun will be waiting for us with the rest of the Guard,' the Viking snarled as he ran.

'Wulfrun will not be here,' the Mercian replied, smiling to himself.

Kraki cursed. 'Wulfrun too? Am I the only one who knew nothing about this plot?'

Hereward held up his hand to slow the other two. The emperor's quarters lay ahead. 'Wulfrun knew nothing at the beginning. But then his love gave him a hard choice – betray his honour, or lose her. He is an honourable man. Though there is no love lost between us, he came to me and warned me of the threat against me.' Hereward remembered the look of despair on the Guard commander's face when he had told all he knew. 'His sacrifice will have cut him more than any blade.'

As his friend opened his mouth to grumble some more, Hereward raised a hand to silence him. He could feel the battle-fury filling his heart with fire. Unsheathing Brainbiter, he stepped into the large hall that bordered the emperor's quarters and looked down on Nikephoros, cowering in a corner. His eyes were wide and wild like a whipped dog's. A new bruise glowed above his right eye. When he saw the English warrior and his allies step into the hall, his lips pulled back from his teeth into a snarling rictus.

'See, now, son of a whore? I spoke truly. Your days are done.' The Mercian could see the emperor's head turning towards the other side of the room.

Hereward followed his gaze. He looked directly into the face of Karas Verinus, the eyes mere pools of shadow under heavy brows, the fists still clenched ready for the beating he had been about to administer to Nikephoros.

Around him, five of his cut-throats were gathered, their clothing stained crimson with fresh blood. Two Varangians lay dead behind them, no doubt men who had rushed to the palace to ensure the emperor's safety.

'If you want to keep your heads upon your shoulders, leave now. This business is all but done.' Hereward heard a note of triumph in Karas' voice, and felt only contempt for this would-be usurper. Here was a man who had known no doubts. He had never faced defeat upon the battlefield, as the English had. His belief in his own power and the blood of the Verini had led him relentlessly to this moment. The Mercian laughed inwardly, and his devil laughed too. How could any man call himself a warrior if he had never tasted loss?

'You are wrong. This business was done long ago. You are like a dying man dragging himself across the field of battle, still believing he has fight left in him.'

Karas snorted. 'You would still fight, even though

there are only three of you? Come, then. I have an emperor to slay and a throne to claim. When Justin arrives, a new age will dawn across the empire.'

'Aye, one drenched in blood,' Nikephoros spat.

For a moment, Hereward closed his eyes and relished the darkness. 'I have walked along the shore of the great black ocean, and I have spoken to Harald Redteeth. He told me of many things, but mostly of death,' he breathed. 'Of my death, and yours.' When he opened his eyes, he hefted Brainbiter, smiling at his sword as it caught the light.

'Harald Redteeth? Your words are meaningless.' Drawing his own sword, Karas took a step forward.

'Justin Verinus will not be wearing that bloody crown,' the Mercian continued. 'His days are ended.'

Karas scowled. 'Justin is not dead.'

'He was not, when he was found drifting in the harbour. Nor when that box was lowered into the hole, weighted with stones, a rag in his mouth and his hands bound. But now . . . ?'

Kraki handed over the sack he had been carrying since he left the cemetery. Hereward glanced in it once, then emptied out the contents.

Black with rot, the head of Justin Verinus rolled across the flagstones.

Hereward watched as the other man's expression turned from horror to despair. Karas staggered back, a wail of grief rolling out. The Mercian had never sensed that the general held any love for the boy, but now he glimpsed in the other man's face something of what he and his kin had shared, which had now been lost for ever, along with all his plans and hopes for his days yet to come. A life building to this moment, and then dashed into nothing. Hereward felt no pity. There was only ice in his heart.

'It is done,' he said.

Karas' men looked at the severed head that lay on the flagstones in front of them. Hereward could almost feel the fight leach out of them. Dropping their weapons, they edged along the wall until they could dash out of the door. Nikephoros' shrieking laughter followed at their heels.

Levelling his sword, Karas spat, 'I will have vengeance.'

Alexios half drew his sword, but the Mercian raised one hand and said, 'He is mine.' Dropping his shoulders, he braced himself. He could see the general had no intention of backing down. Nor had he. He set his devil free.

With a bestial roar, Karas hurled himself across the chamber. His sword cleaved through the air with enough force to have felled a tree. Balancing on the balls of his feet, Hereward spun aside. The blade shrieked across the flagstones, raising a shower of sparks. Karas did not slow. He was consumed by waves of grief, of anger and despair. The Mercian could see that now, and knew it was to his advantage. All the general's skill with the blade had been swamped by that deluge of emotion. Only brute strength remained. Hacking wildly, he was trying to drive his foe into a corner where he could be butchered.

Hereward shrugged his shoulders. Brainbiter felt

comfortable in his hand. He was more agile than his opponent, his wits sharpened by battle-fury, not dulled by despair. Whenever Karas' sword began its arc, he was always one step ahead.

The thunder of blood in his head drowned out the voice of his devil. He felt afire. The world fell away until only Karas' face floated before his eyes. He frowned, recognizing something in those features that he had never seen in the general before, but the battle-fury whisked it away before he could think on it.

His blade nicked Karas' chest, his arm, his cheek. But still the general came at him, thrusting and slashing. Gone was the ruthless and cunning warrior, and in his place a flailing, howling beast. His foot slipped on the blood-slick stone and he went down on one knee.

Hereward felt surprised when he saw a moment's hesitation, and then a rush of contempt. Karas did not hurl himself aside or scramble back. Nor did he raise his blade to defend himself. The general's gaze flickered up, the eyes now haunted.

There could be no doubt. Karas wanted to die. And Hereward knew the devil that always squatted inside him was more than ready to supply that gift. His battle-fury drained away, and he thrust Brainbiter into the general's chest with a cold will.

This was not an honourable death. This was a warrior who could not face a life where defeat was a possibility, a man fleeing like a frightened child. Hereward turned away before the light had died in his enemy's eyes. As he strode across the chamber, he heard the body slump to the flagstones. This man who had thought himself greater than all others had been brought to nothing.

Nikephoros clawed his way upright, but his suffering had taken its toll. He looked more frail than he ever had, the Mercian thought. 'You have my thanks,' he said, his voice trembling as much as his body.

Hereward held up his hand to silence him. 'I swore an oath to protect your life, and I would never break that vow. You will have many days yet to come. But not as emperor.'

His face growing cold, Nikephoros looked from Hereward to Alexios. 'More treachery.'

'The empire is on its knees,' Alexios said. 'On one thing, Karas Verinus spoke true. It is time for a new dawn.'

Nikephoros sneered. 'And you think yourself the saviour?'

Sheathing Brainbiter, Hereward said, 'Do not waste your breath calling for your guards. You know this business is done.'

The emperor's shoulders slumped and he half fell against the wall. 'Good. My bones are weary.' From under his lids, he eyed Alexios with contempt. 'All your promises of returning the empire to glory will turn to dust. You will soon discover this crown is cursed.'

'If God wills it, so be it,' Alexios replied, adding, 'You may think me a liar, but I never sought this.'

'The Comnenoi have always lusted after the throne. Your mother will no doubt drown herself in wine as she celebrates this victory.' Nikephoros turned to Hereward. 'But you . . . a barbarian. Do you truly believe they will reward you with power?'

'I do not seek power.'

'Then what gain is there to you?'

Hereward thought back along those long seasons of plotting, of learning the cunning ways of his enemies, of sowing seeds, not knowing if they would ever sprout. But he had told Alric the truth – he had proved himself the greatest viper in a pit of vipers. He smiled. 'What gain indeed?'

CHAPTER FIFTY-ONE

Ariadne fought her way through the flow of bodies, tears of fear stinging her eyes. The city blurred past – the crowds, the looting, the torches, the fighting. The slaughtered bodies she had seen at the house of the Nepotes still burned in her mind. But she had not been able to find Leo anywhere. That gave her some little hope.

If he had been preparing for the culmination of his kin's plot, there was only one place he could be. Now the burden of the Nepotes' lust for power had been removed, they could flee the city together, find a new home not ruled by death or duty or days long gone.

Skirting the edge of the Great Palace, she raced for the Chrysotriklinos. There were no guards. Only chaos ruled in Constantinople that night.

As she crept into the throne room, her breath burned in her chest in anticipation of what she might find. Yet there he was, still breathing. Ariadne felt her heart leap and a surge of relief that he was still alive.

Leo was sitting in the throne, one leg hanging over the armrest. She opened her mouth to call out to him, but the words died in her throat. He was wearing his jewelled *loros*, the fine clothes that he would, should, be wearing once he ascended to the throne of the empire. But they were splattered with blood.

Ariadne's hand flew to her mouth. 'Are you hurt?' she cried.

Eyes as dead as those of any corpse swivelled towards her and he slowly shook his head.

'I know my mother and father are both dead.' His voice trembled with self-loathing. 'I stood with Varin and cheered him on as I watched them breathe their last. I begged him to let me watch them die.' His voice was a low whine now. And then she knew the source of the blood upon his *loros*. Leo was shaking as if he had a fever. Ariadne felt horror as she looked into his face and thought that she might be staring into the eyes of a madman. 'They died, as Maximos died . . .'

Ariadne's stomach knotted, her pity turning to despair. What horrors the Nepotes' lust for power had inflicted upon all of them.

'Then we are damned together. My brother is dead too,' she said. 'Our kin have drained our lives of joy. But there is still hope for us in this world.'

'For you, perhaps.' Leo levelled his sword at her, the one that his brother Maximos had taught him to use with such skill. Ariadne felt shattered and terrified in equal measure.

Away in the dark, she glimpsed a ghostly figure. After a moment, Varin stepped forward.

'What have you done?' Ariadne cried.

'Place no blame on Varin,' Leo interrupted in a low,

firm voice. 'He did what he always had to do – remove the threat of my kin for his allies. He told me to leave, but I wanted to see their stain wiped away.' His voice rose, cracking.

The Blood Eagle walked closer. Ariadne thought she saw a sadness in his face, a softening that she had never witnessed before. 'Heed her,' he whispered. 'All is now ashes. The emperor has fallen. Karas Verinus is dead. A new age dawns. Go with her from the city and begin anew.'

'And I will say to you what I said before: my sins are too great.'

A clamour echoed from somewhere nearby. Soldiers drawing closer, no doubt driving out what little resistance remained to the Comnenoi, Ariadne thought.

'Do not let them find you here,' Varin said to Leo, with a note of compassion that Ariadne could not understand. 'They will not be kind.'

The Blood Eagle backed away, casting one last look at his former charge before he faded into the shadows. When Ariadne turned back to the throne, Leo too was gone. His sword, his most treasured memento of the brother he had both loved and killed, now lay across the chair.

Ariadne felt a rush of panic. She hurried out of that cursed throne room, along the path that led to the wall where the land fell away sharply down to the sea. Leo was nowhere to be seen, but her heart knew the truth. In that instant, all her emotion drained away and she felt hollowed out. Steeling herself, she pressed her forehead against the cold stone of the parapet and whispered a prayer. Then she looked down.

And God had abandoned her. There, caught in the moonlight on the rock below, lay the broken body of the man she loved.

Hot tears burned her eyes and for a moment Ariadne was blind. As sobs racked her body, she considered throwing herself over the edge to join Leo in death on those rocks. Perhaps that would be the best fate.

But then she felt a hand upon her shoulder, strong and steady. 'You have endured much. But all this will pass.' The voice was low and warm and filled with care. 'You are not alone,' Salih whispered. 'You will never be alone again.'

Ariadne turned and fell into the arms of the man who had become like a father to her. 'Why would he not let me help him?' she said in a small voice.

'This is a lesson you will carry with you for all your days,' the wise man murmured. 'However much your heart yearns to make things right, you can never truly save another. They can only save themselves.'

CHAPTER FIFTY-TWO

Torchlight danced off the golden crown. Flames wavered in every jewel studding that headdress as it was held aloft for God's blessing. Across the Hagia Sophia, a hush fell among the hastily gathered congregation, the few loyal senators and patricians who could be found among the fighting and looting.

Wreathed in incense smoke, Alexios Comnenos knelt in front of the altar, already wearing the ceremonial cloak across his shoulders. Hereward watched his friend as the Patriarch Cosmas lowered the crown on to his brow. At the last, he thought he saw a flicker of doubt in his friend, perhaps worry. But by then it was too late.

Anna Dalassene's face lit up in a smile and she clasped her hands together. Beside her, Maria wiped away a tear.

And then the congregation cried out 'Holy!' and the church echoed with the thrum of prayers and the new emperor's communion, but by then the Mercian's thoughts had already fled that place, to the shores of England where his plot had first flickered into life, through all the hardships and deceits, the sacrifices and the guile, and into the fog of days yet to come. There had been battles aplenty along the way, but the war had been won. And now a new war was waiting to be fought, one to keep secure all that had been earned.

But that was the warrior's lot.

Hereward emerged from the Hagia Sophia into the night. He felt the congregation push past him and stream into the dark. Their faces looked dazed as they struggled to comprehend the monumental happenings of that day. In the square in front of the great church, his spear-brothers had gathered in the torchlight. Hereward strode down the steps to join them, feeling gratitude for their loyalty on the long road. Alric was there. Their victory had done him some good, it seemed. In his face, the Mercian could see no sign of the suffering that he must have endured during his period of captivity.

'We have a new emperor, then,' Kraki grunted. 'Let us hope this one differs from all the other bastards.'

'We have fought alongside this one,' Sighard said. 'We know he is a good man. But I would not take his place for all the gold in Constantinople.'

'Aye,' Guthrinc agreed with a nod. 'Winning a crown is one thing. Keeping it is another.'

'Still your tongues,' Hiroc the Three-fingered mumbled sourly, lowering his eyes.

Hereward turned to see Anna and Maria walking towards the palace, arms linked, flanked by their bodyguards. He watched Falkon Cephalas leave them and walk over.

'Do not fear Falkon,' he laughed. 'He is a friend.'

For a moment, Kraki stared incredulously, and then he shook his fist. 'That dog too? I curse you and the ground you walk on.'

'Falkon serves power, not men. He knew Nikephoros' rule was ending,' Hereward said in a low voice. 'He took little persuading to play his part with Karas Verinus, and then the Nepotes, and then return to tell all he had learned from them.' He paused and shrugged. 'Perhaps a little persuading. A prick from the dagger of Salih ibn Ziyad.'

As he neared them, the man bowed. 'Anna Dalassene requests your attendance at the palace. There is much to discuss.'

Hereward turned back to the spear-brothers. 'You have been patient. If you would wait only a little while longer all will be made plain. I will meet you in the hall beneath the Boukoleon palace and tell you what lies ahead for us.' As he walked away, he raised his hand towards a large figure waiting in the shadows. Varin nodded in reply and slipped away into the night.

Hereward and Falkon walked back to the chamber adjoining the emperor's quarters. The bodies of the guardsmen and Karas Verinus had been removed and all signs of bloodshed had disappeared. Slaves brought flat bread, cheese, olives and wine to the few who had gathered there, ravenous in relief that they had survived the night. Hereward saw the Caesar, John Doukas, standing in one corner with his grand-daughter Irene. The old man was beaming, no doubt pleased that now Nikephoros had been deposed the Doukai once again had a foothold upon power. As an ally of the new emperor he could expect to be well rewarded.

Falkon guided the Mercian over to Anna Dalassene, who threw her arms wide, spilling wine from her goblet. 'My son is emperor.' Her words began to slur. 'All is well.' A slave hurried over with more wine.

'Now that the Comnenoi have power, what will you do with it?' Hereward asked.

'First, we will show that the new emperor is merciful. Nikephoros will be allowed to keep his life, and his eyes. He will live out his days in peace at the monastery at the church of St Mary Peribleptos. And then . . .' When she paused to take a sip, Hereward saw her eyes spark over the rim. Let her enjoy her moment, he thought. She has fought hard and suffered greatly to reach this point.

There was a sudden commotion outside. Hereward turned to see Alexios enter, accompanied by fawning greybeards. The business of the empire never stopped, and the Mercian thought that the new emperor already looked weary. He was still wearing the symbols of his coronation, the jewelled *loros* and the *chlamys*. But when his gaze fell on Maria, Hereward saw his face brighten. She smiled back, the love they shared clear. Now that Nikephoros was no longer a burden, Hereward felt certain that they would soon wed.

It was then that he felt a hand upon his forearm. Anna leaned in and whispered in his ear, 'I need your aid.' He could smell the wine sour on her breath.

He raised an eyebrow at her, puzzled. 'What would you have me do?'

'He has no father, and where he will not heed his mother he will listen to a friend like you, a man he looks up to.'

She paused, and the Mercian watched as Alexios waved his advisers away and made his way to his private quarters. Anna hurried after him, beckoning Hereward to follow.

In his chamber, Alexios threw off his heavy cloak. He poured himself a cup of wine and threw it back. When he looked up, he saw his mother and Hereward waiting there. 'You have what you always wanted,' he said to her, no doubt more harshly than he intended.

'We have it,' Anna corrected. 'This is not power for power's sake, you know that. With you on the throne, this empire can be great again.'

'I am ready for the fight.' Alexios nodded to Hereward. 'Are you ready, my friend?'

'I am.' Hereward thought of all the struggles that lay ahead. But he would enjoy this one night. It had been a long time coming.

'Good. We will seal our long-standing agreement this night.'

'There is one other matter,' Anna said, glancing at Hereward.

'What is wrong?' Alexios narrowed his eyes at his mother. He knew her too well.

'You cannot wed Maria.'

The new emperor waved a dismissive hand. 'Not

now, not so soon. But when Nikephoros is safely sealed away in his monastery—'

'Never.' Anna shook her head firmly.

Alexios looked to Hereward. 'You know of this?' The confusion in his voice was thick, but the Mercian heard a note of fear there too.

'No more than you.' The Mercian felt a pang of pity for his friend. Anna never stopped plotting. She would do whatever she had to do to secure her son's place upon the throne.

'Tell me,' Alexios demanded.

'You know full well the Patriarch Cosmas is loyal to the Doukai—'

'And he will soon be gone and we will have our own man ruling church business.' Alexios poured himself another goblet of wine.

Anna circled him, not meeting his gaze. 'We could not have won the throne without John Doukas' assistance. He bribed the guard to let your forces into the city.' Her voice was soothing, that of a mother explaining something difficult to a child.

The new emperor's knuckles whitened around the goblet. 'What price did you agree for that assistance?' His voice dripped with sarcasm.

'The price,' Anna began, licking her lips. She paused, choosing her words carefully. 'The price for the removal of Cosmas . . . the price we *must* pay to keep all we have gained . . . Irene must be crowned empress.'

Hereward nodded. Now he understood. With the Caesar's granddaughter beside the throne, the alliance between the Doukai and the Comnenoi would be sealed. If this agreement were not made flesh, John Doukas would find some way to undermine Alexios. Power would ebb away quickly. There would be more plotting, bloodshed, and death. Hereward felt hollow. Would these manipulations never end?

Alexios turned to Hereward. Sadness coloured the young man's face. 'What say you?' he asked, his voice breaking.

'There may be a way for you to see Maria . . .'

'Yes,' Anna leapt in, 'there may be.'

But Alexios must have known it was a slender hope. For a moment his head sagged, and then he hurled his goblet at the wall.

Anna nodded. She had betrayed her son, and Maria as well. Alexios had been left with no choice but to sacrifice his love for the responsibility that came with the crown.

Hereward could only stand there, looking at the other man. 'Loss makes a warrior fight harder. Though you feel this pain now, it will make you stronger. The empire will finally have the ruler it needs.'

'I will need your wise counsel in days to come,' he said, his voice flat.

Anna looked towards Hereward and smiled her thanks. As he turned to leave the chamber, he looked back at the young warrior. Alexios' head was bowed, the burden of ruling an empire already heavy on his shoulders.

Now there was only one more thing to do.

CHAPTER FIFTY-THREE

In that hour before dawn, on the edge of the Marmara Sea, the Boukoleon palace was still. Hereward strode through the corridors, his footsteps echoing behind him.

At the entrance to the hall, Ricbert raised a hand in greeting. 'He waits within,' he said, a knowing smile spreading across his ratlike face.

'What does he know?'

'Nothing. Yet.'

Inside, Wulfrun stood like a statue beside the hearth, his Dane-axe upright by his side. He was holding his helm as if he were ready for battle at any moment. Hereward studied the man who had loathed him for so long, who blamed him for the death of his father yet had still come to his aid in the name of honour.

'What do you want?' the commander of the Varangian Guard demanded.

Hereward sat on a stool by a table and took a moment to compose himself. He looked up at Wulfrun. It was a time to speak plainly, he knew. He owed that much to this man who had made such a great sacrifice.

'You are an honourable man,' he began. 'I am in your debt. If you had not come to me when the Nepotes demanded your betrayal, all might well have been lost.'

Wulfrun nodded, seemingly uncaring, but in his eyes Hereward glimpsed a deep well of despair.

'I know the cost you bore.'

'There is no need to speak of these things. What is done is done.'

'There is need. I wronged you, in days long gone when we were both raw. You have borne the burden of that time, and though you may not believe it, I have too. I would make amends.'

Wulfrun snorted. 'You think there is some way to right those wrongs?'

'I do.' Hereward turned his head and called, 'Here. Now.'

The door opened and Varin stepped in. He was not alone.

Wulfrun stumbled back. Her cheeks wet with tears, Juliana ran across the room and threw her arms around him, burying her face in his chest. Her voice but a whisper, she said, 'Can you forgive me? I am filled with sorrow for the harm I have caused you.'

His mouth wide with incredulity, Wulfrun looked to Hereward. He seemed to be struggling to find the words to express his thoughts.

'Leave,' the Mercian said. 'Leave now. And take this woman with you.'

'My . . . my oath . . .' Wulfrun began.

'You have not sworn an oath to this emperor. And he no longer has need of you. Your life is your own.'

Wulfrun stuttered, still at a loss for words. Juliana raised her face to him, smiling. 'Do as he says. There is nothing for us here any more.'

'No more games.' Wulfrun voice was hoarse.

'I am done with games,' she replied. 'I am sick of deceit, and I . . . and my kin . . . have paid a terrible price for it.' Hereward watched a shudder of grief run through her. Her voice became a whisper once more. 'Now I only wish to make amends for how I have treated you.'

Hereward was still unsure how far he could trust this woman. But for now she seemed honest, he thought, and the brightness in Wulfrun's face was clear. Here, for once this night, there was hope.

A look of gratitude broke through Wulfrun's confusion and he held Hereward's gaze. 'Your debt has been paid.' The Mercian saw his face soften. He looked like a different man. 'I have lived the life of the axe for as long as I remember. I found honour, and comfort, in my service to the emperor. But I am ready for this.' His eyes shone with a faraway look. 'A new life . . . ?'

Juliana took his hand and squeezed it. 'I am ready too,' she said in a small voice, which did not yet sound as confident as his.

Hereward stood and walked out with Varin. The Blood Eagle's face was unreadable. With a sly smile, Ricbert nodded as they passed. The Mercian led the way towards the steps down to the dark underground chamber where every Varangian guardsman underwent the ritual of joining. Where every warrior was forced to look death in the eye.

'You thought you had passed your crossroads, but you had not. Now you have a chance to choose another path,' he said as they walked.

Varin's voice rumbled back. 'You placed your trust in me. I will not forget that.'

'There was no other I could trust to do the work you did. All in the Guard told me you lived by honour, and I needed a man who was honourable, who had the courage of a warrior and could kill like a warrior, but a man the Nepotes would never suspect. And those dogs would have suspected any other man in Constantinople.'

'You risked much to find me. And you bested me in the wilds to the east. How could I refuse you? Now . . .'

'Now you have a place with us. You have earned it.'

They came to a halt at the top of a flight of stone steps and eyed each other. Hereward felt the Blood Eagle's cold, unsettling gaze on him. 'Return to the Guard?'

'Return to the Guard. Stand shoulder to shoulder with my spear-brothers. We will have need of a man like you for what is to come.'

Varin nodded. 'Let me think on this.'

As he descended into the dark, Hereward looked back. The giant of a man was waiting there, a statue of stone.

In the long, low-ceilinged chamber only one candle flickered. Hereward looked around the suffocating space. Their lives had changed when they underwent the Varangian ritual here. It was only right they gathered in this place one more time to learn what was to come.

Alric sat against the wall in the circle of wavering light. As his eyes grew accustomed to the gloom, the Mercian made out the spectral outlines of the spear-brothers sprawled around. Kraki, Guthrinc, Sighard, Hiroc, Derman, Hengist, Herrig the Rat. They had undergone so much together. He felt the warmth of their camaraderie.

In the hunch of their shoulders, he sensed their exhaustion, from the years of battles since they had come together, the seemingly never-ending night. He heard that weariness in their muttered greetings. Soon they could rest. But not yet.

'Now, for the first time, we have an ally . . . a friend . . . seated upon the throne.' With each word, he felt the weight that had been resting upon him for so long begin to lift a little more. 'And we have worked hard to put him there.'

''Twould have been good to know that was what we were doing,' Kraki grumbled.

'Aye, I have been guilty of keeping secrets from you, but for good reason. If we failed, there would be no blame placed on you. But we did not fail.'

Silence had fallen. Hereward watched the spear-brothers look up at him. In the candlelight, their faces softened as they understood what a long game he had been playing, and that through it all he had tried to protect them.

'The Comnenoi owe us a great debt, and they will pay it in full.' His deep voice echoed off the stone walls. 'This day I have been made commander of the Varangian Guard, and you, all of you, will be raised up with me. The rest of the Guard will answer to all of you. This is the bargain I made with the emperor's mother long seasons ago.'

Grins sparked in the half-light. Hereward sensed their excitement mounting.

'There will be gold aplenty, that is true, but that is the least of it. We have the ear of the emperor now, in a way no others have had. We have fought beside Alexios and he knows and trusts us. And Anna Dalassene wants only the most trusted to keep her son safe. He is young still, and he needs seasoned men to guide him.'

Hereward looked across the upturned faces of his spear-brothers. They had followed him over the vast sweep of the whale road, across trackless leagues. They had followed him on their journey from farmers and woodworkers and simple folk to warriors. They had followed him from the despair of defeat to this, their greatest victory. The Mercian felt his heart swell with pride. Without them, without their courage, none of this would have been possible.

'Ahead of us lies a great fight. Robert Guiscard and his Norman bastards will be determined to attack. The Turks need to be defeated. But with this new emperor, and with us beside him, there is hope. A new age is dawning here in Constantinople.'

'Then we are truly raised up high,' Sighard murmured. Hereward could sense the wonder in the young man's voice.

'Wise men could steer a clear course, I would say.' Hereward caught Alric's eye as the monk grinned at him in the dancing candlelight. He returned his smile. Alric had always been at his side along this hard road, and knew him better than anyone. He knew what had been sacrificed, and he knew, now, what had been achieved.

'In England, we stared defeat in the face, a defeat that would have broken many men. But we were not crushed. We found the fire in our hearts, and we fought on.' Hereward looked around those faces one more time, as his spear-brothers considered his words. 'We have lost a kingdom. But now we have gained an empire.'

Silence filled the room as the spear-brothers let this realization settle on them. Slowly they began to see the full promise of all the days yet to come. Hereward looked up to the sole narrow window, high up on the eastern wall, and saw the new dawn beginning to silver the sky.

His grin still bright, Alric leaned over and blew out the candle. The darkness swept in.

AUTHOR'S NOTES

As we bring this sixth Hereward volume to a close, I wanted to reveal some of my thinking behind the storytelling.

Every author is faced with hundreds of choices when planning a novel, none more so than the writer of historical fiction. They can be quite small – which historical detail to omit to help the story flow – or very large, such as whether to leave out a huge event that is irrelevant to the central story that's being told. These aren't history textbooks, after all – they are *stories*, and the author's primary responsibility is always to the storytelling, the depth of character, the deep themes, the meaning, and, most potently, how the great sweep of history impacted upon people's lives at the time: the human story.

I had some tough choices to make, right from the very beginning. One might expect a tale about the English resistance to the Normans to show the actual invasion. But in 1066 Hereward was away from his homeland, fighting as a mercenary in Flanders. Could

I really allow such a pivotal event to take place in the background, dismissed in a couple of lines?

Luckily, I had Hereward's adopted brother Redwald to bear witness to that shattering event. I'm sure some readers would have liked more – a detailed, blow-by-blow account of William the Bastard's arrival through to the moment he sat upon the throne. But that is a book for someone else to write. This was Hereward's story, and I had to remain true to that, while providing the necessary context in dramatic form.

And, I must confess, I originally planned to end Hereward's tale at the end of book three, *End of Days*. As I've mentioned before in these public musings, we have only scant evidence for the life Hereward lived, and no knowledge of when his death occurred. We can take a punt and guess it wasn't at the Battle of Ely when King William finally crushed the resistance to his reign – we would most likely have some account of that in other historical mentions of that final struggle in the fenlands.

We have plenty of evidence that many of the surviving rebels, and those nobles who could afford to flee William's brutality, sailed east to find new lives in Constantinople, with the most seasoned warriors seeking to join the highly regarded Varangian Guard.

And as I pondered Hereward's final fate, I thought I noticed an opportunity.

One of the difficulties in teaching history is the understandable necessity to break down the great, glorious sweep of it all into easily understood, easily ring-fenced sections. The Elizabethan Age. The Unification of Italy. The Chinese Dynasties.

But, of course, everything is connected – across time, from then to now, and in any given year, across the world too. At school, like every other child, I learned of the Norman Conquest. But my teacher never felt it necessary to talk about how the Normans were also spreading south and east, influencing the course of history across Europe.

In the second half of the eleventh century, there were two absolutely pivotal events that changed the course of everything up to the modern day. William the Bastard's invasion ended the developing Anglo-Saxon golden age and set England on a new path, for better or worse (as the academics are still arguing). And in Constantinople, the rise of the Comnenoi and the sweep of the Seljuk Turks across the eastern Roman empire had repercussions that are still playing out in the struggles we see on the news almost every day.

With Hereward, I had a chance to show how those two great dramas were linked, while also tying in to the deeper themes that I wanted to examine in these books.

Deciding to follow the English refugees east created a whole new set of problems for me, though. The vast numbers of people involved in the events in Constantinople, high born and low, could have bloated the story beyond all bounds of reason, and dragged it into a dull crawl, if all were detailed here. I had no choice but to wade into them with a machete. No time to give Alexios' brother Isaac much time centre-stage. No time for the ranks of powerful government figures, who all had parts to play, or for the many plotters and backstabbers and throat-slitters (yes, there were many more than you have read about here).

I had to be ruthless, cut everything back to the most essential players. There are times when I think I've been too ruthless, and at times not ruthless enough. But these are the choices that have to be made. Some are right, some are no doubt questionable, but they're my choices and I can live with them. Actually, I *have* to live with them. That's the job.

This is the last story about Hereward, at least for a while. There are more to tell, as you might have gleaned from the book's ending. If you are still interested, I may well return to them in the future. If not, Hereward and the spear-brothers will be battling on in your own imaginations.

For me, it is time to move on to a new era and a new story, one rooted firmly in the Dark Ages. Keen-eyed readers may have picked up on elements in book three which suggested that Hereward was the template for the mythic character of Robin Hood (with apologies to my friend, Angus Donald, who has written some excellent historical Hood novels). A hero, a champion of the common man, hiding out in the greenwood with a band of merrie men which includes a monk, a strongman and more, while battling against a wicked sheriff (of Lincoln, not Nottingham) when the country is in the grip of a tyrannical king.

In a completely different way, my next project will also tackle the theme of how harsh reality becomes myth. It's a generational story, following a bloodline that may be blessed or may be cursed, and its working title is *Pendragon.*

ACKNOWLEDGEMENTS

To my editor, Simon Taylor, for his always-excellent
advice and guidance.

James Wilde

His thrilling, action-packed series rescues a near-forgotten English hero from the darkest of times and brings him to bloody but brilliant life!

HEREWARD

1062. King Edward is heirless and ailing, and William, Duke of Normandy waits for the moment when he can seize the English throne. Hopes of resisting the would-be conqueror come to rest with just one man: Hereward . . .

HEREWARD: THE DEVIL'S ARMY

1067. It seems all was lost at Hastings. The iron fist of William the Bastard has begun to squeeze the life out of this conquered land, but for one who stands in his way. He is Hereward, and he is England's last hope.

HEREWARD: END OF DAYS

1071. Five years have passed since the Normans' crushing victory at Hastings. England reels under the savage rule of its new king. But Hereward plans an uprising that will sweep the hated Norman king from the throne.

HEREWARD: WOLVES OF NEW ROME

1072. The battle has been lost. The Norman king William is victorious. For the beaten English rebels, the price of defeat is cruel: exile. It falls to Hereward to lead them across a war-ravaged Europe to Byzantium.

HEREWARD: THE IMMORTALS

1073. Under a merciless Eastern sun, Hereward and his men plan a daring rescue mission. But within the corrupt heart of Byzantium there are those who would see the English warrior fail and meet his end as a feast for the ravens . . .